**Larissa Ione** is a *USA Today* and *New York Times* best-selling author. She currently resides in Williamsburg, Virginia, with her husband and son.

Please visit Larissa Ione online:
www.larissaione.com
www.facebook.com/OfficialLarissaIone
www.twitter.com/Larissa Ione

*By Larissa Ione*

*Lords of Deliverance series*:

Eternal Rider
Immortal Rider
Lethal Rider
Rogue Rider

Apocalypse: The Lords of Deliverance Compendium

*Demonica series*:

Pleasure Unbou
Desire Unchain
Passion Unleash
Ecstasy Unveiled
Sin Undone
Reaver

*Moonbound Clan seres*:

For my readers and my friends. How lucky I am that they so often overlap. I love you guys!

# REAVER

## LARISSA IONE

piatkus

PIATKUS

First published in the US in 2013 by Grand Central Publishing,
A division of Hachette Book Group, Inc.
First published in Great Britain in 2013 by Piatkus

A CIP catalogue record for this book
is available from the British Library.

ISBN 978-0-349-40076-1

Printed and bound by CPI Group (UK) Ltd, Croydon, CR0 4YY

Papers used by Piatkus are from well-managed forests
and other responsible sources.

MIX
Paper from
responsible sources
FSC
www.fsc.org   FSC® C104740

Piatkus
An imprint of
Little, Brown Book Group
100 Victoria Embankment
London EC4Y 0DY

An Hachette UK Company
www.hachette.co.uk

www.piatkus.co.uk

# Acknowledgments

First of all, I want to thank everyone on the Grand Central Publishing team for everything they've put into this book, with special thanks to Madeleine Colavita for all her help. And a massive thank-you goes to my editor, Amy Pierpont. Oh, my God, we did it!!!!

Special thanks go out to Kim Whalen for being a great shoulder and agent. Yay, Reaver!!!

And thank you, Bryan, for being home when I needed you. Now that you're home full time, the rest of this crazy journey is yours to share too, so brace yourself!

# Glossary

*Agimortus*—A trigger for the breaking of a Horseman's Seal. An agimortus can be identified as a symbol engraved or branded upon the host person or object. Three kinds of agimorti have been identified and may take the form of a person, an object, or an event.

*Boregate*—Portals that allow demons to travel inside Sheoul. The precursors to Harrowgates, Boregates are either unpredictable or inflexible. Some run back and forth between two realms while others take users to random locations within Sheoul.

*Daemonica*—The demon bible and basis for dozens of demon religions. Its prophesies regarding the Apocalypse, should they come to pass, will ensure that the Four Horsemen fight on the side of evil.

*Dermoire*—Located on every Seminus demon's right arm from his hand to his throat, a *dermoire* consists of glyphs that reveal the bearer's paternal history. Each individual's personal glyph is located at the top of the *dermoire*, on the throat.

*Fallen Angel*—Believed to be evil by most humans, fallen angels can be grouped into two categories: True Fallen and Unfallen. Unfallen angels have been cast from Heaven and are earthbound, living a life in which they are neither truly good nor truly evil. In this state, they can, rarely, earn their way back into Heaven. Or they can choose to enter Sheoul, the demon realm, in order to complete their fall and become True Fallens, taking their places as demons at Satan's side.

*Harrowgate*—Vertical portals, invisible to humans, that demons use to travel between locations on Earth and Sheoul. A very few beings can summon their own personal Harrowgates.

*S'genesis*—Final maturation cycle for Seminus demons. Occurs at one hundred years of age. A post-*s'genesis* male is capable of procreation and possesses the ability to shapeshift into the male of any demon species.

*Sheoul*—Demon realm. Located deep in the bowels of the Earth, accessible to most only by Harrowgates and hellmouths.

*Sheoulghul*—Tiny, extremely rare crystal spheres that allow angels to partially charge their powers in Sheoul. The origin of these crystals is a closely guarded secret, and little is known about them, but some users claim to have heard them make weeping sounds.

*Sheoul-gra*—A holding tank for demon souls. The place where demon souls go until they can be reborn or kept in torturous limbo.

*Sheoulic*—Universal demon language spoken by all, although many species also speak their own language.

*Ter'taceo*—Demons who can pass as human, either because their species is naturally human in appearance or because they can shapeshift into human form.

*Watchers*—Individuals assigned to keep an eye on the Four Horsemen. As part of the agreement forged during the original negotiations between angels and demons that led to Ares, Reseph, Limos, and Thanatos being cursed to spearhead the Apocalypse, one Watcher is an angel, the other is a fallen angel. Neither Watcher may directly assist any Horseman's efforts to either start or stop Armageddon, but they can lend a hand behind the scenes. Doing so, however, may have them walking a fine line, that, to cross, could prove worse than fatal.

# *Prologue*

Fate was not a word angels tossed around lightly. But as Zachariel, First Angel of the Apocalypse, wrote the final chapter of *Verrine/Harvester: An Unauthorized Biography*, he couldn't help but think about how fate had screwed her over.

And so it was that, five thousand human years ago, the angel Verrine fell in love with the angel Yenrieth. But Verrine, in her innocence, fled from his affections and sent him into the waiting arms of another.

Verrine finally realized her mistake, but it was too late. She came upon her beloved Yenrieth fornicating with the succubus Lilith.

Unbeknownst to Yenrieth, Lilith became pregnant. Verrine, however, was aware of the pregnancy and for reasons known only to her, she kept the knowledge from Yenrieth. She did, however, swear an oath to find and watch over Yenrieth's offspring.

In time, Lilith gave birth to four infants, three boys and a girl: Reseph, Ares, Limos, and Thanatos.

After many years of searching in secret, Verrine finally located the boys, who had grown up with human families, placed there by Lilith.

But the girl, Limos, had been betrothed to Satan and had made her life in the underworld. Only when Limos emerged from the dark depths of hell did Verrine feel as though she could finally tell Yenrieth about the existence of his children.

But as fate would have it, Limos's arrival in the human realm was disastrous.

Yenrieth's children, upon learning from Limos that they were not human but were, in fact, half angel and half demon, started a war between the earthly and demon realms, causing destruction and chaos that bordered on Armageddon.

As punishment, Yenrieth's offspring were cursed to become the Four Horsemen of the Apocalypse, their fates to be determined by prophecy. Should the Seals that bound them to the curse break, they would become Pestilence, War, Famine, and Death, but whether they fought on the side of good or evil had yet to be determined.

No one knows what became of Yenrieth after this, but Verrine, in order to hold to her personal vow to watch over his children, approached three archangels with a plan—to infiltrate hell and use whatever means at her disposal to be assigned one of Sheoul's most coveted tasks: Sheoulic Watcher of the Horsemen. She intended to act as a spy and manipulate events in order to prevent the demon bible's version of apocalyptic prophecy.

Three archangels, Metatron, Raphael, and Uriel, approved her request and, knowing she would never see Heaven again, Verrine became the fallen angel Harvester.

It took three thousand years of proving herself to her father, the fallen angel and lord of the underworld, Satan, before she was granted a position as Watcher. For the next two thousand years she covertly helped the Horsemen keep their Seals from breaking and pretended to work against each of the Horsemen's Heavenly Watchers, Shiresta, Barabus, Gethel, and Reaver.

And when, in the Year of our Lord 2010, a Seminus demon named Sin inadvertently broke Reseph's Seal and turned him into the demon known as Pestilence, Harvester's work began in earnest. The *Daemonica*'s version of the Apocalypse had begun.

Harvester, corrupted by thousands of years of evil, performed tasks that would eat at her soul and scour away what little goodness was left in her heart. But ultimately, her actions saved humankind, and the Apocalypse was averted. All worked out according to plan...until Gethel, a traitor to Heaven, betrayed Harvester to Satan.

And Harvester, unable to ask the very people she saved for help, was dragged to Sheoul to suffer an eternity of torment at Satan's hands.

Zachariel paused to dip his angel-feather pen into the sacred ink blended from the blood of twenty archangels.

Crimson drops dripped from the nib as he lifted it from the crystal bottle, and he wondered how much more he should write. Yenrieth had been scrubbed from the history books and from the memories of all but a select few, and Zachariel wasn't sure how much he should reveal. His own memories of Yenrieth had been returned just recently, and only so he could record Harvester's story.

Blood ink spattered on the desk, and Zachariel realized the finality of the situation. Harvester was gone forever. There was no more to write. Thanks to Harvester's sacrifice, humanity was safe, and so were Yenrieth's children. She, more than any angel in history, had shaped the future of all the realms.

Harvester was a fallen angel. And a fallen hero.

Zachariel let the pen fall back into the bottle, and with a silent prayer for Harvester's soul, he closed the book.

# One

~~~~

In any other building in the world, the sight of a hellhound lying on the floor with a baby in its mouth would send people screaming in horror or scrambling for weapons.

In a castle belonging to one of the Four Horsemen of the Apocalypse, people didn't bat an eye.

Reaver ignored the shaggy black beast that bared its teeth at him as he strode across the great room. Hellhounds hated angels, and the feeling was mutual.

"Thanatos," Reaver called out, "Cujo is slobbering on your son."

Thanatos poked his blond head out of the library doorway. "That's why Logan gets a lot of baths."

The hound, a puppy itself at around two hundred pounds, flopped onto its side and allowed Logan to tug on its fur and ears as the infant climbed on top of the beast. Logan was going to be a soggy, furry mess by the time his mother, Regan, got home.

It had been months since Reaver had been here, and not much had changed. The fire that burned practically year-round was going in the hearth, vampire servants bustled between the cavernous rooms, and the mouthwatering aroma of fresh bread wafted from the kitchen. Regan had added personal touches here and there, replacing some of Thanatos's ancient weapons and gory paintings on the walls with tapestries and pictures of the local landscape. Throw rugs now covered the hard, cold floors, and baby toys lay scattered like colorful land mines that squeaked in shrill protest when Reaver's booted feet accidentally stomped on them.

The keep's massive wooden doors flew open behind Reaver, bringing a chilly blast of late spring Greenlandic wind through the entrance. Ares, Reseph, and Limos came in with the breeze, Ares in shorts, a T-shirt, and flip-flops, Reseph in jeans and nothing else, and Limos in a glaringly orange maternity sundress. When she saw Reaver, she grinned, and despite being five months pregnant, she tackled him in a fierce embrace.

He'd always loved her enthusiasm, even before he learned she was his daughter, and he hugged her close. He just wished he'd been able to give her much-needed hugs when she was a child. Wished he could have been there for her first steps, her first words.

If only he'd known about her. And Ares. And Thanatos. And Reseph.

"'Sup, Pops?" Limos pulled away, taking her tropical piña colada scent with her. "Where have you been? We haven't seen you in months."

Time ran differently in Heaven, so it felt like only days to Reaver. And maybe he'd been a little hesitant to visit.

For years he'd been the Horsemen's Heavenly Watcher, but the dynamic of their relationship had changed since he'd discovered they were his offspring. He'd been fired as their Watcher, and more important, he wasn't sure how to be a father to five-thousand-year-old legends.

Worse, he didn't know how to be a *grand*father. He was over five thousand years old and technically could be a grandfather thousands of times over, but he didn't feel old enough to be a grandfather even once.

"I've been in the Akashic Library trying to find something… *anything*, that'll help track down Gethel," Reaver said, and Thanatos growled at the mention of the Horsemen's ex-Watcher, an angel who betrayed Heaven and nearly killed Than's son. "I even searched her home in Heaven, but it's been ransacked by Enforcers already."

Enforcers, Heaven's angel lawkeepers, had made finding the renegade angel a top priority, their zealous pursuit spurred by the fact that the entire underworld was buzzing about her rumored involvement in some sort of plot against Heaven. Intel from the Heavenly spy network indicated a countdown was also involved. But a countdown to what?

"It should *not* be this difficult." Frustration lashed Reaver all the way to his wing feathers. He'd been searching for eight months without a single lead. "She isn't technically a fallen angel, so she can't hide in Sheoul—" He broke off, wheeling around at the sudden sensation of evil emanating from the doorway.

"My ears are burning." Tiny flecks of light materialized into a shape. Gethel's shape.

Instantly, the Horsemen flicked their fingers over the crescent-shaped scars on their throats, activating their armor and their weapons. Snarling, the hellhound leaped to his feet, somehow sweeping Logan beneath his big body as everyone put themselves between the child and Gethel.

"Limos!" Than shouted. "Get Logan out of here."

Reaver didn't hesitate. He blasted the angel with nuclear-grade direlight. The blue spear of sizzling light whispered through Gethel's body and blew up the keep's massive wooden door. Gethel, unharmed, merely smiled, even when he sent an arc of fire at her head. The flaming column passed through her like an arrow through fog.

"How the fuck did you do that?" Thanatos advanced on her, sword leveled at her throat, but Reaver suspected the Horseman's weapon would be as useless as his own. The souls Than stored in his armor—the souls of those he killed—swirled at his feet, anxious to kill. "How did you get in here? My keep is warded against anyone but my Watchers and Reaver flashing in."

"The child I carry lent me his power." Gethel touched her stomach, and Reaver's mouth went dry at the sight of the bump under her palm.

What kind of child could she possibly be carrying? Power of that magnitude in any species was almost unheard of.

The answer came to him like a poleax between the eyes. A Radiant, or Shadow Angel, as some called them, would be powerful enough to blow through Than's wards. But there hadn't been any angels of that class around for centuries. If Gethel was pregnant with an angel who could travel freely through both Heaven and Hell, the archangels needed to know.

The hairs on the back of Reaver's neck stood up, and

half a second later, the Horsemen's Sheoulic and Heavenly Watchers, Revenant and Lorelia, flashed in.

Ares's leather armor creaked as he stepped closer to Gethel, his two-handed sword poised to strike a lethal blow. "Explain."

Gethel dragged out a dramatic pause. "I'm going to give birth to Lucifer."

*Bullshit.* Lucifer, Satan's right-hand man, was dead. Reaver had seen the fallen angel torn to pieces with his own eyes. So what was Gethel's game?

"You mean Lucifer's child?" Reaver hoped not. Any spawn of Lucifer's would be as powerful as most archangels.

"Lucifer himself," she said sweetly, and Reaver's stomach wrenched with disbelief. "I was chosen to be the vessel that will give him physical form again." She eyed Thanatos's sword. "Go ahead and run me through. I'm not really here. My precious Lucifer has the power to project my image to the moon if I want."

A thunderous rumble tore through the castle, and then two archangels dressed in business casual slacks and shirts slammed to the ground in twin rays of golden light. Before anyone could react, Raphael and Metatron swept the Horsemen and Revenant, their evil Watcher, aside like flies, leaving them lying unconscious on the ground. Lorelia stood there looking stunned and grateful to be left conscious.

Reaver snared Raphael's arm. "What did you do to them?"

Irritation flickered in the angel's expression, and Reaver knew he was close to being laid out by some über-powerful archangel weapon.

"They'll recover." Raphael gestured to Gethel. "When we get hold of you, you *won't* recover."

"You are an angel, Gethel." Metatron's silver-blue eyes flashed lightning, but his words were measured. Controlled. The calm before the tempest. "You can stop this madness before it's too late."

"Why would I do that? I'm carrying the second most powerful being in Sheoul." She drummed her fingers on her belly. "His power will rival even yours."

"How is this possible?" Lorelia asked, obsessively twisting the ruby ring on her pinky. "Reseph destroyed Lucifer months ago."

In truth, Reseph's demon half, Pestilence, had also played a key role in Lucifer's messy demise, but Reaver wasn't going to split hairs right now.

"Lucifer was destroyed," Metatron agreed, never taking his eyes off Gethel. "But his soul was sent to Sheoulgra. Given the right, albeit unlikely, conditions—"

"He could be reborn," Raphael finished sourly. "But under what circumstances?"

Metatron closed his eyes as Gethel smirked, waiting for him to solve the puzzle. "Only Satan is powerful enough to sire a reincarnated fallen angel of Lucifer's status. The mother would need to be someone pure and holy who fell from grace."

"Or an angel who betrayed Heaven and Earth," Reaver said grimly. "Gethel."

Gethel clapped. "Bravo."

Raphael glared at Reaver. "If you'd killed her when you had the chance, this wouldn't have happened."

*Way to stab me where it hurts, dickhead.* Reaver's failure to kill the golden-haired wench during their last battle ate at him like acid. But that didn't mean he liked being taken to task about it by a puffed-up archangel who had parked his butt safely behind his monstrosity of a desk while the human realm suffered under a demon invasion and near-apocalypse.

"If any of you had gotten off your pampered asses to, I don't know, *help*, maybe she'd be dead by now," Reaver said, wondering if he should throw in a few expletives for emphasis. Ultimately, he decided not to push his luck. Either archangel could turn him into a juicy stain.

"You really should have killed me," Gethel said, twisting the knife Raphael had already stabbed him with. "Now I'm under the protection of both Satan and Lucifer." She patted her belly again, as if she was carrying a sweet, innocent baby and not, literally, the spawn of Satan. "Granted, my little boy isn't as strong as he could be yet, but I'm about to rectify that. Harvester's blood, extracted with the Dark Lord's own pressing machines, will nourish him." Fat black veins started to spread from her fingers to her arms, neck, and finally, her face, and her voice went low. "And then you will all know his wrath. All of Heaven will feel it."

Gethel's image faded away, and Reaver's heart plummeted to his feet at the mention of Harvester. Until five months ago, Reaver had believed she was the enemy. Raphael's revelation that she'd been working with Heaven all along, that she'd fallen from Heaven in order to watch over the Horsemen, had knocked Reaver for a loop.

But what had really blown his mind was that the archangels refused to rescue her from Satan's prison. Her service to Heaven and mankind deserved better.

Plus, Reaver wanted answers. He needed to know why she would give up everything to watch over children who weren't even hers.

Lorelia smoothed her hands down the front of her gray business jacket and matching skirt as she looked at the empty space where Gethel had stood. For at least the tenth time, Reaver wondered how she'd ever been chosen as Watcher. She'd always come across as a little mousy, a lot inquisitive, and definitely more scholar than warrior.

"What was Gethel talking about?" she asked.

Metatron spoke up, his voice still calm, but an underlying current of anger charged the air around him. "Lucifer's power was second only to Satan's *before* he died; being born as Satan's son will only make him stronger." Like most archangels, Metatron rarely put away his wings, and now the silver wingtips that matched the streaks in his dark hair fluttered at his feet. "Worse, the rare reincarnation of any fallen angel results in fractures in Heaven's very foundation."

"But Lucifer isn't just any angel," Raphael said, his voice going hoarse as the implications of Lucifer's rebirth sank in. "His birth will cause cataclysmic events in Heaven. Quakes. Floods. Volcanic eruptions. Angels and humans in Heaven will be caught in the disasters and die, lost forever."

Lorelia asked, "How does Harvester fit in with this?"

"She's Satan's daughter," Reaver told Lorelia. "Feeding Lucifer her blood can only make him stronger."

"She's not just his daughter," Metatron reminded them grimly. "She's the only one of his children conceived while he was still an angel. Even though she's fallen, her blood will give Lucifer some talents and powers that are usually exclusive only to Heavenly angels."

"We have to find and destroy Gethel before Lucifer is born," Raphael, angel of the freaking obvious, said.

"And how do you propose to do that?" Lorelia asked.

Metatron and Raphael looked stumped, but Reaver had an idea that could not only take care of Lucifer but could force the archangels to do what they should have done months ago.

"We'll have to spring Harvester from Satan's prison."

"Absolutely not," Raphael barked.

Metatron snorted. "Impossible. Any rescue attempt on our part will confirm Heaven's role in her espionage against Satan, and it'll start a war—"

"Yeah, yeah," Reaver interrupted. "A war between Heaven and hell will mean death, destruction, and rivers running with angel blood, blah, blah."

Funny how the archangels were concerned about this war when they hadn't been all that worried about an apocalypse in the human realm. But then, most angels liked to bury their heads in the clouds and pretend humans and demons didn't exist.

"It's wrong that she's imprisoned," Reaver argued. "She was helping our side."

Raphael shook his head. "She was well aware that if she was ever caught, she'd go down as a lone wolf who was working her own evil agenda. Her cover was blown, she got caught, and it's over."

"I still don't understand," Lorelia said. A summoned copy of *A History of the Watchers of the Four Horsemen of the Apocalypse* popped into her hand, and she immediately started flipping through it. Yup, scholar. "How will rescuing Harvester help our cause?"

Reaver chose his words carefully. Raphael and Metatron needed to believe Reaver had no ulterior motive. That he didn't want to rescue Harvester in part so he could piece together the past he'd lost when his memories of being Yenrieth were ripped from his mind. He'd asked for his memory back, over and over, but he'd been met with refusal every time.

But Harvester had known Yenrieth. She'd given up her wings for his children. Clearly, Yenrieth had meant something to her once, even if she didn't remember what he looked like.

"As Satan's daughter," Reaver began, "Harvester can sense her siblings. She can find Lucifer even if he's inside Gethel."

Lorelia scowled. "What's to keep her brothers and sisters from finding Harvester after she escapes?"

"Harvester's ability to sense Satan's offspring is unique," Metatron answered, "for the same reason her blood is stronger than that of her siblings. She was conceived in Heaven before Satan was expelled."

"No." Raphael crossed his arms over his chest and pegged Reaver with a hard glare. "Nyet. Nein. Non. Nei. Nu. Na. Shise. Yai. You aren't rescuing Harvester. Is any of this getting through to you?"

Reaver smiled. "You're wrong about *shise*. That's Sheoulic for fungus. The word you're looking for is *shishe*." Idiot.

"Why am I not surprised by your fluency in the universal demon language?" Raphael's own smile was chilly. "Did all your demon friends and lovers teach you?"

Reaver didn't take the archangel's bait. His best friends were demons, but he hadn't been intimate with a demon in years. Not since the day he earned his wings back. And right now, his friends weren't the issue.

"If *you* won't mount a rescue for Harvester, let me do it. Give me command of a flight of battle angels."

Raphael scoffed. "You want *command* of an entire flight? You're barely capable as a battle *soldier*."

"I'm more powerful than any battle angel, and you know it."

"But you can't follow orders. How are you supposed to lead if you can't follow?" Metatron sounded almost reasonable. Wrong, but reasonable.

Raphael's shrewd gaze fixed on Reaver as if stripping him down to his very essence. Reaver actually looked down to make sure he was still clothed in jeans and a navy button-down.

"We appreciate your wanting to help," Raphael said in the same tone someone might use to pat a child on the head. "But even if we did decide to rescue Harvester, you'd be the last person we'd send. She hated Yenrieth. She'd be more likely to hand you over to Satan than let you rescue her."

Reaver frowned. "But she gave up her wings for his—my—children. Why would she do that if she hated me?"

Raphael's mouth puckered like he'd licked a rotten lemon. "I've wondered the same thing." He waved his hand, dismissing the subject and Reaver. "We'll take it from here."

"You can't do this—"

Raphael waved his hand again, and Reaver's voice cut out. "We can do whatever we want."

*Screw you*. Reaver hoped they could read his mind.

"Don't even think about rescuing Harvester," Metatron said. "You won't make it out of Sheoul, and even if you do, we'll take your memory from you again, but not before raining fire down on you with such force that you'll beg for death."

Normally, at this point he'd flare his wings out in defiance. Or flip them the not-so-holy bird. But if there was ever a time when Reaver needed to exercise control and feign compliance, now was it.

However, playing nice didn't mean he had to roll over like a chastised puppy. "Can I at least have my memory back?"

He was tired of no one remembering him, tired of not remembering anything beyond the last thirty years. He'd only recently pieced some bits of his past together, but there were still far too many holes in his angelic timeline. If he could just get some of that back maybe he could finally feel whole. His memory loss had always bothered him, but after learning that he was a father—to the Four Horsemen, no less—getting his past back had become a priority. How could he be a good father if he didn't know why he'd abandoned them for five thousand years in the first place?

Not to mention the fact that as the Horsemen's father, it was he who was fated to break their Seals to begin the biblical Apocalypse, one of the last measures meant to stop Satan in the final days of the prophesied war between Heaven and hell.

"No," Metatron said. "And stop asking." He strode over to Revenant and nudged him with a toe as he lay on his side. Reaver wished the archangel would give the evil Watcher a swift kick in the ribs.

"Reaver." Raphael's voice was hushed as he pressed an object into Reaver's palm. "I mean it. Stay out of Sheoul." He joined Metatron, leaving Reaver to check out Raphael's gift.

His breath caught when he saw the grape-sized rough crystal in his hand. He'd seen only one in his thirty years of memories, and that *one* was in his possession, lifted off Gethel a few months back.

He ran his thumb over the *sheoulghul*, a device that allowed angels to charge their powers in places angels couldn't normally access a charge.

Like Sheoul.

But why would Raphael give him something like this? Did he *want* Reaver to go after Harvester?

Well, well. Weren't archangels full of surprises. Reaver had no doubt the guy would deny helping Reaver in any way, but for now, he was going to take it as a sign.

A sign that pointed straight to hell.

# *Two*

⌒

That hell was all fire and brimstone was a common misconception, and while there most certainly were areas of blistering heat and flames fifty stories tall, Harvester thought the freezing cold was much worse.

But that was because she was in a torture chamber whose blizzard-like atmosphere froze her lungs with every breath. Not that taking breaths was easy, given that she was facedown and being pressed between two blocks of ice.

Tomorrow she might be back in the fires, or she'd be tossed into a pit full of ravenous hellhounds, or she'd be impaled on a thick pole and put on display in Satan's living room, where anyone who entered could do whatever they wished to her.

Those were the most pleasant of the thousands of scenarios she could be faced with.

She marshaled all her strength to take a breath, but

what little air she took in felt like it consisted of tiny razor blades. Blood splashed from her nose and mouth, freezing almost instantly on her lips and skin.

A prickling sensation stung her neck muscles, which should have been frozen solid, and she knew she was no longer alone.

"Harvessssster." Venom, one of Satan's Torture Marshals, spoke in his silky, snakey voice. The yellow-skinned bastard's shuffling footsteps came closer. "It's time to move you."

A shiver went through her. She hoped he'd move her to a cell where she'd get a few hours of rest and some food, but that happened so rarely that hoping was akin to dreaming. Most likely, she was in for more misery.

"On a ssscale of one to one hundred, I'll bet your dess-sire to die is clossse to one hundred, yesss?"

One hundred? One *million* would be more accurate.

"Your father wantsss to sssee you."

*No. Oh . . . no.* A single tear formed in her eye, freezing before it could fall.

"He isss having a feassst tonight. You will be the centerpiece on hisss table. Quite an honor."

*Forgive me for not being excited, but last time, I was the predinner entertainment, and then I was part of the meal.*

"You also have a visitor."

Visitor?

Another prickly sensation joined the first, and her gut twisted as a female voice filled the chamber. "Oh, my. You do look awful."

Gethel. That *bitch*. The former angel had betrayed Heaven in the worst way, and now, if Harvester's senses were working properly, it would seem that Gethel was pregnant with Harvester's half sibling.

Daddy had been busy.

"I wanted to be the first to tell you that I will be giving birth to Lucifer."

If Harvester could throw up, she would have. But there was nothing in her crushed belly. Lucifer's rebirth would send shockwaves through Heaven. Literal shockwaves that would cause death and destruction.

"And this is where you come in." Gethel cleared her throat as if preparing to give a speech. "He'll be born full-grown. The birth, of course, will kill me, but I'll die a glorious death, don't you think?"

Glorious? No. But with any luck Gethel would suffer the way she deserved.

"You, Harvester, will nourish him when he's born. Instead of milk, he'll need blood. And instead of being cradled in the arms of his mother, he'll be cradled between your welcoming thighs. And when he's finished with you, he will destroy everything you hold dear. The Horsemen. Their children." Her voice dropped to a low growl. "Reaver."

That was where Gethel was wrong. Harvester did not hold Reaver dear. She hated him, and if she never saw him again it would be too soon. Okay, yes, she'd always been fiercely attracted to him and certainly wouldn't kick him out of bed for picking his teeth with bones, but she still hated him.

He'd stirred those dual desires from the day they'd met at Ares's Greek manor. He'd been assigned as the Horsemen's Heavenly Watcher shortly before Reseph's Seal broke and initiated the demon bible's apocalyptic prophecy. He'd flashed onto Ares's beach, and Harvester had zapped him with a bolt of lightning before he'd fully materialized.

*"Who are you?" Harvester stood, feet glued to the sand, stunned at her own actions. She'd sensed his arrival and her first instinct had been to strike. Sure, she'd always been one to shoot first and ask questions later, but she wasn't usually* this *quick on the draw.*

*The newcomer angel peeled himself off one of the many ancient stone columns that dotted Ares's island, his charred T-shirt trailing wisps of smoke and his sapphire eyes seething. With a snap of his fingers he returned fire, nailing her between the eyes with some sort of invisible sledgehammer.*

*Crushing pain nearly knocked her to her knees. Bastard. She threw another bolt at him, but he was ready, and he wheeled gracefully out of the way.*

*"Knock it off!" he yelled. "You're Harvester, right?"*

*She narrowed her eyes at him. "Maybe." Damn, he was hot. Smoking hot. Literally. His jeans were still smoldering.*

*"I'm Reaver. Gethel's replacement." He strode toward her, and the closer he got, the more she wanted to light him up again.*

*Something about him pissed her the hell off, and she had to wonder if they'd met in battle in the past. Had to be a battle, because she'd have remembered a one-on-one meeting with him.*

*Or a one-on-one anything.*

*She held up her hand. "Stop now or I'll fry you to a crisp." Tiny streaks of lightning danced between her fingers, poised to make her threat a reality.*

*He blatantly, infuriatingly, took two more steps, ignoring her warning before halting just out of arm's reach. "Why did you attack me?"*

*"You're a stranger."*

*"A stranger? You're kidding, right? Because it's not like I zapped in here with candy and a white van with blacked-out windows." He stepped closer, and she turned up the electric charge in her hand. "Also, you aren't twelve. So why did you attack me?"*

*"How was I supposed to know you weren't going to attack me? It's not like angels pop out of thin air all the time just to wish me a nice day."*

*His full lips twisted into a sneer. "Don't fuck with me again, Fallen."*

*Fallen. Of all the insults he could throw at her, of all the vile slurs, he chose the only one that really stung. The only one that struck her like a physical blow. All other cheap barbs rolled off her back because they were either ridiculous or true. But this one... she'd fallen from grace to help superior asshats like the angel standing before her, and she was tired of putting up with holier-than-thou self-importance from dicks like him.*

*She blasted him. Straight up put him on his ass again. And God, it felt good.*

*Smiling at the feathers floating down all around her like the aftermath of a teenage girl's pillow fight, she flashed the hell out of there.*

So, yeah, she hated him, hated him even more simply *because* she lusted for him in a way she hadn't lusted for anyone in almost five thousand years.

Not since Yenrieth, the angel who had claimed her heart. And then stomped on it before mysteriously disappearing forever, not only from all the realms but from memories, as well. Oh, Harvester remembered how he'd made her feel, but his face was a blank. He could have been a toad-headed orc for all she knew.

The sound of grinding gears and clanking chains filled the cavern, and Gethel and her obnoxious chatter was forgotten. As the giant block of ice lifted, Harvester inhaled her first full breath in...what, days? Again, the pain of her lungs filling with shockingly cold air sent a storm of agony through her.

Then the real pain set in as a layer of skin peeled off her body with the block of ice. Unable to scream through her frozen throat, she shrieked in her head, until her skull seemed ready to explode.

The block swung free, leaving her crushed, skinless from her ankles to the back of her neck, and unable to move as Venom looped a razor-sharp chain around her ankles.

Gethel moved into Harvester's field of vision, her frilly red maternity top filling Harvester's view. Helpless, Harvester watched as the angel bitch slashed her wrist with a dull knife before holding a crystal goblet to catch the blood streaming from the wound.

Harvester's head spun in sickeningly slow circles. Eventually Gethel pulled the goblet away, letting Harvester bleed into a gutter on the floor. Not that bleeding on the floor was anything new.

Gethel squatted next to Harvester and put the cup to her lips. "Lucifer will feed from you himself when he's born, but you can nourish him now, as well. With every swallow, tremors will rock Heaven. You are both so very connected."

*Crazy bitch.* The only person Harvester was connected to was Yenrieth, and that hadn't turned out so well.

*"Give me your hand."*

*Verrine didn't hesitate, even though she had no idea what Yenrieth was doing with a ceremonial blade. She trusted him, and she especially liked it when he touched her.*

*Very gently, he turned her hand over, palm up, and put the tip of the silver knife to the skin under her thumb.*

*"I'm going to connect us forever," he said, and she jerked.*

*"That's forbidden," she said in a gasp. "Only mated battle angels can do that."*

*"I'm a battle angel."*

*"But I'm not. And we aren't mated." Not that she wouldn't mate him if he asked. But right now he was proposing something very much against the rules. Heart racing, she yanked her hand away. "We'll be punished."*

*"Not if we don't tell anyone." He put the blade to his palm and drew a slow, shallow cut from the base of his pinky to the heel of his thumb. "We have to do this. I can't explain why. I just know that someday it's going to make sense."*

*Verrine's gut churned. Yenrieth had always known things, and he'd always been right, so she didn't question his intentions or his reasoning. But this was a substantial angelic offense. Not to mention that it would create a permanent link between them, and given that angels were immortal, it wasn't an act to be taken lightly. Not even if you'd loved the person asking you to link since the first day of Demon Hunting Basics class.*

*And yet, she held out her hand. Allowed him to slice*

*her palm the way he'd cut his. The pain was fleeting, gone the moment he twined his fingers with hers. Their blood ran together, and Verrine was lost in a moment of bliss so pure that all she could do was moan with the glory of it.*

*"We're linked," he whispered. "We'll forever be able to find each other, no matter where in the universe we are."*

He'd been wrong. On the day he disappeared from Heaven and memories, she lost the ability to feel him. It was as if he'd never existed. She'd searched for him for years, had made a nuisance of herself by questioning everyone she thought might have answers, but she'd come up empty. Not even the archangels had offered up any explanations.

She supposed the fact that no one remembered Yenrieth could explain why, but *someone* had to know something. Only after she'd lost her wings and gone to Sheoul had she given up the search, but that didn't mean she didn't sometimes wonder what had happened to him.

Gethel drained the goblet, and Harvester swore that an aura of power pulsed around her now, as oily and dark as a puddle of tar poison in Sheoul's Boneyard region. She wiped her mouth with the back of her hand and sighed contentedly.

"I'll see you at supper," Gethel said, all cheery. Harvester hoped Gethel was experiencing morning sickness. All day long.

Gethel slipped away as Venom tugged on the chain connected to Harvester's ankles, and she slid off the bottom block, taking another layer of skin from her body. The pain kept her from feeling the landing on the floor, at least.

Harvester felt herself being dragged over uneven, rocky ground, and as her body thawed, her agony jacked higher.

For the ten millionth time, she replayed the moment, thousands of years ago, when she'd stood before three archangels and said, "I want you to kick me out of Heaven so I can infiltrate Sheoul as a spy and earn my way to being the Horsemen's Watcher. I can work to subvert the *Daemonica*'s version of the Apocalypse."

The archangels had laughed until they realized she was serious. Raphael had thrown a full-blown angel tantrum that humans felt as a dust storm that swept across the Holy Land. And then Metatron and Uriel had joined in to try to talk her out of it, even as they agreed that if her plan worked, it would be the greatest Heavenly coup in history. If she failed, she'd suffer like no angel ever had.

Turned out that she'd succeeded... but she was still suffering like no angel ever had.

"The Dark Lord will break you tonight." Venom dropped the chain and crouched next to her to grip her face in his scaly hands. "You *will* tell him how much Heaven knew about your actionsss."

"Nothing," she croaked. "I swear." The lie came easily, which was, no doubt, why Satan didn't believe her. Thousands of years of living in Sheoul had chipped away at the angel she once was and had made many things simple. Lying. Destroying. Killing.

All she'd ever wanted was to be good, so it was ironic that in order to *do* good, she'd had to become bad. She'd had to make everyone she cared about hate her. She'd had to lose everything, from her self-respect to her wings to her dreams of having friends and a family with Yenrieth, the only person she'd ever loved.

The only thing she had left was knowledge, and that was something she would hang onto until her last breath.

Life as she'd known it was over, but she could still do good. All she had to do was keep her mouth shut while enduring an eternity of torture.

# Three

⌒

Reaver was about to rush in where angels feared to tread. "I guess that really does make me a—"

"Fucking idiot."

Reaver stared at Eidolon, Underworld General Hospital's head doctor. "I prefer 'fool.' Also, only a fucking idiot would call an angel a fucking idiot."

The demon doctor stared back, his dark eyes glittering with gold flecks. "A fool would merely *consider* entering hell without a plan. Only a fucking idiot would seriously intend to saunter into the Prince of Evil's living room in the very center of hell to kidnap his little girl. Against orders. And without a plan."

Harvester wasn't a little girl, but the doctor had a point. Reaver had done a lot of insane, stupid things in his thousands of years of life, had broken more rules than he could count. But disobeying the archangels to rescue a fallen angel who happened to be Satan's daughter was worse than all the other broken rules combined.

Well, impregnating Lilith, queen of the succubi, and fathering the Four Horsemen of the Apocalypse five thousand years ago was right up there. He was *still* being punished for that.

If Reaver pulled off this newest stunt, he'd be lucky if he lost only his wings. And that was assuming he survived to lose his wings in the first place.

"I have a plan," he muttered.

Eidolon parked a tray of surgical tools next to the exam table Reaver was sitting on inside the makeshift tent room in Underworld General's parking lot. As an angel, Reaver couldn't enter the hospital, so it was fortunate for him that the tent had been set up to handle the recent increase in patient volume.

"And your plan is?" Eidolon prompted.

"Ah...it mostly involves sneaking in and sneaking out."

Wraith, Eidolon's blond, blue-eyed brother, snorted. "Because you're *so* subtle." Reaver couldn't believe those words had come out of Wraith's mouth. Wraith, who was as subtle as a plane crash. Mr. Subtle pushed off the tent support he'd been leaning against. "So what's in it for you?"

"I'll have the personal satisfaction of knowing that if everything goes well, I'll be preventing a Heavenly catastrophe."

Wraith nailed him with his shrewd gaze, and Reaver knew instantly that the demon didn't buy his reason for what he was planning.

But Mr. Subtle was also Mr. Contrary, and instead of calling Reaver out, he shrugged. "I'll go with you."

"As much as I'd appreciate your help, everyone in the

underworld knows who you are." Reaver cocked an eyebrow at the Seminus demon, a rare species of incubus that were human in appearance. "You're a beacon for trouble."

"Hey." Wraith had a particular talent for playing wounded. "I saved the world. And I *helped* save it, like, a million times."

"I love how he makes it sound like the rest of us sat around and drank beer while he was saving the planet." Eidolon crossed his thick arms over his chest. On his right arm, his *dermoire*, a tattoo-like tapestry of paternal history every Seminus demon bore, blended in with his black scrubs.

"Do the Horsemen know about your dumbass non-plan?" Wraith asked, and Reaver stiffened.

"No." He shot each of them a meaningful stare. Sin, the demon brothers' only sister, rolled her dark eyes. "And I'm trusting you to not tell them."

As expected, Eidolon gave a respectful, if reluctant, nod, and so did Sin, but Wraith could never make things easy.

"Why not?" he asked. "They're the most powerful beings on Earth. And you're their daddy. They're going to want to help."

"That's why they can't know," Reaver said. "If they know what I'm planning, they're going to either try to stop me or try to help me. Either way, there's no force on Earth that can stop them once they get something into their collective heads. But there are forces in Heaven that can. And those forces will do whatever it takes to stop them from springing Harvester, including hurting their mates and children."

Besides, they'd been through enough in the last few

years. It was time for them to enjoy their lives with their new families.

"Then let us help," Sin said. "Wraith has a neon arrow pointing to his little pin head, but your Heavenly bullies won't recognize the rest of us."

"You'd be surprised. But no, I won't put any of you at risk." He held up a hand to stop Wraith from saying what Reaver knew he was going to say. "I know your charm will keep you safe from most dangers in Sheoul, but if word gets out that *any* of you helped me, Underworld General itself will be a target for Satan's minions."

"I hate to tell you this," Eidolon said as he gloved up, "but what I'm doing now is helping you. Strip."

Reaver unbuttoned his shirt. "You know what I mean."

Eidolon gestured to Wraith, who tossed him a glass vial. The tiny objects inside clinked as the container met Eidolon's palm.

"I had to kill three *lashers* for those, so treat them well."

"Three?" Reaver asked. "I only needed two *lasher* thyroid glands. One for each wing."

Wraith shrugged in his beaten-to-hell leather duster. "The third *lasher* tried to decapitate my mate."

Yeah, that would do it. Wraith, like all five of the Sem siblings, was extremely protective of his mate and offspring.

Eidolon took Reaver's shirt and tossed it to Sin. "This is going to hurt a little. Or... a lot."

Local anesthesia didn't work well on angels. Figured.

"You'd think angels wouldn't be big babies," Wraith said.

"I can deal," Reaver said. "It can't be that bad."

Eidolon swabbed the base of Reaver's wings with alcohol. "I'm inserting two gland sacs full of concentrated evil into your wings. Imagine someone drilling into your body and then leaving the drill bits inside."

Yeah, this was going to suck. But without a way to mask his "angelness," as Sin liked to put it, Reaver would attract every demon in Sheoul. He'd be dead within a day, once his Heavenly powers ran out.

"So if we can't help, why did you ask me to meet you here?" Sin asked.

"Because I could use a favor," he said. "You used to run an assassin den. Do you still have any pull with the current assassin master of your old den?"

"Maybe." Sin played with the long black braid falling over her shoulder. "Why?"

"I can't use most of the Harrowgates in Sheoul, and I have limited flashing abilities. I need a guide to get me in and out."

Reaver hated needing a guide for anything, but he needed all the help he could get for this particular mission. As a bonus, all assassins were skilled fighters, so if Sin could arrange it, Reaver would have command of his own Sheoul special ops team. Raphael and Metatron could shove the flight of angels he'd asked for up their asses.

"I can probably get Tavin on board for you. He's been everywhere," Sin said. "And as long as you pay, he can't be accused of helping an angel infiltrate hell."

Excellent. Tavin had been instrumental in saving Limos's husband's life a while back. Of course, a few days later Tavin had tried to kill Arik, but still, as far as demon assassins went, Reaver could do worse than having Tavin on his team.

"I'll also need someone who can feed Harvester. She'll need to drink blood to regrow her wings." Because wings were an angel's source of power, Satan would have had them removed immediately. Without them, no angel— fallen or not—could flash to another location, and their fighting abilities were severely limited. "And do you have someone familiar with the B'lal region of Sheoul?"

She shook her head. "No one is familiar with Satan's personal playground except his inner circle. And dead people. But I know a Nightlash demon who has made it as far as the Mountains of Eternal Suffering. And I'm pretty sure I can get you a werewolf assassin who likes to be fed on."

Reaver looked up at the chains looping across the tent ceiling supports before turning back to her. "How much is this going to cost me?"

She appeared to consider that. "One penny for each assassin," she chirped. "And a favor."

"What favor?"

"I don't know yet. Could be anything." She blinked at his flat stare. "What? I'm a mercenary. And a demon. I can't fight instinct."

Wraith grinned. "It's like we're twins."

Eidolon muttered something under his breath as his gloved fingers pressed firmly at the base of a wing anchor. "Reaver, I need you to take a deep breath. And don't flinch or summon your wings."

Angels didn't "summon" thier wings, but reminding Eidolon that wings morphed into a liquid form to melt under the skin of an angel's back when not in use was stupid, given that the demon was holding a scalpel.

"I'm tougher than Wraith seems to think—*holy shit*!"

Pain drilled into Reaver's back, exploding up his spine and knocking his ability to see, hear, or think right out of his skull.

He felt hands on his shoulders as someone braced him from the front. Another stab of agony nailed him. E, inserting the second pod of concentrated evil. Reaver would have taken a header if not for whoever was holding him upright.

Someone else took one of his hands. Sin. Her small palms cradled his hand, squeezing gently. Gradually, as the pain waned, his vision cleared. The outline of Wraith's big body appeared through fuzzy waves of gray mist.

There had been a time, years ago, when Reaver's opinion of these demons had been less than favorable. As an Unfallen angel employed at the hospital, Reaver had been steeped in bitterness and self-pity. He'd been bred to battle demons, and instead he worked with them. Healed them.

Now these Sems had become his family, which was even more bizarre considering he'd been restored to a full-blown angel.

"Done." Eidolon's fingers smoothed over the bilateral incisions he'd made beneath Reaver's shoulder blades. "The *lasher* glands are going to slowly release hormones that'll mask your angelic signature, but you're on a ticking clock. You've got, at most, thirty days before they run out. Less than that if you hit parts of Sheoul where time runs faster than here." Eidolon stepped around in front of Reaver and trashed his gloves. "There might be a slight side effect."

Reaver didn't like the sound of that. "Side effect?"

"*Lasher* glands are a hot item on the underworld black market because they can boost some species' power. It's possible that because you're an angel, the effect could do the opposite in you. It could cause your powers to either warp or drain rapidly."

Perfect. Because the cards hadn't been stacked against him enough.

"You sure we can't go with you?" Sin asked.

"I'm sure. But E? I might be needing a job after I lose my wings."

He was only half-joking, and Eidolon knew it. "You always have a place here," Eidolon said solemnly. "You know that."

"Good luck, man." Wraith clapped him on the shoulder. "For an angel, you don't suck."

"Ditto. For a demon . . . well, you do suck."

"Because I'm half vampire?"

"Sure," Reaver said. "Let's go with that."

Wraith beamed. "So," he said, "you really think having archangels string you up by your halo is worth saving this Harvester chick?"

Yes. "Even if stopping Lucifer's reincarnation isn't a good enough reason to rescue her, she still deserves it," he said. "She saved the world."

Wraith shrugged. "So did I, but I don't see you offering up your holy ass to save *me*."

"Are you suffering unspeakable horrors at the hands of Satan?"

"No," Wraith said, "but sometimes I have to eat hospital cafeteria food."

Reaver sighed. Wraith was a hundred-year-old child. "She also saved Reseph's life when he was a kid, and she kept watch over all four of my children while they were growing up. And she might be able to help me put together some pieces of my past."

"She remembers you? Does she know who you used to be?"

He shook his head. "She might remember Yenrieth, but she was taken to Sheoul before even *I* learned the truth of who I was, so she wouldn't have connected me with Yenrieth."

Sin looked up from her cell phone. "I met her a couple of times. She was a heinous bitch."

Reaver had thought the same thing for so long. The fallen angel had taunted him at every turn, defied him whenever possible, fought him until they were both bloody, and tortured him on one occasion. Now he was going to risk his tail feathers to save her.

"It was all an act," he said, but the burning skepticism in Sin's eyes said she wasn't buying it. He wasn't sure if he bought it, either.

Eidolon shouted through the tent opening at a passing vampire paramedic, something about checking the duty schedule, and then he turned back to Reaver. "How do you know where she's being held?"

"Gethel mentioned Satan's pressing machines," Reaver said, and Sin shuddered.

"He has his own blood wine label," she said. "His pressing machines are supposed to both chill the blood and squash it out of you."

Reaver couldn't even begin to imagine the horror of being "juiced," and the idea that it was happening to Harvester only made him more eager to get her the hell out of there. Literally.

"His pressing machines are located in his main dungeon complex," Reaver said. "That's where she'll be."

Wraith shoved his hands in his jeans' pockets. "How

long before we consider you overdue and mount a rescue party?"

"Never." Reaver shrugged into his shirt. "If I don't come back, it's because I'm either dead or in a situation that's too dangerous to get me out of."

"Oh," Sin said brightly—and sarcastically. "You mean like the situation Harvester is in."

Seminus demons were annoying no matter what gender. "Yes. Like that."

She punched him lightly in the shoulder. "Good. Glad we're clear. Try to come back soon or we'll come after you."

"Don't do anything dumbass-ish, my fine feathered friend," Wraith said.

Eidolon clasped Reaver's hand. "Good luck. Something tells me you'll need it."

Luck? No, Reaver needed something more powerful than that.

He needed a miracle.

# *Four*

⌒

Five days. Reaver and the three assassins Sin had hooked Reaver up with had been traveling through Sheoul for five days. Felt like five years. They'd been attacked by seventy-one different breeds of demons, over a hundred plant species, and more demonic animals than Reaver could keep track of.

They'd been scalded in torrential rains of boiling water. Nearly frozen by blasts of liquid nitrogen in a region of ice and snow. And they'd been singed by rivers of lava that leaked through stone retaining walls as tall as the eye could see.

Making matters worse, Tavin, the blond Seminus demon Reaver had been acquainted with for a couple of years, kept telling Reaver that they were still in the "upscale" parts of hell.

So far, the biggest dangers were environmental, since Reaver's powers were more than enough to deal with most minor demons. The most pressing problem was that he recharged slower here even with Raphael and Gethel's *sheoulghuls*, and as Eidolon predicted, his weapons sometimes went wonky.

Earlier, he'd summoned a ball of fire to throw at a *croix viper*, and the ball of flames had expanded to twenty times its size before growing teeth, claws, and a tail. The fire-animal had then devoured not just the *croix viper*, but every demon within a hundred-yard radius. Another assassin, a werewolf named Matt, was lucky to have escaped its fiery wrath. Reaver had been forced to destroy his own weapon before it ate the guy alive.

Fortunately, all three assassins turned out to be excellent fighters. Tavin's ability to explode eyeballs with a touch was especially impressive. It had definitely come in handy against a ten-foot-tall demon with butcher-knife-sized teeth and two dozen eyes.

*Pop! Pop! Pop!* Eyes everywhere. Some powers were meant for fun.

"How many times have you been to Sheoul before this?" Matt asked warily as he pulled his brown- and black-singed hair into a low ponytail.

"Thousands," Reaver said. "Hundreds of thousands." He shrugged. "It was nothing like this, though. Angels are extremely limited in where we can go and how long we can stay. Coming here is usually a quick in and out." He took a bite of some ugly little animal Tavin had caught and roasted over their fire. They'd camped on the banks of the Inferno river, in a region Reaver had never explored before. "Get out before the devil knows we're here."

"Just like that country song," Tavin chimed in from where he was sitting next to Matt.

The third assassin, Calder, was on patrol, which was fine with Reaver. The Nightlash demon smelled of cigarettes and mildew, and he was a crude, violent bastard on the best of days. Once, Reaver had even been forced to stop him from assaulting a female enemy following a battle. Reaver might have actually killed the fucker if not for Tavin and Matt pointing out that what made Calder abhorrent to Reaver made him an asset in Sheoul. And of the three assassins, he was the only one familiar with the regions surrounding Satan's stronghold.

Reaver cocked an eyebrow at Tavin. "You don't strike me as country guy."

Tavin snorted. "I'm not. Our assassin master took Sin's idea to make an inspirational playlist of every song that mentions hell and run it on a constant loop in the assassin den."

"I'm guessing you're not as enamored with the music?"

"Only if *enamored* is code for wanting to slit your wrists just so you can hear the sound of your blood pumping out instead of the twang of some annoying human yammering about sin."

"Ah. In that case, I've been *enamored* a few times myself."

"By annoying music?"

Reaver shot Tavin a pointed look. "By annoying, yammering demons."

Tavin took a swig of water from his canteen. "And people say angels aren't funny."

"Who says that?"

"Everyone," Tavin said, and Matt nodded in agreement.

Well, Reaver couldn't dispute that. Most angels he knew were all serious and dour. The ones who weren't were sweet and happy and...floaty. Like Mary Poppins on an acid trip and a pot of coffee. Reaver didn't know which was worse.

Standing, Tavin stretched his arms and worked the kinks out of his neck. "I'm going to go find a female. You gonna get some rest?"

Reaver shook his head. "I need to log our travel today. Go." He waved the demon away. "I'll plot out our trek for tomorrow."

"Just make sure we take the southern route through the Razor Eyelets. The northern track will put us at the desert edge of Satan's region. We don't want that."

Reaver didn't ask why. If Tavin didn't want to go there, it must be bad. The demon was fearless and resourceful, but he didn't have a death wish.

Matt left to join Calder on patrol as Tavin took off for a Harrowgate he'd sensed a quarter of a mile away. Reaver kicked back with his journal and noted the day's events, including mapping out the areas they'd been through, places no angel had ever seen. His journal would be a priceless record if he survived the trip home, likely studied for centuries by the greatest minds in Heaven.

Of course, he probably wouldn't be around to see how the fruits of his efforts paid off. Not if the archangels had their way. Rains of fire, severed wings, maybe death… those were what he had to look forward to.

Shoving his possible impending wingectomy and death aside, he recorded the demons, plants, and animals he'd come across, including descriptions, strengths, and weaknesses he'd observed, and the locations where he'd found them. He finished with personal notes about the journey so far, and then he tucked the book away and dug out the crude maps Tavin had brought with them.

They didn't have far to go, maybe two days' travel, but the remaining distance was going to be brutal. In approximately five miles, they'd hit the Wall of Skulls, a massive barricade that surrounded an entire region and extended hundreds of feet upward. The things that guarded the openings varied from nearly microscopic parasites that drilled into the body in search of vital organs to massive dragon-like beasts with teeth as tall as three-story buildings. Then there were the squads of vicious, eyeless Silas demons that patrolled the ramparts, killing intruders to add to the skulls lining the walls.

Next, they'd have rivers of lava, dead forests full of pain-feeding monsters, and an entire region dedicated to torture devices to navigate before reaching Satan's territory.

From there, Reaver would be on his own. Their group would draw too much attention, so the plan was for him to sneak in to Satan's torture complex, grab Harvester, and meet up with Tavin, Matt, and Calder for the journey home.

That was the plan, anyway.

In the distance, something shrieked. Something else screamed. And a few somethings snarled. Here, in hell's underbelly, those were probably comforting sounds. No doubt someone had developed a sleep app with the lulling white noise of pain, misery, and fighting.

Ah, Sheoul.

Reaver closed his eyes and put his head back against the rock wall. *Hold on, Harvester. I'm coming.*

But would she welcome him or fight him? She hated him, and if the archangels were to be believed, she'd accepted her fate a long time ago. She might resist an attempt to rescue her.

Not that it mattered. Reaver was saving her if he had to kill her to do it.

In this case, death could only be a relief.

For the first time since Harvester had been brought to Sheoul for an eternity of torment, she wasn't miserable. Oh, she wasn't exactly comfortable, what with the way she was naked and hanging by her wrists over a pool of bubbling acid, but at least she wasn't freezing or burning or being tortured.

Granted, she couldn't see, since her eyes had been gouged out a few hours ago, but the pain from that had dissipated as her body tried to heal and make new peepers. She couldn't hear very well, either; her most recent torturer had driven thin spikes into her ears and shattered her eardrums. Again, the pain was long gone, and she was pleasantly numb.

So as long as she was by herself in this room, either forgotten or left to grow agonizingly hungry and thirsty, she was going to enjoy the break.

Enjoy. She was going to *enjoy* something while enduring an eternity of torture. The very fact that the word *enjoy* had broken through the gray matter of her brain at all was a measure of how high a threshold for pain and how low a threshold for pleasure she now had.

She wanted to laugh. A hysterical, mindless laugh that would end in tears. Except she had no tear ducts.

Deranged laughter bubbled up but never got the chance to surface. A faint tremor prickled her skin.

Again. And again. The vibrations came in a steady beat, and she choked on a sob when she realized what they were.

*Footsteps.*

Cold terror knotted every one of her muscles, locking her up so hard she could barely breathe. As miserable as she was now, at least she was alone. No one was making her scream in agony. No one was demanding answers from her with sharp objects or torturing her with bloody threats they always followed through on.

The tremors grew stronger. Someone was coming closer, and dread made her empty stomach churn.

Warmth spread over her back. Whoever was in the room was just inches away.

"Who are you?" Harvester felt hands on her, felt the whisper of someone's words against her cheek, but she couldn't hear or see, and even her ability to think was being stripped away by impending panic.

The chains looped around her wrists came free. She dropped toward the acid pool below, but even as she started to scream, a hand covered her mouth and she was cradled firmly against a very broad chest.

This was a new torture. Usually while she was either blind or deaf or both, they struck her or cut her or worse—making her go mad with anxiety over where the next pain would come from and how bad it would be.

This was far more horrible. Whoever was hauling her away was being gentle. She didn't like gentle. Gentle always resulted in pain. Mental or physical, it always hurt.

She trembled, waiting for it. This asshole would skin her, or he'd stab her with a red-hot iron. Or he'd impale her on a spike. Maybe he'd violate her over and over before handing her off to friends. Perhaps he'd trick her into trusting him, and then he'd turn on her.

No matter what, it would be agonizing.

The whisper came again, a light, warm caress of air on her cheek. Soft lips brushed her skin, and she wondered what species of demon they belonged to. He was likely hideous, but she was sure he was male. Every place her body was in contact with his was rock hard and there was a very masculine note to his scent—which was surprisingly pleasant.

And familiar. But why?

She wracked her brain for the answer, but fear of the unknown and the pain of the last round of torture kept her brain too occupied to delve deep into the mystery. All she could do was wait for him to take her to wherever her new, fresh hell would take place.

The lips again. Speaking against her forehead. The male's hand came up to tuck her head against his chest in what she could almost believe was a protective gesture before suddenly, he was moving fast, his movements jerky and violent. Twice he almost dropped her, and she lost count of the number of times he banged her against something. Each time, those lips would caress her skin, and deep in his chest, a rumble would vibrate through her body.

What was going on?

It seemed like they went on this way forever, with him sprinting like a madman through an obstacle course, and then occasionally stopping and going very, very still, with only his chest rising and falling as though he were panting. His heartbeat was a fast tap against her chest that never seemed to slow down. How could he go on like this? Surely his heart would explode or he'd collapse. And where were they going?

She lost track of time, and she thought she might have

even fallen asleep once. Sleep that was brought to a painful, abrupt halt when she fell out of his arms and tumbled over what she assumed were sharp rocks.

As she lay on the ground her ability to hear cut in and out like a bad radio signal. The earth around her shuddered and shook...a battle was taking place. She had no idea where to go or how to protect herself, so she curled into a ball and hoped she was out of the way.

Gradually, the sounds of battle died away, and the male returned, his scent now carrying the distinct tinge of blood, sweat, and combat. Normally, she'd find those scents sexy. Now they just made her shiver with the unknown.

His palms came down on her head and her breath jammed in her lungs. What was he going to do to her? His hands roamed over her body and she cringed, waiting for a violation. Thankfully, after a rapid check from her feet to her head, he picked her up and they were off again, heading God knew where for God knew what.

Again, she lost track of time as he moved, sometimes running, sometimes skidding to a halt. Twice more he put her down to fight, and twice more she scented him when he returned. The second time, she welcomed his attention, because as frightened as she was, so far, he hadn't hurt her.

Silky soft lips brushed her cheek again. "There... can...in...rest."

She started. Words? She'd heard him! Finally, her hearing was coming back online. "Who..." She swallowed, but her mouth might as well have been a desert. "Who are you?"

"It's...I...you'll...okay. Tav will...and rest."

The words were louder this time, but no clearer. Her heart started to pound. What should she do? Plot an escape? Help him with whatever it was he was doing? She hated this. Hated not knowing what was going on or what she should do. Worst of all, she hated not knowing what she should feel. Fear? Gratitude? Both were emotions that didn't come easily to her.

She was far more comfortable with hate.

The male stopped and smoothed his finger over the shell of her ear. The telltale tingle of healing energy entered her body and, as if the world had suddenly gone from peaceful night to daytime in the city, sounds flooded her ears. In the distance, there were shrieks and barking noises. Somewhere close by, the distinct rattling of crispy tree leaves in the breeze joined the male's labored breathing.

"Tell me," she rasped, "your name."

"It's me," he murmured in a voice that filled her with disbelief. Dread. Relief. Emotions that didn't mix well. Like fear and gratitude. Love and hate. "It's me. It's Reaver."

# *Five*

⌣

"R-Reaver?"

Reaver held Harvester's frail body tight against his as he navigated the final steps of a winding ledge that dropped them into a world of weird. "It's me. It's okay. We're safe."

Relatively safe, anyway. *Relative* meaning that they weren't dead. Yet. He just hoped the same could be said for Tavin, Matt, and Calder. When he'd left them to sneak into Satan's realm, they'd been engaged in a battle they'd initiated as a diversion. It had been a risky move, and Reaver could only pray they'd make it to the rendezvous point.

A hunter's horn sounded in the distance and was answered by another, closer horn signal. Satan's minions hadn't gained ground, but they were spreading out. *Damn*.

He scanned the landscape of thorny plants, hills of blackened earth and trees, and twisted, abandoned structures. Nothing moved.

He looked down at Harvester, and as before when he first saw her hanging over a pit of acid, he felt sick to his stomach. He didn't like Harvester even though he was grateful for the things she'd done, but she didn't deserve this; her naked body too thin and mottled with bruises and ligature marks, her once silken black hair tangled and dull, and worst of all, missing her gorgeous green eyes.

Under ideal circumstances, an angel could heal from even the most heinous injuries within hours. But these were far from ideal circumstances, and Harvester's source of power, her wings, had been severed. Without wings or medical assistance, it could take weeks, even months, for an angel's body to fully heal.

"I can't risk healing you more than I did," he said. "My power isn't reliable right now, and I could do more harm than good."

"Reaver," she croaked, as if he hadn't spoken. "Why ... how ..."

"Shh." He tucked her face into his chest, quieting her. "We're going to meet up with some friends, and then I'll answer all your questions."

Reaver and the assassins had worked out a plan A and a plan B. Plan A had been shot to hell when iron gates had prevented Reaver from getting out of Satan's realm to the south, where his companions would have been waiting. Now, with demons in pursuit, they were on their way to plan B. Hopefully Tav, Matt, and Calder had realized quickly that Reaver's escape route had gone bad.

Inhaling the stench of rotten vegetation that permeated this section of Sheoul, he started away from the skeletons of some burned-out buildings and toward a mountain range as expansive as the Rockies. He moved swiftly, outrunning the sounds of pursuit and pausing once to blast a group of imps with a ball of lightning. The sphere struck the leader, and from there sent electrical strikes at each of the surrounding imps, frying them all in a handy eight-for-one.

Harvester slept in his arms, barely stirring when he stopped to listen for anyone following them. By the time they neared the plan B meeting site, Reaver was sure they'd lost the demons—temporarily. Reaver wasn't naive enough to think they were off the hook. The demons chasing them were only the first wave, the security detail unlucky enough to be guarding the dungeon Harvester was kept in.

Once Satan got wind of this, if he hadn't already, Reaver and Harvester were going to have legions of minions on their heels.

A trail carved into sheer canyon walls dropped them into a narrow valley, where he found Tavin near a dense copse of twenty-foot-high larva-nettle bushes that bit like snakes. Worse, the bastards implanted their larva into the victim, and anyone unlucky enough to play host to the spiny larva died a week later when branches started popping out of their bodies.

Wisely, Tavin had positioned himself several feet away.

"Dude." Tav stepped out from behind a gnarled tree trunk, his crossbow up and ready to nail anything that moved. "I can't believe you fucking did it. Man, when all hell broke loose from inside Satan's realm, I figured you were a goner."

"If you can't get us out of here soon, I still might be."

"I'll get you out of here, but we still have a three-day journey to a spot where you can flash us out."

Three days. They might not last three hours if they ran into Satan's minions. "Where are Matt and Calder?"

Tav used his bow to gesture to a path that wound between trees and jagged stones. "Calder's scouting the route ahead. We lost Matt in the Valley of Screams, but he knows this is where we're supposed to meet." Tav's voice, normally level, was strained. "I hope the warg's okay. He's my drinking buddy. Plus, he's supposed to introduce me to his sister. She's a porn star. Fucking cool."

Reaver hoped Matt was okay, too, but for different reasons. Reaver liked the guy, but more important, Matt had agreed to be Harvester's blood source. Now they were stuck waiting for him. Without blood, her wings weren't going to heal quickly enough to help them, and without wings, she was almost powerless.

He shifted Harvester in his arms. "She needs to heal. Can you zap her?"

"No can do," Tav replied. "I drained myself. Didn't you see all the dead *croucher* demons at the top of the canyon? The ones with popped eyes?" He jerked his thumb at his own chest. "My work. I'm awesome."

Well, Reaver couldn't explode eyeballs, but he had other tricks up his sleeve, and they needed to take shelter. He turned to the larva-nettle bushes and froze them with a mere word, turning them into ice-glazed salads.

Harvester squirmed in his arms. "What's happening?" Her voice was so raspy he could hardly understand her.

"We're at our rendezvous," he said. "I'm going to put you down."

"Bastard." She clung tightly to him. "Don't go."

Only Harvester could push someone away while simultaneously keeping them close. She was the most contradictory person he'd ever met.

And the fact that she wanted him to stay near was an

indication of how traumatized she was. He'd seen her in emotional and physical pain before, and her response had always been to retreat like a wounded animal.

"I'm not leaving." He ran his hand over her hair in long, soothing strokes, but she didn't release her iron grip on his shoulders. "I promise. I have to clear out a place to rest, but I'll be only a few feet away, and Tavin will be here with you. Do you remember him? He tried to kill Arik that one time. Limos still gives Tav the evil eye for nearly gutting her husband."

"It was nothing personal," Tavin muttered. "I *am* an assassin."

Harvester nodded, but Reaver still had to peel her off him. He placed her gently on the ground, where she wrapped her arms around her knees and huddled, her body shaking. She wasn't cold, not in this sweltering heat. But he knew too well how trauma and fear manifested, and he hoped that once she'd eaten, rested, and cleaned up her strength and stamina would return.

But would *she* return? She could be a world-class wench when she wanted to be, but he much preferred that over the quiet, frightened Harvester. This new Harvester could have him softening toward her, and he'd learned that she was a master at exploiting soft spots.

Tav gave him an I-got-it-handled nod, and as quickly as Reaver could, he wrestled iced-over branches aside and burrowed his way into the center of the bush. At their cores, larva-nettles were hollow, creating a natural hideaway that few would bother trying to search. Once the thing thawed, it would ignore whatever had secreted itself inside it and would go back to defending itself against anyone who came close.

He removed a blanket from his backpack, spread it on the ground, and went back outside.

Tavin grabbed Reaver's arm and lowered his voice. "We can't stay here long. Matt can catch up."

"I know." Reaver looked over at Harvester, who was still curled up tight, her forehead resting on her knees as she rocked slowly back and forth. "But she can't continue like this. We've traveled for hours and she hasn't improved. She needs rest." He eyed the Sem. "If worse comes to worse, are you okay with letting her feed from you?"

Tavin snorted. "I'm always okay with having a female's mouth on me."

Reaver bristled. "Feeding *only*."

"Chill, buddy. She's in bad shape, and I do have standards."

Reaver wondered if Tav's standards meant he didn't do fallen angels, or if his standards were about not screwing badly injured people. Hopefully both.

"Glad we're clear," Reaver said, giving Tav an uneasy look. Ingesting incubus blood made a lot of species mad with lust, and the energy expended on sex would lessen the healing effects of the blood.

Plus, the idea of Harvester getting naked with the demon made Reaver uneasy. And the fact that he was uneasy made him even more uneasy. Why should he care whom she had sex with?

"Clear as a False Angel's tears," Tavin said. False Angel tears were toxic to many, so Reaver wasn't sure how to take that. "But if you're worried about it, why don't you let her suck on you?"

Reaver's cock jerked, clearly taking the suck thing the

wrong way. "Because it'll drain my powers, and worse, angel blood can turn fallen angels into mindless beasts." Harvester was difficult enough to deal with *now*. "We'll take turns standing watch. Can you take the first shift until Calder gets back?"

"Yup."

"Let me know right away when Matt gets here."

At Tav's nod, Reaver gathered Harvester in his arms, slipped back inside the bush, and placed her on the thin layer of wool. She simultaneously scooted away from him and gripped his wrist with bruising force until he gently peeled her fingers away.

"I have food and clothes," he said as he dug through the backpack for a canteen, a bottle of honey, and another blanket.

Crouching in front of her, he draped the second blanket over her shoulders and wrapped her carefully.

She said nothing as he gathered the ends and tucked them into her trembling hands. It wasn't until he put the canteen to her lips and she'd taken several swallows that she finally spoke.

"Do you have an *aurial*?"

Shit. Asking about a weapon designed specifically to kill angels didn't bode well. "No," he lied.

She let out a ragged breath. "Then how do you plan to kill me?"

"Kill you?"

"Aren't you here to destroy me?" She sounded almost disappointed.

"Nope." She didn't need to know that he'd mentally prepared himself to do exactly that if circumstances called for it. He wouldn't allow her to suffer at her father's command for all eternity. He popped the cap on the honey and held it up. "Open your mouth."

She swatted blindly, knocking the honey to the ground. "Are you taking me to be tortured?" Fisting his T-shirt, she tugged him close, her sudden strength fueled by desperation. "I can't... I can't take more. I know you hate me, but please, I'm begging you. Kill me."

"I'm here to rescue you, Harvester." Reaver cupped her cheek, hating how gaunt it felt, how papery her skin was under his fingers.

Bewilderment left deep grooves in her forehead as she released him. "But... why?"

Once again, he held the honey up. "Open your mouth, and I'll answer your questions." When she hesitated, he added, "It's just honey."

She went taut, and he wondered if she was remembering how, when she'd held him captive in her home, she'd spooned honey into his mouth after he'd taken a brutal beating from Pestilence. He didn't push her, and he breathed a sigh of relief when she finally opened up and allowed him to squeeze a small glop of the life-giving sugar onto her tongue.

Almost instantly, her color improved, and under her sunken eyelids, new tissue began to form.

"That's my girl," he murmured.

She hissed, flashing fangs as she struck out again, catching the honey bottle with her elbow and barely missing raking him with her nails. "I'm not your girl."

"Well," he said, not bothering to hide his smile from her sightless eyes, "the good news is that the honey gave you back your sparkling personality."

"And the bad news?"

"The honey gave you back your sparkling personality."
She huffed. "You didn't answer my question."

Yep, she was back, but he couldn't find it in himself to be irritated.

"You want to know why I'm here?" He reached for the honey bottle. Again. "It's because I know the truth about you. I know you've been Heaven's spy since the Horsemen were cursed."

Harvester's fingers tightened on the blanket and her mouth worked silently for a few heartbeats. "Who told you?"

"Raphael." He squeezed more honey into her mouth.

The pink tip of her tongue swept her bottom lip to catch a sticky drop that clung there. Damn, even as torn up as she was, she exuded a smoky sexuality that had made Reaver crazy from the moment he met her. Sure, she'd attacked him for no reason and he'd hated her instantly, but hatred hadn't put a damper on the insane desire he felt whenever she was near.

He'd made a conscious effort to avoid her whenever he could because, like it or not, Reaver didn't have a lot of willpower when it came to lust.

And then she'd forced him to consent to the very thing he'd been trying hard to not even think about.

*"You agree to pleasure me at the time of my choosing."*

Harvester wouldn't thank him for saving her, of that he was sure, but at the very least, he'd make sure she let him out of the ludicrous bargain they'd struck last year when she'd rescued him from Sheoul-gra.

"Raphael?" She frowned. "I still don't understand. Why would the archangels send you?"

"They didn't."

"They...*didn't*?" Dropping the blanket, she grabbed his shirt again, this time in both fists. "Tell me they know you're here. *Tell me*."

"They *didn't* know I was here," he said, putting effort into keeping his voice light and calm, even though he wasn't feeling it, "but we stirred things up pretty good. They've probably gotten word by now."

"Oh, no," she whispered. "Oh...*no*." Releasing him, she opened her eyes. They'd fully formed but were crystal clear, not yet capable of sight. "They're going to destroy you, Reaver."

She said it like he wasn't aware of that fact. And why did she care, anyway? "It'll be okay—"

"No, it won't! You fool!" she spat out. "You've signed your own death warrant."

The blanket had pooled at her hips, leaving her upper body exposed, but she didn't seem to notice. Reaver noticed, but not because her breasts were perfect and he knew how they looked in a skimpy bikini top. He noticed because of the light pink lash marks crisscrossing her chest, and a dark cloud of anger descended on him. He suddenly wanted to lay waste to every vile creature who had laid a finger on her.

He told himself his reaction was ingrained in his battle angel DNA—he'd always felt an intense desire to kill demons who harmed people. He told himself that, but for some reason he heard Eidolon's voice in his head saying bullshit. The demon had always been a straight shooter.

And look at that, Reaver was an angel with a demon on his shoulder.

"Don't worry about me right now." He settled the blanket around her shoulders, but again, it went ignored and fell open in front. "You need to save your strength to heal."

"I'm not worried about you, and healing is pointless," she replied. "You've got to kill me. Let Satan think you pulled a lone wolf and did it to get back at me for kidnapping you and helping Pestilence. The archangels will be furious that you went against their orders, but you'll probably keep your wings. It'll be a win-win all around."

"I'm not killing you, so stop asking. We need you to track down Gethel, and we have to do it fast. She's pregnant—"

"With Lucifer," Harvester interrupted. "I know. Gethel wants me to be his Binky."

"Binky?"

"His pacifier." She tucked her legs under her, and he was glad to see some of the abrasions had healed. "He'll be born fully grown, and he'll need the blood of a sibling to help him achieve full strength. She already made a meal of me to make him stronger."

Damn. "If we can kill him before he's reborn, he won't be using anyone as a Binky."

One curvy shoulder shrugged under the blanket. "I'm not helping you track him down, so you might as well kill me now."

"Why won't you help?"

"Because."

He ground his teeth. "Whether you help or not, I'm not killing you, and that's final."

"You're as stubborn as ever."

"*I'm* the stubborn one?" His mind churned with reasons she would refuse to help find Lucifer, but only one made sense. "You're refusing to help find Lucifer just so I'll kill you."

"Maybe," she said, "I'm refusing because I'm evil and Lucifer is going to be my brother. Ever think of that?"

She wasn't serious. She couldn't be serious. But she'd never been easy to read, and her expression right now would earn her a first-place ribbon at a mule show.

"I don't believe you," he ground out.

"Then maybe you'll believe me when I say you're going to regret not killing me."

"*That* I believe." He cursed, rethinking this entire rescue. "We'll find Lucifer without your help." How, he had no idea. Just surviving the journey out of Sheoul was going to be difficult enough.

"Good luck." The irritation in her tone was mixed with exhaustion, and a moment later, she yawned.

"Let me get Tav in here. You need to feed." As much as he hated the idea of her feeding from the incubus and getting all jacked up, he hated the fact that Harvester was so damaged even more.

Her sightless eyes shot wide. "No one touches me. Not until I can see."

He didn't want to be a dick and argue, but with his powers so compromised and probably every demon in Sheoul after them, they needed her to be as strong as possible.

"You need to regrow your wings—"

"I said no," she snapped, the color rising in her face. "Don't you see that I'm *blind*?"

Saying she was blind was the closest Harvester had ever come to admitting to having any kind of vulnerability. Bile rose in his throat at the level of desperation she must be feeling, and though it went against every instinct, he gave her more time to come around.

"We can wait until you wake up." Hopefully Matt

would be back by then. Werewolves, with their human origins, provided more nourishment than demons, by far. Very slowly, he reached for her. She flinched when his fingers brushed her shoulder. "You need to get some rest."

He urged her to lie back on the ground. She went without an argument, which told him how tired she was. Harvester never did anything without a fight or a cutting word.

Closing her eyes, she curled up under the blanket, and within a couple of heartbeats, she was breathing in a deep, even rhythm.

But just as Reaver breathed a sigh of relief that she was asleep, she stiffened and gasped in alarm. "My father," she croaked. "I can feel him. He's coming for us, Reaver. Satan's coming."

# *Six*

Very little frightened Revenant.

But right now, standing in Satan's living room, he was scared shitless and sweating bullets inside his black leathers.

The Dark Lord's rage was a force of nature that rocked the building, knocking over statues and shattering pillars and putting deep cracks in the walls, the floor, the ceiling. And in Rev's skull.

Revenant clutched his head in his hands as Satan's roar of fury blasted his eardrums. Blood ran from his ears, his nose, his mouth.

But he was far, far better off than the werewolf hanging from a hook in the middle of the room, his body shredded and studded with nails, blood streaming from a gaping hole where his eye used to be.

"Someone stole her," Satan snarled. "Someone took her right out from under my nose." He roared again. "*How?*" He grabbed the werewolf by the throat. "You helped. Tell me who took my daughter from me or I'll carve out your other eye and eat it while it's still warm."

The guy admitted to being an assassin, which meant he likely couldn't talk about who hired him even if he wanted to. The assassin's oath was binding on a magical level, and while the spell could be broken, doing so would take time, and it would kill the assassin. And Revenant had a feeling Satan wanted to kill this guy with his bare hands. Or, as he was sporting right now, claws.

The male groaned, his blood-streaked face a mask of agony. Then he screamed when the king of all demons drove one long, sharp claw through his pupil.

"I want her back." The black veins under Satan's skin visibly pulsed with the force of his anger. "I want my beloved Harvester back where she belongs. On a skinning block, writhing in blood-soaked misery."

Beloved? Skinning block? Satan had a strange way of showing affection. Revenant really wished the demon would stop sometimes referring to him as "my son," which, as far as he knew, wasn't true.

*Please let it not be true.*

Satan popped the werewolf's eyeball into his mouth and chewed thoughtfully. After a moment he wheeled around to Revenant, and Rev's bowels turned to water.

"You said Metatron and Raphael paid a visit to the Horsemen. Did they discuss rescuing Harvester?"

"No, my lord. Not that I heard." The bastards had rendered him immobile, deaf, and blind. When he'd come to, all of the angels were gone, including Reaver and Lorelia. "I don't think the Horsemen even know of her status as a plant for Heaven." They'd been as confused—and pissed—as Revenant when they'd gained consciousness.

Satan snarled, his mood going suddenly sour. "I want Harvester and the heads of those responsible for stealing her. And I swear by all that's unholy that if angels are involved, I'll devastate Heaven. Once that angel-infested realm is nothing but smoldering ash and there's no one to save the weakling humans, I'll turn my legions loose on the earthly realm."

Revenant nodded with as much eagerness as he could muster. He hated angels and thought humans were an annoying infestation on an otherwise nice planet, but the idea of turning Heaven and Earth into replicas of Sheoul didn't sit well. He'd never been to Heaven, but he liked the Earth the way it was. The colors were vibrant. The air was fresh, the sunlight pleasant on the skin. Best of all, it wasn't crawling with demons. Well, it was, but mostly, they remained hidden behind human masks.

But if Satan had his way, everything would change. He'd been wanting war for eons, and now he might have his excuse. Even more important, he now had the means to carry through with his threat. Lucifer's birth would be the opening salvo that would strike the Heavenly realm like a magnitude million-point-nine earthquake, weakening its very foundations and paving the way for a demon invasion.

A demon invasion Satan would organize should Harvester admit to her espionage, or should her rescuers be either angels—or backed by angels. Any of those scenarios meant that Heaven had broken a substantial law that archangels themselves had drafted along with both the Sheoulic and Heavenly Watcher Councils. And if they'd violated the statute that stated that neither Heaven nor Sheoul could plant an agent inside the enemy Watcher ranks, the penalty was a matter of souls.

In this case, Heaven would default a hundred thousand souls to Satan. Plus an angel of his choice.

"Can't another of your children feed Lucifer?" Revenant asked, and he swallowed dryly as Satan rounded on him again.

"Of course," he growled. "But she's the oldest of my progeny, and the only one conceived while I was still an angel. Her blood is ten times more powerful than any of my other sons and daughters. I need the bitch." Reaching up, he rubbed one of his horns. "And I'm not even close to being done punishing her for betraying me."

He turned back to the werewolf, and with a vicious swipe, he ripped into the male's belly. Blood and organs spilled onto the floor. The warg's screams faded away, but before the poor jackass could die, Satan partially healed him with a flick of the wrist.

*Partially*, because you never wanted your torture subject to be pain free.

"Go back to your duty, Revenant. Bypass the Watcher Council and come directly to me if anything happens with the Horsemen or their Watcher." He sneered. "They might know more than they're saying."

It was against Watcher rules to break the chain of command—even if Satan himself requested it. But the fuck if Revenant was going to point that out, so he merely bowed. "Yes, my lord."

"And Rev," he said silkily, "don't let me down, or you'll take Harvester's place on the skinning block." He gestured to the door with his blood-coated clawed hand. "Send in Blight."

Rev sucked in a sharp breath. Blight commanded all of Satan's militaries.

"I'm sending an army after Harvester. When they find her, they will drag her and her rescuers back by their intestines." Satan smiled at the barely conscious werewolf. "And you…you *will* talk. And then I get a hundred thousand extra souls to enslave in my armies, and Heaven and all its happy inhabitants will fall into my hands."

And once Heaven fell, there would be nothing to stop him from taking over the Earth next.

# Seven

Tavin's shout screamed through Reaver's brain.

He dove outside through the opening in the larva-nettle bush and came face to ass with a giant stegosaurus-sized beast. The creature was pawing at Tavin as the Sem tried to wedge himself between two boulders. Calder was twenty yards away, coming at them at a dead run, but Reaver doubted he'd get here before the thing got to Tavin.

"Hey!" Reaver yelled. The demon wheeled around with a snarl, its gaping maw large enough to swallow him whole.

Digging deep into his perilously low power reserves, Reaver blasted the thing with liquid fire that tore into the demon's chest, splattering blood and gore on the parched earth. The beast screeched, but didn't slow down. It swiped at Reaver with bony, clawed hands that dripped with the hair and meat of whatever creature it had tangled with before it found them.

With the stench of burnt flesh swirling around him, Reaver spun out of its way while simultaneously hurling a ball of lightning at its head. The lightning veered off course at the last second, a victim of Reaver's unpredictable powers, and fizzled into a harmless shower of sparks.

Calder, the claws on his hands and feet extended, leaped into the fray, slashing at the demon's hindquarters as Tavin extracted himself from the safety of the boulders.

His power failing miserably, Reaver went old school and hurled a stone into the demon's jaw. Roaring, it lunged awkwardly, partially crippled by Calder's efforts. Reaver hit the ground in a roll to avoid snapping jaws that would have cut him in half. As he popped to his feet, he summoned a shear-whip, and in a single, fluid motion, he leaped onto the demon's spiny back and brought the white-hot scourge down on the beast's skull.

The whip cut deeply into its skin, leaving steaming gashes all the way to the bone. The demon roared and threw itself backward, smashing Reaver into the rocky cliff surrounding the camp. Pain speared every bone in Reaver's body, and his thoughts scattered like spilled marbles.

He bounced off a rocky outcrop before hitting the ground in a messy sprawl. Momentarily stunned, he lay there as the thing clamped its paw on top of him, caging him inside a prison of bony fingers and razor-sharp claws.

Man, he hated these giant things. They couldn't kill him—very few demons could—but they were capable of serving up a world of hurt that could leave him defenseless for days. Worse, the commotion might attract Satan's minions.

With renewed enthusiasm, he energized his hands with

iced fire and jammed them between the demon's fingers. Frost streaked through the creature's hand and up its arm, leaving trails of chilled vapor billowing in its wake.

Excellent. The demon would retreat…ah, *shit*. Ice froze the demon's hand to the ground, trapping Reaver as the beast fought Tavin and Calder with its other arm and its clawed feet.

"Reaver!" Tavin's voice sounded above the demon's pained screams.

"I'm here," Reaver called out. He summoned a giant mallet and prepared to smash his way out of the prison of the demon's palm. "You guys keep the bastard busy."

"I'm open to suggestions, asshole," Calder yelled. "Wait…standby!"

A massive crash buckled the ground, shattering the demon's frozen hand and releasing Reaver. The demon lay dead a few yards away, bled out from a gut-spilling gash in his belly, courtesy of Calder, who was bent over, trying to catch his breath. But where was Tavin?

Reaver scrambled over a pile of boulders. "Tav? Man, where are you?"

Calder joined in Reaver's frantic search, until finally, the Nightlash demon shouted. "There!"

The Seminus's arm was poking out from under the dead beast's hindquarters.

Fear made Reaver clumsy as he rushed to Tavin, and he nearly passed out with relief when he found the Sem caught in a small space between the demon's leg and a rock.

"You okay?" Tavin didn't respond. Anxiety spiked again as Reaver sank to his knees. "Tav?"

Blood soaked the ground around Tavin, pooling and

mixing with the other demon's darker blood. A faint scritching noise rose up, and the dirt began to vibrate, sending chills up Reaver's spine.

*Carnage maggots.*

"Get to safety," Reaver told Calder. "Now."

The demon eyed the larva-nettle bush. "What about the fallen angel?"

"The bush will protect her," Reaver yelled, his patience shot. "Go!"

Hastily, he dragged Tavin out from under the demon's leg and heaved him over his shoulder. The ground rumbled hard enough to make him stagger. In seconds this patch of battle-chewed earth would become a feeding ground for great white shark–sized grubs that fed on blood and dead flesh, but they wouldn't turn down a live meal either.

The ground between Reaver and Harvester erupted with maggots, cutting off his path. Shit. He spun sharply and hauled ass up a mound of boulders, narrowly avoiding the snapping jaws of a maggot that burst out of the ground like a damned porpoise out of water.

"I hate Sheoul," he breathed, as he laid Tavin out on his side on a flat rock and kneeled beside the still unconscious Sem. The stench of blood, bowels, and death filled his nostrils, and his heart plummeted to his feet. It was worse than he'd thought.

Tavin had been gutted from the back. Broken bones pierced organs that were spilling out of the two-foot gash, and Reaver had a sick feeling he'd left a few vital innards on the ground below.

"Damn you," Reaver muttered.

Even if Reaver possessed the ability to get the demon

to Underworld General, he wouldn't survive the time it would take to get there. Reaver was Tavin's only hope, and healing him was going to take every drop of Reaver's power. He couldn't afford the loss, but neither could he afford to lose Tavin.

But there was also the very real possibility that his healing power could go awry, twisted and corrupted by the *lasher* implants. He could kill Tavin just as easily as heal him.

Reaver wasn't even going to think about the fact that healing demons with angelic power was sort of... frowned upon by his angel brethren. He'd broken a lot bigger rules than that in just the last day.

Tavin sucked in a weak, shuddering breath. As he exhaled, his body went slack with the familiar death sag.

Reaver was done with the overthinking crap.

Power tingled up from his core, spreading across his skin. He placed his hands on Tavin's head and funneled everything he had into the demon. Sweat formed on his brow as Tavin's organs and bones began to mend and his heart began to beat.

Clenching his teeth, he dragged power from the deepest depths of his very bones, channeling it into Tavin until he sputtered and choked.

Tavin groaned in tandem with Reaver as his healing ability trickled down to nothing. Drained to the point of near-unconsciousness, Reaver lurched forward, nearly landing on Tavin as his muscles turned to water. He collapsed onto the hard stone and let himself lay there, panting and sweating. Next to him, Tavin breathed in deep, steady draws. The Sem was out of the woods.

"Reaver?" Tavin's voice was raspy and rough. Pretty

normal for a guy who had been teetering on the wrong side of death.

"Yeah?" Reaver didn't sound so hot, either.

Tavin exploded up to crouch on his haunches next to Reaver, his mangled T-shirt hanging off him in bloody strips, one hand covering his personal Seminus glyph on his throat. "What the fuck did you do to me?"

"I saved your life." Reaver sat up, irritated at the demon's utter lack of gratitude. "And you're welcome."

Tavin's blue eyes sparked with gold, which meant he was either horny or annoyed, and Reaver hoped to hell it wasn't the former, because the guy wasn't going to find a female anytime soon.

"No... what did you *do* to me?"

Demons. They didn't make sense at the best of times. "What are you talking about?"

Tavin moved his hand. Reaver leaned in for a closer look. Had the symbol changed? Reaver thought it had been some sort of string or rope.

"Ah... what was your symbol?" Reaver asked.

"*Was?*"

"Is," Reaver said. "Was, is... whatever. What's the symbol you see on your neck every day when you look in the mirror?"

Tavin's cheeks blushed pink. "It's a worm."

"Worm?" Most Sems had more masculine symbols, or at least, symbols that weren't... worms.

"Yes, worm." Tavin gnashed his teeth. "What's wrong with it? It feels different. *I* feel different."

The ground rumbled as the maggots began to move away. It wouldn't be long before they'd be gone and he could get back to Harvester. Reaver smoothed his fingertip over the thin black lines and gray shaded details of Tavin's new glyph. A prick of pain stabbed his fingertip, and he drew back with a hiss.

"Well," Reaver said as he stared at the blood welling on the pad of his finger, "no one is going to make fun of you for having a worm on your neck anymore."

Tavin glared. "Why not?"

"Because your worm turned into a viper." He held out his bloodied finger. "And it bites."

Tavin fell back onto the rock and stared up into the endless black above. "Remind me to never travel with an angel again. Especially not you."

"I doubt you have to worry about that," Reaver said.

Because after this trip, chances were that he would no longer be an angel.

# *Eight*

It had been a long time since Harvester had awakened feeling rested and comfortable. She was hungry and a little thirsty, but her mouth wasn't so parched that she wanted to drink her own tears, so that was something.

Warm arms were wrapped around her, and at her back, a big male body was bracing her, holding her securely in place. Strangely, instead of feeling trapped and shackled, she felt secure. Safe. How long had it been since she'd felt safe? She couldn't remember.

No...that wasn't true. She'd been an angel once, living among her kind, never worrying about losing her life or being subjected to endless torture. Now she was...where?

Sudden panic squeezed her in a vise grip and she sat up with a cry. The arms caging her tightened, and when she struggled, they squeezed even tighter.

"Harvester. It's me. It's Reaver."

She went still. Reaver? It all came back to her, but it sure as shit didn't make her feel any better. She no longer felt the shockwaves from her father's searing rage, but that wasn't necessarily a good thing. When Satan was calm, he was plotting death and destruction. She and Reaver were in grave danger, and it was only a matter of time before the enemy—or the good guys—found them.

"Release me," she ground out.

His arms fell away, and she scrambled to the other side of the little cove he'd made for them in the center of the larva-nettle bush. She was naked, but she'd lost her sense of modesty thousands of years ago, and besides, they had bigger problems than her lack of clothing. At least she had her sight back.

Yay for eyes.

Reaver remained on the ground, lounging on his side, head propped on one hand as if they didn't have a care in the world. As if he hadn't been holding her as carefully as if she were made of glass. Why would he do that? Maybe he was trying to throw her off balance with the nice-guy act. But if he thought he was going to sweet-talk her into looking for Lucifer, he was more of a fool than she'd believed. She'd done enough for Team Good. She'd done her time and paid her dues.

Besides, she couldn't sense her evil unborn brother. Not at a distance. She was too drained, too weakened by months of torture. Hell if she was going to tell Reaver that, though.

"We need to get out of here," she said. "We've been here too long. Trackers are going to find us."

"I know." Sitting up, he gestured to his backpack. "There are clothes and protein bars inside. Get dressed and eat while I check the situation outside. We'll head out as soon as you're ready. Tavin said we're only a three day journey from a place where I should be able to flash us out of here. Three days, and we'll all be safe."

Safe. Reaver might be an optimist, but she was a realist. They'd never be safe. He slipped away before she had a chance to ask where they were. They couldn't be that far from Satan's stronghold. She could still feel the sinister vibration that emanated from Sheoul's very center and called to her blackened soul like a beacon.

No, they were close to hell's beating heart.

With a shudder, she dug through Reaver's backpack and scarfed two of the protein bars as well as an apple she found in one of the pockets. She gulped water from the never-empty canteen, a handy angelic vessel that usually held nectar. Unfortunately, most Heavenly nectars were poisonous to fallen angels. Reaver had thought ahead, the wily little halo-head.

Finally feeling as though her gut wasn't a bottomless pit, she checked out the clothes Reaver had brought. The matching bra and underwear were…pink. Bright. Hideous. Payback, she supposed, for the kitten-dotted pink sweats she'd given him when she'd gotten him out of Sheoul-gra.

She slipped on the hideous pink crap and held up the black tank top. Not bad. She wasn't going to complain, for sure. He could have humiliated her with another pink thing to wear. But as much as she hated to admit it, Reaver might be an arrogant ass, but he wasn't stupid. Pink outerwear would make her stand out too much in a place where more people wore burlap, scales, or other people's skin than actual clothes.

The black leggings fit perfectly, almost as if he'd rifled through her closet for them. The midnight-black leather knee-high boots were plain but serviceable, and again, she wasn't about to gripe.

Of course, she wasn't going to thank him, either. The idiot had started them on a fool's quest, and even if they survived the journey out of Sheoul, would they survive the punishment the archangels would dole out? Harvester wouldn't bet on it.

Reaver returned as she was tucking all the supplies back into the pack.

"One of our companions has gone missing, but Tavin's healing powers are restored. I'll get him in here—"

"No." She swallowed dryly. "I told you."

"You aren't blind anymore."

No, she wasn't. But she'd been at the mercy of too many people, and the thought of yet another stranger putting his hands on her, channeling power into her...

"Harvester," Reaver said softly, "even if you won't let him heal you, you need to feed."

"I know." If she didn't, it could be weeks until she could do basic things, like sense Harrowgates, let alone grow her wings back.

They wouldn't survive weeks down here, and even if she didn't care about her own life, she couldn't condemn everyone in the party to death because of her stubbornness. Or her fear.

She blinked in utter shock. Had she really just considered other lives besides her own? Maybe Reaver's angelic goodness was rubbing off on her like itching powder on her skin. Great. Now she was torn between being glad and wanting to shower. She'd survived by committing herself to an evil way of life. Being nice got people killed.

"Harvester?"

*Right. Get it together. You spent five thousand years in Sheoul and only five months in Daddy's torture playground. Don't be a pussy.*

"Yeah," she said abruptly, surprising even herself. "I'll do it. I'll feed." She stood, hoping he didn't notice that she wobbled.

He noticed. "You okay? We can hang out here for a few more minutes."

"I don't need your pity," she snapped, realizing she was being a bitch, but she didn't know how else to be.

Oh, she remembered her time as a trusting, nonbitchy angel, but those days were long gone, and the walls she'd erected when Yenrieth crushed her had been fortified into an impenetrable barrier that didn't allow for breaches.

"I don't pity you, Harvester."

"He says, his voice dripping with pity." She waved her hand dismissively. "Whatever. Can we go? I'll feed outside. With you there," she added, and then instantly regretted it.

She sounded needy and pathetic, and she swore if he said something nice right now, she'd rip his throat out with her fangs.

Trying to get a read on what he was thinking, she eyed him, which had never been a hardship. Tall and obscenely muscular, he had a body to die for and a wavy blond mane women would kill for. Add to his rugged good looks his deep sapphire-blue eyes, a mouth made to make even angels imagine wicked things, and a dangerous dose of irresistible sexuality, and he was the epitome of masculine beauty.

Then there were his wings. They were tucked away right now, but they were magnificent. Lush and pristine white with azure-tipped fringe feathers, they made her want to get them dirty as they rolled on the ground. Fighting or fucking, it wouldn't matter. Better yet, both at the same time.

"You done sizing me up?"

Oh, she could size him up all day. Even among angels, all of whom made supermodels appear average, Reaver was special. A low-level current of power reverberated in the very air around him, something she felt under her skin like a caress.

"I'm wondering how you made it all the way to Satan's stronghold if you can't recharge your powers down here." Reaching out, she dragged her finger down the center of his T-shirted chest and over his washboard abs. He was smoking hot, and she resented how easily he made her admire him. "I'm also curious about why you aren't radiating an obnoxious angelic glow that should be attracting every evil being in Sheoul."

"You make it very difficult to like you." Expression shuttered, he gripped her hand and moved it away. Prickly asshole. "I'm carrying a couple of *sheoulghuls*. The power I can draw from Sheoul with them is amplified by the *lasher* glands I had implanted under my wings to mute my angel glow."

"Impressive," she murmured, and her own wing stumps throbbed painfully. "And creative."

He rolled one powerful shoulder. "I have friends who think outside the box."

Friends. A startling twinge of something...envy, maybe...pricked her. When she'd been a full-fledged angel, she'd had lots of friends and a best friend in Yen-rieth. She'd been happy then. Could she be happy again? She'd given up on her dreams of having a normal life a long time ago, but if it was possible...damn, she had five thousand years of evil baggage to shed and she didn't even know where to start.

Getting out of here might be a good place to begin.

"Are you as powerful down here as you are above-ground, then?" *Say yes.* A "no" meant the likelihood of them getting out of here was abysmal.

"Not even close," he said, and her heart sank. "I can't replenish my power as quickly, and when I use it, the results can be unpredictable." Bending, he grabbed his backpack. "I was hoping you'd have some power in reserve."

She automatically rolled her shoulders to feel her wings, but only the lingering sensation of ghost limbs greeted her. Deep inside her wing anchors, angelic energy tingled, but only a whisper.

"I have a little. Maybe enough to cripple a single demon."

Reaver cursed. "Once you use it, how long will it take to replenish?"

"Several hours." Which sucked. She'd rather be blind than powerless. Deaf than weak. Dead than vulnerable.

Reaver considered that. "Once you feed from Tavin, you'll be a lot more useful."

Useful? She'd be *useful*? "I'm more than useful, you haloed ass." She sniffed. "You forget where you are and who I am. I am Satan's daughter, and we're in my domain."

Not that any of that meant anything since she had no idea what region they were in, and right now, being Satan's traitorous daughter only increased her visibility.

"Trust me, I can't forget where we are," Reaver muttered, as he looped the pack's strap over his shoulder. "But you know, you could at least *pretend* to be grateful that I risked my wings, life, and soul to rescue you."

He was right. But she couldn't afford to be grateful. Gratitude meant owing him, and owing people meant they had a hold on you.

"I didn't ask you to save me," she snapped. "I made my choices with my eyes wide open and no false hope that I'd get out. Ever. So save the guilt trip for someone who cares."

Reaver watched her as though trying to strip away every protective layer. She felt it as tangibly as she'd felt her torturer's skinning knives, and anxiety robbed her of her breath.

"Stop it!" she croaked. "Stop looking at me."

Frowning, he reached for her, but in her mind, it wasn't his hand. It was her father's, and his claws dripped with blood.

Terror squeezed her heart in an icy fist. She screamed, the sound ripping from her throat in a raw, hot rush.

"Reaver! Shut her up!" Tavin's voice penetrated her horror, but something wasn't right. Even as the clawed hand in her mind morphed back into Reaver's, fear still clung to her like a dire leech.

The ground shook and a concentrated swell of evil descended on them like a cloud.

"Shit." Reaver grabbed her hand and dragged her out of the shrub, which he'd iced over again. Outside, in the muggy air above, demonic critters swarmed, their wings clacking like bones striking more bones.

And beyond the inky cloud of flying things, standing on a blackened ridge, was an army.

Satan's army.

# Nine

⌒

Tavin was used to being chin-deep in trouble. Hell, he was in trouble more often than he wasn't.

But as he and Calder stood behind a wall of stone and thorny bushes and scanned the massive army that seemed to stretch for miles on the cliffs above them, he was aware that this was a special kind of trouble.

"Stupid bitch," Calder hissed. "Her scream brought them right to us."

Reaver came from out of nowhere and clamped his hand around Calder's throat. When he spoke, his voice was low but dripping with menace. "Say that again, and I'll feed you to that army."

Calder nodded, his already pale skin going even paler.

"I don't think they see us," Harvester whispered from behind them. "If they did, they'd be here already."

Point made, Reaver released Calder and gazed up at the two-story-tall horned goat-man who appeared to be the leader. "I think you're right. But we can't get out of here while they're surrounding the valley."

Tavin nodded. The army was in their direct path to one of the few small zones where Reaver could flash out of Sheoul. The demon's goatlike eyes took in the immediate area, but he didn't focus on any one thing, including where Tavin, Calder, Reaver, and Harvester were concealed between bushes.

"They're going to search the valley. We have to make a break for it." He gestured behind them, where massive fissures left deep clawlike marks in the sheer cliff faces. "They'll never find us in those."

"And we might never find our way out," Harvester said. "There are thousands of tunnels that extend for hundreds of thousands of miles beneath the mountains."

Tavin let his homing senses do a quick sweep of the area, and he got a faint hit to the northwest. "There's a Boregate inside one. Not too far."

Reaver frowned. "What's a Boregate?"

"They're like Harrowgates," Harvester said. "Except you can't control where they go. And some of them can only go back and forth between two places."

"And they're all different sizes," Tavin said. "They're unpredictable as hell, and a pain in the ass, but I don't think we have a choice."

"Damn," Reaver breathed. He looked over at Harvester, who gave a nearly imperceptible nod. For a few, tense heartbeats, Reaver seemed to consider their predicament, and then he gave Tav the go-ahead with a thumbs-up gesture.

Fucking awesome. Assuming they didn't get slaughtered by Satan's forces, Tavin would be out of here in a few hours. Gesturing for everyone to follow, he ducked low and darted between a row of stone pillars. The army rumbled above them, and Tavin's heart nearly stopped when he looked over his shoulder to see hundreds of demons starting down the hill into the valley.

"Hurry," Harvester barked, as if Tavin wasn't already moving as fast as he could without drawing attention to their movement.

A sudden blast of heat came in a massive wave from ahead, scorching his skin and making the snake on his neck wriggle. He scratched at it viciously. The thing bit him. Fucker.

"Which way?" Reaver asked.

Tavin gestured to the crevice glowing red in the distance. They ducked around a stony outcrop, and the heat became a blistering, nonstop wind. As they rounded a bend, the path opened up into a broad expanse of mountainside that dripped with lava.

"There." Squinting against the hot blasts of air, he pointed to a passage between lava flows. "The gate should be a few miles in."

The passage turned out to be a maze of tunnels and bridges over muddy rivers and molten streams, and twice they had to leap over collapsed sections of pathway. Finally, as the stench of brimstone and sulphur swallowed them in a cloud of steam, Tavin sensed the Boregate within a few yards.

"We're here—"

Reaver's shout cut him off. "Watch out!"

Instinctively, Tavin ducked. Something whistled past his head. Shouts rose up over the sound of Calder's curses.

Tavin spun around and threw out some curses of his

own as the hot mist cleared, revealing a dozen eyeless Silas demons spilling out of a *Y* junction and onto the path in front of them.

Calder dropped one with his crossbow before Tavin's blades cleared their sheaths. Several demons broke away from the pack and charged them, their mouths gaping wide with tiny, sharp teeth.

Reaver, eyes on the leader, coolly tucked Harvester behind him and fired off some sort of icy weapon shard at the lead Silas.

The demon went down, a hole in his chest from the ice shard. The demon behind him met the same fate from the same shard and so did the third and fourth. By the time the shard reached the fifth Silas, it had melted to the size of a pencil, and it shattered on the demon's sternum.

The Silas cackled. It cackled until Tavin slit its pasty white throat. Blood splashed onto his hand, and at the same moment, the snake bit deep into Tavin's neck.

What the—

Suddenly, everything became a blur he saw only through a haze of red. It was as if Tavin was dancing on air, striking out at whatever came within reach of his blades. He felt no pain, but neither did he feel the need to protect himself.

There was only the insane, driving desire to kill. And not just kill, but cause pain. He heard himself laughing maniacally as he toyed with one of the demons, cruelly carving out two holes in its face where its eyes should have been.

*Tavin.*

*Tavin!*

Someone was calling his name. He didn't recognize

the voice. He turned toward it. A male he thought he should know was staring at him. All around the blond male—an angel?—were dozens of Silas bodies, some of them boiling in pools of liquid fire. A black-haired female stood nearby, her body swaying as if she could barely hold herself up.

The desire to kill revved up again, and he launched a blade at the female. The angelic male dove in front of her, knocking aside the blade. He hit the ground and rolled, hissing when his shoulder hit a stream of lava.

Tavin was going to make him drink the lava. And then he was going to fuck the female. The Nightlash demon grinning with bloodlust as he hacked off a Silas's head could watch until Tav finished. Then the Nightlash would die.

The snake kept chewing on his neck, filling him with hot, stinging juice. It made him strong. Fearless. This was fucking awesome.

"I'm going to make you scream, female." His voice rumbled with savagery. "You're mine." Drooling in anticipation, Tavin leaped at her, but the blond male hit him with a full-body slam. They both grunted and crashed down on the burning stone.

*Tavin. Stop it!*

He felt a buzz of energy enter his body, and then a sting in his throat, and for a moment, everything went dark.

"Tavin?"

Tavin lifted his lids. Reaver was sitting on him, a knife in his hand and a concerned look on his face.

"W-what . . . happened?"

"Shit." Reaver disappeared the dagger. "I don't know. But you need to get to Underworld General. Fast."

Tavin struggled into a sitting position, aided by Harvester, and looked down at himself. Blood poured out of dozens of gashes. Bone was visible in places where flesh had been stripped by the Silas's blades, and his right knee was crushed so badly his lower leg bent at an awkward angle.

"Oh...fuck."

"Yeah." Reaver yanked him into his arms as Harvester led them to the shimmering curtain of light ahead. The Boregate. "You went berserk when the serpent glyph bit you. You tried to attack Harvester. I had to stab it to make it let go." He cursed. "Hold still."

Nausea bubbled up in Tavin's throat as Reaver's power sifted through him. The snake writhed, and Tav joined it, pain screaming along all his nerve pathways.

Calder's voice cracked over the sound of Tavin's pulse pounding in his ears. "Let him die. He's a danger to all of us if he goes ape-shit again."

The asshole was right, and Tavin was mercenary enough to know he'd have said the same thing. But fuck... Tav wanted to live. Hand trembling, dripping with blood, he extended his middle finger at the Nightlash male.

Reaver's breath became labored, and Tav felt the angel's power become a trickle. "Dammit," Reaver rasped. "I can't."

"You're out of power?" Or maybe it was corrupted. At this point, Tav figured corrupted healing would be better than none at all.

"No," Reaver said, his voice thick with regret. "But I will be if I heal you any more than I just did. Calder's got a point. You're a danger to us all, and I can't afford to drain my power."

Loss of blood made Tavin lightheaded as he grabbed his belly, which was slit open and threatening to spill his organs.

"Damn you, Reaver," he rasped. "You cursed me with this fucking snake with an attitude problem, and now you're going to let me die?"

"No," Reaver swore. "We'll take the Boregate and get you help."

"Ah, Reaver?" Harvester stared at the Boregate. "*We* won't be taking the gate anywhere. It goes to the Deathsands region. I'm pretty sure it's a one-way trip to a warg-run gambling casino."

"That's good, isn't it?" Reaver asked. "They should have a nearby Harrowgate."

"Yes," she said. "But this Boregate fits only one passenger. And it won't come back until someone uses it from the other side."

Since they'd come to rescue Harvester, Tavin figured she'd be the one to take the Boregate. But shockingly, Reaver heaved Tavin into his arms and shoved him inside the coffin-sized gate, propping him against the pitch-black walls.

"Go," Reaver said. "Someone at the casino should help you to Underworld General. Hurry."

"But—"

"Go, you fool," Harvester snapped. "We'll find another way."

Weakly, and with a shaking hand, Tavin tapped the squiggly Sheoulic *GO* symbol carved into the smooth ebony wall. As the gate closed and the two angels disappeared from view, the snake hissed.

Gods, Tavin hated snakes.

As the gate carrying Tavin away closed, Reaver said a silent prayer that the demon made it to safety. Then he said another for himself, Harvester, and Calder. They were going to need every prayer Reaver could come up with. They'd just lost a damned good fighter, and now they'd have to rely on Calder to locate a Harrowgate. If they lost Calder, they were fucked.

"He'll be okay, Reaver," Harvester murmured, and he slid her a surprised glance. Was she actually...comforting him? "Now quit moping and get us out of here."

That was more like it. "You're all heart, Harvester." But hey, the fact that she'd been nice, even for only a moment, was progress.

Scowling, she crossed her arms over her chest. Under the surface of her skin, bruises lingered, and he realized that without Tavin, they were down to Calder for her to feed from. Reaver was going to make sure he was breathing down the bastard's neck as Harvester bit into it.

"I have no heart," Harvester said, but it was a lie. He'd seen glimpses of it over the last few years, though at the time he hadn't recognized it for what it was.

Although the tenderness in her eyes when she'd asked to hold Thanatos's son, Logan, for the first time had been crystal clear and, perhaps, the first true hint that she wasn't what she'd seemed.

Reaver cursed under his breath as Calder slipped away to scope out the route ahead, leaving Reaver and Harvester to catch up.

They found Calder standing motionless on the trail a few hundred yards ahead, and Reaver's heart leaped into his throat. The path continued across a rickety wooden bridge, but the dilapidated state of the bridge was the least of Reaver's worries.

Above them, far up on the sheer rock faces that surround them, demons perched on ledges and narrow trails. One, a horned demon with a goatlike snout, looked down, and Reaver swore the beast smiled as he caught Reaver's eye.

Reaver's gut clenched. They'd been spotted.

The demon raised his hand in a sharp command. Three demons holding the leashes of creatures that resembled scaly skinned bears snapped into action, vaulting from ledge to ledge in a rush toward them.

"We are so fucked." Calder leaped onto the suspension bridge, and the way it groaned with age and fatigue made Reaver's clenched gut drop to his feet.

Harvester's hair swirled around her softly rounded shoulders, caught in a balmy breeze that billowed up from the chasm in front of them. "Aren't you King of the Obvious."

"Be nice," Reaver said. "We need Calder to find a Harrowgate." He scanned the surroundings, looking for any way out of here that didn't involve crossing a highly questionable bridge. "Unless you can sense them now."

"Fuck off."

So that was a no. Harvester would never admit that there was something she couldn't do.

"Fuck both of you," Calder said with a flash of razor-sharp teeth. "I'm going."

The bridge creaked under his weight and swayed perilously over the gaping canyon, but he continued across, his feet sometimes knocking boards loose or punching right through them. Far below, in the blackness of the pit the bridge spanned, something shrieked.

Reaver held his breath until the Nightlash was across. The approaching demons were halfway down the cliff face now.

"Hold my hand," he said to Harvester. "We have to run. If the bridge collapses, I'll fly us across."

He just hoped it didn't come to that. Flying in Sheoul was like trying to fly in water. The effort involved in even short flights would drain an angel in mere minutes.

Taking her hand, he darted across the bridge. As they stepped on firm ground, a bear-toad howled.

The demons were on the other side of the bridge, where Harvester and Reaver had been standing just moments before.

"Run!" Harvester yelled, as if Reaver needed the prompt.

They hauled ass through the mountain tunnels with Calder in the lead. Vines dripping with acid grabbed at them like octopus tentacles, and their feet crunched on demon remains littering the ground. The obstacles didn't slow the bear-toads, and the sounds of their pursuit grew louder with every passing moment.

"We've got to take a stand," he said, as they leaped across a wide stream flowing with a brown gelatinous substance that smelled like rotting flesh.

"I can feel a Harrowgate nearby," Calder yelled back. "I'll find it." Before Reaver could protest, the demon put on a burst of speed and dashed off, disappearing in the murky darkness ahead.

"Shit." A vine grabbed at Harvester, and she yanked it out of the wall by its roots. Blood dripped from her palm where the acid had eaten her skin away, but she didn't seem to notice. "The demons are close."

Too close. Reaver could practically hear the bear-toads'

growls. They were in for a battle, and they had to find a place to fight that would give Reaver's team every advantage they could get.

They ran hard, finally slowing when the passage widened into a cavern, its ceiling extending so far into the darkness that Reaver couldn't see it. Massive, sharp stalactites jutted like fangs from above, and spiky stalagmites erupted from the floor.

Exit tunnels on the far wall sat just beyond a pool of oily black stuff that Harvester eyed like it was poison. When she actually said, "It's poison," he wasn't shocked.

"I guessed that."

"You *guessed*," she said. "I *knew*."

"Why is everything a competition to you?" Calder had better have located the Harrowgate, because if they had to spend another day down here, Reaver was going to kill her. Or himself. "We need to work on our—" He broke off at the low-pitched drone of a howl.

Harvester wheeled toward the opening they'd come through. "Here they come."

*Dammit.* He had no idea which of the tunnels Calder had taken, and even if he did, he couldn't risk getting caught by the demons in a narrow space where he couldn't fight.

They had to make their stand here.

The battle angel in Reaver leaped into action, rapidly taking a tactical measure of their surroundings, escape routes, and potential weapons. He and Harvester had the advantage if they struck first, hitting the enemy as they filed out of the crevice that opened up into the cavern.

*Calder, where the fuck are you?*

He glanced over at Harvester, and for a brief moment

he drank in the sight of her facing in the direction of the enemy, her expression feral, her lithe body squared for battle. The clothes he'd chosen for her left little to the imagination, clinging to every curve, every muscle. And to every bone that lay too close to the surface of her skin. He hated that her hips and ribs stood out so starkly.

But she wasn't afraid. After all she'd been through at the hands of demons, the only vibe she was giving off right now was the electric tingle of anticipation.

She wanted revenge.

*Good girl. Hold onto that.* "Do you have enough power to summon a weapon?" he asked.

When she shook her head with obvious reluctance, he held out a dagger. "It's a—"

"Dragon Biter," she finished. "I know. Goes through thick hide and scales like butter. I used to have one before it was stolen by a Bathag I let get a little too close to me."

"Why?"

She looked at him like he was an idiot. "Why do you think? I wanted something from him."

"Sex?"

She snatched the dagger from him. "Why does sex automatically come to mind?"

The bear-toads howled, their bloodthirst carrying through the tunnels like a banshee's wail and sending a chill up Reaver's spine. "Maybe because you blackmailed me into having sex with you for twenty-four hours at some random time of your choosing?"

A thick shock of hair fell over her eyes, and she thrust it back with an impatient shove. "You know, most males wouldn't whine about having to have sex."

"Most males wouldn't be having sex with you," he

pointed out, and were they really doing this when demons were almost on them?

"Most males should be so lucky." She reached into her boot and fished out a stone. "But does it really matter if I wanted sex from a Bathag?"

No, it didn't. But for some reason, he didn't like the image that was now searing itself into his brain, of her rolling around with some pale-skinned, silver-haired mine-dweller.

"I don't care who you sleep with." Another howl rang out, chillingly close, and he summoned his power, what little there was, readying it for battle.

"You sound a little grumpy for someone who doesn't care."

Her tone was singsongy, meant to goad him into a fight, but they'd have one of those soon enough. The steady pounding of running footsteps came from only a few yards away, and he put himself in front of Harvester.

Who, naturally, moved into the path of the enemy.

A bear-toad burst into the cavern a split second ahead of its master, its gaping maw exposing several rows of sharp teeth. Reaver hit it with a blast of balefire as it leaped at Harvester. The thing screeched and went off course, crashing through a stalactite before crumpling into a steaming pile of goo.

The bear-toad's handler, a fifteen-foot-tall demon from a species Reaver couldn't identify roared with fury. Harvester hurled her blade, catching the creature in its throat. The Dragon Biter sprouted claws from the handle and sank them into the demon's elephant-like hide. The dagger would now use its claws as leverage to push deeper and deeper, until either it came out the other side or the demon died.

The demon didn't seem inclined to die anytime soon. It came at Reaver with a weapon that looked like a crude cross between a sword and an ax, and with the first swing, it nearly caught Reaver in the chest. He leaped back, shoving Harvester out of the way as he fired off another round of balefire.

The demon swung his blade, deflecting the cylinder of balefire and sending it into a stalactite hanging low from the cave ceiling. The other demons and their bear-toads charged into the cave, and suddenly the battle turned violent, bloody, and desperate. A blade came out of nowhere, spinning wildly through the air at Harvester's head. Reaver flew upward in a flare of wings and knocked the sword away, but a crushing pain and tug on his leg brought him crashing down on top of the bear-toad clamped down on his calf.

He kicked the bastard in the head, then jackknifed up and slammed his fist into its jaws to deliver a one-two punch of physical strength and angelic power. The animal released Reaver's leg, its skull crumpling like an eggshell.

Reaver didn't have a chance to bask in victory. Across the poison pond, the demon Harvester had impaled with the Dragon Biter finally went down, but that still left her battling the remaining two demons with nothing but her fists and feet, which under normal circumstances wouldn't be easy. Harvester's weakened condition left her on the defense. The remaining bear-toad was in a full-out charge, her throat in its sights. She was holding her own, but barely, her graceful spins and leaps slowing with every move.

One of the demons got in a lucky strike, nailing Harvester in the sternum. With a grunt, she crashed to the ground, only to be stomped on by the second demon.

"Harvester!" Reaver bolted to his feet, ignoring the pain in his leg, and flicked a shower of drill sparks at the demons even as he took flight. He went for the closest target, the bear-toad, reversing course at the last second to drive both boots into its hindquarters. The creature flipped head over paws and splashed down in the poison pond.

Reaver didn't give the thing a glance. He went after the demons, who were now swatting at the sparks, but wait... why weren't the fiery pinpricks drilling into their flesh?

He got his answer when one of the sparks came at him. No longer pure spark, it had warped into a winged insect with a needlelike spike protruding from its eyeless face. Son of a bitch. Now he and Harvester had to battle not only the demons but whatever new hell had been bastardized by his magic.

Extending his wings, he shot upward into the stalactites, drawing off a swarm of the sparks. The massive effort of flight down here slowed him as he flew toward the ceiling and at the last second, he banked hard and dove. The sparks spattered all over the rock like paintballs, leaving behind tiny wisps of sizzling smoke.

He used his downward momentum to skim the ground and scoop up Harvester a millisecond before one of the demons brought a sledgehammer down on her head. She wrapped her arms around his neck and held on tight, her fiery skin burning against his.

"Thank you."

Her barely audible words of gratitude astonished him so completely that he pitched forward and nearly did a header into the poison pool. He recovered just before he hit the dissolving body of the bear-toad, and in one seamless swoop, he dropped Harvester on her feet and slammed into a demon. They both tumbled like bowling pins into a pile of boulders.

Reaver, panting with exhaustion, still managed to recover first and swipe the male's sword. Spinning, he brought the blade down on the demon's thick throat, severing its ugly head. He pivoted, ready to make a matching set of headless hellspawn, but midturn, a searing, biting agony ripped through his back.

Muscles locked, he went down, catching a glimpse of a shiny black rope in the demon's giant fist. What the hell? A whip that could paralyze an angel? Not good.

In his frozen position he couldn't see Harvester. The demon with the whip took off, leaving Reaver to stare at the ground, helpless to do anything but blink his eyelids.

The sound of fighting rang out, the clang of metal on metal, grunts of pain, thuds of dull objects striking flesh. And finally, a splash and a scream.

Harvester? He thought his pulse was racing and his heart was pounding, but he couldn't feel anything. All he knew was a breath-strangling anxiety he couldn't quell no matter how many times he told himself that it must have been the demon that went into the pool.

Footsteps approached. Reaver swallowed. The paralytic agent was wearing off, but it was taking its sweet time.

"Reaver?" Harvester kneeled next to him, and he would have breathed a sigh of relief if he could. She rolled him so he was on his back, looking up into the blackness. "You were hit with an anti-angel weapon my father invented. He's creative that way. You'll be okay. It wears off quickly."

She put her hand on his chest and leaned in so he

could see her face. Her cheeks were smudged with dirt
and her bottom lip was split open, but she appeared to
be unharmed. And yet, as she looked him over, her eyes
grew haunted.

"It sucks to be helpless." Her voice was so quiet he
barely heard her. She stroked his face with her fingertips,
and his heart lurched in his chest at her gentle touch. He
felt her thumb swipe his jaw, and it came away with blood.

Suddenly, her gaze, which had been full of tormented
shadows, became...hungry...as she looked down at the
pad of her thumb. Her lips parted to reveal rapidly length-
ening fangs.

*Don't do it...don't do it...*

She did it. She moaned as she slid her thumb into her
mouth. She sucked greedily, eyes closed, and shit, he was
torn between watching her fellate her thumb and worrying
that the taste of his blood was going to lead to her wanting more. If she fed from him while he was paralyzed and
unable to stop her, she could be swept away by bloodlust
and drain him. He wouldn't die, but he'd be comatose for
days. Weeks, maybe. They'd never get out of here.

And where the *ever-living fuck* was Calder? Not that
Reaver wanted that bastard to come back while Reaver
was helpless. The assassin might be a professional, but
he was also a demon with powerful, cruel instincts, and a
vulnerable angel might be too much of a temptation.

"You taste...incredible. Like sex." She swirled her
tongue around the tip of her thumb as if giving him a
visual to go along with her words. Damn, that was hot.

Her eyes popped open, and anxiety spiked. They were
still green, but flecks of the deepest, darkest black were
spreading, swallowing the whites.

Her evil was starting to show. Had his blood done that to her?

Her lips curved into a sinister smile. "We were in a similar situation not long ago. You were helpless. At my mercy."

No shit. She'd cut off his wings and kept him immobilized and miserable, then she'd tried to get him addicted to marrow wine. At the time, he'd believed she'd enjoyed herself. But now he knew she'd been playing for Team Heaven...so had her enjoyment been an act? Or had all that time in Sheoul corrupted her enough that she truly had loved every minute she'd spent hurting him?

Harvester slid her hand up to his throat and lightly stroked his skin. Or maybe it felt light only because he was so numb.

"I didn't want to do it, but orders are orders, aren't they?" There was actually a thread of remorse woven into the dense malevolence in her voice. Or maybe that was wishful thinking on his part. "You know what's funny?" He loved how she asked questions when he couldn't answer them. Harvester had really never needed physical implements of torture. Talking alone was adequate. "I liked having you at my place. I didn't like for you to be in pain..." She licked her lips, catching a smudge of his blood that lingered in the corner of her mouth. "Well, not much pain."

Her fingers trailed up and down his jugular, and both alarm and his hackles rose. Would she do more than talk him to death? She could wreck him with the Dragon Biter if she wanted to.

Or drink him into a coma.

"I was supposed to hurt you more than I did. I was

supposed to blind you." She brought her palm to his cheek and smoothed her thumb over the sensitive skin under his eye. "But don't make the mistake of thinking I held back out of compassion. I have none."

Maybe not right this minute, but he was still going to call bullshit. He'd been on the receiving end of her care after Pestilence had beaten him half to death. He wondered if she was even aware that she was lying.

"I held back because I dislike being told what to do."

Well, they had that in common. But he still didn't buy that she'd spared him pain out of an unwillingness to follow orders. But why the hell was she yammering on like this? Although he supposed there was nothing else to do while they waited for his paralysis to wear off.

"So," she said, as if she hadn't just rehashed one of the weirdest and worst times of his life. That he knew of, anyway. Anything could have happened during the thousands of years that were a black hole in his memory. "What shall we do to pass the time?" She grinned, a real wicked I'm-a-naughty-girl special. "I wonder if every part of you is as hard as your limbs." Her gaze traveled down the length of his body, and if he hadn't been stone-cold frozen, he'd have hyperventilated.

She wouldn't.

Would she?

"Oh, chill out, you uptight pile of feathers. I'm not going to take advantage of your...stiff...condition. We have a little pact that will address that, don't we?"

Yes, they did, but why she'd made him agree to pleasure her was still a mystery. He'd nearly vomited at the time he'd sworn to uphold the deal, but now that he knew the truth about her...okay, he still wasn't thrilled. But the more she stroked his skin, the more she watched him with those half-lidded eyes, the more he wanted her to keep doing it.

And when she leaned even closer, until her lips were a mere feather's width away from his, the more he *wanted*. Period.

# Ten

Harvester really liked having Reaver at her mercy. He'd always driven her crazy with his pompous holier-than-thou attitude, and while she would never admit this to him, he usually seemed to have the upper hand when it came to their verbal sparring. It was a rare treat to have him silent and unable to argue.

Plus, the taste of his blood had been like a one-two punch of lust and loathing, reminding her how much she both despised him and wanted him. She hated that she wanted him, so she was going to punish him for it and take full advantage of his unfortunate circumstance for as long as it lasted.

"You think I'm an evil, skanky bitch, don't you?" she asked, relishing the fact that he couldn't answer. Smiling, she brushed his silky hair back from his eyes—a face like his should never be obscured.

"I'll bet you're wondering if I've been corrupted by all those centuries spent in Satan's service. Am I right?"

Even though he was paralyzed, the whip's effect was wearing off, and his expression was enough to let her know that yes, she was spot-on.

"Let me satisfy your curiosity." She trailed a finger over his satiny lips, remembering how they'd felt on hers when he'd kissed her to seal the deal they'd made in Sheoul-gra.

Good grief, the boy could kiss. The last time she'd been brought to her knees by a mere kiss was with Yenrieth.

Funny how she couldn't conjure up an image of what he looked like, but she most definitely recalled how he made her feel. Most of the memories were good ones that made her smile and made heat bloom between her thighs.

The rest . . . she couldn't go there. Not only was it point-less, because he was gone and wasn't ever coming back, but her time with him had been so long ago. She needed to concentrate on the future, uncertain as that may be.

"But I'm not sure *corrupt* is the word we should focus on," she said. "I prefer . . . *grow*. I had to grow up fast down here."

Reaver's blond eyebrows climbed.

"Yes, I was an adult when I fell. But I was so naive. I wasn't a battle angel like you, so I didn't have the kind of contact you have with demons. I mostly dealt with humans. Stupid, evil humans I was charged with deliv-ering justice upon, but humans nonetheless." She trailed her finger from his mouth to his ear and spent a moment stroking the soft skin of his lobe. He was so . . . warm. "As you can imagine, I was in for a bit of a shock when I entered Sheoul. Looking back, I can see that I should have thought the whole thing through a little more. I defi-nitely should have prepared better."

Her cover story explaining her expulsion from Heaven,

that she'd killed humans for fun, had been a good one, and the fact that Satan was her father only made it more believable. Bad genes and all that. But the reality of life in Sheoul had been more of a shock than she'd expected. The realization that her father truly was the epitome of evil had been devastating. For the first few decades as a fallen angel, on some lofty level she'd actually believed there was a kernel of good in him, a remnant of who he'd been as a Heavenly angel.

Not so much.

But what did that mean for her? Sometimes she didn't know if there was any good left in her, either.

"Ah, well." She dismissed the thought with a wave of her hand, not wanting to delve too deeply into questions she was afraid to be answered. "Hindsight is twenty-twenty, isn't it?"

Reaver took a deep, shuddering breath as his lungs unfroze. She didn't have much time to drive him crazy. Which was fun. Maybe a little therapeutic, too. Oh, she wasn't baring her soul or some shit, but since he already knew she'd fallen on purpose and with the cooperation of three archangels, he might as well know some of the story.

Let him see for himself just how evil she'd let herself become.

"The first two hundred years were the worst. Demons and other fallen angels love to torment the newbie, you know."

She thought about that. Reaver had lost his wings once, booted out of Heaven and into the human realm as an Unfallen. But he hadn't entered Sheoul, which would have turned him into a True Fallen, a fallen angel with no hope of ever being redeemed. Remarkable, really. Few Unfallen lasted long in the human realm. The temptation to enter Sheoul and be given new wings and powers as a True Fallen was too great.

"No, you wouldn't know. Just trust me." She smiled down at him. "You don't trust me though, do you? Is it because I'm a fallen angel, or is it because it's not in your nature to trust easily? Either way, you're right not to trust me."

She shoved to her feet, wincing at the multitude of bumps and bruises she'd taken during the battle. Worse than all of it, though, was the throbbing ache in her wing anchors. Unlike her other injuries, the pain of her wings trying—and failing—to regenerate was going to intensify and spread through all of her bones until she was crippled with the agony of it.

Harvester dug the canteen from out of Reaver's backpack. Returning to him, she straddled Reaver's body and sank down on his hard abs. "Are you tired of my talking yet?"

Reaver's expression softened, but was she reading him wrong? He couldn't possibly *like* hearing her ramble. Could he? Because if he did, she'd have to stop.

Except she kind of liked that he was listening.

Way down inside the murky deep freeze that was her chest, something stirred. Something bad, like angry wasps. Or butterflies. If she were human, she'd think she was getting sick.

She popped the cap on the canteen and carefully tilted it against Reaver's lips. Water spilled into his mouth, and he swallowed eagerly. She kept giving him drinks in small doses until he blinked at her.

"Is that a 'no more'? One blink for more water, two for no more." He blinked twice. "You do know that if I was feeling evil I'd keep making you drink, right? It would be like angel waterboarding. We could make it a sport. How entertaining."

Reaver rolled his eyes. No sense of humor, that one.

"You're going to be talking soon, and that'll ruin all my sinister plans to torture you with inane babbling, you know."

One corner of his mouth turned up, knocking loose a crystal bead of water that had lingered on his bottom lip. The drop ran along the seam of his lips, drawing her gaze. Never in her life had she wanted water as badly as she did at this moment. His lips parted, and his tongue swept out to capture the drop.

She swallowed as if she'd been the one to taste the glistening bead, and she found herself leaning into him, rolling from the hips to slowly plaster her upper body against his. Was it her imagination or were his eyes darkening from radiant sapphire to a bold, lavish navy blue? Could he actually be turned on?

His clean scent invaded her senses, permeating every cell in her body. He always smelled good, even when he was covered in dirt, ash, blood, and the remnants of battle. It never took long for that honey-spiced angel fragrance to saturate his skin and obliterate everything else.

She wanted to kiss him. To taste those full lips again. The weird thing was that she always took what she wanted, but for some reason, she was hesitant about this.

Kissing Reaver would annoy him. Maybe even piss him off.

Right. Decision made.

She sealed her mouth against his. Months ago when they'd kissed to seal the sex deal there'd been an instant sense of familiarity the moment their lips touched, a bizarre and disturbing *rightness* that shook her to the core.

Nothing had changed. The feeling was still there. The strange rightness should scare her, and it did, but it also felt so good she wanted to weep, and that was something she hadn't felt in a long time.

It was almost as if she was Verrine again, and she and Yenrieth were lying in a meadow together, soaking up the sun. She'd been so happy at times like that, and the only thing that would have made her happier was if she'd been sure he felt the same way about her as she felt about him.

Clinging to those precious memories, Harvester thrust her tongue between Reaver's velvety lips. For a heart-sinking moment he did nothing, but when she flicked her tongue against his, he responded with a low moan that flowed through her like a caress.

Sliding her hands upward from his shoulders to his neck, she traced the tendons that strained under his skin and the veins that pounded beneath her fingertips. A rumble started low in her belly, the hunger she needed to take care of soon but that always grew worse when she was aroused.

The taste of Reaver's blood had only whetted her appetite, and the thought of sinking her teeth into Reaver's warm flesh and taking the ultimate nectar that composed an angel's blood made her fangs throb and lengthen.

She'd been disgusted by the idea of feeding when she'd first fallen, but gradually, she'd learned to tolerate it. Then like it. And now it was a pleasure she looked forward to.

Especially if she got to feed from an angel.

She didn't care that drinking from an angel brought out her evil side.

A shudder of anticipation ran through her, followed by unwelcome reservations. She no longer had to play fallen angel, did she? Yes, she was technically a True Fallen, and she had all the needs that came with it. But she was supposed to be a good guy underneath her evil veneer. Shouldn't she be at least *trying* to be decent?

Reaver's teeth pinched her bottom lip, gently, and all her self-doubt faded into the background.

"Reaver," she whispered against his mouth.

The next thing she knew Reaver flipped her onto her back and slammed his heavy body on top of her. His smile was cold as he looked down at her.

"Come on, Harvester," he said, his voice husky, unused, and so damned sexy even when he was trying to intimidate her. "Did you really think I'd let you get the upper hand?"

"Of course not," she said bitterly. "The great Reaver doesn't let anyone get the upper hand. He doesn't let anyone in, does he?"

He frowned. "Where is that coming from?"

A sudden stab of anxiety pierced her gut. Where, indeed. She had no idea if Reaver let people in or not. And why in the realm of fuck would she care, let alone be bitter about it?

Something was happening to her, and whatever it was, she didn't like it. She used to know exactly who and what she was. Even when she was hanging from hooks in Satan's living room, she knew what she was, even if what she was amounted to nothing but a slab of meat.

But since the moment Reaver stormed into her life to rescue her, everything she knew was turned upside down. Was she good? Was she evil?

Only one thing was certain: For the first time in her life, she was lost.

⌒

Very little could confuse Reaver. Harvester not only confused him; she twisted him into knots. His body reacted to her even as his brain tried to make sense of the things she said and did. No one else had ever done that to him. At least, no one whom he could remember.

"Well?" he prompted. "What makes you think I don't let people in?" She was right, but how did she know that?

"I don't want to answer," she said crisply. "Now who has the upper hand?"

She shoved against him, a halfhearted effort. She was testing the waters, determining if she was strong enough to unseat him. She wasn't, even though his body was still recovering from the paralyzation and was numb from the thighs down. Everything above that was in full operational mode. Everything was working *too* well, in fact, leaving him breathless, hot, and aching after Harvester's kiss.

"I'm still on top of you," he said. "So I wouldn't get too cocky."

She arched under him, blatantly rubbing against his erection. *Oh… yeah.* Forbidden pleasure jolted him all the way to his balls.

"I'm not the *cocky* one." She smiled, all innocence and sugar. "So now that you have me under you, what do you plan to do to me?"

Plan? Or want? "I don't plan to do anything to you." He started to push away, but she grasped his biceps, digging her nails into his skin to hold him.

"Wait."

Tired of her games and her taunts, annoyed with himself for becoming aroused by the one person in the universe he knew would use it against him, he snapped. "What?"

Hurt darkened her eyes but was gone so fast he'd have missed it if he blinked. "Nothing. Get off me." She shoved at him, this time in earnest, but he didn't budge.

He made an effort to soften his tone this time. "Tell me what you wanted."

"Fuck off."

He looked down, trying to get a read on her, but he kept getting derailed by the dark circles under her eyes. She was healing from her torture experience, but far too slowly, and they might still have a long way to go.

"Tell me, Harvester, how did you perform Heavenly good deeds for five thousand years and not get caught?"

She laughed, but he failed to see what was so funny. "Easy. I didn't perform any good deeds. I fell from Heaven in order to gain a position as the Horsemen's Watcher and derail the *Daemonica*'s Apocalypse if and when the time came." She dug her nails into his chest, and he swore she purred when he felt a twinge of pain. "If something wasn't related in some way to the Apocalypse, I ignored it. It would look pretty suspicious if I ran around rescuing kittens and defending humans from demons now, wouldn't it?" She writhed, struggling to escape his hold. "Release me."

"I can't help you if you don't tell me what you want."

"I don't want your help."

So damned stubborn. "You might not *want* my help, but you need it." He shifted his weight and eased to the side, giving her some room so she wouldn't feel trapped. "We need to work together to get out of here alive. You know that, right?"

She sprang away from him like a frightened rabbit and settled on her haunches a few feet away. "Of course I know that." He thought her face was a shade paler than it had been a moment ago. "I just don't like it. And I don't trust you. I don't understand why you would risk so much to rescue someone you hate."

*Because you watched over my children.* Remembering why he was here erased all his animosity. She was difficult, volatile, and infuriating as hell, but he owed her a million times over, and so did every human and angel in existence. But could he risk telling her the truth? If what Raphael said about her hating Yenrieth was true, she'd blow a gasket if she found out Reaver was the very angel she detested.

Maybe he should test the waters a little.

"Wouldn't you rescue someone you hated if they saved all mankind and prevented an apocalypse that would have killed countless angels?" he asked.

"No."

"Not even if that someone was Yenrieth?"

She hissed, baring her fangs, and he knew Raphael hadn't jacked him around on how she felt about Yenrieth.

"Especially not him." Her hands clenched into white-knuckled fists. "Why would you even bring him up to me?"

"You gave up your wings to take care of his kids. He must have meant something to you, even if you hate him now."

"He *did* mean something to me, but that was in the past. Now I would rather see him rot for all eternity than save his miserable soul," she growled, and he wondered what he'd done to her to make her hate him that much. "So shut up about him and tell me why you did this. You're not an angel of justice. You're a battle angel."

"So I can't want to make sure someone who does a great service is rewarded for their actions?"

"Oh, I think you absolutely want that," she said. "But it's not your priority. You were bred for war, so it's in your nature to write off people as collateral damage if their lives are sacrificed for the greater good. If the archangels didn't want you to come, then they're well aware that the greater good will be served by my being tortured for all eternity." She stood in a fluid, lithe movement that drew his appreciative gaze. "So why would you, a battle angel who should consider me a casualty of war and an acceptable loss, risk *starting* a war to save someone you hate?"

"You aren't an acceptable loss, and I don't hate you," he said, surprising even himself with his honesty. But that didn't mean he liked her. His feelings for her were as complicated as the history between Heaven and hell.

Her snort of derision set his teeth on edge. "Even if you loved me, I wouldn't understand why you saved me."

"Have you ever loved someone?" he blurted out, and whoa, that came out of left field.

But suddenly, he wanted to know the answer. He couldn't imagine her in a relationship, and he was beginning to wonder how prickly she'd been even as an angel. Who in their right mind would put up with her?

*As Yenrieth, I must have.*

The thought sucked the air right out of his lungs. It

had popped into his head as easily and inexplicably as his question to her about loving someone. Being in Sheoul must be getting to him.

"Irrelevant," she said. "You don't love me, so that's not why you did this."

"It's a simple question."

"And I have a simple answer. Fuck off." Harvester even offered him a helpful visual aid in the form of a hand gesture.

He flopped onto his back and stared up at the craggy ceiling. "If you keep saying that, you'll forget how to talk like a polite person." Something whacked him in the head. "Ow." He sat up and glared at the stone wobbling next to him. "What was that for?"

"For fun." She scooped up his backpack. "Are we leaving or what? I'm tired of waiting for Calder."

Despite his curiosity, he welcomed the change of subject from past loves, because he definitely didn't want to get into why he'd rescued her again. He wanted to tell her that he was the angel Yenrieth, to explain that the Horsemen were his children and he was grateful for what she'd done, but now wasn't the time. He had a lot of questions about his past and who he'd been as Yenrieth, and until he broke down the massive wall around her, he couldn't expect any real answers. If anything, giving her important information like that would hand her a huge advantage over him, and that was something he couldn't risk. She was far too unpredictable and, likely, unstable after months in Satan's dungeon.

Of course, Reaver thought she'd been unstable *before* her own father imprisoned her.

"We don't know where Calder went." He gestured to

the far side of the cavern, where two different tunnels meant two different possibilities. "We could guess, but if we choose wrong, we'll lose him."

They couldn't afford another loss. Reaver hadn't known Matt well, but he hoped the guy was okay. Tavin, though...Reaver was going to steep in guilt until he got confirmation that the Sem had made it to Underworld General.

Harvester hadn't moved.

"Harvester?"

She still didn't move. In fact, he thought she might be shaking.

"Harvester," he prompted, more urgently this time.

Her gaze flipped up to his. "We have to find him, Reaver."

She licked her lips, and he caught a glimpse of her fangs, longer than usual, and he felt like a dolt. She needed to feed, and they were out of time.

He shot for a tone that wasn't dripping with sympathy— she'd hate that—or that wasn't overflowing with impatience. "You can feed from me."

"No." She backed up, crying out when she bumped her wing anchors into a stalactite that hung so low it nearly touched the ground. When she spoke again, her voice was laced with pain. "I might lose control. And it's against Heavenly law for you to willingly give your blood for food."

The control thing was an issue for sure, but since when did she care about Heavenly law? "As you've pointed out before, I tend to bend rules."

"Bend? You wouldn't be *bending* a rule. You'd be breaking it over the ass of an archangel."

The visual almost made him laugh. "Don't worry about that." After what he'd done, what was one more broken law?

"I'm trying," she said tightly, "to not make things worse for you with the archangels."

He actually did laugh at that, even as he appreciated her concern. "I hit the height of worst when I rescued you."

Her chin came up, and he braced himself for a mulish conversation. "I'm not feeding from you."

He wasn't worried about a broken rule that no one would find out about anyway. His concern was that drinking his blood could, potentially, drain his powers as it replenished hers. He could scarcely afford to lose any strength, and he wasn't sure how much he could trust Harvester if she was significantly stronger than he was.

"Why are you being so obstinate? A year ago, you'd have jumped at the chance to suck me dry."

"A year ago, I was pretending to be an evil bitch."

"And now?"

"Now I don't know what I am!" she shouted. "I used to know, and now I don't, and it's all your fault."

*Ah, damn.* For so long after he'd lost his memory, he'd wandered aimlessly, not knowing who he'd been and unclear on who he was, other than an angel who had been given the boot from Heaven for saving the life of a human child who had been fated to die.

So yeah, he'd been directionless, but at least he'd been able to start life with a clean slate. Harvester didn't have that. In her case, she'd spent the majority of her life in the service of Sheoul. She might have fallen from Heaven on purpose, but she'd truly become a fallen angel. Was she going to be able to re-adjust?

One thing was certain. Offering to help her was only going to send her into retreat mode, and arguing with her would do the same. All he could do was give her space, something he was *so* not good at. So screw it.

"You're a fallen angel, Harvester," he said. "But you aren't evil." Hopefully. "That means you can be whatever you want." He moved toward her, noted the way her breaths came faster as he drew nearer. "But you can only be what you want if you survive. Which means you need to feed from me. No more bullshit. Do it or give me a damned good reason why you can't."

"Fuck off."

"There you go," he growled. "Run to your standard answer when you don't have a real response."

"You don't understand, you fool," she yelled. "Is your halo squeezing your skull so tightly that your brain can't get blood? Feeding from you will fuck me up. I did it once. I fed from an angel, and it made me do...horrible things. I killed the angel, Reaver. I couldn't stop, and *I killed him*."

Crushing sadness at the angel's death...and at Harvester's obvious regret, sat like a lump in Reaver's belly. But they had no choice, and he couldn't let up on her now.

"You won't kill me. I won't let you."

He backed her against a boulder, and she yelped again when she banged her wing achors against the stone. She must be in so much pain, but even now she was schooling her expression as if she hadn't made a sound. He spared her his pity and tapped his throat.

"Now, bite me."

Her eyes locked onto his neck and the force of her hunger crashed over him like a tidal wave. This time, she wasn't going to refuse. A sudden stab of unease pierced his chest, even though he knew they needed for this to happen or they weren't going to survive.

Then again, if she fell into a sinister haze of bloodlust while he was powerless, drained by her feeding, she might just revisit the time when she'd tortured him. When she'd done her evil best to get him addicted to marrow wine.

Maybe they should wait a little longer for Calder—

As fast as a *croix viper*, she struck, sinking her fangs deep into his vein.

And then the world shifted under his feet.

# *Eleven*

Eidolon was having a great day. Which was notable, because ever since Pestilence had come through the hospital like a rabid tornado and killed half his staff and destroyed a fuck-ton of equipment, most days were shit.

Underworld General had been understaffed for months, and he'd had to do an emergency hire of untrained people in order to keep the hospital operating at the most basic levels. He was paying to have several *ter'taceo*—demons who passed as humans—attend EMT, nursing, and medical schools, but obviously that took time. Time he didn't have.

What was getting the hospital through in the meantime was the hiring of demon species who already possessed healing abilities as part of their breed makeup. Which meant he'd hired dozens of Seminus demons.

It hadn't been easy—Sems were rare, even for incubi. But thanks to Sin's prior relationship to Tavin when she'd been his assassin master, Eidolon had been able to bring several of his brothers on board.

Things were finally getting better. He was even getting ready to expand his medical practice by building an urgent-care clinic that would be connected to Underworld General via an internal Harrowgate. He'd chosen his in-laws, Gem and Conall, as well as a False Angel named Blaspheme to run the place.

Eidolon finished stitching up a Mamu who had split his head open while attacking an elderly human male. Eidolon had no idea if the human had survived, and he didn't ask. His job wasn't to judge. Usually. He'd been raised by Justice demons, so judging had been trained into him at an early age, and every once in a while he couldn't help but deliver a little hospital justice. Like using stitches instead of his much less painful healing power. Or operating without anesthesia.

Little things. Little things that gave him an immense feeling of satisfaction.

"Keep the area clean," he told the Mamu. It was pointless to talk about cleanliness with a demon who thrived in filth, but some habits were hard to break. "You'll need to make an appointment to have the stitches removed."

The Mamu hissed, his black lips peeling back from pitted, pointy little teeth. "Appointments. Fuck appointments. I can do it myself."

"That's your choice." Eidolon stripped off his gloves and trashed them. "See the front desk about payment." He got out of there before the Mamu bitched about that, too.

"E!" Blaspheme's voice called out from the other side of the emergency bay.

He jogged over to one of the exam rooms, where Blas

and a red-haired Sem named Forge were working on a Sem lying on a table.

"Handing this one off to you." Blaspheme shoved a clipboard at him. "I've got a pregnant Sora in exam one I need to prep for delivery." She gestured to the Seminus demon patient. "He asked for you."

She swept out of the room in a blur of golden hair and purple scrubs. He moved to the patient and was shocked to see Tavin lying on the table.

"Holy hell, Tav." The guy had been minced, but Forge's healing ability was sealing up wounds nearly as quickly as Eidolon could do it. "What the fuck happened? Where's Reaver?"

"Screw Reaver," Tav muttered. "He did this to me."

Eidolon blinked. He didn't get struck dumb often, but he couldn't see Reaver turning on someone like this. "You'll have to be more specific."

Tavin sat up, fighting Forge when the other Sem tried to hold him down. "This," he said, yanking down the collar of his shirt.

Eidolon peered closely at the glyph. "I thought you had a worm—"

"I did." Tavin cursed. "Reaver healed me. It did something... I don't know what. But when it was done, I had this viper that fucking *bites*."

Eidolon brushed his finger over the snake and yanked his hand back when it struck. "That's interesting."

"Interesting?" Tavin flopped back down on the exam table. "Maybe you'll find it interesting how, when I sliced into a demon and got blood on my hand, the damned viper latched onto my throat and injected me with shit that made me go crazy. I went into some sort of berserker mode. Nearly killed myself without even knowing it. I tried to...hurt...Harvester, too. Would have, if Reaver hadn't stopped me."

It sounded almost as if Tavin had entered *s'genesis*, the final stage of a Seminus demon's maturation, when they turned into monsters who cared only about sex. And they would take it in any way they had to, which often meant trickery and violence.

Eidolon frowned. "You said this happened when you killed a demon?"

At Tavin's nod, Eidolon strode to the door and shouted at a nurse to fetch Idess, another in-law. As an ex-angel of sorts, she was the closest thing to an expert on an angel-powered...whatever-it-was plaguing Tavin.

While he waited, he helped Forge heal Tavin, who spent the entire time bitching about angels. Eidolon said a silent thanks when Idess showed up, her chestnut hair secured in a long, tight ponytail by a series of gold metal bands.

"What's going on?" she asked.

Eidolon pointed to Tavin's symbol. "Do you recognize that?"

Narrowing her honey-colored eyes, Idess leaned in close. But not close enough to get bitten, he noticed. "That looks like a patron cobra."

"A what?" Eidolon and Tavin asked in unison.

She inhaled a deep breath. "It's a symbol angels used to brand people requesting protection from demons. But this makes no sense. Not only is it slightly altered—this snake has fangs—the symbol hasn't been used in thousands of years." She frowned down at Tavin. "How did it get there? Only an angel could do this."

"Reaver did it."

She blinked. "*Reaver?*" She looked as baffled as Eidolon felt. "Why would he do that? The patron cobra can't be used on demons."

"It wasn't intentional," Tavin said. "His powers are all fucked up."

"Oh." Idess's expression went slack. "*Oh.*"

"Oh, what?" Tavin croaked. "I don't like the sound of that."

Neither did Eidolon.

"I think," she said slowly, "that instead of protecting you, it's fighting you. See, if the symbol is cast on a human, it gives the bearer strength and focus and the ability to fight demons with extra skill. The snake also comes alive and fights the enemy. But because you're a demon, it's battling you, too."

Tavin closed his eyes. "That's great. That's just fan-fucking-tastic." When he opened his eyes again, they'd gone gold with anger. "So you're saying that every time I fight a demon, this is going to happen?"

"I can't say for sure," she said, "but I'd guess that's the case. It might attack you randomly, as well."

"Found that out already." Tavin uttered a juicy Sheou-lic curse. "I have decades left on my assassin contract. This . . . this is not good."

Red lights flashing on the wall indicated that an ambulance was arriving with a critical patient, and Eidolon's adrenaline spiked. He loved a good emergency.

"I gotta go," he said to Tavin. "I'll work on this, see if we can come up with a way to reverse it." He glanced at Idess. "Can you look into it as well?"

"You bet." She smiled reassuringly at Tavin, but the

look she gave Eidolon was the exact opposite. Basically, poor Tav was screwed.

*Reaver, what have you done?*

*Reaver, what have you done?*

Plugging into Reaver's vein was like plugging into an electric socket. Harvester had fed from an angel before, but to her relief, this was different. Better. *Way* better.

No longer worried about turning into a heinous beast, she drew deeply, greedily.

Hot blood splashed into her mouth, a silken cascade of the most coveted substance in the underworld. It was as if Harvester had bitten into a live wire while orgasming. Wetness flooded her sex as blissful effervescence flowed through her veins and ecstasy sizzled over the surface of her skin.

Clinging tightly to Reaver's shoulders and clamping him firmly between her thighs, she swallowed, her pulse growing stronger with every pull on his vein. She'd only ever experienced this once before.

With Yenrieth.

This was what sex between angels felt like. This was what Neethul marrow wine was created to imitate. Harvester used to guzzle the stuff like iced tea on a steamy day in the Styx river basin. Now she realized that marrow wine was a massively pathetic substitute for the real thing.

This was sensual. Decadent. Literally divine.

If Heaven could be summed up as a flavor, it would be Reaver's blood. She needed more.

"Easy, sweetheart." Reaver's husky voice rumbled through her, adding another layer of euphoria to her senses. "You can take more later. I'm not going anywhere."

*You promise?* The question popped into her head as if it were a natural thing to ask. Whatever. She'd be horrified later. Right now, all that mattered was how Reaver's lifeblood made her feel. How *he* made her feel.

He'd broken another huge rule for her, and he'd done it so easily, as if he weren't committing a wing-severing offense. The knowledge laid her out, gutted her emotionally.

And it made her so hot she wanted to rip his clothes off with her teeth. Moaning at the thought, she rocked against him, letting her sex roll back and forth over his erection. She thought she heard him moan, too, and was his breathing as frantic as hers?

"Hey, Harvester." Reaver stroked her back as he spoke, breathless and hoarse. "You need to stop now."

No stopping. Her entire body vibrated at a frequency that threatened to blow her apart in a dark, seething storm of ecstasy...

Dark...seething...no, that didn't seem right. Her angel-blood-addled brain couldn't focus anymore. Reaver's Heavenly light and power was infusing her, making her strong. Warping into darkness and evil and—

"Harvester." Reaver's voice, more urgent, rolled through her. "Stop."

His hands, which had been caressing her back and running through her hair, were suddenly on her shoulders in a biting, painful grip. Growling, she doubled her efforts to take his blood. Somewhere in the back of her mind she knew she should stop, but she crushed the thought with coldhearted ruthlessness.

She was a fallen angel, after all. Evil. Satan's daughter.

Suddenly, Reaver tore away from her. Blood sprayed

from his torn throat, calling to her like a juicy hamburger called to a starving man. She dove for him, but he wheeled out of the way.

"You . . . I remember—holy shit." He stared at her like she was both a stranger and an old enemy as he slapped his hand over the wound in his neck. "Something's wrong with you."

Something was wrong with *her*? She laughed, and even to her own ears it was a sinister sound.

"Nothing's wrong with *me*, angel." Her voice was warped. Guttural. Demonic surround sound. "It's you. You're glowing. You're an angel in hell, and now everyone is going to know it."

# *Twelve*

⌒

Metatron barreled through the halls of the Archangel complex, his heart racing, his powers skating on the surface of his skin. Screams reverberated off the walls and pillars, and under his feet, tremors rocked the ground.

He skidded around a corner at the entrance to the Crystal Chamber, and for a moment, he froze at the incomprehensible sight of a Soulshredder tearing apart an angel.

A *demon*.

No demon had ever set foot in Heaven, let alone inside the Archangel buildings.

"Metatron!" Raphael's shout rang out from somewhere behind him.

Metatron hurled a flaming dagger at the Soulshredder, taking it out with effortless ease. The thing shrieked as its body combusted, raining greasy ashes onto the gold-and-gem-tiled floor.

Whirling in the direction of Raphael's shout, he

ducked the swing of another Soulshredder, but before he could destroy it, a sword cleaved the evil beast in half. It collapsed, and with its death, the overwhelming, almost crippling sense of evil in Heaven vanished.

Behind the creature, spattered in demon blood, was Raphael. Disbelief and anger etched deep lines in his face, and Metatron wondered if he looked as shaken as Raphael was.

"This is madness," Raphael breathed, his voice laced with a rare note of fear.

Oh, he didn't fear demons; he feared for the future, just as Metatron did. Not since Satan led a rebellion that divided Heaven and cost thousands of angel lives had an event of such proportions rocked Heaven.

"This goes beyond madness," Metatron said grimly. And, he could admit it, *shakily.*

Raphael recovered his sword and cleaned it with a mere thought. "There's no way Lucifer has been born already."

Metatron reached deep into his rattled psyche for an elusive measured calmness. "This isn't Satan's doing."

Raphael frowned. "Then whose?"

"There's only one answer." Metatron didn't even have to guess at this. He *knew.*

Raphael's eyes shot wide. "*Reaver.*"

"And Harvester. It's the only thing that makes sense."

Raphael's face mottled with anger, but the emotion was a lot milder than Metatron would have expected. The other archangel had always hated Reaver, but Metatron had no idea why.

"He did it. I actually went through with it. He rescued her and put us all at risk. That fool!" Raphael made the sword disappear, though Metatron suspected he'd like to run it through Reaver's chest. "We have to post combat units at every mass exit point from Sheoul, and we have to get structural teams to find the weak spots in the Heavenly membrane."

He groaned out loud at that last part, because Heaven was...huge. It would take thousands, if not hundreds of thousands, of years to inspect every nook and cranny.

"It's time to tell the others," Metatron said grimly.

Time to let all the other archangels in on what Metatron, Raphael, and Uriel had done five thousand years ago when they'd erased all memories of Yenrieth. No one else knew that Reaver was Yenrieth, father of the Horsemen, destroyer of entire villages and towns. No one knew how truly powerful Reaver was, and that Metatron had been forced to bind his powers when Reaver was very young.

And no one except Metatron knew that Reaver and Harvester, as Yenrieth and Verrine, had blood-bonded.

Under normal circumstances and with their memories intact, they'd have felt each other no matter where they were in the universe.

But when Verrine fell and she became evil, the bond went into a hibernation of sorts. It should have stayed that way...unless Harvester tasted Reaver's blood.

Metatron had feared this, had feared what would happen if the bond was awakened while Reaver was in Sheoul. Now he knew. The powers Metatron had sealed within Yenrieth were starting to leak out. Warped and twisted by his Sheoulic environment, they were punching holes in the very fabric that separated Heaven and hell.

There was pounding of feet, and then a dozen senior archangels burst into the chamber. A dozen more flashed in and the room, its gold-veined crystal walls vibrating, went opaque for privacy and expanded to accomodate the crowd.

Gabriel was the first to speak. "What is going on? I just killed a demon... *in my home.*"

"I found one in my pool," Michael said as he instantly changed his garb from a soaked robe to pin-striped black slacks and a Green Bay Packers green-and-gold jersey. From century to century, the angel thought he had a handle on current human fashion, but he rarely got it right.

Metatron met each of his brothers' gazes before focusing on the spilled bowl of fruit near the body of the angel the Soulshredder had killed. Sorrow made his heart clench, but mourning would have to wait.

"It's time," he said grimly, "that you all knew the truth."

*Hold onto your balls, everyone, because if you thought things were bad now, just wait. They were about to get much, much worse.*

Raphael flashed himself straight from the Archangel complex to the Emerald Knoll, a grassy hill surrounded by a moat that flowed in a circular river. Lorelia was waiting for him, her golden hair glinting in the sunlight. An ancient Chinese text floated nearby, but she wasn't reading. Instead she was pacing and flapping her dove-gray wings with the speed of a hummingbird. When she saw Raphael, she ran to him.

The book hit the ground.

"Raphael." Her hands fluttered nervously at her sides. "I heard demons broke in. Is it true? Has Lucifer been born?"

"Demons, yes. Lucifer, no." He smiled tightly. "We have another problem. Tell me, do the Horsemen know Reaver's whereabouts?"

She shook her head. "Not that I know of."

"Ask them."

"Of course," she said. "But why?"

"I have a task for you," he said, intentionally ignoring her question. That was the great thing about being an archangel. Niceties and explanations weren't necessary. "It's going to be dangerous. And delicate."

"Name it." Lorelia had been a guardian angel of unborn infants before her assignment to the Horsemen, so this was going to be right up her alley.

"As you're aware, Gethel is pregnant with a bouncing baby reincarnated Lucifer." At Lorelia's nod, he continued. "Obviously, we can't let her give birth. We sent assassins the moment we heard about her pregnancy, but their chances of successfully taking her out are slim. No doubt she's heavily protected and most likely residing in a region of Sheoul that our assassins can't enter."

The archangels had first approached their network of demon spies, but finding someone willing to put down Satan's lover and his unborn son was beyond impossible. Demons might be as dumb as doorknobs, but they weren't suicidal. Darkmen, as conjured assassins, had no such self-preservation instinct.

"What does this have to do with me?"

"We need a backup plan." Another backup plan, anyway. Raphael had set the first one in motion when he'd given Reaver the *sheoulghul*. He'd suspected that the idiot might try to rescue Harvester, and now it was only a matter of time before he paid dearly for that stupid move.

"What kind of backup plan?" Lorelia asked.

Raphael swallowed his distaste at what he was about to say. Regret was the price of being an archangel, of setting aside personal feelings in order to do what was necessary to win a war.

"I need you to perform a *fetaelis mortcaesar* on Limos."

"Limos?" The color drained from Lorelia's face in an almost comical rush. "You...you can't be serious."

"Do I look like I'm kidding?"

"But the risks—"

"Limos is the only person I'm aware of, in any of the three realms, who can do this. She's immortal, so she'll survive. She's pregnant, which is critical. She's farther along in her pregnancy than Gethel by a matter of a couple of weeks, which is a bonus. And Satan's blood has run through her veins since she was betrothed to him as a child. Also a critical requirement. Can you think of anyone else who matches those prerequisites?"

"Of course not, but—"

"Are you arguing with me?"

She swallowed audibly. "No, my lord. But it's against Watcher rules. Even with your orders, I'll be punished. Unless you've spoken to the Watcher Council."

"No. This is an archangel matter. I told you this was going to be dangerous. I'll do what I can to ensure a light punishment, but ultimately, it's up to both Heavenly and Sheoulic Watcher Councils."

He just hoped his plan worked. He'd be the hero who saved Heaven. If it failed, he'd end up before the Archangel Council and face punishment of his own.

Lorelia shifted her weight as she chewed her bottom

lip, and he knew she was going through all of the pros and cons.

*Pros: Save Heaven.*

*Cons: Too many to list.*

She needed an incentive. "Tell you what," he said. "Do this, and I'll assign you to the FCU."

Her astonished breath told him he'd both hooked her and reeled her in. "You'd really do that? You'd assign me to the Fabled Cities Unit? I know people who have been trying for a thousand years to just get on the waiting list."

Everyone wanted to be assigned to FCU detail and rightly so. Who wouldn't jump at the chance to visit lost cities and mythical locales? And not just visit them, but go back in time to experience the rise and fall of entire ancient civilizations, some of which had been erased from human and even angelic knowledge.

"There's an opening if you want it." Besides, once the task was done, she'd have to avoid the Horsemen for the rest of her life. They'd kill her for what she was going to do.

Suddenly eager, Lorelia wrung her hands like a villain from an old silent film. "When do you want this to happen?"

"As soon as possible. We might not be able to kill Gethel, but with your help, we can make sure that Lucifer's birth takes place under our control, where we can kill him before he takes his first breath."

"How do you think I should handle it? Revenant isn't going to let me just walk up to Limos and rip the child from her womb."

True. The Horsemen's Sheoulic Watcher existed to give the Heavenly Watcher trouble. And to keep Heaven from stealing an advantage in the ever-present tug-of-war between Heaven and Sheoul.

"You've got powerful anti-Horsemen weapons. Start a fight. Make them take the first swing so you can use self-defense as an argument with the Council. And be sure to demolish them all so they're out of commission for a while. We need six Earth hours to complete the ritual."

"What about Lucifer? How are you going to take him from Gethel?"

"We need the physical presence of only one of the infants to perform the ceremony. Lucifer's soul will be forced out of Gethel remotely." He lowered his head, hating that it had come to this. But war was war, and Heaven would do what it must to win. "Do your job right, and Limos will have no way of knowing we switched her child with Gethel's, and that the life we put back inside her is Lucifer."

At least, no one would know until he was born. Then the horse shit would hit the fan. The Horsemen had wreaked havoc upon the Earth once—badly enough that history had been erased and rewritten. The archangels had done it before, and they could do it again. The Earth and its inhabitants might suffer, and that was regrettable.

But Heaven would be safe.

# *Thirteen*

Reaver stared at the beast Harvester had become, his mind torn between focusing on the fact that he was glowing and the fact that while she'd been latched on, connected to him in a way that seemed more intimate than anything he'd ever done, he'd remembered things about his past with her. Yenrieth's past with Verrine. The memories had been fleeting and broken, as if they'd been whirling inside a tornado and he could catch only bits and pieces as they flew by.

Harvester stared back at him, her normally green eyes as black as the oily pools dotting the landscape around them. Black and blue veins ran like a road map of evil under her gray skin, and her lips, usually lush and as smooth as a fine merlot, had blackened and peeled back to reveal a mouth full of sharp teeth. She was taller. Larger. And two horns jutted from her skull like railroad spikes.

"We're going to slaughter you down here, angel." She charged him, swiping at his face with claw-tipped hands.

"Shit." He spun, caught her from behind, and threw her to the ground.

His blood had strengthened her, but she was still no match for him. Not yet. Once she was fully healed, they'd be on even footing. He knew from experience that she was his equal in almost every way.

She popped to her feet with a hiss. "You're going to die."

"*Verrine!*" His bellow rumbled through the cave, breaking free rocks and dust that pelted them and swirled through the air. "This isn't you. My blood did something—"

"It *is* me!" she screamed, and he swore the air pulsed around her. "I'm not Verrine. I'm hell's daughter. Evil runs through my veins. You wasted what was left of your pathetic life to rescue a monster."

"You aren't a monster."

"No?" She took a few steps toward him, her hips swaying in that dangerously seductive way she had that drove Reaver crazy with lust. "Want to know what's going through my head right now? Because I guarantee you'll change your mind." She whirled around as Calder burst into the cavern.

"I found the way out!" Calder gave Harvester a double-take. "Damn, bitch, you're ugly." He gestured to the tunnel he'd emerged from. "Come on, I'll show you. We can be in the human realm in an hour—"

Calder's head exploded like a balloon full of strawberry jelly and cream cheese. Gore splattered on the cave walls and dripped down the stalactites to form gooey puddles on the ground.

"*What the fuck?*" Reaver leaped away from Harvester,

whose finger and thumb pointed like a gun at the demon's remains.

Smiling, she brought her hand up and pretended to blow smoke from her finger pistol. "Bang."

Still stunned, Reaver choked out, "He was going to get us out of here."

"Whatever," she said with a shrug. "He was an asshole."

Yes, he was. But he was an asshole they needed. "He was our ally!" he shouted.

"Ally?" Harvester laughed, a crackly, paper-thin sound. "Do you know how many good guys I've killed since I fell? Thousands. Humans, demons, angels." Closing her eyes, she breathed deeply, as if inhaling the scent of her victims' misery. "I fucking loved it." She shivered and opened her eyes.

*To survive Sheoul and earn a place as Watcher, she had to do things that hardened her heart and blackened her soul.*

Raphael had called it. Reaver wasn't sure what he'd expected from Harvester post-rescue, but this wasn't it. He'd hoped that Verrine was somewhere inside the fallen angel, and now that he had a few memories in his head, he truly couldn't reconcile this Harvester with the angel who had, in the human realm, healed children and animals. Who had brought him manna drops after he'd been mangled in a battle with demons.

Who had kissed him.

"Damn you, Harvester," he breathed. "Whatever is going through your head is happening because of my blood. Or my glow. It's affecting the evil side of you, but you can fight it."

She raked her hand through her hair, exposing more of her polished black horns. "It's easier not to."

"Since when has doing the right thing been easy?" He inched slowly closer, careful to keep her from feeling trapped. "It wasn't easy to give up your wings, was it? It wasn't easy to do the things you had to do to prove your loyalty to Satan, but you did it."

A tremor shook her, so subtle he'd have missed it if he'd blinked. But then it was gone, and her malevolence burned in her coal eyes once more.

"It was difficult...but only at first." She licked her lips and moaned with pleasure. "Do you know how quickly you learn to love the rush other people's misery provides?"

He took another step closer. "Listen to me. You're an angel. Your mother is an angel, and your father, bastard that he is now, was an angel when you were conceived. There's more good in you than evil no matter how much Sheoul has changed you. Fight this, Harvester."

She blinked, and when she opened her eyes, they were bloodshot, but at least the whites were...white instead of inky black. "You remind me of someone."

*Yeah*, he thought. *I remind you of me. Of Yenrieth.*

"Purge your powers," she said roughly, and he went taut with suspicion. "You have to get rid of the glow." Her clawed hands flexed at her sides. "It makes me want to... hurt you."

She was right—if feeding from him had drained the *lasher* implants and with them, their angel-masking ability, the only way to dampen his angelic signature was to drain his powers. But what if she was lying and he wasn't radiating an angelic aura? What if she wanted him to drain himself so he'd be weakened and vulnerable?

"Do it," she purred. "Expend yourself."

Could he trust her? And did she have to make it sound so dirty?

Harvester's expression tightened, and all over her body, the veins winding in erratic paths beneath her skin began to pulse. "Do you think I'm going to slaughter you once you've depleted your power reserves?"

"The thought had occurred to me."

"I won't." She clenched her teeth as she spoke, as if her brain was trying to keep her mouth from talking. "My word is all I have. I won't go back on it. I keep to my oaths."

*I keep to my oaths.* Another snapshot of memory. He saw Verrine on her knees, sobbing as she pleaded with him. *I keep to my oaths. Please, Yenrieth, you have to understand.*

Understand what? What oaths? What was that all about? Had he trusted her then? Could he trust her now?

Harvester was starting to pant. "Once you do it, I should return to normal. But hurry. I can't hold back for long."

Shit. Even if he could settle Harvester down or knock her out, he couldn't walk around Sheoul like some sort of divine beacon. He'd be dead, or worse, taken prisoner within hours.

"Stand back." He gestured to the far side of the cave, near Calder's body. "Over there."

With a displeased growl, she moved with him to the exit, and he didn't like the way she kept staring at him like he was a juicy steak. And not one to be savored.

Reluctantly, he prepared himself, knowing this could be the dumbest move he'd ever made. And that was saying something, because he'd made some whoppers.

Gathering every drop of his power, he threw out his hands and sent a blast of energy at the far side of the cave.

*Please, Yenrieth, you have to understand.*

Verrine's words blindsided him again, knocking him so mentally off balance that he lost control of the divine lightning. The *lasher* implants might be drained of the ability to mask his aura, but they still managed to morph his power into a superstrong wrecking ball of white-hot fire that plowed into the cavern wall. An explosion shattered the air and hurled them a dozen yards down the tunnel. Through a thick plume of dust, he could make out tumbling boulders and falling slabs of earth.

"The cave's collapsing," he breathed, and then he stopped breathing as the tunnel they were in began to fold like a house of cards. "Run!"

He grabbed Harvester's hand—no longer clawed—and sprinted over the uneven ground as the ceiling behind them buckled.

"You're still glowing," Harvester shouted above the roar of the destruction. "But it's faint. I might only be able to see it because your blood is in my veins."

He wasn't that relieved. Now he was an angel in hell with no powers, no disguise, and no idea how they were going to get out.

# Fourteen

Two days later, they were still stuck in Sheoul, but at least Harvester had gotten them out of the mountain caverns. They'd been forced to run blindly from the collapse, and then from a constant stream of enemies. The *sheoulghuls* gave Reaver a partial recharge, but he had to constantly discharge his powers to keep his Heavenly aura muted— and to keep Harvester from going evil again. But the close confines of the tunnels meant he wouldn't broadcast the glow very far, which had allowed him to hold a small amount of energy in reserve to handle minor threats. Like an orc he blasted while they'd been on the run. He hadn't even slowed down to do it.

Harvester, at least, was stronger now, and she'd been able to take out several enemies with some low-level fallen angel weapons.

But she drained her powers quickly and while she was able to recoup them faster than before, she was still operating at far below her normal threshold. Worse, she was unable to either flash them anywhere or sense Harrowgates. With their powers depleted, they'd taken a dive into a swift underground river in order to lose the enemies on their heels.

Endless miles of trying to keep their heads above water later, they'd been thrown out of the mountain darkness and onto the shore of an eerie, orange-glowing realm where everything was grotesquely gaunt and exaggerated, all Tim Burton and a touch of crack.

Now, dripping wet, exhaustion making them shuffle almost drunkenly, they entered a ramshackle village teeming with tall, inky-black creatures that resembled upright Borzoi dogs, with their narrow heads and skinny bodies.

"No sudden movements," Harvester whispered. "Walk very slowly at first, or the carrion wisps will give chase."

"Carrion wisps?"

She nodded. "The name is misleading, because they don't eat carrion. They like their meat still moving."

Reaver eyed the things, which were coming out of their soot-colored smokestack-like dwellings to follow behind them as they made their way through the center of the village. "How do we keep from being moving meat?"

Her still-damp hair clung to her shoulders as she shrugged wearily. "Don't look tasty."

*Don't look tasty?* Brilliant.

He looked beyond the village, to a forest of black, leafless trees that sprouted from the ground like skeletal zombie hands punching up from graves. Looked like they were going to be walking into a Halloween portrait.

Talk about your postcards from hell.

"I don't suppose you know where we are," he said.

"Sure I do." The teasing spin on her words amused him despite the fact that they weren't in the best shape or situation. "We're in the middle of nowhere."

"How helpful."

Another shrug. "I try."

She was her usual flippant self, but days spent on the run with no rest was taking its toll on her. On Reaver, too, if he could be honest with himself.

"You're loving this, aren't you?" he muttered.

"Loving what? The fact that now I'm the one with all the power and knowledge?" Reaching back, she tied her damp hair into a messy knot. "Yes." She gazed up at the sky, which was a little less bright than it had been a few minutes ago. "We need to find shelter. It's getting dark, and in this realm, everything has to take shelter at night. Here, the darkness kills."

"You couldn't have mentioned that when we first washed up on the riverbank?"

She glared. "Right. Because that's the first thing I thought of while recovering from two days of swimming and fighting off demon fish things. Also, we need to move faster."

Reaver was on board with that. The carrion wisps were inching closer, and now there were maybe a hundred of them, all sizing Reaver and Harvester up for a meal.

They picked up the pace, their boots clacking painfully loudly on the uneven cobblestone road. The eerie quiet of the place was so unsettling he decided he'd rather listen to Harvester.

"Obviously, you know where we are," he said. "Do you know how to get us out of here?"

"Yes." She frowned. "No. I still can't sense Harrow-gates. But if we keep moving to the north, we should arrive at the Pavilion of Serpents in a few days. It's one of the few places you can flash us out of Sheoul from."

As they walked she tugged at her wet tank top, airing it out and peeling it away from places where it had molded to her body. Really, she could leave it wet and plastered to her curves. Reaver might hate her, but he'd never denied that she had a spectacular body.

Except he didn't really hate her anymore. The thought came out of nowhere, was a surprise to him, but he wasn't going to deny it. The slivers of memories that had come to him when she'd taken his vein had brought back emotions as well. He'd cared for her when he was Yenrieth. He might have even loved her. And before any of those memories had returned, he'd already accepted that she'd done evil for the sake of good, and he understood how she'd become what she was.

So no, he no longer hated her. But that didn't mean he trusted her.

"So what's your plan for us when we get out of Sheoul?" Harvester asked. "You can't take me to Heaven unless I'm bound with angel twine, and even if you have that, don't you think the archangels are going to just toss me back to Satan?"

He actually did have angel twine tucked away in his pack, but he hoped he wouldn't have to use it. The dental-floss-thin thread, if used to bind a fallen angels' wings, allowed passage into Heaven. It also bound their powers while in Heaven. Handy stuff.

"They aren't going to send you back," he said.

She rubbed her bare arms as if chilled, but it was a

million degrees in this freakshow realm. "How can you be sure?"

He bared his teeth at a carrion wisp who came a little too close, and the thing backed off. They were getting bolder. "You'll be the most important asset the archangels have ever seen. After five thousand years in Sheoul, not to mention the fact that you're Satan's daughter, you have powerful intel. They won't be able to afford to let you go again."

He studied the faded slash marks on her arms and shoulders, wondered if the emotional scars she bore from her time in Satan's dungeon were healing as fast as her physical ones.

"And," he added, "you can help them find Lucifer. That's your ace. They need you."

He could almost feel the wall around her fortifying itself. "I told you I'm not helping."

"You said that so I would kill you."

"No," she said, her voice thickened with anger. "I said it because I don't give a shit what happens to anyone in Heaven. Especially not the archangels." She stopped in the middle of the road, and so did the herd of carrion wisps. Her gaze met his. "You can't trust them, Reaver. Never trust them."

Surprised by her vehemence, Reaver hesitated, feeling as though he should comfort her even if he didn't know why.

"I don't." He hefted the backpack higher on his shoulder. "But what makes you say that?"

Her smile was bitter. "I say it because I used to trust them. If there was anyone I thought I could count on, it was the archangels."

"Until..." he prompted.

"Until I was ordered to take you captive," she said, and an uneasy sensation rolled through him. "You can't trust any of them. Especially not Raphael."

"And why is that?" he bit out.

"Because," she said softly, "it was Raphael who ordered your capture and torture."

Harvester rarely got a chance to see Reaver struck dumb. Now was one of those moments, and she was going to savor it a little.

And maybe she wanted to savor it because even when he wasn't being all luminous, like now, something about him still got to her like a poisonous rash, irritating the part of her that was dark and damaged.

She so badly wanted to scratch that itch.

Her body was tight with tension and the kind of restlessness that demanded relief. Making her even grumpier, her wing anchors felt like they were on fire. They were trying to heal, but they required fuel. She needed to feed again, but damn, she was still experiencing the ragey effects of the last feeding. What she couldn't figure out was why, when she'd fed from Reaver, she hadn't gone evil right away, the way she had when she'd fed from Tryst, the angel she'd killed thousands of years ago.

Guilt tore at her, cozying up to the thousands of other guilt-inducing acts she'd committed over the course of her life.

"Raphael?" Reaver finally growled. "*He* wanted you to cut off my wings and get me addicted to marrow wine? Why?"

"He needed you out of the way so you wouldn't stop me from doing what I had to do to stop the Apocalypse."

A tempest brewed in Reaver's blue eyes, making them swirl with clouds and lightning. Sexy. She'd always loved a man with a temper.

"My ass. You could have gotten me out the way without torturing me." He narrowed those stormy eyes at her. "So whose idea was that?"

She started walking again, hoping to outrun her own deeds, but no, Reaver kept up, his scorching glare a reminder of what she'd done.

"Well?"

"Raphael's."

They'd met in a realm-neutral Central American cave, where she'd asked the archangel to reconsider, but he'd been dead set on making sure Reaver was incapacitated and in pain. When she'd outright refused, he'd threatened to take the one thing she cherished. The one thing she still had left of Verrine's life: her memories of Yenrieth.

It didn't matter that some of the memories were terrible. The majority were from happy times when she and Yenrieth were learning to hunt demons or ride horses, or when they were just lying in a meadow and watching shepherds with their sheep. Those memories were what she hung onto when she lost faith in the reason she'd started on the fallen angel path in the first place. They'd given her a purpose. And more than anything else, including saving the world and giving the Horsemen peace and happiness in their lives, her memories of Yenrieth had given her an escape when she was hanging from chains in one of her father's many dungeons.

*"You already have more memories than you should,"*

Raphael said. *"You don't remember what he looks like, but you remember everything he did. No one, except perhaps Lilith, has even that. To everyone else, he only exists in the histories of the Four Horsemen of the Apocalypse."*

*She still had no idea why it was that she had memories no one else did, and Raphael never answered her when she asked. He was such a dick.*

*"You hellrat bastard," she spat. "Reaver's pain means so much to you that you're blackmailing me to make it happen?"*

*"Yes." Raphael brushed a cobweb off his shoulder. "Now, do you want me to take the memories of Yenrieth from you?"*

*"No." Fury roared through her, joined by pain as her body morphed, against her will, into her demon body. She hated when she went all Hulk from rage or angel blood, but that's what being a fallen angel was. Evil and ugly. "I'll do it."*

*Raphael shrank away from her in disgust. "Good." He disappeared, but his voice hung in the air for a few more seconds. "Make it hurt. And don't let me see you like that again. You're hideous."*

Yeah, Raphael was all heart and asshole.

"Did you enjoy hurting me?" Reaver asked, his voice as angry as his gaze.

Ouch. She supposed it was a legitimate question, given how she'd done all she could to make him believe she'd loved every minute of his misery, but for some reason, she no longer wanted him to think the worst of her. Maybe there really was part of her that was still good. She'd done a lot of things for the good team, but she'd never truly felt as if *she* was good. Especially because the things she'd done in the name of good had been reprehensible.

Like torturing Reaver.

She looked ahead, avoiding his gaze. "Did you enjoy it when you found Gethel torturing me with *treclan* spikes?"

"No."

"Well, there you go."

They walked in silence for a while, the carrion wisps still following like sickly ghosts.

"Harvester," Reaver said, his voice calmer now, "why did you choose to fall?"

"I needed to watch over the Horsemen."

Reaver's golden mane had dried in perfect, shiny waves that fell across his cheeks and jaw as he inclined his head in a slow nod. "I know. But why were the Horsemen so important to you?"

She considered her answer, but everything sounded so lame. *Because I was in love with their father. Because I made a promise. Because I was an idiot.* Finally, she settled on, "You wouldn't understand."

He cursed, low and long. "I really hate it when people say that. You have no idea what I'll understand and what I won't. Pet peeve of mine. So why don't you try me."

His tone set her temper on edge, and no matter how many times she repeated to herself that she needed to refuse to let her evil side reign and make an effort to talk instead of argue, she still spit out an irritated, "Why should I?"

A muscle in his jaw twitched. "Maybe because I risked my wings to rescue you."

"I didn't ask you to," she reminded him for what felt

like the millionth time. "And if you're going to hold that over my head for the rest of my life, why don't we part ways now and let me fend for myself."

Reaver closed his eyes and breathed deeply enough for her to hear. "Once, just once, can you not fight me?"

She owed him and she knew it, but being indebted to anyone, especially Reaver, was unacceptable. When she owed someone, that debt became a weapon, as she'd learned after many, many lessons. And while Reaver didn't have anything worth blackmailing her with, he knew more about her vulnerabilities than anyone alive.

Still, she was grateful, and he deserved better than her fallen angel attitude. "I swore to Yenrieth that I would take care of his children."

Reaver missed a step. "He was aware that you were planning to fall for the sake of his children, and he *let* you?"

"No one *lets* me do anything." She flicked a spark of power at a carrion wisp that was close enough to have her by the throat in two bounding leaps. The thing yelped and slunk to the back of the pack.

"But he *knew*?"

"Not exactly," she said and sighed. "My oath was more to myself. On the very day his children were conceived, I swore I'd watch over them. He didn't even know Lilith was pregnant."

Reaver's throat worked on a swallow, and when he spoke, his voice was hoarse. Impossible for him to believe she had once been decent, she supposed.

"Why? Why would you swear to something like that?"

She thought about lying, or not answering at all, but she knew Reaver well enough to know that he wouldn't let this go. And again, he'd rescued her. She owed him.

"Because." It was her turn to swallow. And avert her gaze. "I was in love with him."

She snuck a peek at Reaver, but his expression went shuttered, utterly unreadable. Maybe he was having a hard timing imagining that she might have had feelings for someone. "So you remember him?"

"I remember events," she said, maybe a little harshly, but dammit, it kind of stung that Reaver would be so floored by the idea that she'd loved someone. "But I don't remember what he looked like. No one does."

It was a long time before Reaver replied. "Was he... were you two..."

"No." This was so humiliating. "I pined for him for decades, but to him I was only a friend. Then, one day, he kissed me."

That had been the best day of her life. She and Yenrieth had been practically inseparable, best friends who honed their fighting skills together, who pulled pranks on humans and other angels, and who even skinny-dipped in crystal pools together. He'd never looked upon her with lust, but she'd been unable to see his magnificent body naked without practically drooling.

"I was a virgin," she said hoarsely. "I was saving myself for him, but when he finally pulled his head out of his ass and kissed me, I panicked like a lamb in a storm and fled. And he ran straight to Lilith's bed."

Well, bed of grass, anyway. He'd fucked the demon on the bank of one of the pools he and Harvester had swum in, and Harvester had come upon the aftermath. She'd been gutted by what she'd seen, and to this day the memory still had the power to cut deep.

Reaver muttered something that sounded like *fucking*

*idiot* as he kept his gaze focused on the forest ahead, never looking in her direction. He was probably disgusted by her stupidity, just as she was.

"What happened then?"

"I sensed that the succubus was pregnant." Looking down at her boots as they walked, she wondered what would have happened if she'd handled things differently. Some angels possessed the gift of clairvoyance, but she wasn't one of them. How handy *that* would have been. "I should have told Yenrieth right then, but I was afraid he'd chase her into Sheoul and get himself killed. He was so damned impulsive and hotheaded, and he was still a novice battle angel. Even with the kind of power he had, he wasn't experienced enough to enter most of Sheoul by himself. Plus, it was sometimes dangerous to upset him."

He stiffened. "What do you mean, with the kind of power he had?"

"He was the most powerful battle angel I've ever seen," she said. "Hell, I think he could have given Raphael a run for his money, and Raphael is a fucking archangel."

She allowed herself the smallest of smiles. Yenrieth was always getting himself into trouble, and her with him. But the fun they'd had had been worth the lectures and menial labor they'd been given as punishment.

"So I decided to wait to tell him about the pregnancy until I could find the children myself." Unfortunately, that plan got derailed when she found Lilith first...and the bitch had threatened the children's lives if Harvester spilled the beans. "But it didn't really matter, because the encounter with Lilith changed Yenrieth. He became bitter and angry. Even his already considerable powers seemed to expand."

Finally, Reaver turned to her. "Expand?"

She contemplated how to explain this without sounding crazy. "He could do things I've never seen any other angel do when he was battling a demon. It was almost as if he could absorb the demon's abilities and use them himself."

"How?"

"I have no idea." She took a deep, weary breath. "I used to follow him into Sheoul to keep him from going anywhere novice angels were forbidden to go. I was sure he'd get killed while he was looking for Lilith—"

"Wait...why was he looking for her? He knew she was pregnant?"

She shook her head. "He hadn't known she was a demon when he slept with her, and he wanted to kill her for using her succubus tricks to seduce him. His pride was one of his biggest flaws." In the distance, a lone howl rang out, and the hairs on the back of her neck stood up. Hellhound. Nasty things. "Obviously, he never found Lilith, but he slaughtered a lot of demons while he was searching, and I swear he was able to recharge his powers down here."

Reaver's blond brows shot up. "That's impossible without a *sheoulghul*."

"I know that," she said, not bothering to conceal the *duh* tone in her voice. "Maybe he had one, but they don't allow for *that* much power. It was very strange."

"Did you ask him about it?"

Her belly growled, and she realized they hadn't eaten in days. Worse, her wing anchors were throbbing reminders that she needed blood. Maybe she could feed from one of the carrion wisps, because there was no way she was taking Reaver's vein again. That had caused way too

many problems, and the idea that she might hurt him...
she didn't want to think about it.

She nodded at him...and had to force herself to not
look at his throat. "He claimed he didn't know what was
going on. So...I went to Raphael."

Reaver's eyes widened. "Behind Yenrieth's back?"

"That's a little harsh," she said, a little too self-
defensively. She'd felt like she was betraying him at the
time. Maybe she still did. "I was worried about him. He
was on a self-destructive path that was going to land him
on the wrong side of Heaven."

"Do you think maybe he wouldn't have gone as nuts
if you'd told him he was a father instead of hiding such
a critical secret from him?" Reaver's voice dripped with
accusation, as if *he* was the one she'd lied to.

"Fuck you, Reaver." She punched him in the arm the
way she used to do to Yenrieth when he pissed her off. "It's
easy to cast judgment when you're five thousand years in
the future and looking back on the should-haves, isn't it?"

He cursed on an exhale, and when he spoke next, he'd
managed to moderate his tone. "So what did Raphael do
when you went to him?"

"He told me to keep an eye on Yenrieth, which I did, in
between my Justice duties and looking for his children."

"And you found them?"

"I found all but Limos," she said. "I knew where she
was. I just couldn't get to her."

Lilith had farmed out three of the four children to
human parents, swapping their human infants for hers.
Years later, Harvester learned that Lilith had sold the
human babies to demons. For what purpose, Harvester
didn't ask. Didn't want to know.

The fourth child, Limos, had remained with Lilith. Limos had been raised to be evil and had been betrothed to Satan as a youth. It wasn't until Limos left Sheoul to find her brothers that Harvester had finally seen Yenrieth's daughter for the first time.

"Raphael told me you saved Reseph's life once. Is that true?"

"Maybe. There's no way of knowing if he'd reached immortal maturity at that point. But yes, I took him from a burning building when he was a child. His human mother was a worthless priestess whore who left him to fend for himself for days at a time."

Reaver's jaw clenched, but what he'd just gotten angry about, she had no idea. He was pretty attached to the Horsemen, so maybe he didn't like the idea that Reseph and Limos had gone through tough childhoods. Ares's had been brutal as well, being raised as a warrior, but his parents had, at least, cared for him. Thanatos had been the lucky one, gifted with wonderful parents in a tight-knit community.

Too bad he'd gone crazy and killed most of his clan after being cursed as a Horseman. Thanatos might have had the best childhood, but he'd been given the worst curse and had suffered the most because of his actions.

The carrion wisps were closing in again, their agitation growing as the orangeish light that gave the region its extra-eerie atmosphere began to dim for nightfall. She picked up the pace as much as she felt she could.

"So," Reaver said, his square jaw still tight, "when did Yenrieth finally learn he had three sons and a daughter?"

She shivered despite the arid heat in this horrid place. "Not until after they were cursed as Horsemen. Limos told him. I'm still not sure if she did it to be cruel or if something deep inside her really wanted a father. At the time she was still very much under the influence of her evil upbringing."

Again with the tightness, except now it was Reaver's entire body that had gone as taut as a Darquethothi hide bow string.

"What did he do?" Reaver's voice was little more than a growl.

"Today's humans might say that he went…ballistic." The memory made her sweat, not because of the fact that he'd practically gone into orbit with rage, but because that was just the beginning. "Raphael tasked me with trying to calm him down, and it worked…until I admitted that I'd known about Lilith's pregnancy since conception."

Reaver's footsteps became heavier, striking the stones under his soles with such force that the ground shook. "Was he angry with you?"

Her shiver turned into a full-body shudder. "He would have had to come down a hundred notches to be merely angry."

*"You knew? All this time you knew I was a father, and you didn't tell me? I trusted you. I've trusted you more than I've ever trusted anyone."*

*"I'm sorry," she cried. "At first, I didn't want you to get yourself killed. Then I found Lilith seducing a human. I tried to force her to tell me where the children were, but she was furious that I knew about them in the first place. She threatened to kill them if I told anyone. I had to wait until they were old enough to take care of themselves. But then Limos wreaked havoc with the boys and it all went so badly. She told you before I could." She fell to her*

*knees in front of him, tears streaming down her face. "It was all for you. I wanted to tell you sooner, but—"*

*"But what?"* He seized her biceps and lifted her roughly to her feet. *"You had no right, Verrine. None. I would never have betrayed you like that. This is payback, isn't it? Payback for fucking Lilith instead of you."*

"He hated me," she whispered. "He was so cruel."

"What did he do?" Reaver stopped in the middle of the road as if there weren't hundreds of demons slinking closer and closer. "Harvester? What did he do to you?"

She kept walking. It was stupid to have told him any of this. Now all that shit she'd worked so hard to bury was surfacing again, and it hurt more than anything Satan's torture crew had done to her.

Reaver grasped her arm and swung her around, and she clenched her teeth at the stab of fire that shot through her wing anchors. "Tell me."

"Why? Why do you give a shit what happened?" She jerked out of his grip, earning another searing blast of pain. "Are you getting off on knowing I lost the only male I've ever loved? That he crushed me under his boot like garbage? Is that fun for you?"

"No." Reaver reached for her again, this time to brush his knuckles over her cheek. "I just want to know what kind of person he was. He sounds like an asshole."

She slapped him. She slapped him before she even knew what she was doing, and when the crack of flesh on flesh echoed through the village, everything stopped. The creatures froze, and so did she and Reaver.

"Don't say that," she rasped. "You didn't know him. He trusted me, and I betrayed that trust."

"You did it to protect him."

She barked out a bitter laugh. "Or maybe I did it to have power over him, like he said. Or maybe he was right when he told me I did it to punish him for fucking that demon bitch instead of me. I am Satan's daughter, after all."

"Harvester might have done that, but not Verrine."

She snorted. "You didn't know Verrine. How can you say that?"

"Because Verrine sacrificed herself for Yenrieth and his children. She wouldn't have done that if she was the kind of person who would betray him out of a power trip or revenge."

"Whatever." Suddenly feeling the weight of the last four days without rest, she rubbed her eyes with the heels of her palms as she started down the road again. "Can we just drop it?"

Reaver fell in beside her. "We can't drop it. I want to know what he did to you."

"You really are a hellhound with a bone, aren't you?" He didn't reply. Not that she expected him to. "Fine. You really want to know? Yenrieth, that bastard, after he was done ripping me a new one, disappeared for months. When he finally came back, he was his normal self again." She grimaced. "That should have been a clue."

"How so?"

"He...pretended to want me. I still loved him, so I gave in." She closed her eyes, trudging blindly on the bumpy road.

God, she'd been a fool. Yenrieth had found her in her quarters. There had been no talk. Yenrieth had simply blown in as if he'd belonged there, swept her up, and kissed her until she opened up like a night-blooming rose. She'd been so happy, so filled with love for him that she hadn't even considered any possibility other than that he'd finally come around and realized they were meant to be together.

What a fucking stupid, blind twat she'd been.

"I gave him my virginity. And he…" Heat scorched her cheeks. She opened her eyes, wishing she'd done the same thing back when Yenrieth had come into her room to seduce her. But truly, would anything have changed? She'd wanted it, and like a spineless fool, she'd been weak enough to take it any way he'd give it. "I'm done with this conversation."

Reaver ignored her. Shocking. "He used you and threw you away, didn't he?"

*I've fucked demons who were less disgusting than you.*

Pain lanced her, as fresh and raw as the day he'd said those words to her.

"What a bastard," Reaver growled, taking her nonresponse as a yes. "After what he did, why would you have been willing to fall? Why would you have given up everything for a jerk like him?"

"I told you," she said quietly, "you didn't know him. He wasn't always like that." They were almost to the village boundary. The forest beyond would provide some cover and escape routes. "And I made a promise. Pathetic as I was, I loved him in spite of everything. He came to my rescue so many times when I got in over my head with demons. And he always brought me my favorite rare irises to cheer me up. And once, when I caught him mourning a child he was too late to save from a demon, he told me that every child who died on his watch took a piece of his soul. I think I fell for him that day."

She inhaled a shaky breath. "He loved children…and

I should have told him about his own sooner. If I had, maybe he could have saved them before the curse was cast upon them."

She'd waited until they were adults for their own protection, but by then Yenrieth had forgotten about his vendetta against Lilith, and he'd also seemed to have lost a lot of his powers. Harvester had kept putting off telling him out of fear that he'd go crazy again, and this time, he'd truly end up dead. She shouldn't have allowed her fear to rule her head. How many people had paid horrible prices because of her actions?

She searched Reaver's face for judgment, but his expression was blank. Scarily blank. "So what it comes down to is that I kept my oath to watch over his children, and I volunteered to become a spy. After I was cast into Sheoul, I never saw him again. I don't even remember what he looks like." The tears she'd been trying so hard not to shed stung her eyes. "Reaver? How can I remember every cutting word he said, every warm touch of his fingers, and not remember what he looks like?"

# Fifteen

Reaver's stomach rolled. He was responsible for what Harvester had become. As Yenrieth, he'd been a real piece of work, hadn't he?

And how messed up was it that he hoped Yenrieth had gone through centuries of hell for what he'd done to Verrine. But screw it, aside from the brief memories that had come to him in the caverns Reaver didn't remember anything, and to him, Yenrieth was a stranger. Hell, Yenrieth was a stranger to everyone except Harvester.

But why? What had Yenrieth done to deserve such an extensive memory wipe? If what he'd done was that bad, why had he not been simply cast from Heaven and straight into Sheoul?

"I'm sorry, Harvester," he murmured.

"I didn't tell you any of that to get your pity," she said sharply, but the bite was dulled by the hitch in her voice. "I told you because you rescued me, and you deserve to know why I did what I did. But it was a long time ago. I'm over it."

Clearly. He kept his opinion to himself, however. Being kind to Harvester always ended badly.

The howl of a hellhound rose up, followed by another… and another. The carrion wisps began a frantic squirre-lesque chatter.

Up ahead, dark shapes began to take form as they crept out of the forest shadows. The telltale outline of buffalo-sized hellhounds grew into fully realized forms that shot toward the village like giant, furry bullets.

Crimson eyes zeroed in on Reaver and Harvester.

"I don't think they're here to hunt carrion wisps," Harvester whispered.

Reaver cursed. He didn't have enough power to slow a single hellhound let alone an entire pack.

"I have an idea," he said, keeping his gaze on the rapidly approaching predators. "Do you have enough power to put up a shield between us and them?"

"Yes, but it'll be good for only a moment."

"Do it. Stay behind me and don't say anything."

Her eyes flashed with temper. "Excuse me?"

"Do you want to be eaten or dragged back to Satan… or both? No? Then shut up and get behind me." Yeah, he was going to pay for that later, but for now, she glared daggers and obeyed.

The hellhounds came at them, their long strides eating up the distance. Reaver squared his stance and waited as Harvester cast an invisible shield between them and the hellhounds. The first wave of beasts hit the shield and bounced off like rubber balls on a window.

The shield collapsed and before the animals could

recover, he grabbed the leader around its thick neck and wrenched it to the ground. He sank his fingers into the hellhound's fur at the base of its skull and used the last of his power to project images of the hellhounds that protected the Horsemen's families, followed by an image of their queen of sorts, Ares's mate, Cara.

Hot, fetid breath and serrated growls surrounded him as the other hounds crept in close. Gaping jaws dripping with drool opened near his head. Reaver tensed, waiting for the thing to clamp down.

For a long time, nothing happened. And then, as if he was at ground zero for a nuclear blast, the lead hellhound forced images back at him. Reaver's mind reeled, spinning inside his skull and careening around so fast he couldn't pull the images together. He gripped his head and fell back as everything the hellhound had seen in the last few days downloaded into his brain.

"Darkmen," he gasped, releasing the beast.

Harvester's hands framed his face, and her gaze searched his. "Reaver? What about darkmen?"

He shook his head to clear it, but he could still see the black-robed hunters in his head. "The hellhounds saw darkmen. Nearby."

"Nearby?" She whistled through her teeth. "This is bad."

On that, Reaver agreed. Darkmen weren't something anyone wanted to deal with. The conjured, shadowy men carried with them the powers of angels, which was no surprise, since they were controlled by them.

The archangels had sent assassins.

# Sixteen

The Horsemen were at it again. Their tropical parties were legendary, even among legends, and once again, they were preparing to put the female Horseman's beach hideaway to use as a pig-roasting, margarita-guzzling, volleyball-playing bash.

Clearly, with the *Daemonica*'s apocalyptic prophecy averted, the Horsemen had nothing better to do.

Revenant changed his hair from short to long, from brown to dirty blond as he strode toward them, his boots kicking up the warm sand as he walked. He fucking hated sand. And naturally, two of the four Horsemen lived in Sand Central. Limos and her mate, Arik, liked the tropical Hawaiian shit, and Ares and Cara made their home on a private Greek island. Most people would consider their homes to be paradises.

Most people were morons.

But hey, Revenant wasn't elitist when it came to

classifying morons. Morons existed in all races, from humans to angels to demons. He might have to hang with demons because he was a fallen angel, but that didn't mean he couldn't see their faults. Evil was more interesting than good, but truly, most evil beings were dumber than fence posts.

He slowed as he got closer, an irritating tingle on the back of his neck alerting him to the arrival of the female angel who appeared in front of Limos.

The moment the Horsemen saw him, they swiped their fingers over their armor symbols on their throats and went from beach attire to suits of armor in a split second.

"'Sup, Horseboys and Horsegirls?"

"Revenant." Lorelia curled her lip in disgust. "You always have the worst timing."

"You *both* have terrible timing." Thanatos folded his arms over his bone-armor breastplate. "What are you doing here? Has Gethel been found?"

"You know I can't discuss Gethel." Revenant loved annoying all these assholes. "I'm here to deliver some other news. But I'll let my Heavenly counterpart go first." He grinned. "Ladies and pure goodness first. I'm polite that way."

"You don't know what polite is, Fallen," Lorelia said, all snooty-like.

"That was rude," Revenant said, doing his best *I'm-so-hurt* impression. No one bought it.

Lorelia huffed. "Have any of you seen Reaver lately?"

Limos, looking like a slightly pregnant armadillo in her samurai armor, narrowed her violet eyes. "Why?"

Revenant was curious about that as well.

"Because I asked," Lorelia snapped. "Have you seen him?"

Everyone clammed up tight. Stupid angel. Had she not figured out that these hard-headed horseshits didn't do demands well? He'd learned that you definitely caught more horseflies with honey than with blood.

In the uncomfortable silence, Revenant studied his nails. Then brushed a bit of dust off his leather coat. Then used his boot to scratch his name in the sand. It was fun to draw attention to the awkwardness.

Finally, Lorelia ground out, "My superiors want to know where Reaver is. It's important."

"We haven't seen him in weeks." Ares's hard leather armor creaked as he ran his hand through his short reddish-brown hair. Known also as War, he tended to keep things simple and to the point. "No idea where he is. He does this sometimes."

"Now, why are you asking?" Reseph, his beach-bum platinum hair gleaming in the sun, bounced a volley-ball from hand to hand as if he didn't have a care in the world. His carefree attitude was deceptive though; of all the Horsemen, he'd proven to be the most dangerous. The human world was still recovering from the hell he brought down on it as Pestilence.

Revenant had liked him better as Pestilence.

"None of your business," Lorelia said icily. Revenant wondered if she'd noticed the huge-ass hellhound creeping up behind her. Ares rarely went anywhere without one of the fucking things.

"You're the grumpiest Watcher ever," Reseph said. "I thought Gethel was bad. And Harvester. And Revenant—"

"I get your point," Lorelia interrupted. She shot him a

look of disgust. "It must have been so much easier to deal with you when your mind was broken." She turned to Revenant before she could see Reseph's expression darken. Why was she antagonizing them like this? "Maybe you could share why you're here?"

"Gladly." He was so going to take advantage of being the good cop. Any opportunity to make a Heavenly puke look bad was worth jumping on, and Lorelia was making it easy. "The underworld is abuzz with the news that your ex-Watcher, Harvester, has been rescued from Satan's favorite torture chamber."

"So?" Thanatos, whose Horseman name was Death, stared at Revenant, his yellow eyes flashing with impatience.

"So…" Lorelia drawled, her tone contemplative, "if Reaver is missing, maybe he's involved with Harvester's escape."

Limos scoffed. "Why would Reaver help that bitch? She tortured him, tried to start the Apocalypse, and helped Pestilence try to kill Thanatos's son."

"I'd like to know the answer to that, as well," Lorelia said.

"Maybe he didn't go to rescue her," Reseph offered. "Maybe he went to kill her."

Ah, so they *didn't* know Harvester had allegedly been a spy for Heaven. Granted, it wasn't common knowledge even in Sheoul; Revenant knew only because his Watcher Council had filled him in and Satan had, for some reason, included Rev in his inner circle. But Revenant would have thought Reaver would share the information with the Horsemen, given that Harvester's machinations had helped them behind the scenes.

"Well?" Limos tapped her foot in the sand. "Are you going to tell us?"

He was tempted to reach out and strangle her, but that would ruin the good-cop thing he had going. Plus, she was pregnant, and while he didn't give a shit about the brat, he had rules to follow, and the rules said he couldn't strangle pregnant biblical legends or in any way harm said biblical legends' children.

"Harvester is a traitor," Rev said. "She was working for Heaven."

All eyes went comically wide and fixed on him.

"Yup. True story. Heaven arranged her espionage plan *before* she fell."

"Are you really saying," Ares began in his deep, resonant voice, "that she infiltrated Sheoul in order to be a spy? She didn't actually fall?"

"That's what I'm saying. Apparently, everything she did was done to avert the Apocalypse and help you guys defeat Pestilence." He shrugged. "She hasn't admitted to it, even under severe torture, but it's pretty obvious what happened."

"But she was working *with* Pestilence," Limos protested.

"She *pretended* to be working with him." Revenant couldn't hide his disgust. He'd always been more of a stab-you-in-your-chest kind of guy than a stab-you-in-the-back sort. He liked his enemies to know he was coming. "I don't know the whole story, but Reaver learned the truth around the same time he learned he was your father."

Lorelia let out an impressive snarl. "That stupid angel," she spat out. "If he went after Harvester, then *he's* the traitor. His foolish actions could start a war between the realms. We're already dealing with what Lucifer's birth could bring about if he's born."

*If?* Odd way to phrase that.

"You're talking about our father." Limos's voice cracked like a whip. "So I'd be very careful what you say next."

"Spoiled brat." Lorelia's dove-gray wings flared high. Girl was pissed. Although...there was something a little off about her anger. It was...overdone, and again he wondered what she was up to. "You do not speak to me in that way."

Thanatos stepped closer to the Watcher. "She speaks in whatever way she wants to. Especially to angels with sticks up their holy asses."

Oh, this was getting good. Revenant wished someone would make popcorn.

Lorelia roared in anger and struck out with a lash of power that lifted Thanatos off his feet and hurled him into the side of Limos's party hut. Thanatos went through the wall like a cannonball.

"Bitch!" A sword appeared in Limos's hand, and the yellow flower in her hair wilted.

Revenant contemplated extra butter on his popcorn as in a blur of motion, Limos went after Lorelia. The angel flashed out of the way and materialized behind her.

The next few seconds were a shock of thunderous booms and flashing light as Lorelia hit Limos with a blast of acid fire before following up with blows for Ares and Reseph when they tried to help their sister.

Revenant dove to the ground to avoid the aftershock of a particularly powerful downburst of Angel Storm. Shit, that bitch was out of control. Screw the popcorn; she'd have scorched the shit out of it.

Summoning his own power, he rolled to his feet, prepared to defend himself. But the scene he was faced with...*unholy hell*. He stood, stunned, as he took in the carnage. Lorelia, her arm bleeding from what looked like a bite from the dead hellhound a few feet away, crouched next to Limos, her palm hovering over the Horsewoman's abdomen. She and her brothers had been...demolished. They'd heal in time, of course, but right now every one of them had been pulverized.

Revenant once told them he could blow them up inside their armor and pour them out like a liquid.

Lorelia had just done that.

Fury built in his chest. *"Lorelia!* We have rules." He stalked her, the anger bubbling up and getting hotter with every step. "You can't wreck the Horsemen just because they piss you off. *You broke the rules.*"

She came to her feet and didn't meet his gaze as she tucked something into her pocket. Then, before he could grab her, she flashed away. But that didn't mean she was *getting* away.

Rules meant order. Without order there was chaos, and unlike most Sheoul denizens, Revenant *hated* chaos.

So Lorelia was going to pay for what she'd done to the Horsemen. Not because he liked them, but because what she'd done to them was against the rules. And rules must be followed.

But so must orders, and after he found Lorelia and beat the truth of why she'd made toast of the Horsemen out of her, he had an appointment to make. An appointment he dreaded.

With Satan.

The emergency department was slammed.

Medical staff rushed to triage incoming patients, mostly innocent victims of Satan's armies as they chewed a path through Sheoul. From what Eidolon could gather, the armies were both searching for "Satan's renegade daughter" and preparing for a battle with Heaven. Refugees were fleeing Sheoul if they could, and if they couldn't, they were holing up and trying to keep out of the path of the Dark Lord's war machine.

Apparently, Satan's troops didn't differentiate between friend and enemy when they were on the move, and the ED was stretched beyond its limits with survivors. The hospital hadn't been this packed since the apocalyptic events brought about by Pestilence. Even the parking lot was once again packed with the wounded.

Gem, his mate's twin sister, jogged up to him with a clipboard, her black and blue hair pulled into two pigtails on either side of her head, exposing the enchanted tattoo around her neck that helped keep her from shifting from her human form to her demon one.

"Remember that wolf shifter you treated last week?" she asked. "And the month before that? She's back. Broken leg. I think her mate might be responsible, but she won't say much."

The Justice demon in him clawed at his chest, battling with the doctor he'd become. The winner would be the doctor though; the patient's injuries came first. The mate could be dealt with later. That was Wraith's specialty.

"I'll check her out." Eidolon took the clipboard, but before he could glance at the patient's paperwork, the emergency room's Harrowgate flashed, and a mostly human male, Arik, burst out of it. His mate, Limos, was in his arms.

At least, Eidolon assumed it was Limos. The female looked like she'd gone through a paper shredder before being glued back together by a blind person.

"Help," he croaked. "Help her."

Eidolon shoved the clipboard at Gem. "Have Grim handle the shifter." The Sem, one of Tavin's brothers, hadn't been here long, but the guy had a powerful healing ability, and Eidolon trusted him to be sensitive to abused females.

"You got it." Gem took off as Eidolon sprang into action, ushering Arik to the closest open exam room.

Blaspheme joined them, holding Limos's head as Eidolon helped Arik settle what was left of the Horseman onto a table. Gods, she was messed up. He'd been a doctor for decades and had never seen anything like this.

"What happened?" Eidolon let Blas perform the ABC's—airway, breathing, and circulation—but the procedure was more protocol than necessary in this instance. Limos was immortal. Fucked up beyond recognition, but immortal.

"I don't know." Arik was trembling so hard his teeth chattered. "We were going to have a party. I got back to our place with a keg." He inhaled a shaky, tormented breath. "I found her like this. Her brothers...they're the same. I couldn't...I couldn't bring them all...fuck..."

Eidolon didn't bother gloving up. He placed his hands on Limos's torso and channeled his power into her. His *dermoire* glowed as his healing gift winged its way down his right arm. There was too much damage to focus on a single injury, so he spread the healing wave evenly through her body. In his mind's eye, he could see internal organs plumping up, muscle fibers knitting together, and bones fusing.

Sweat beaded on Eidolon's brow as Limos started to come together like a jigsaw puzzle, but he didn't have enough power to bring her even halfway back.

Blaspheme knew. "I'll get Shade."

She took off like a shot, leaving him with Arik, who was about to come apart at the seams. Eidolon got that. Didn't matter that Arik's mate was immortal. Arik saw only her pain and misery.

"She's in bad shape," Eidolon said, "but she's going to be fine. I'll have Shade or Forge help to get her back with a minimum of suffering."

Arik nodded, but he was still shaking like a leaf. "What about the baby?"

Eidolon sucked in a sharp breath. He'd forgotten Limos was pregnant. The last time he'd seen her, she hadn't been showing yet. He drew back his power and focused it in a concentrated laser into Limos's womb.

"Oh, shit," Arik breathed. "You've got to save it."

Eidolon wanted to. Gods, he wanted to. "How far along is she?"

"Almost five months." Arik spun around and jammed his hands through his short brown hair as he walked back and forth across the obsidian floor where Limos's blood was pooling in shiny wet puddles. "Fuck, I'm going to destroy whoever did this. *Fuck!*"

The curtain swished open and Shade entered, his dark head bent, his gaze glued to his phone. "Blas said you needed me. And why did I just get a text from Thanatos's mate saying the Horsemen had been attacked? Limos is missing—" Shade cut off at the sight of the female on the table. "Hell's fires, is that her?"

At their nods, Shade raced over and palmed Limos's forearm. His biceps glowed along the lines of his *dermoire* as he channeled his power into her.

Eidolon eyed his brother, but he couldn't get a read on

him. Shade's gift wasn't the same as Eidolon's and wasn't as useful for healing, but it was powerful in its own right. Shade was able to manipulate bodily functions, to make a heart start beating or force bone marrow to create red blood cells.

Eidolon glanced at Arik, judged him to be justifiably unstable, and lowered his voice. "Remember, she's pregnant."

Shade's head came up. "Fuck." Closing his eyes, he concentrated.

Eidolon kept his healing energy spreading through Limos as Shade probed her womb. Her skin and extremities had almost fully formed now.

But there was no baby bump.

"Well?" Arik gripped the table near Limos's head so hard his knuckles turned white. "How's the baby?"

Very slowly, Shade's eyes opened. Eidolon didn't like what he saw.

"I'm sorry, Arik," Shade murmured. "The baby is gone."

# Seventeen

⌒

Revenant stood outside the exam room where Limos was being attended by Underworld General staff. The baby was gone? Lorelia had killed Limos's child? Revenant felt the blood in his veins begin to steam, and as usually happened when he was pissed, his hair went from the sandy color he'd chosen today to jet black.

When Lorelia was punished for what she'd done, he wanted to be there. He wanted to see her bleed.

He hadn't been able to make that happen earlier; the angel had flashed from Hawaii, and Rev hadn't been able to follow her Watcher signature. Which meant the cowardly bitch had gone to Heaven.

A blonde female in ridiculous purple scrubs dotted with blue hearts came out of the exam room, and he grabbed her arm. "You. When will Limos be released?"

She rounded on him, a nasty smile curving her bloodred lips. "Let go of me or you'll lose your hand."

An idle threat, given the hospital's antiviolence ward, but it was cute that she tried. He let his gaze travel down the length of her voluptuous body. Her scrubs and lab coat didn't hide nearly as much as she probably thought they did. Nice breasts. He could even admire them while pretending to be fascinated by her name tag.

Very deliberately, he held her arm for another five seconds, and then he dropped his hand. "Answer me, Dr. Blaspheme."

"Fuck off."

She strode away, and damn, her ass was so fine that he wasn't even angry. No, he was intrigued. No one told him to fuck off. At least, not if they weren't sure they could match his strength.

Or his cruelty.

When she reached the end of the hallway, he flashed in front of her, halting her in her tracks. "Answer," he repeated.

"I neither work for you nor am I mated to you, so I don't have to respond to your rudeness. And if I was mated to you, I'd respond with a blade to your balls. So I repeat, fuck off."

He got hard. Brutally, painfully hard. He could so easily imagine this hellcat in his dungeon, her wrists bound with silk, her skin pink from his leather lash as she submitted to him in every way he asked her to.

"What species are you?"

She stiffened as if he'd offended her. "I'm a False Angel. Not that it's any of your business."

False Angel? Odd. She didn't read like one. Didn't act like one. False Angels were known for their teasing, seductive natures and malicious tricks. Not to mention their sex drives. This female should be creaming herself over him, drawn to his darkness and his power.

Time to try another approach. "If you answer my question, I'll let you suck my cock."

Mostly, he was testing her with his crude suggestion. Mostly. If she wanted to give him a blow job, he wouldn't object. He'd tell her exactly how to do it. How to lick him from his balls to his crown. How to swallow him deep and hum on the backstroke. How to use her teeth to balance pleasure and pain.

He shivered with the exciting possibilities.

"Really?" Clapping in exaggerated delight, she gave him the most superficial smile he'd ever seen. "You'll let me put a total stranger's piss hose in my mouth while my knees scream in agony on the hard floor? Right here in front of everyone? Gosh, such a hard thing to pass up. But you know, I'd rather eat Ebola pudding than let your sad little dick near me." She wiggled her fingers as she slipped past him. "Toodles."

Oh, he needed to tap that.

He waited until she was out of sight, and then he headed back to the emergency department, where a gaggle of Seminus demons had gathered, heads together with a dark-haired female who bore faded Seminus markings on her right arm that, if she were male, would make sense. Sems were *exclusively* male, and their female mates took the markings on their left arms, so what the hell? He wondered if her marks were tats, and then he realized he didn't give a shit.

He recognized Eidolon and tapped him on the shoulder. "How is Limos?"

Eidolon's dark eyes flashed with irritation. "Take a seat. I'll get to you when I can."

"Dumbass," the female muttered.

Revenant hissed. "Who the hell are you to talk to me like that?"

He eyed each of the Seminus males. He knew Eidolon and had seen the blond one, Wraith, hanging out with Thanatos. But the other other male and the female were strangers.

"I'm Sin." She gestured to the group of males. "These are my brothers."

"Ridiculous." He snorted. "There's no such thing as a female Seminus demon."

Sin rolled her eyes. "Clearly, my existence renders your statement...stupid."

"Your existence is not in the natural order. You should be executed," he said, and her brothers all growled.

"Your mama must not have liked you much," Sin muttered.

Wraith's lips peeled back from an impressive set of fangs. Was the guy part vampire? That wasn't normal, either. "Can't imagine why that would be."

Revenant had no idea if his mother had liked him or not. "Tell me what's going on with Limos. When will she be released?" They all glared, and he clenched his teeth. These insects should give him what he wanted without him having to dig for it. "I'm her Watcher. Tell me."

Finally, Eidolon got the bug out of his ass and gestured for him to move to an area with little more privacy. When they were away from the others, he shook his head gravely.

"Limos was injured beyond what anyone here can heal, but we got her to about seventy percent. She's resting now and can go home tomorrow. She'll need a couple of days to recover. She doesn't know about the baby yet," he said, and Revenant felt a twinge of ... something. Couldn't be sadness, though. "Do you know what the hell happened at Limos's place?"

"Yes." The weird sensation plucked at him again, and this time, it was almost painful, as if his body were trying to reject a foreign emotion the way it might reject a transplanted organ. His chest tightened and his skin grew clammy and that was enough of that. He needed to change the subject. He gazed off in the direction the False Angel had gone. "Tell me about Dr. Blaspheme."

"After you tell me what happened."

Frustrating demon. The rare intelligent ones were the worst. "The Horsemen's Heavenly Watcher had a nuclear meltdown."

"Why?"

"I don't know." He really didn't. Her actions hadn't made sense. If she were that volatile, she should never have been assigned as a Watcher. So what had made her go berserk enough to mince the Horsemen and kill a baby? Unless ... unless she hadn't killed it. He thought back to the aftermath, when she'd been crouched over Limos, her palm hovering over her belly. When she stood, she'd looked ... guilty. And what had she put in her pocket? "Wait ... Limos's child ... you said earlier that it was gone. You mean dead?"

Eidolon glanced over at Limos's room. "Given the extent of her injuries, as well as those of her brothers, we're assuming the baby didn't make it."

Assuming. Revenant didn't like assumptions. He liked cold, hard facts. Assumptions were for assholes. But call him an asshole, because Lorelia's behavior earlier was starting to make sense, and he suddenly didn't think the infant had been incinerated.

The doctor stood there as if expecting a response to the bad news, and social convention probably dictated that Revenant should give him one that wasn't full of curse words. So he nodded politely.

But inside, he was fuming. Lorelia had intentionally baited the Horsemen into a fight, giving her an excuse to blast them all and take the baby. And there was only one reason she'd have done that.

The archangels were planning a switcheroo with Gethel's kid. Clever bastards. Too bad for them that Rev was more clever.

"Now," he said, done with the fake polite shit. "Blaspheme."

Eidolon bared his teeth. "She's off-limits to you."

The doctor turned on his heel and strode back to his siblings. Off-limits, he'd said. Not bloody likely. That False Angel intrigued Revenant. He'd never been fascinated by a False Angel before, but something about Blaspheme made him twitchy. She had a secret, and he wondered how hard it would be to get it out of her.

Later, though. Right now he had more pressing matters.

He turned toward the exam room where Limos was with Arik and various staff members. He began to chant, low and quiet, until all around him, the air started to hum. With a thought, he gathered the vibrating air together into a single ball of energy that filled his palm.

"*Stora ilsh ka'aport.*" The ball flew invisibly from his hand and shot into Limos's room, where it settled over her belly to form a shield. "Fuck you, Lorelia. You and your Heavenly brethren can kiss my ass."

Raphael's bellow of rage rocked the ancient Karnak temple complex, cracking walls and toppling pillars that had stood since 1500 BC. They were in the human realm, but occupying the same space in a different realm was the Sheoulic equivalent, a demonic temple used for sacrificing pregnant females.

They'd planned this down to the second. They'd positioned themselves perfectly. Even the damned stars were favorably aligned.

The ritual, performed only once before, should have worked. Raphael had performed the other one, so he knew how to do it.

Uriel grabbed his arm, but Raphael spun out of the way and the other angel caught a fistful of his robe's silky sleeve.

"Calm down." With a wave of his hand, Uriel airlifted a two-ton stone to the top of the pillar it had fallen from. "We're not here to destroy this place."

"No," Raphael snarled, practically choking on his fury. "We're here to swap Limos's child with Gethel's, but the *ritual failed*." He rounded on Lorelia, who had gone as pale as the full moon above. "What did you do? Every chant we tried failed to send Lucifer into Limos. *Every* chant!"

"I—I didn't do anything—"

"Limos's womb wouldn't accept him. You had to have done something. That was our only shot at destroying Lucifer!"

"Listen to me." Lorelia's ivory lace gown swished in the yellow dirt as she moved toward him. "I'm telling you, nothing I did would have caused her body to repel Lucifer. Nothing. They share blood. Her body should have recognized that."

"Then what happened?" Sweet heaven, he wanted to scream again.

Uriel righted a fallen statue and then wiped his hands as if he'd manually moved the five-ton goliath. "Could anyone have known what we planned?"

"Like who?" Raphael asked.

"I don't know." Uriel was wearing his usual drab brown tunic and gray breeches, and he blended in with the scenery as he paced around, looking for debris to clean up. He could be annoyingly OCD. "But if someone knew, they could have done something to Limos."

Lorelia nodded. "It's possible she ingested herbs or a potion that would render her body inhospitable to Lucifer. Or perhaps a spell encased her in repellant magic."

But who could have known? He'd kept this between the three of them for a reason. Had either Uriel or Lorelia betrayed them? Had Lorelia, in her enthusiasm to level the Horsemen, said too much or behaved strangely? The smallest thing could have given the Horsemen something to go on. They weren't fools, after all.

He swiped the tiny clouded marble out of Lorelia's hand and held it up to the moonlight. He could crush it between his fingers like a grape. And while he'd rather not, he would if doing so served the greater good.

But it wouldn't, so Limos's baby, its essence reduced to the marble he was holding, would live.

But that didn't mean he was done with it.

# Eighteen

An hour before darkness fell, Harvester and Reaver discovered an abandoned shack to hole up in just a few miles from the carrion wisp village.

Harvester, her power humming through her body at maybe a fourth of her capacity, set displacement wards on the trail behind them to throw off the Darkmen. Naturally, she pointed out that even if Reaver had been at full strength, he couldn't have placed the wards. Only evil magic could fool an angelic assassin.

"See, I'm more than useful," she said, enjoying the way the vein in his temple throbbed with annoyance. "Now discharge your powers. I can make out your glow, and it kind of makes me want to stab you."

He used up his power to demolish a couple of the eerie black trees that populated the area, and by the time they stumbled through the shack's open doorway, Harvester's stomach was growling embarrassingly loud for food. But worse, her entire body was snarling with the need for blood, and her wing anchors throbbed so viciously that any shoulder movement felt like she was being struck with an ax.

She couldn't feed from Reaver again. Feeding from him had turned her into a monster she hadn't wanted him to see. She shouldn't care, should revel in Holy Boy's disgust. But truthfully, every time she went all Monster Mash, she disgusted even herself.

Besides, it fucking hurt when the horns drilled out of her skull.

The windowless one-room dwelling was dusty and smelled like mold, but there was a gel-like sleeping pad large enough to fit two extra-tall people and a stone trough, which was presumably a toilet. It wasn't the Hilton, but considering the last time they'd rested it had been inside a parasitic bush, this was luxury.

Reaver cast a glance outside through the crack he'd left in the doorway. "I'll keep watch while you get some sleep."

"I'm not tired," she lied. She was fucking *exhausted*.

"You're going to sleep," he insisted as he dropped his backpack onto the dirt floor and dug out the canteen. "Here. Drink."

Her first instinct was to rail against his command no matter how parched she was, but immediately on the heels of that impulse was genuine gratitude. Huh. Maybe there was hope for her after all.

"So demanding," she said, settling on a combination of both acceptance and indifference. Sinking down on the gel mattress, she took the canteen, downed as much as she could handle, and then took the protein bar he offered. "Thank you."

He cocked an eyebrow, as if shocked that she took the time to offer thanks. *Yeah, well, join the club. Right there with ya, buddy.*

She tore open the chocolate-covered whatever-it-was as Reaver opened his own. The thing was waxy on the outside and had the consistency of sawdust on the inside, but it tasted better than anything Harvester had ever had.

*With the exception of Reaver's blood.* She shoved that thought into the back of her mind and ordered it to stay there.

Reaver finished his protein bar and sank onto the mattress, putting his back against the wall so he was facing the door. He folded his hands across his abs, and she let her gaze take him in from his broad chest to his powerful shoulders. His black T-shirt, torn and frayed at the seams, clung to him like a second skin, revealing every flex of his muscles.

And his arms...holy hotness, they were strong, yet gentle. She'd seen him demolish demons with them, but she'd also seen him cradle a newborn infant with care. As she ogled his tan biceps, they rippled as if demanding attention.

Even Reaver's *muscles* were demanding.

"You should get a tattoo," she blurted. She loved tattoos.

He grinned, and she felt a silly flutter in her breast. "A long time ago, I made a bet with Eidolon. He said I'd find a mate. I bet him I never would. So now if I ever take a mate, he's going to make me get the Underworld General caduceus tattooed on my ass."

"Why?" Seemed like a stupid bet for an immortal to make. Never was a long, long time.

"I don't know," he muttered. "You'd think he'd want me to tattoo it somewhere everyone would see it."

"Not the tattoo," she said impatiently. "The bet. Why did you say you wouldn't take a mate?"

One massive shoulder rolled in a lazy shrug. "At the time, I was Unfallen. I had no future. I wasn't going to enter Sheoul to complete my fall, and the likelihood of earning my wings back was pretty much nil. Who would want me?"

Was he fucking kidding? Who *wouldn't* want him? Just looking at him was practically orgasm inducing. He was powerful. Loyal. And he'd stop at nothing to protect those he loved. He'd even sneak into hell to steal Satan's prize possession in order to stop Lucifer. Any female would be lucky to have him.

Even Harvester, who had hated him for years, could see that.

"And now?" she asked quietly. "Do you think you'll find a mate now that you're a halo-fied angel again?" She didn't know why she was asking. Wasn't even sure she wanted an answer.

His sapphire eyes locked onto hers, and her heart did a crazy flip. "Assuming I don't get stripped of my wings or executed for rescuing you...maybe."

The way he said it, low and rough, was downright erotic, as if he was right now picturing his mate. Naked.

Harvester's body went all kinds of hot.

"Harvester," he said, in that rough voice that made her sex throb.

"What?" she found herself leaning toward him, heard her pulse pounding in her ears and felt her lungs struggle for oxygen.

"Lift up your shirt."

She sucked in a hot breath. "My shirt?" Her hands were already on the bottom hem.

"I'll do it." Very gently, he gripped her shoulders and turned her. "I want to see how your wings are healing."

"Oh." She went utterly cold with disappointment. She wasn't sure what she'd been expecting, but that wasn't it.

"If it makes you feel any better," he said, a dry teasing note in his voice, "I'm not a doctor, but I played one for years."

"Yes," she drawled, "that's much better." She wondered if he'd enjoyed working at Underworld General. She'd never thought of him as the doctorly type, but as he peeled her tank top up and smoothed his warm hands up her back, she decided she liked his bedside manner.

"Your scars are gone," he murmured, and she swore she heard his heartbeat pound a little harder, a little faster. So did hers.

His touch was tender as he probed the aching area near her shoulder blades. "Can you extend your wings yet?"

"I'll try." She hoped the slight breathlessness in her words came across as pain and not a reaction to his hands on her body.

Then the pain definitely came through as she tried to bring her wings out. Bone erupted from the slits in her back, and by some miracle she didn't cry out.

"That's good," he said. "You've got about two feet of framework. All bone, but once you feed, you can probably double that and add some tissue."

Retracting her unformed wings, she jerked away from him and yanked her top down. "Not from you."

"Are we really doing this again? You," he growled, "are the most stubborn, difficult, infuriating person I have *ever* dealt with."

"Aw." She fluttered her eyelashes. "You say the sweetest things."

He shook his head as if she were a lost cause, and maybe she was. "We need you to be able to sense Harrowgates. It's only a matter of time before your father's forces find us, and if darkmen are on our trail, we need to get out of Sheoul. Now."

"No." This time her refusal carried less resolve, and even as she formed an argument—a pathetic one—her fangs lengthened and throbbed, and all the starved cells in her body started to quiver. "Feeding does strange things to me."

He barked out a husky laugh. "It does strange things to me, too. You need this, angel." Casually, gracefully, he relaxed his long body and crossed his legs at the ankles. "Come on. I'm right here. It's just blood. No big deal. Just like last time."

*It's just blood. No big deal.* Except it was a big deal. It was a huge deal for her to turn into an ugly beast, and Reaver was all, *Go ahead, stick your fangs in me.* And wait...he'd said *angel.* Usually he called her *fallen.*

It was the nicest thing anyone had ever said to her. Warmth spread through her and emotion she couldn't identify bubbled up inside her. It overflowed from the sealed container she'd kept all her touchy-feely feelings inside since she'd fallen, and while her inner demon wanted to blow her stack and rip Reaver apart for being nice and tapping into that container, she couldn't.

She needed to feed, she needed to build her strength,

and as much as she hated to admit it, she needed Reaver. Like it or not, he was her lifeline, and she had to grab hold and not let go. Otherwise, if they got caught, his sacrifice would have been for naught.

"Seriously?" he asked, in a gravelly voice that told her how tired he was. "Do I have to force you?"

She snorted. "As if you could."

With a flick of his fingernail, he opened a vein in his throat the way he had last time. The heady, intoxicating scent of blood hit her like a blow, short-circuiting every thought that didn't revolve around feeding.

She locked on to the crimson stream dripping down his neck, following the tendons that stood out starkly under his bronzed, perfect skin.

"Take it." His eyes were heavy lidded now, his body relaxed, and her mouth watered.

He didn't have to tell her again. In a heartbeat she was on him. Straddling his thighs, she opened her mouth over the cut. She wasn't going to use her fangs, not this time. With her fangs, blood flowed too fast. She took too much. If she could drink slowly and limit her intake, she should be able to control her renegade Satanic DNA.

The first drops of blood hit her tongue, and she gasped as the sensation of grabbing a live wire ripped through her. She could feel the bones in her back begin to knit and form more framework for her wings and the ecstasy of angelic sex made her writhe. Images flashed in her head. Erotic images of Reaver slipping his hand under her shirt and sliding his palm up her thigh. Of him kissing her breasts, tonguing her nipples. Of him licking his way down her naked body to her sex.

"Verrine," he whispered. "I want you. Damn...I remember you."

*Yes.* Reaver's voice filtered through her ears and heat flamed across her skin as the fantasies played out and his blood flowed over her tongue. But...no, this wasn't right. The images in her head weren't part of a fantasy. They were memories, and while Yenrieth had said he wanted her, just that once, he hadn't said anything about remembering her.

And Reaver definitely wasn't the angel who had made her come three times *before* he took her virginity.

*Yenrieth.*

That son of a bitch. Leave it to him to interrupt her time with Reaver.

*Fool. It was Reaver who interrupted the memories of Yenrieth.*

She jerked upright, so startled by that thought that she couldn't focus on feeding. Reaver was breathing hard and staring at her as if he'd seen a ghost, but if anything, she'd seen a phantom. A phantom lover.

The memories of her night with Yenrieth had been with her for thousands of years, and other than the fact that she couldn't remember what he looked like, they had never altered or dimmed. But somehow, today, they'd not just changed; they'd gotten better.

Or maybe Reaver's blood running through her veins was messing with her head.

"Why did you stop feeding?" His voice carried a strange hitch to it, but as he threaded his fingers through her hair, his touch was astonishingly tender. "What's the matter?"

*Oh, I'm picturing your head between my legs, your*

*mouth at my sex while you fuck me with your tongue. Why?*

She probably shouldn't lead with that. Still a little dazed from the trip down memory lane, she murmured, "I don't look like a demon, do I?"

He used his free hand to tilt her chin up and down and from side to side, making a big production of deciding if she had gone all beastie. She tried to read him, to get a hint of what was running through that handsome head, but his eyes gave nothing away.

Finally, his gaze met hers, and oh, she'd been wrong about his eyes giving nothing away. They were filled with heat, longing, and the vaguest sense of...familiarity? Déjà vu? They hadn't had sex before, but they'd both seen each other naked. That could explain it.

Except that, back in the cavern, she'd felt that same familiarity. A rightness that didn't make sense.

Frankly, the mystery was starting to piss her off.

"You don't look like a demon," Reaver said, his voice gravelly, and she wondered how he'd sound after a long, hard night of sex. "You need to get some rest. Let my blood heal you."

She shifted on his lap, nearly moaning at the feel of his hard shaft pushing against the fly of his jeans. She loved that she could affect him that way. Perhaps it was time that she demanded what he owed her.

Sex.

Erotic tension bloomed between them, thick and heavy, almost as if he'd read her thoughts. Maybe she didn't need to invoke their deal. Maybe he'd sleep with her willingly.

And maybe she was a big idiot. Just because he'd res-

cued her didn't mean he'd lower his lofty standards to
screw a fallen angel. So yes, she could demand that he
fulfill his end of their bargain... except that all of a sudden, forcing him to pleasure her seemed like a real shitty
thing to do.

Huh. Looked like her moral compass was starting to
point more and more toward Heavenly north.

Which scared the shit out of her. She wanted to be
good. She did. But wouldn't that mean lowering her
guard? She'd lowered her guard with Yenrieth, and he'd
nearly destroyed her.

But maybe she could start small, like magnanimously
telling Reaver she'd let him out of the bargain.

"Reaver—" She spoke at the same time he said, "Harvester," and because she was feeling all unselfish and
good, she patted him on his chest and said, "You first."

Dear Lord, his chest was firm. She patted a little longer
than she should have, but hey, she still had a long way to
go to be a totally upstanding person.

To her heart-stopping, mouth-dropping shock, he
placed his hand over hers. "Why did you kiss me back at
the cavern?"

Too flustered to form a clever response, she said simply, "To annoy you."

He laughed, a hearty, soul-deep sound. "You do that a
lot. You always have."

*Always have?* He made it sound like they'd known
each other for centuries. "Did it work?"

"Oh, yeah." He shifted, lifting his hips, and the motion
put his erection fully against her sex as she straddled him.
"It annoyed me. It would annoy me if you did it again."

She inhaled sharply. Was this a challenge? Or was he

issuing an invitation? Harvester didn't like invitations. Invitations were commands veiled in the pretense of having a choice.

So she'd take this as a challenge. She never turned those down.

Drawing on rusty seduction skills she hadn't used in what seemed like forever, she leaned in, angling her face toward his. She paused when only a whisper of air separated their lips. His eyes darkened and grew heavy-lidded, and she felt an abrupt sense of relief. He wasn't pushing her away. He wasn't making her feel like an idiot for wanting to kiss him.

It shocked her how much that mattered to her.

Reaver's heartbeat thrummed rapidly against her palm, speeding up as her mouth hovered over his.

But she wouldn't give him what he expected. At least, not yet. Reaver had taken the lead for most of the journey so far, and it was time she took control. And kept it.

Lowering her head, she dragged her mouth on a lazy path from his throat to his jaw, where she nipped him hard enough to make him hiss. His hands dropped to her waist, gripping hard when she soothed her little bite with her tongue before moving on to his mouth. His lips met hers eagerly, and she started to think that maybe taking the upper hand wouldn't be as easy as she'd thought.

He licked at her, forcing her lips open. With a groan, he rolled her under him so he was pinning her, moving between her legs in a slow, sinuous motion that made her writhe to get him even closer.

"Damn," he whispered against her lips. "Just like I remember. You feel...perfect. Beautiful."

A wave of heat washed over her with so much force

she didn't bother asking what he remembered. She knew he appreciated her body...hell, he'd always gone for the females who dressed on the trashy side, so she used to dress as provocatively as possible just to mess with him. What better way to drive him crazy than to make him hot and bothered for a female he detested?

But she hadn't ever believed he thought she was beautiful.

Reaver shifted so they were both on their sides. His hands gripped her hips, guiding her as she ground against him, the weird gel mattress moving with them. It was as if they were in the sky, mating on air currents, angel style.

She wedged her hand between them and palmed his arousal, and his harsh, ragged breath vibrated her all the way to her bones. Even with the thick barrier of his jeans she could feel the hardness of him, the impressive size, the heat that radiated into her skin.

Enough playing. She didn't do foreplay. Yenrieth had set the bar, and even though he'd destroyed her emotionally after it was over, she hadn't been able to take her time with anyone since.

And it wasn't like they had all the time in the world to have sex anyway. No, this had to be a quickie. Maybe once she fucked him she'd be over whatever it was about him that made her crazy. Since the very first time she met him on his first day of Watcher duty, she'd been drawn to him like a scissor moth to an open eye, which had never made sense. It still didn't. This was too hot, too intense.

Her skin shrank at the thought. This kind of intensity was bad. She was too involved, and Reaver had to know it. Knowledge was power.

She would never allow any male to wield the kind of power over her that Yenrieth had.

*Too late.*

Panic built in her chest even as desire bloomed between her legs. His hand drifted to her butt, and her desire flared hotter, edging out panic and roaring to victory.

*Well played, Reaver. Well played.*

Sex could be just sex. That's all it ever had been for her. She wasn't a young, stupid angel giving her virginity to the male she loved.

She was quite capable of separating her emotions from her physical needs.

Telling herself all the lies she needed to believe, she dragged her fingernails up his length, smiling at his combined hiss and moan of pleasure. At the button at the top of his fly, she stopped, letting herself toy with the brass disc for a heartbeat.

*Yes. This was going to be good.*

She flicked the button and tugged on the denim, and the fly opened with a series of muffled pops. Reaver's cock sprang free, a broad, dusky column pulsing with thick veins. Finally, after all these years of curiosity, she took him in her palm.

He gasped, followed by a soft curse that was more of a moan. Oh, she loved those sounds—there was nothing hotter than a male in the throes of pleasure, nothing more beautiful than Reaver as he threw his head back and panted, his parted lips glistening from their kiss. In her hand he was rock hard under velvety-smooth skin, and as much as she wanted to pump her fist and take him higher, she wanted to savor this moment more.

She supposed she could take a *little* time for foreplay.

A desperate craving unfurled in her belly and reached into places she'd forgotten she had, awakening a beast she wasn't sure could be put back in its cage. No, she was sure. She'd always been able to have casual sex... in fact, she preferred a no-strings roll in the hay.

But the desire she felt right now was nothing like what she'd felt for those casual flings.

Squeezing lightly, she swept her thumb back and forth at the silky tip of him, loving how his entire body jerked with each slow pass. She threw her leg over his and got even closer, so ready to take him inside her the moment they got their clothes off.

Suddenly, he gripped her wrist. "No... Harvester. We can't."

"We can," she whispered against his throat. "I'm healed." Except for her wings, but the bones were knitting together swiftly now, the pain dulled from the feeding.

"It's not that." He lifted her as if she weighed nothing at all and set her aside. Sharp, lashing pain scored her heart as he sat up and buttoned his jeans. "I'm not doing this with you."

What the hell was going on? Harvester struggled to jump-start her lust-addled brain and make sense of what he was saying. Her body was juiced, her feminine parts were aching, and her heart was pounding.

Swallowing dryly, she sat up and braced herself against the wall. "What's the problem?"

Shoving to his feet, he swore, long and loud. "What's the problem? It's you, Harvester." He gestured between them. "It's us. This can't work."

Very slowly, as if she were bleeding to death, something

drained out of her, leaving her colder and more hollow than ever before. She'd trusted him to not reject her, and didn't it figure that he'd waited until she'd truly let down her guard to do it.

"Of course we can't work," she said, welcoming the bitterness that seeped into her voice. Her old friend was back. "You're a pure, holy angel of goodness, and I'm Satan's evil whore of a daughter. So yeah, *we* can't work. Thanks for pointing that out, Captain Obvious. But we can fuck."

Reaver's eyes were like jeweled drill bits, boring so deep inside her she was afraid he'd seen her darkest secrets.

"Tell me," he said softly. "If Yenrieth were to return, what would you do?"

Yenrieth? How dare he conjure that name right now? What did Yenrieth have to do with anything?

"Who cares?" She stood, suddenly feeling the need to be on even footing with him. "Yenrieth hasn't been seen in thousands of years. He's dead."

"And if he wasn't?"

"Why? Are you afraid I'm falling in love with you or some shit? And then Yenrieth will magically return to sweep me off my feet and leave you in the dust?" She poked him in the chest. "Because I have news for you. I'm not falling in love with you, Yenrieth isn't coming back, and, if he did, I'd be more likely to kill him than let him sweep me to anywhere." She fisted the hem of her tank top and peeled it off over her head. "So get over yourself and fuck me, dammit."

Reaver's expression was a mix of anguish and disgust

and, as far as she could tell, aimed at her. Was she that repulsive to him?

Her eyes stung, and she hated herself for it. Feeling suddenly, stupidly exposed, she covered her breasts with her arms.

"I can't." Reaver's voice was guttural as he wheeled around and stared at the wall. "I remember. I loved you."

She blinked, her bafflement taking the edge off her anger. "What are you talking about? Did you hit your head?" She eyed his throat. "Did I drink too much blood? Are you okay?"

"I loved you," he repeated, because it hadn't sounded crazy enough the first time. "But I remember the hate too."

"Yes," she said carefully, because she didn't want to set off the madman. "You hate me."

"And now I know why." He clenched his jaw so tight she heard a crack. "You told me what you did to me, and I understood. As Reaver, I got it."

As Reaver? She was beyond baffled now, was starting to get scared. Something was very wrong with him.

"But as Yenrieth I hated you. I can feel that now. Like it was yesterday."

Oh, God. She breathed a huge sigh of relief. "I think somehow our memories are getting jumbled up together. Weird stuff happens in this region, and with the *lasher* implants and your *sheoulghuls*—"

"Dammit, Harvester, listen to me." Pivoting, he dragged both hands through his hair over and over, almost obsessively, as if whatever was scrambling his brain could be calmed by a scalp massage. "I came to rescue you to find Lucifer, but I'd been planning to do it all along anyway.

Because of the Horsemen. What you did for them. They're my children," he said, and it was as if all her bodily functions seized up under an adrenaline overload. He was freaking high. He couldn't be their father because their father was—"I'm Yenrieth."

# Nineteen

⌒

Reaver couldn't believe he'd just admitted the truth to Harvester. At the worst possible time. But dammit, images had slammed into him while she was feeding, knocking him so off balance that it felt as if he was in two places at once—the present and the past—and only Harvester could shed light on the dark holes in his memory.

He'd remembered moments with Verrine, more flashes of their exploits together, but this time they were a little longer, and this time, they came with the raw emotions he'd felt when the memories had been made.

He'd loved her. He didn't remember why he hadn't acted on how he'd felt, but he was certain he'd loved her. So when Harvester had kissed him, he'd felt like everything was right. It had been like coming home.

But then she'd touched him, stroked him, and even as his lust built, searing hatred had scorched his heart. The memory of why he'd bedded Verrine had slammed into him, along with the rage he'd felt when he, as Yenri-eth, had learned that Verrine had kept the existence of his children away from him for almost thirty years.

Now all of those emotions were swirling around in his head the way they had five thousand years ago, fresh and poisonous, and mixed with everything Reaver knew and felt, as well.

He didn't know what he was supposed to be feeling right now, and he was pretty sure Harvester was in the same leaking boat.

She stared at him, and her eyes glazed over with disbelief and confusion. Her mouth opened. Closed. And then he saw it. The moment it all sank in.

Her face went ashen with devastation. "Oh no," she whispered. Her entire body began to shake. He could smell her fury, her sense of betrayal, and it sliced him wide open. "No. You...oh, gods, *no*."

"Harvester—"

"Shut up!" she rasped. "Don't you speak to me, *Yenri-eth*. Don't you ever speak to me again."

Closing his eyes, he waited for it. When it came, he was ready, but it was still the most painful slap he'd ever gotten, not because of the force but because behind it was a female whose agony transferred straight to him.

"How long have you known?" She was screaming now, her anger so great that her powers were seeping into her tirade and blistering waves of heat seared his skin. She snatched up her tank top, her eyes blazing with raw hatred. "Where have you been for the last five thousand years, you bastard?"

He didn't reply, but it wasn't because she'd told him to never speak to her again—he was pretty sure that would be impossible given that she was asking questions she demanded answers to. No, he didn't reply because he couldn't. He didn't know where he'd been prior to the last thirty years or so. And he was pretty sure she wasn't ready to hear anything he had to say.

"Answer me!" Tears streaming down her face, Harvester lunged at him.

He caught her by the shoulders and wrenched her to the mattress. She might be more powerful than him right now, but he was physically stronger, and once he had her on her back, he used both his strength and his weight to keep her from hurting herself or him.

He just had to hope she was too angry to think about blasting him with her powers. He'd also like it if his cock wasn't still in *let's play with the hot female* mode.

"Harvester." He jerked his head back to avoid getting whacked in the face by her flailing arm. "I don't know where I was. You know I can't remember anything but the last thirty years."

"*Liar!* You've lied about everything else, you fucking asshole."

She rocked her head up to bite his shoulder, and *shit*, that hurt. He shifted to gain leverage and muscled her into the mattress with his forearm over her throat. He kept the pressure light, not wanting to hurt her, but he also didn't need to have any bites taken out of him.

"Listen to me," he said roughly, because it wasn't easy to talk when you were fighting off a snarling hellcat. "I'm not lying. I didn't even know the truth about myself until a few months ago, after you were taken to Sheoul."

Eyes shimmering like wet emeralds, she glared up at him, practically frothing with rabid fury. "What," she ground out, "do you remember?"

"Not much. I can get brief glimpses of my past with you, but most of it is jumbled together. There's no context." He paused as a strange vibration began to buzz the air outside. The sharp, shrill sensation of terror skated over his skin.

"It's night." Harvester's gaze tracked around the room as if seeking the source of the vibration. "Nothing can move now. We're safe for a couple of hours."

Safe. He was stuck inside a twelve-by-twelve shack with a fallen angel who hated him. There was nothing safe about any of this. Not for him.

"Now get off me," she snapped.

"Do you promise you won't try to kill me?"

"No." If glares were daggers, he'd be bleeding out from massive trauma right now. "But if I wanted to kill you, I'd have given you the Calder treatment already."

She had a point. He eased off her, but he braced himself for a possible surprise attack. Harvester had always fought dirty. Instead, she sat up calmly and tugged on her tank top.

Now what? He'd rather have her upset and yelling than eerily silent, like a dormant volcano on the verge of a catastrophic eruption.

"Damn you, Reaver." Harvester scooted to the far side of the mattress and sat there, staring at him with glassy, bloodshot eyes. "What do you want from me?"

"I don't want anything from you." Well, that wasn't entirely true. He wanted more answers about his past.

And he wanted her forgiveness for what he'd done to her as Yenrieth. The anger over the secret she'd kept from him still lingered, but it was nothing compared to what she must be feeling. He'd had five months to come to grips with who he was. She'd had five minutes.

"You don't want anything from me." Acid dripped from her voice. "Just like old times."

"Don't," he said as he reached for her. "Don't do this."

She jerked away from him. "Don't touch me. Don't talk to me." She flopped down on the mattress, putting her back to him and shutting him out as effectively as a brick wall. "Leave me alone."

"Harvester—"

"I said, leave me the fuck alone!" She didn't turn over, just kept up the impenetrable wall routine. "Just give me some fucking space. Can you do that? Can you follow a command for once in your life?"

The pain in her voice flayed him to the bone. He might be feeling residual hate, but the love he'd had for her was there, too, and while both were tempered by his experiences with her as Reaver, that only seemed to make it worse.

Because as far as he could tell, he'd been a major dick as Yenrieth, and Reaver had no idea how to reconcile who he'd been with who he was now. All he knew was that he was the source of Harvester's pain. Every single stitch of pain she'd endured for the last five thousand years could be laid on his shoulders.

Bracing his back against the wall, he searched his brain for more memories as he waited for Harvester to process everything. He figured he had about five minutes before she ripped into him again, and sure enough, she sat up with a snarl, her eyes flecked with black.

"How did you learn the truth?"

"Reseph told me." Man, he couldn't have been more shocked. "He found out from Lilith."

"Lilith," she spat out, and beneath her skin, her veins

began to blacken and rise to the surface. "I want her dead. I want her to suffer—"

"She's dead," he said before she got more worked up. "Reseph destroyed her."

A low, menacing growl came from deep in her chest, and the tips of her horns erupted through her hair. "I hope he tortured her. I hope he did to her what he did to me." A shudder shook her, and he reached for her again, but she hissed and knocked his hand away with a flare of power that singed the hair on his arm. "Were you upset about losing your lover?"

Shit. She was starting to go over the edge, and once that happened he'd be screwed. As calmly as he could, he said, "You know I wasn't. I hated her, remember?" He doubted she saw the irony in *him* asking *her* if she remembered.

"*You fucked her.*" Suddenly, pain clamped down on his skull and pressure compressed his chest. "You hurt me."

"Harvester," he croaked. "Stop."

She didn't listen. Her eyes went ebony with irrational fury as she slammed her hands into his ribs and sent a blast of electric agony into his body. Clenching his teeth, he groaned and dug deep for the last drop of power he had.

With a whispered command, he released it into the air, enveloping them both in a bubble of exhaustion. It was a last-ditch move that affected them both, and even as she began to return to normal, he felt his eyelids droop.

Harvester slumped to the mattress. "What," she said tiredly, "did you do?"

*Oh, nothing. I just made us both vulnerable to anyone or anything that happens upon us.* He just had to hope she was right and that nothing moved during the night in this realm.

Her eyes closed, and she let out a delicate snore. He

tried to stay awake, but he was definitely falling victim to his own weapon. His muscles turned to pudding and he fell onto the mattress next to her. With another little snore, Harvester rolled over, bumping her forehead against his. Closing his eyes, he listened to her breathe. He was willing to bet that very few males had ever listened to her sleep. She wouldn't want to be that vulnerable.

How lonely would that have been? He reached out and carefully tucked her closer, until she was curled into his chest, her arm across his waist. This felt familiar, and when a memory of them lying, fully clothed on a beach of white sand, popped into his head, he knew why.

Damn, but she'd been warm back then.

Floating on a raft of regret, he drifted off...

And woke to the sound of screams. Harvester jackknifed into a sit next to him. "What is it?"

"I don't know." He leaped off the bed and threw open the door. Outside it was dawn, and a mob of carrion wisps were screeching at something that seemed to be fighting its way from the center of the group.

"A darkman," Harvester breathed. "Impossible. How the hell did he find us? My wards should have thrown him off track for days."

"Worry about that later." Reaver scooped up the backpack. "We've got to get out of here."

She grabbed his wrist in a bruising hold. "Wait. Something's not right."

"Maybe your wards were defective. It doesn't matter. We have to go."

"My wards were fine. The darkman tracked us somehow." She scowled. "Did anyone give you anything for the journey?"

"The *lasher* implants. Why?"

"Because supernatural objects can be enchanted to become homing beacons for darkmen. Only an angel could do that. Did the *lasher* implants come into contact with any angels that you know of?"

He shook his head. "Wraith would never have let them out of his sight once he had them. There's no way—" He broke off as the answer hit him like a punch to the gut. "That *bastard*."

"What is it?"

"The *sheoulghuls*." He dug the crystals out of his pocket. "Raphael gave me one."

Her eyes snapped up to his. "Holy fucknuts," she whispered. "I told you not to trust him."

"And you were right." Reaver's voice was wooden to his own ears. "He knew I'd come after you, and I fell right into his trap. I led the darkmen straight to you."

Once again Revenant stood before Satan, and once again he wished he was anywhere but here. *Anywhere*.

Most demons and fallen angels, and even a few humans, would sell their own children at meat markets for the privilege of serving the Dark Lord. It was, after all, an honor to be considered one of Satan's inner-circle minions. People dreamed of one day being at his side and in his service.

Those people were fucking stupid.

Only a stone-dumb idiot would want that. Satan's lackeys rarely lived long. One screw-up and it was the ax. The literal ax. The Dark Lord didn't believe in second chances.

He was also a big fan of shoot-the-fucking-messenger.

"You said your news is important." The demon king

turned away from the warg he'd been torturing for days. "It had better be. I'm about to break this werewolf assassin's oath and find out who stole Harvester."

It was important, all right. Revenant just hoped Satan didn't freak out and do the shoot-the-messenger thing.

"Were you aware that Limos was pregnant?"

Satan's growl indicated that he knew, and Revenant wondered what happened to the unlucky bastard who'd delivered the baby news. Limos was supposed to have been Satan's bride, and he held a grudge.

Revenant continued quickly, before his boss had time to get angry. "I believe the archangels are attempting—or already have attempted—to switch Gethel's and Limos's babies in the womb."

The legendary Big Bad pivoted around. "They did what? How do you know?"

"Because the Horsemen's Heavenly Watcher mangled the Horsemen. It was...bizarre. When she was finished, Limos's baby was gone. Not dead. Gone."

Satan went quiet. Too quiet, and Rev could practically hear the tension crackling in the air. Finally, he wandered over to a tray loaded with implements of torture and selected a rusty butter knife.

"If they have Limos's child," he said in a terrifyingly calm voice, "they can perform the ritual remotely within a brief window. When did this happen?"

"Recently." Rev kept his eye on the knife, not wanting to find himself with a knife *in* the eye. "I found her at Underworld General. I bound her womb so it won't hold any child but her own."

"Excellent. I'm starting to think you should be working for me instead of babysitting Horsemen."

*Oh, fuck no.* Revenant's sense of self-preservation was way too strong to want such an *honor.*

Whirling in a blur, Satan launched the knife. The thud of the dull blade punching into the werewolf's gut echoed through the chamber, followed by the male's low moan.

Satan, now empty-handed, clapped and a female fallen angel named Knell entered.

"My lord?"

"Increase the guard around Gethel and fetch the Orphmage Gormesh. Have him conjure a protection enchantment for Lucifer. He's in my guest quarters." He glanced over at Revenant. "He brought the ingredients and incantation I needed to break the warg's assassin oath. Now the fun begins."

Knell bowed and left the chamber. Satan strode over to the werewolf, who was hanging from a huge wooden cross. He wrapped his hand around the warg's throat.

*"Mephormus etalia exodushem."*

The warg sucked in a sharp, asthmatic breath. Satan leaned in, lowered his voice. "Who are you working for?"

"Reaver," the warg moaned, and this time it was Revenant who inhaled sharply.

Rev braced himself for an explosion of Satan's fury, but to Rev's shock, the king of demons merely tossed the werewolf to the ground and watched him until he died, a victim of the broken oath's death sentence.

"I knew Heaven was involved," Satan said, his voice still eerily calm. "But Reaver...he's an interesting development."

What the fuckity fuck? Why wasn't the demon having a nuclear meltdown? And why would he think that Reaver's involvement was "interesting"?

"My lord," Revenant said, as unobtrusively as he could. "What do you want me to do?"

Satan's lips turned up in a bloodthirsty grin. "Tell Knell to belay my last order. I have another job for the Orphmage."

Revenant cocked an eyebrow. "Sir?"

Satan laughed, a maniacal sound that congealed Revenant's blood. "My armies are on the move, waiting to get into Heaven, but right now, all battles with angels will have to be fought in the human realm until Lucifer's birth shatters Heaven's walls."

Revenant wasn't about to say "Duh," but...duh.

"I'm tired of waiting. The Orphmage is going to change the game. He's going to accelerate the timetable." Satan ran his tongue over sharp teeth. "Lucifer is going to come early."

# Twenty

Son of a bitch!

Reaver was going to destroy that archangel. Somehow, if he survived the darkmen, he was going to make Raphael pay for this.

He tossed the *sheoulghuls* onto the cabin's dirt floor, but Harvester snatched them up. "It's too late to get rid of them. The enchantment has already marked you as a target." She shoved the crystals back into his pocket. "I think I know a way to fix it, but we have to go."

She said it as if he wasn't aware of the urgent need to get the hell out of here.

A shrill, wet scream came from outside. The darkman was closer. They were out of time.

"We can slip past while the demons are distracting him." He shot her a glance. "You ready?"

"No," she said so nastily that he knew her nap hadn't smoothed the way for reasonable dialog about their past.

"I was thinking I'd take up knitting while I wait for him to kill me."

He ignored that and held out his hand to her. "Come on."

With a blatant sneer at his offer, she brushed past him and slipped out into the throng of carrion wisps.

Swearing quietly, he followed her as she crept around the skinny demons and used the trees and brush as cover.

"We need to head north." Harvester shoved a fat, leafless branch out of the way and darted into the shadows. "Toward the mesa in the distance." A crossbow bolt, no doubt made of *aurial* material, impaled a tree trunk mere centimeters from his head. "Shit—Reaver, you're glowing!"

Reaver wheeled around in time to see another bolt fire from the darkman's crossbow. He dove at Harvester, taking her down as the bolt screamed over their heads. Reaver rolled behind a fallen log and blasted the asshole with a stream of hellfire that drained every last bit of Reaver's power.

The flames caught the darkman in the torso, knocking him backward and sending his crossbow flying.

"The glow's gone," Harvester breathed.

"Good." He already had a bull's-eye on his chest. There was no need to add neon lights and a flashing arrow pointing at it.

Reaver shoved Harvester down the path they'd started on, but she stopped so suddenly he crashed into her.

"Lucifer," she gasped. "I can feel him." She gasped again. "Oh, shit. I can feel my father, too. He's ahead of us."

An icy fist closed around Reaver's heart. "How close?"

Terror flashed in Harvester's eyes as they shifted to the darkman, who was up and charging in their direction. "I don't know. Close. We have to hurry."

"Won't we be exposed when we hit the Scythe Plains?"

"We're stopping before we get there. But we need to run or Satan's army is going to cut us off." Harvester took off at a jog, leaving Reaver no choice but to follow. "The entrance to Persephone's Playground should be over the next ridge."

He stumbled like a toddler learning to walk. "Persephone's Playground? It's real?"

"Yup. No violence allowed. If we can get through the barrier, the darkman can't hurt us."

"What about your father?"

"He's the exception to the 'no violence' rule."

Figured. Satan was the exception to every rule.

They pushed hard, running where they could, scaling inclines when they had to, and once wading through a river that ran red with the blood of something extremely large that had been wounded or killed upstream.

They reached the ridge as another darkman topped the knoll, his white teeth flashing inside the pitch-black hood. Reaver didn't hesitate. He tackled the thing as it loosed a razor-sharp disc designed to separate heads from bodies before returning to the thrower. They went down in a heap of fists. The darkman tried to wriggle free, his shadowy substance creating a slippery hold, but Reaver had to hang on. Darkmen had few weaknesses, but physical combat was one of them.

He pounded the darkman in the face—at least, what should be his face. There was nothing under the hood but a mouth.

The thing let out a silent scream that Reaver could feel like a million stinging nettles digging into his muscles. He hit it again, hoping to shut the bastard up, but the stinging only grew worse.

"Reaver!"

He cranked his head around just as the darkman who had been chasing them struck Harvester with a summoned club. She launched sideways and plowed into a tree, snapping the trunk in half. Wood splinters showered them, raining down hard enough to give a vampire nightmares.

But Reaver wasn't a vampire, and he snagged a thick stake out of the air and brought it down through the darkman's gaping mouth, pinning him to the ground. It wouldn't kill him, but it would hold him long enough for Reaver and Harvester to get out of there.

*If* they could neutralize the other assassin.

In a black blur, the darkman launched a blade. The weapon sliced through the air on a collision course with Harvester's heart. Reaver shoved off the staked darkman and lunged. Searing pain ripped into his shoulder as the dagger clipped him on the intercept. He landed next to Harvester and careened off the jagged stump she'd created when she'd crashed into the tree.

"Bastard." She snarled at the assassin, kicking out her legs and catching the darkman in the ankles. He didn't go down, but his attempt to keep his balance gave Reaver the opportunity to pluck the dagger out of the ground where it had impaled itself and hurl it back at the creature.

The blade caught the assassin in its nonface, and the sensation of stinging nettles wrapped around him again. At Harvester's hiss, he knew she was getting the pincushion treatment, too.

"Come on," she rasped as she tugged on his hand. "We need to get inside Persephone's Playground."

His backpack had fallen off at some point, and he grabbed it as they bolted past the two thrashing assassins. Harvester released him to scale an incline. At the top, she came to a halt next to a massive crystal carved into the shape of a goat-headed demon skull.

"There." Harvester pointed down, into the bottomless canyon that dropped sharply on the other side of the ridge. Creepy animals clung to the sides or skittered in and out of crevices and holes, and in the darkest rifts, glowing eyes stared out.

"There, what?"

Harvester bit into her wrist and dripped blood onto the crystal carving. Crimson rivulets ran down the skull's forehead and into the eyes and nostrils and finally reached the pointy teeth. There, Harvester's blood was sucked inside. Next to them, an opening and staircase appeared out of thin air, disappearing into the canyon.

"Let's go." Harvester leaped into the chasm and took the stairs two at a time. Crazy female.

The opening and stairs disappeared behind them as they ran, leaving them in an earthen tunnel, and Reaver wondered what would happen if they turned around and tried to go back up.

"Do you hear that?" Harvester looked over her shoulder at him. "Music. We're almost there."

"I wasn't expecting a concert." Laughter and voices joined the sound of music.

Harvester stopped on the stairs as the tunnel gave way to a huge, cavernous area filled with hundreds of species of demons, colorful tents offering food and drink, jewelry, toys, weapons, and a lot of things Reaver couldn't identify.

"It's not a concert. It's a market," she said. "But it's not just any market. You know how, in the human realm, there are places where evil gathers to see blood spilled at dog fights or to sell human children? Well, in Sheoul there are places where nonevil people can meet with their own kind and not be judged."

"So none of these people are evil?" He eyed a tall, white-haired Neethul male testing a sword edge at a yellow tent nearby. Most Neethuls made their living in the slave trade, and those who didn't still found vile ways to support themselves.

Harvester shrugged. "Oh, he's evil. But just like a Christian white-bread male might fall to temptation and sneak out for a night of drinking and debauchery, people like the Neethul sometimes get the urge to be rebels and visit the other side of the tracks now and then. The good side."

So this was an evil being's version of rebelling. No doubt all the evil ladies got hot for a rebel "good boy."

Reaver frowned. That didn't even sound plausible.

"So what now?"

"Now," she said, "I should leave you to fend for yourself. *Yenrieth.*"

He was wondering when she'd start up on him again. He had a feeling he was in for a long, long day. And an even longer eternity.

"You wouldn't do that," he said, and she snorted.

"Clearly, you don't remember all the times you pissed me off."

Actually, one memory did flare up, a time when he'd

teased her about screaming like a little girl when a suckling pig burst out of a forest where they'd been hunting hellrats. She'd blown her stack, whacked him with a summoned stick, and stormed off.

"I know you're capable of it," he said, "but I know you won't. You want answers too bad." Answers he doubted he could give until he had his full memory back.

"Arrogant ass," she snapped. "Come on. We need to get the darkman enchantment from the *sheoulghul* removed." She waved him forward. "This way."

They picked their way through the crowd, weaving between tents and demons, and just when Reaver thought he'd seen it all, he nearly jumped out of his skin when a fangy demon dressed like a clown popped out of a box as they passed by a circus-themed tent.

Harvester cocked a black eyebrow at him, and heat flamed his cheeks. "Clowns are freaky," he muttered. "And demon clowns? Man, they're in a freaky category of their own."

"Aw." Harvester shot him a snarky, fake pout over her shoulder as she slipped between two demons haggling over the price of some sort of fish. "Reavie-weavie is afwaid of a widdle cwown." She trailed her finger along the rim of a wine barrel as they passed. "Speaking of Limos, you know, your *daughter*, how are the Horsemen?"

Awkward. Reaver suddenly felt like his boots were crunching on eggshells.

"They're fine," he said warily. "Limos is pregnant."

Harvester looked back at him in surprise, and with the tiniest hint of a smile. "Good. She's been wanting that for a long time." She turned into another row of tents. "Do they know about me? Who took my place as Watcher?"

"They don't know," he said. "I thought if I told them they'd want to help me rescue you." He side-stepped to avoid getting shouldered by a hell mare someone was leading through the market. "Your replacement is a douche named Revenant."

Harvester skidded to a halt and wheeled around. *"Revenant?* That puffed-up, ill-tempered hellswine?"

"I see you've met him."

She snarled. "That by-the-book hardass has been after my job for decades. He even tried seducing me, as if I'd give up my job after enough orgasms. Fool."

She jerked her hair back from her face so hard it had to hurt, but what Reaver really wanted was for Revenant to hurt. Just because.

"Does he know he can't insult Limos without getting the boys all riled up?" she asked. "He needs to know that. And he really needs to know not to mess with Battle. Ares's stallion hates fallen angels. Although I guess it'll be funny to watch him learn that on his own." She laughed as if picturing the scene in her head. "Ooh, and I can't wait for him to mess with Than's vampires. Thanatos will hang Revenant from the southwest tower of his castle for that."

"Not likely," Reaver said. "Watchers got a defensive upgrade to protect against angry Horsemen."

"Really?" Harvester scowled. "I could have used that once or twice."

"I know," he said quietly.

"You don't know anything," she snapped.

It had been nice to chip through the layer of ice that encased her, but now they were back to the way it had always been. Him trying to get through to her, and her putting up walls as fast as she could.

She spun back around and moved even faster toward wherever she was going.

"I know what Pestilence did to you." He could guess, anyway.

"Yeah? Good for you. But compared to what my own father and his minions have done, Pestilence was a little boy playing at war spoils. I'm over that trauma, so shut up about it."

Yup, she sounded over it. But not being completely dense, he didn't voice that thought.

She stopped in front of a black tent, where a humanoid female was arranging beads on a string, chanting as she worked.

Harvester spoke to her in a language Reaver didn't know, and a moment later, she turned to him. "She can remove the tracking enchantment. But it's going to cost both *sheoulghuls*."

He lowered his voice and spoke into her ear. "Without the non-enchanted *sheoulghul*, I can't recharge down here."

"If you're dead you can't recharge either," she pointed out. "Unless you have anything else in that backpack to bargain with, it's both *sheoulghuls* or nothing."

Damn. This was bad. He hadn't been able to hold onto much power or he'd glow, but every little bit helped. If he couldn't recharge, he was going to not only be fully dependent on Harvester, but he would be a liability to her as well.

Some rescuer he was.

Cursing to himself, he handed over the *sheoulghuls*. The shopkeeper smiled like she'd won the lottery as she carefully took the crystals and secured them in a leather pouch that looked suspiciously like human skin.

Man, he hated demons.

The shopkeeper disappeared inside her tent, and when she returned a minute later, she was carrying a bowl of green paste.

"Give me your hand," she said, and Reaver did as she'd demanded.

Harvester propped a hip against a tent support, her stance relaxed and casual, but he didn't miss the way she was watching the crowd like a hawk, her sharp eyes assessing every individual who walked by. She was so different from the young, innocent Verrine, who, no matter how many times he'd told to be alert to her surrounding, would get distracted by the smallest things, like a butterfly landing on a flower.

The sudden memory and wash of tender feelings made him jerk as the demon poured the green stuff into his palm. She glared, wiped spilled drops off her hand, and continued, starting up an incantation that made his ears ache. He glanced over at Harvester, but if she noticed the painful buzz, she wasn't letting on.

The demon ended on a high note that made Reaver wince, and then he damned near shouted when, out of thin air, she produced a golden nail and punched it through his hand.

"What the—" He cut off with a strangled yelp as she yanked the nail back out.

Blood poured onto the ground, and her voice became a clipped, harsh bark. "Done."

His bleeding stopped, and in an instant, the hole sealed.

Harvester pushed away from the tent support. "You're clean. Let's go." She took his hand and started to jog. "Daddy's here."

Reaver's gut hit the floor. "Here? As in, inside this place?"

She nodded. "I felt him operate the entrance."

She picked up her pace until they reached a series of portals in the wall. Harvester stopped in front of the third one, its opening constructed from the giant bones of gargantua demons and larger than any of the others, at least as wide as a semitruck's trailer was long.

"What's this?"

"It's another Boregate. Sort of." She took his hand with only the smallest of dismissive sneers. "We have to walk through together or we'll end up in different places."

This didn't sound promising. "What do you mean, different places?"

"I mean that there's no map inside. This Boregate drops you wherever it wants to. Could be anywhere in Sheoul, though it usually takes you someplace that makes sense. It's almost as if it reads your needs. But every once in a while they'll drop you in the place you least want to be."

"Like your father's realm?"

"Exactly." She smiled with exaggerated perkiness. "But the good news is that he's not there right now. See? I can see the bright side of things."

"You're a real ray of sunshine."

"That was uncalled for." She tugged on his hand. "You ready?"

No, but they didn't have a choice. They stepped through the gate and into what appeared to be a black box.

"Now what?" he asked as the gate snapped shut. And remained shut.

Harvester didn't answer. Didn't have to. The expression on her face said it all.

They were trapped.

# Twenty-One

Oh, this was not cool.

Harvester cursed as she paced around the black room, which, like almost everything else in Sheoul, was lit by an unseen light source. Not that it did much good. The inky walls, floor, and endless ceiling seemed to absorb the light, leaving them able to see in only about a ten-foot radius no matter where they moved.

"Fuck," she snapped.

"Why hasn't the gate dropped us anywhere?"

She rubbed her eyes with the heels of her palms. Couldn't anything go right for them? Just once?

"These Boregates are glitchy. Sometimes they do this. Just hold you in these stupid boxes."

Reaver looked up as if searching for a way out. She wished him luck. "For how long?"

"Until someone else tries to use the gate and un-glitches it." Frustrated, she kicked at the wall. "I suggested that

someone grab Bill Gates and get him to install a new operating system, but apparently, he's not a demon." At Reaver's eye roll, she nodded. "Right? I was surprised, too."

Reaver leaned against a wall as if they didn't have a
care in the world. How could he relax in a place like this?
The claustrophobic crush was going to end her.

"Aside from the fact that we're trapped for the moment,
are you okay?"

"Why wouldn't I be okay?"

"I don't know, maybe because your über-evil father
was within seconds of grabbing us?"

"Spare me the false concern," she said tightly. "I'm
fine."

Yep, the way her hands were shaking and her voice
was frayed with anxiety hinted to all kinds of *fine*.

"Whatever." Reaver threw up his hands. "I was just
trying to be nice. You know, things normal people do."

"Are you kidding me? We aren't normal people. And
nice? That's how you want to play this? You drop a big
bomb on me, *Yenrieth*, and you want to be all *nice*?"

During her time with Satan's torturers, Harvester had
been drawn and quartered not once but twice. It had been
a huge spectacle, the premeal entertainment for two of his
dinner parties.

But as agonizing as the experiences had been, they
hadn't even come close to what she'd felt when Reaver
confessed his identity.

She still couldn't believe it. Couldn't believe that five
thousand years after Yenrieth disappeared, he was standing in front of her. How was she supposed to process this?
*Could* she process this?

Hell, she might be in total denial if not for the fact that

her intense hatred and baffling attraction to Reaver finally made sense. So did the memory of sex with Yenrieth, where Reaver's face had filled in the blank holes. Reaver had been in the memory because he'd actually *been there*. Now she knew why kissing him felt so familiar. And why, the first time she'd met Reaver, she'd sensed him before he'd fully materialized. That had never happened with anyone else before.

"Fine," he said. "You're right. We're not normal. We're the most fucked-up, star-crossed lovers in history. So let's not play nice." His penetrating stare seemed to look right through her. "Maybe you can tell me why you ran away that day when I kissed you."

"The day you fucked Lilith, you mean?" And wasn't that a prick to the heart. That single decision, to flee from a kiss, had led to all of this, but she wasn't ready to take the entire blame. She rubbed her sternum as if that would ease the pain that still lingered all these centuries later. "I ran away because I was afraid. I had no experience, and you...you were a whore." His jaw hardened into a stubborn line, and she dared him to deny it. "You still are, aren't you? Your exploits with demons are well known."

Reaver's expression turned cold. "How do you know about the demons I've been with? And, by the way, that was in the past, when I was an Unfallen."

She let out a dubious snort. "Are you really asking me to believe you've been a model of angelic purity since you got your wings back?"

"I've never been a model of angelic purity," he said roughly, and she wondered if the note of bitterness in his voice was real or imagined.

"No shit." She sauntered up to him and stabbed her

finger into his breastbone. "So now that you have some memories back, maybe you can tell me where you went after you seduced me, took my virginity, and then told me I disgusted you."

Inhaling a ragged breath, he closed his eyes. "What I did to you . . . I'm sorry—"

She jabbed him in the chest so hard he winced. "I don't give a hellrat's ass about your apology," she snapped. "Where did you go?"

He opened his eyes, and while she was gratified to see a shadow of hurt in them, she also felt a little bad about putting it there. Emphasis on *little*.

"I don't know. My new memories are limited to me and you."

"How convenient." She spun around, paced to the far wall, and then came back at him. "What else do you remember?"

"I remember going to you after I found out I was a father. You were the first person I told. I confided in you." The hurt in his eyes morphed to blue-fired anger. "But you already knew. You'd known for fucking *years*."

Guilt ripped into her with such force that her knees nearly buckled. But she couldn't let her pangs of conscience derail her need for answers.

"So you remember that, but do you remember any of the shit you did to me? Do you remember how I did everything you ever asked of me, including giving you my blood so you could bond us?"

"Shit." He scrubbed his hand over his face. "I remember that. It was a few months before Lilith. We'd just advanced in novice demon hunting training."

"And you wanted us to be able to feel each other if we got into trouble."

He hesitated, and the air inside the Boregate grew thick with tension. "There was more to it than that." He stepped closer, and the musky scent of his skin filled her nostrils. "I didn't tell you the rest."

A sinking sensation filled her chest cavity. "You lied?" God, she'd been such a fool. Such a stupid, lovesick, spineless, idiot.

"Only because the truth would have sounded crazy."

She crossed her arms over her chest. "And what was the truth?"

"That we needed to do it." He shoved his hand through his blond mane, leaving it messy and begging for her touch. Even though she hated him right now. "It was just a feeling I had, something we had to do, but I didn't know why."

"And now you do?"

"Maybe," he breathed. "I think the bond is what's helping me get my memories back."

"Well, good for you. Glad I could help."

He ignored her sarcasm. "I am, too."

She drank in the sight of him as he stood there, his chest heaving as though they'd sparred with their fists instead of with words. And now, she realized, in all the memories she had of Yenrieth, he was no longer faceless. The angel who laughed with her, played tricks on her, and had brought her to the most amazing orgasms was the male standing in front of her.

"So what now?"

He propped one boot casually behind him on the wall. Because yeah, this was all just so run-of-the-mill. "Now we wait for this Boregate to take us somewhere."

"That's not what I'm talking about and you know it."

"Do you really think now's the time to discuss our future? We don't know if we're going to survive the rest of the day let alone the next century."

He was right, but his dismissal still stung. For thousands of years she'd wondered what she would do if Yenrieth reappeared, the scenarios ranging from a cheesy joyful reunion in which they'd run at each other and she'd leap into his arms to her killing him in a fit of rage.

Most of her imaginary reunions involved him falling to his knees and begging forgiveness while she listened patiently until she'd had enough. Then they had wild, intense sex and he swore to never let her go again.

What a joke. Of all the fantasies she'd come up with, none of them had involved them being on the run from Satan and darkmen.

"Let me ask you something." She squared her shoulders, wincing at the sudden, intense itching in her back as her wings regenerated. A good sign, but annoying. "After you found out I knew about your children, when you seduced me, did you *want* to have sex with me, even a little? Or was it all for revenge?"

His gaze hit the floor, but not before she caught a glimpse of shame. "I don't remember."

"My ass," she spat out. "You must have some idea. Some feeling."

"The feeling I get from that day is anger. So if I had to guess, I'd say it was all for revenge." His eyes snapped up to hers, as brutally cold as his words, and her chest constricted around what was left of her shriveled heart. "Was that what you wanted to hear? Or should I have lied?"

She'd have been fine with a lie, and how fucked up was

that? Son of a bitch, he could throw her off balance, and if there was anything Harvester hated more than being tortured, it was being unsure of herself and her emotions.

"Fuck you, Reaver." Irrational anger gripped her in sharp talons as she spun away from him, needing as much distance as she could get in the damned shoebox they were trapped inside.

His exasperated voice followed her. "You asked."

She braced her forehead against the opposite wall, letting the cool stone soothe her. But it didn't do much to alleviate the anguish building inside her.

Shuffling noises filled the room and she tensed as she felt him come closer. "In case we don't make it out of Sheoul, I need you to know I'm thankful for what you did for my sons and daughter. I can't thank you enough." He swallowed audibly, an almost pained sound. "I owe you more than I can ever repay."

"That's a dangerous thing to say to a fallen angel, you know."

"Maybe. Depends on the fallen angel."

She laughed bitterly. "If you're counting on me to wipe the slate clean and tell you to go on your merry way, you're sadly mistaken. I'm not Verrine anymore. I've had to do things to survive that would make your feathers molt."

"You think I don't get that?" He made a sound of frustration. "I'm not Yenrieth anymore, either. But we're both paying for things we did when we *were* those people. Maybe it's time to stop."

Closing her eyes, she took a deep, rattling breath. She wanted to cry. She wanted to scream. He'd hurt her so badly that she wasn't ready to let go of the pain. And maybe it wasn't as much that he'd hurt her as it was that she was an evil bitch who was more about revenge than forgiveness.

No, she definitely wasn't Verrine anymore.

"You want to stop paying for what we did as Verrine and Yenrieth? What about what we've done as Harvester and Reaver?" Pushing away from the wall, she swung around to him. "I smashed you under a mountain. I tricked you and tortured you. Can you really get past that?"

His eyes raked her from head to toe, as if he was trying to see the angel he'd once known. "I already have. But what about you? You said everything you felt for me, as Reaver, makes sense. I know you hate me, but what else?"

"What else?" Her first instinct was to tell him to fuck off. But they both needed a little honesty and a lot of answers now. "Lust," she said boldly. "I despised you, but that didn't stop me from wanting to screw your brains out every time I saw you."

Heat flared in his eyes, and she smiled inwardly. "That's why you made that deal with me in Sheoul-gra."

"Well, I couldn't very well admit I wanted to fuck you, could I? You'd have laughed in my face."

"Yes," he admitted. "I would have."

Even though she'd known what he was going to say, it still felt like he'd kicked her in the gut.

"Release me from the deal, Harvester."

Her heart kicked against her ribs. "What? Never."

"Why not?"

Because now it was more important than ever. It was the only hold she had over him. The only weapon she had against the only person in the world who could still crush her heart.

"Because I said so," she snapped.

Reaver looked down at the ground, his golden mane falling forward to hide his expression. It took forever before he finally looked up, and when he did, his eyes held a predatory gleam that took her breath away.

"Do it." He moved toward her, his broad shoulders rolling like a lion on the prowl. "I betrayed your trust once. Now I'm asking you to give me another chance."

Harvester's pulse pounded in an erratic rhythm as he drew closer. The air between them grew thick with a sultry, erotic heat she felt on her skin like a sunburn. This was how it had been the day he seduced her. He'd been so sure of himself, so confident that she'd give in. And she had.

Then he'd crushed her.

"Why should I?" Her voice was humiliatingly hoarse.

"Because you don't need anything to hold over my head." He stopped a foot away, an unyielding wall of muscle that blocked her view of everything but him. His voice lowered to a sensual drawl. "You don't need a verbal contract between us."

Was he saying what she thought he was saying? That he'd have sex with her even if she didn't force him to? Or was this a repeat of that wonderful and horrible day so long ago? What if he was tricking her to get out of the deal?

"Harvester," he said, but in her head she heard an echo of "Verrine." "Release me. Trust me."

She couldn't. She wouldn't. It would be too easy for him to hurt her again.

But she wanted to be good. How could she do that if she was clinging to a bargain she'd intended to use selfishly? Maybe doing as he asked would be a first step toward making amends for five thousand years' worth of evil deeds.

Her pulse pounded in her ears as she considered his

request and her possible response, all weighed alongside her desire to shed some of the darkness that had become as much a part of her as her skin.

She could do this. But if Reaver made her regret it, she'd gut him with her teeth.

"I...release you." She waited for him to gloat or laugh or *something*, but he just stood there, his half-lidded eyes smoldering. "Ah...now what?"

"You tell me." He licked his full lips, leaving them glistening in the diffused gray light of the Boregate. "Do you want to test me? See if releasing me from the deal was a smart thing to do?"

Was this a trick? She narrowed her eyes at him. If it was, he was playing it very, very cool.

She could do cool even better.

"Sure," she said, kicking off her boots. "Let's see if I made a mistake." Bending, she peeled off her leggings, which left her only in the ridiculous pink panties and her skimpy black tank top. "Are you going to fuck me even without the deal?" She hooked her thumb in her panties' elastic waistband and waited.

And waited.

Finally, Reaver shook his head, and a cold ache drilled a cavern in her chest. "No, I'm not."

Still reeling with shock that Harvester had actually taken a huge step toward trusting him by letting him out of the sex deal, Reaver gave Harvester a moment to let what he'd said sink in. It killed him to let her think he'd gone back on his word, but he wanted her to be very clear on what he was about to say next.

As hurt gave way to fury that built like steam in that slim, athletic body, he closed the distance between them and put his mouth to her ear. He shivered at the sensation of her delicate, smooth skin against his lips.

"I won't fuck you," he whispered. "But I'll make love to you. I'll do what I should have done all those years ago."

For some reason, she cried out and shoved him away. "I don't want that," she shouted. "I can't. I need...I need..."

Shit. Meltdown time. He'd pushed too fast and scared her. Not that she'd ever admit to being afraid of anything, let alone her emotions.

"What do you need?" he said quietly. "I'll give it to you." He had a feeling she needed control, especially now, in the midst of chaos, life altering revelations, and an uncertain future.

For an unbearably long time, she didn't say anything. Finally, she blurted out, "I need you to take off your shirt."

*Good girl.* It didn't matter what request she'd made of him, he'd have done it. He was just happy she hadn't demanded that he hop on one foot while singing a show tune or some shit.

"Done." As he lifted his shirt over his head, the cinnamon-clove scent of Harvester's arousal filled the room.

Raw hunger gleamed in her eyes, replacing the pain and distrust as he tossed the torn garment to the ground. "Good."

She caught her tongue between her teeth as she studied him, and damn, he could so easily picture her in the throes of orgasm, her head back, mouth open, silky ebony hair spilling over her shoulders and breasts. She'd be radiant, beautiful, and she could bring a male to his knees.

That thought, of course, put an image in his head of him on his knees in front of her as he kissed her belly on a blazing path to that sweet place between her legs. He'd lick her until she screamed his name, and then he'd do it over and over, swirling his tongue inside her satin channel as he listened to her sexy little mewls of pleasure.

*You've already done that.*

Yes, he had. He suddenly remembered doing it to Verrine. He'd been all about revenge, but his plans had gone awry the moment he'd gotten her naked.

His rigid erection strained against his fly, aching like a son of a bitch. How long had it been for him? Too long. Way too long. He hadn't been with a female since he got his wings back, was given Watcher duty, and...met Harvester. Oh, he'd had plenty of opportunities with angels who saw him as a forbidden temptation, a rebel angel with a mysterious past, but for some reason, he hadn't taken up any of them on their offers, no matter how blatant or aggressive. And he'd always gone for the aggressive ones. Only now did he realize why.

Deep down, he'd wanted Harvester.

She slid her hand inside her panties, and he groaned as her fingers rubbed in slow circles under the material. "You sure you don't want to fuck?"

Yes. No. *Shit.*

He clenched his teeth, unable to give her an answer. There was nothing he wanted more—aside from getting out of here alive—than to wrap Harvester's long, slim legs around his waist and pound into her until they'd either killed the sexual tension screaming between them or they killed each other.

But he wanted to take it slow. Or, at least, to show her that what they were doing was about more than orgasms.

Because his feelings for her might be jumbled up in a tangle of remembered and forgotten events, but one thing was certain: He'd claimed her when he'd done the blood-bonding thing. Their relationship had been five thousand years in the making, and he wasn't about to let it go, now or later.

They just needed to get out of Sheoul, destroy Lucifer, and get Harvester off Satan's most wanted list first. Oh, and Reaver had to survive the archangels' punishment.

No problem.

"Reaver, you said you'd give me what I needed," she gritted out, when he didn't reply quickly enough to please her. "I need to fuck. No mushy shit."

She was still stroking herself, faster now, and his breath followed suit.

"Agreed," he said. "But it won't be a fuck to me."

"Bastard." The word was harsh, but her tone was almost weary, as if maybe she was as tired of their battles as he was. "Now strip."

Her order made him smile. She very well might want to strip him herself, but the need for control outweighed her personal preferences. That was okay. Next time.

He fingered the top button on his fly and hesitated, loving how she was holding her breath in anticipation, her mouth open slightly, her green eyes as dark as a forest at night.

"Hurry," she commanded him.

Very deliberately, he unbuttoned his fly slowly, revealing what was beneath in tiny increments. *Pop.* He exposed a tiny *V* of flesh. *Pop.* The *V* was bigger now, and the head of his arousal emerged, resting heavily against the denim. *Pop.* His shaft strained against the remaining buttons as if sensing freedom. *Pop.* Harvester began to pant. *Pop.* Freed, his arousal sprang loose, practically throbbing with the need to get inside her.

He kicked off his boots and lost the pants in rapid succession, done with the teasing. When he was standing before her, fully naked, Harvester purred.

"Now that," she said in a husky voice that rumbled through him in an erotic tremor, "is more like it."

They both stood, several feet apart, staring through space thick with sexual tension. Reaver's body practically shook as he watched Harvester stroke herself, her full breasts rising and falling with her rapid breaths.

"Touch yourself," she demanded.

He palmed his shaft, and abruptly, her scent grew stronger. She liked to watch, did she? Okay, he'd play that game. Gripping his cock firmly, he slid his fist down and back up, noting how her ivory skin flushed and her pupils dilated.

"Faster," she whispered, and oh, yes, he could do faster.

Her arousal fed his, hot, potent, and as he pumped his fist up and down his length, a climax built like steam in a pressure cooker. He wasn't going to last, not if she kept stroking herself, her gaze fixed on watching him.

Extracting her hand from her panties, Harvester strutted toward him, her hips swaying hypnotically. She stopped a foot away, close enough that her heat scorched him. With a teasing smile, she put her glistening fingers to his mouth.

"Taste me," she murmured.

Lord have mercy, he thought, as he closed his lips around her fingers and sucked. Her honeyed flavor burst on his tongue, making him groan and sparking another piece of memory. He'd given her three orgasms with his tongue all those years ago, and although he'd been wracked with the need for revenge, he'd also been desperate to wring every drop of pleasure out of her that he could.

"If we weren't in a box that could drop us in the middle of a volcano at any second, I'd have you on your knees right now, angel." Sliding him a naughty smirk, she withdrew her hand from his mouth and kissed him, just a peck, but it was enough to make the ground shift under him. "I'd see if that talented tongue of yours could take me to Heaven again."

"I'll get you to Heaven one way or another," he swore.

"Now," she breathed. "I want to be there now."

She covered his hand with her own and pressed her thumb to the tip of his cock. His hissed at the intensity of her touch, and when an electric friction sizzled down his shaft and into his balls, he shouted. An out-of-control buzz spread from her hand through his entire body as it brought him as close to orgasm as he could get without tipping over.

"You're using your power." Damn...just...*damn*. She kept it going, channeling a masterful sexual talent into him that left him straining and panting on the verge of climax for far too long, and yet, he silently begged her to keep going.

Releasing him, she stepped away and shoved her panties down. "I'm ready. I want you to—"

He didn't let her finish. He'd lost his ability to follow orders five minutes ago.

With a low growl, he grabbed her hips and spun her into the wall. His cock prodded her rear as he captured her wrists with one hand and jerked her arms up over her head so she was caged between his body and the wall and at his mercy.

"Reaver," she gasped.

Burying his face in her hair, he slid his hand between her legs and lightly caressed the plump lips of her sex. Her moan encouraged him, and he used one finger to delve into her slit. Her arousal coated his fingertip as he eased it into her core, testing her readiness and making her rock into his hand.

Now. He needed to have her *now*.

Shuddering in anticipation, he guided himself inside her slick channel. He filled her, but she filled him too, with her scent, her warmth, her very essence. It was as if she was the only female in the universe, wiping out everyone else he'd been with in the past. She was suddenly his everything.

He wished they had time to do this right, but aside from the fact that they were inside a box that could open up into the middle of Satan's army, the option to go slow had been forfeited when Harvester decided to turn her hand into a fallen-angel-powered sex toy.

Lunging, he seated himself to the hilt, lifting her off the ground with the force of his thrust. They both shouted at the intensity of their joining, and then, in a mindless frenzy, he drilled into her. The slap of flesh on flesh joined her cries of pleasure, the wet, erotic sounds taking him higher and higher.

"I didn't...order you...to do it...this, oh, *yes*...way." Harvester spoke between moans and panting breaths.

He was close. So close. "Orders aren't my strong suit," he rasped.

The truth was that after what he'd done to her as Yenrieth, the last thing she needed was for him to see her at a time when she was the most vulnerable, those fleeting moments when pleasure took away the capacity to defend yourself or guard your emotions.

He wouldn't take that from her.

He wouldn't take anything from her ever again. But from this point on, he'd give her whatever she wanted. Which was easy, because what she wanted right now was an orgasm.

"Ask, and you shall receive," he murmured into the thick mane of hair at the nape of her neck.

"I won't ask," she moaned. "I can't."

Closing his eyes, he stopped moving and just held her, his cock pulsing inside her, so close to climax that if she clenched he'd be done.

"You don't need to." He released her wrists and slid his palm down her arm, a slow caress over her perfect skin. Inhaling her warm clove scent, he nuzzled the back of her neck, a graceful, feminine place that was often neglected. The hitch in her breath told him she liked it as much as he did. "I won't fight you anymore, Harvester." He pulled back so his shaft was almost free of her molten core before plunging deep again. They moaned in unison. "I'll never give you a reason to not trust me."

"I'll never trust you," she croaked.

"That's okay." He pumped his hips again, shuddering at the rasp of his flesh against hers. "You don't have to."

Harvester's fingernails raked the stone, scoring it with thin gray lines. "Stop it." She inhaled a ragged breath. "Just stop it."

Not happening. He sensed that they were at a tipping

point, a critical place that would determine the course of their relationship forever. He'd hated her for so long, desired her at the same time, and it was time to stop the game of Ping-Pong they were both playing with their emotions.

If it took Harvester longer to catch up, he'd wait.

He pumped into her slowly, showing her with each stroke that he could take care of her without the brutality she was no doubt used to. That she probably expected from him.

"Fuck me hard." She pushed back against him, her insistent grinding motion making him suck air. "Damn you, stop with the slow, tender shit. I don't want it, you haloed bastard."

Clenching his teeth and conjuring the least sexy things he could in his mind—hellhounds...so not sexy—he slowed even more.

He kissed a blazing trail to her ear. An overwhelming need to hold her, protect her, make her his washed over him. Oh, claiming Harvester wouldn't be easy or, likely, smart. But this was a second chance for both of them, and this time, he wouldn't let them fail.

"I told you to stop it!" Her nails grated on the stone. Tendrils of smoke drifted up from the score marks.

He thrust again, and ripples of pleasure hummed down his shaft to his balls. "No."

"Stop!"

Another thrust. Faster. Harder. More ripples that made him groan. "Come."

"I hate you."

"I know."

Harvester cried out, her tight sheath clenching around

him and pulling him so deep he cried out himself as he grasped for control. "I. Hate. You."

"Come, dammit," he said into her ear as he rocked into her in a wild tempo that vibrated the walls around them. "Make me spill everything I have into you. Only you. You'll have all the power, Verrine."

That did it. She shouted both a curse and a prayer, her body tightening and jerking under him. Ecstasy engulfed him and he came violently in a flash of blinding light.

And just as she'd scored the wall, she'd scored his soul. Again.

He felt it, the mark she'd left thousands of years ago, and it was almost as if nothing had changed. She'd marked him back then, but he'd been too fucking stupid to know.

This time, she'd marked him but *she* didn't know.

# Twenty-Two

*Thank you, wall.*

Harvester kept repeating her mantra of gratitude as she leaned against said wall, its cool stone easing her fever and lending much-needed support. No way would her shaky legs hold her up if she wasn't sandwiched between Reaver and the rock surface.

God, that had been good. Amazing.

And devastating.

Reaver hadn't followed her orders. Instead, he'd taken over and gave her not what she wanted but what she needed. Somehow the bastard had known she was trying to protect herself, trying to keep her emotions at bay, and like the son of a bitch he was, he'd been patient and kind. And beneath the sexual intensity, there'd been a tenderness that would bring her to tears if she thought about it.

*I'll never give you a reason to not trust me.*

What kind of shit was that? Why would he say that?

The only reason she'd survived as long as she had was because she learned to not trust anyone. Trust got you killed. Or worse, it got you tortured.

Some quack human psychologist would probably say that her inability to trust started before she was even born, when her father rose up against the other archangels and started an insurrection. If he'd truly cared about her and her mother, he wouldn't have done that, right?

But according to him, he'd done it *for* her. For her mother. And she'd actually believed him. Over the course of her time spent in Sheoul, he'd told her how the other archangels plotted against him because he had been recognized in the womb as a potential Radiant, the most powerful of all angels. He'd told her he'd loved her mother, even though their mating had been arranged in hopes of producing another potential Radiant.

It hadn't, but he'd told Harvester that he'd loved her from the moment of conception, and that he wished he'd have been there for her birth.

And then, on the day she'd needed him to prove everything he'd said was true, he'd branded her a traitor and sentenced her to an eternity of the most unimaginable torture he and his minions could devise.

So, okay, she had trust issues. And daddy issues. And probably some new issues with sharp objects.

"Harvester?" Reaver slapped his palms on the wall and pushed off her so she wasn't squashed, but he didn't withdraw from her body the way he had when he'd taken her virginity.

*Where are you going?*

*As far away from you as I can get.*

Thrusting the painful memories aside, she sighed. "What?"

"We should get dressed."

She'd expected Reaver to ask if she was okay, or to maybe apologize, so his casual, common-sense suggestion threw her, and she laughed.

"I guess we should."

He combed through her hair with his fingers, a silly gesture that was somehow more intimate than anything they'd just done. Tingling warmth washed over her, and her stupid heart did a fluttery little jig. This was that sappy, cuddly moment all the romance books and girl magazines waxed on about, wasn't it? Not that she read those things, but one couldn't avoid the chatter from women with overactive ovaries.

Dammit, this whole thing had gone terribly wrong. Or terribly right, she realized. She'd released him from the deal they'd made, and he'd proved she was right to do it.

He'd wanted to have sex with her. And he hadn't kicked her to the curb yet, so that was something.

But that didn't mean she fully trusted him, and she needed to keep in mind that with the exception of her mother, everyone she'd ever known had disappointed her.

"Are we getting dressed or what?" she snapped.

Reaver sighed, and his hand fell away. She felt an instant pang of regret for ruining the moment. When he withdrew from her body, the pang got worse.

She heard the rustle of clothing as he got dressed, and in the dark silence, she did the same. Once clothed, they stared at each other.

"Well, this is awkward," she said, and he laughed. God, he was gorgeous when he did that. Everything about him just...glowed.

Glowed...*shit*. He was throwing light like a nuclear

power plant, and she hadn't even noticed. The over-whelming hatred that usually came with his angelic aura didn't bother her either.

"Reaver, you're glow—"

The black box fell away, and in a flash of light, they were dropped into another realm. A realm where every-thing was dreary and gray, even the massive pyramids that sat atop an ocean of sand.

"Oh, fuck," she breathed, as a crushing wave of evil swallowed her whole.

"What is it?"

She glanced over at him and drew in a sharp breath. His aura was gone, confirming her suspicion about their location; in this realm, there was no light except for the ever-present hazy luminescence that kept the realm in a constant state of blah.

She wondered if she should sugarcoat what she was going to say. But screw it; she'd never sugarcoated any-thing in her fallen angel life.

"Remember how I said the Boregate knows where you need to go?"

"Yeah...and we need to get to the human realm. This isn't it."

"No," she said. "This realm belonged to Lucifer. I guess it still does, because I can feel him."

Reaver's sandy eyebrows shot up. "So Gethel must be here." She nodded, and Reaver swore. "This could be bad. He gazed into the distance. "Or it could be good. If we can get close to Gethel, we can take her out."

"How? You can't even kill a hellrat, and I'm operating at less than half power. Not to mention the fact that Gethel will be heavily guarded."

"I can take out a hellrat," he muttered. "I just can't replace any power I spend, now that the *sheoulghuls* are gone."

"No, I mean you that you can't use your powers here because you're an angel. Even if you were at full strength it wouldn't matter."

He swore. "I love how things just get worse and worse."

A feeling of doom settled over her like a shroud as she looked ahead at the city that had been the basis for the ancient Egyptian city of Thebes. Even the Egyptian gods had been based on the denizens of this realm, animal-headed demons who had gotten off on convincing primitive peoples of their godliness.

"Well, we can't just stand here. Is there a way out? Now that we know where Gethel is, we'll go to the archangels," Reaver said, all logical and crap. Except she knew something he didn't.

"Yep, there's a way out. The exit is through a single Harrowgate."

The smug expression on Reaver's face fell. He knew what she was about to say, but she gave him credit for at least trying to remain optimistic as he asked, "Where's the Harrowgate?"

She pointed at the city. "In the very center. Right on Lucifer's doorstep."

"Fuck," Reaver breathed.

"We already did that. But if you're saying that we're *fucked*, I'd say you're right."

The journey to the city didn't take long, and aside from one hawk-headed Horus demon trying to rob them, it was uneventful.

But as they approached the gates to the massive city, Reaver had a feeling things were going to get a lot less dull.

Khepri demons—scarab-headed humanoids—guarded the gate, their skinny antennae swiveling like radar dishes. Flanking them were Sobeks, their humanoid bodies too small for their giant crocodile heads.

Reaver had never encountered any of these demons, which Harvester said no longer traveled away from this realm, but the stories of their cruelty went well beyond the realm's borders.

He leaned close to Harvester, and her scent made his body stir again.

"Are they going to let us in?"

"Of course," she said, as if he'd asked an insanely stupid question. "It's letting us out that'll be the problem if they find out who we are. And they probably will."

Harvester was definitely a glass-half-empty person, wasn't she? But she was right, and the guards opened the gates that were tall enough to allow entrance to Godzilla. Inside, the gray that defined the outskirts of the city was replaced by rich reds and greens, golds and silvers. Great pillars and statues dotted the city, which could have stood in Egypt and no one would have known the difference.

"Charming place," he muttered as they moved past Neethul slave markets and arenas where demons fought to the death.

Harvester nodded enthusiastically, as if he'd been serious. "I know, right? There's a pub a few blocks over that serves the best pomegranate wine in all of Sheoul. Costs a fortune, but it's so smooth. You'd never know they use Soulshredder blood to make it."

"Sounds lovely."

"I hear sarcasm." She *tsk*ed. "What is it humans say? That sarcasm is the lowest form of humor?"

He shrugged. "Only for people who don't get it."

She laughed, and he missed a step. He'd heard Harvester laugh before, but there had always been an evil undercurrent to it, a morbid amusement that came from things normal people wouldn't find funny. But this was a pure, bubbly laugh of genuine delight, and it filled him with the strangest giddiness, like a feather was tickling his heart.

As if she felt it too, she slid him an almost shy glance, a lopsided smile curving her luscious mouth. He didn't say anything, because by now he knew that calling attention to anything pleasant would turn her back into an acid-tongued fishwife. Idly, he wondered if Eidolon had anything for her particular brand of demonic bipolar disorder.

"We're almost there," she said, pulling him to the side of the road to avoid being trampled by an elephant-like creature being ridden by an Anubis.

Almost there. If everything went smoothly, then in a few more minutes the nightmare would be over. This part of the nightmare, anyway. They still had to face the archangels, and the things they could do to him made all the miseries of Sheoul seem like a day at an amusement park.

The Harrowgate hung between two gold columns at the top of hundreds of steps that led to a building Harvester said was Lucifer's palace.

"Will we be able to walk right into it?"

"I doubt it," she said. "Gethel will probably be heavily guarded.

At the top of the steps, demons milled about, but it was the armed Silas demons standing nearby that hot-loaded a massive dump of adrenaline into Reaver's veins.

"Shit," Harvester said, her voice so low he barely heard her. "Silas demons are coming up behind us."

Reaver cast a covert glance back, and yep, they were being flanked. When he looked ahead, Silases were moving toward them, too.

They were blocked.

Instinctively, Reaver reached for his power, but there wasn't so much as a spark. Harvester had been right. He couldn't even kill a hellrat.

"I don't suppose you have any tricks up your sleeve," he asked.

"I have a lot. Unfortunately, they won't work in this situation." She shot a covert glance at the Harrowgate. "I say we forget Gethel for now and make a break for it."

As much as he'd love to end Gethel and Lucifer right now, he had to admit that without their full range of powers, any attempt would be suicide. But that didn't mean he was admitting defeat. No, right now the smart thing to do was to escape and live to fight another day.

"On three," he said. "One." The demons behind them began to jog. "Two." The demons in front of them raised their swords. "*Three.*"

He and Harvester bolted toward the gate, scattering civilian demons like bowling pins. Harvester flung several bursts of lightning at the Silas warriors, turning them to ash. They were within five yards of the gate when a net fell on them, the threads shrink-wrapping them so tightly that their skin sliced open, their blood sizzling when it hit the mesh. Pain tore through Reaver as they crashed to the ground, kicking and fighting, but the netting only squeezed tighter, until they were back-to-back and unable to move more than fingers and toes.

A huge male Nightlash shoved through the throng of Silases, his clawed feet clacking on the stone. "Harvester and Reaver. Slag will be rewarded with such riches for this." His sharp teeth dripped like someone had rung the dinner bell. "I am Slag."

*No shit.* Demons were so damned stupid. Before he could say as much, a demon cut the net away. Reaver shoved to his feet and lunged for Slag, but his limbs where heavy, if he was trying to run through Jell-O.

"The net," Harvester blurted as a Silas yanked her upright. "It's like the whip that paralyzed you in the cavern."

There weren't enough curse words in enough languages for this situation, Reaver thought. But he made a noble attempt at saying them all when icy metal collars that matched the bracelets on Slag's wrists were clamped around their necks. Tight.

"Obey, or..." The demon tapped one of the bracelets, and Harvester fell to the ground, screaming in raw, desperate anguish. Gasping for breath, she clawed frantically at the collar.

"Stop it," he shouted. "Let her go!"

He dove at the Nightlash, but in half a heartbeat Reaver joined Harvester on the ground. Excruciating agony tore through him, as if the collar had sprung spikes that pierced so deeply he felt them in his gut.

It took forever for the pain to ease, and even then, he couldn't function properly, his limbs flopping around and his head dangling on a neck that wouldn't support it as they were dragged into the palace. Raised voices came from ahead...both familiar, and Reaver's stomach bottomed out.

"This," Harvester rasped, "is going to be bad."

Reaver groaned. "You have a flair for understatement, you know that?"

Slag punched Reaver in the back of the head. "Shut up."

Reaver and Harvester were jerked around and forced onto their knees as Gethel and Revenant approached. Gethel's spun-gold hair fell in sparkly waves around her shoulders, but gone was the luminescence that used to surround her. Her eyes had turned as black as ink, and her once lush, shiny wings were shriveled, the feathers curled and frayed. Angels who stayed too long in Sheoul were prone to decay, and Gethel, carrying the spawn of evil, had gone rotten to the core.

Of course, her core had gone bad a long, long time ago.

Her one-shouldered emerald tunic clung tightly to her hugely rounded belly, where her hand rested protectively. Hard to believe someone with such a black heart could be protective of anything. And how had Lucifer grown so much, so fast? Maybe because he was to be born fully grown? If so, Gethel was going to be extremely miserable for another four months.

Good.

Fast as a snake and from out of nowhere, Gethel backhanded Harvester hard enough to knock her into Reaver.

"Bitch," Reaver snarled. That earned him a blow from Revenant that made his ears ring.

"It's good to see you both." Gethel's smile as she rubbed her belly made all the hairs on the back of Reaver's neck stand up. "Extra special to have you here, Reaver."

She grinned, flashing fangs, apparently a pregnant-with-the-spawn-of-Satan upgrade. Or downgrade, depending on how you looked at it.

"Special seeing you, too," Reaver drawled. "I don't think I had a chance to congratulate you the last time I saw you. I hope you suffer in agony for days before Lucifer bursts from your hideous body."

Gethel blinked with exaggerated shock. "That's a little harsh. As a father yourself, I'd think you'd be more sympathetic to the plight of a pregnant woman."

Reaver shrugged. "A pregnant woman, yes. But a psychopathic pregnant troll...can't get on board with that one."

She went down on her haunches in front of him. "It doesn't matter if you can get on board or not. It's too late anyway." She folded her hands over her huge, evil lump. "See, we've accelerated Lucifer's growth. Instead of months, he'll be born in weeks. Maybe days. The clock is ticking, Reaver, and you're almost out of time."

An icy blast of *oh, shit* blasted through him. "You crazy bitch."

He got another whack upside the head. "Let me take them to the Dark Lord." Revenant's deep, eager voice resonated through the opulent marble auditorium.

"I've already sent word to him." Gethel's mouth turned up in a smile that sent a chill skittering up Reaver's spine. "Satan will be here any minute."

# Twenty-Three

Her father was on his way.

Terror shrunk Harvester's skin. They'd managed to stay one step ahead of Satan this entire time, and now, within sight of a Harrowgate, they were going to die.

And that was if they were lucky.

"Was it worth it?" Revenant seized Reaver by the throat and yanked him off the ground. "Was leaving your family vulnerable in order to rescue a traitorous female worth it?"

"She's not a traitor to *my* side," Reaver choked out. He sucked in a wheezing breath. "Wait...my family. Vulnerable?"

Harvester wondered the same thing. She'd call the Horsemen a lot of things, but *vulnerable* was not one of them.

Revenant, his annoyingly luxurious black mane obscuring his face, leaned in as if to tell Reaver a secret. "They're recovering from an unfortunate accident. Very sad." He didn't sound very sad, but there was definitely an odd note in his voice. "It was so against the rules."

"Accident?" Reaver sucked a gurgling breath. "Rules? What rules?"

"The ones you like to break." Revenant heaved Reaver across the room.

Reaver hit a pillar and crumpled to the ground, bits of stone and dust showering him as he tried to push to his hands and knees. Revenant launched at him, and with a sick, twisted smile, Slag tapped his bracelet.

Reaver grunted, and for a brief moment, Harvester got off on his pain. Malevolence was a faint vibration shimmering along every nerve ending, feeding into her pleasure centers like an erotic drug. Daddy's DNA was just the gift that kept on giving, wasn't it?

*You're an angel. Your mother is an angel, and your father, bastard that he is now, was an angel when you were conceived. There's more good in you than evil. Fight this, Harvester.*

Reaver's words in the cavern came back to her in a rush. Her mother...she'd died only three hundred years ago, an innocent casualty of a small uprising in Heaven, according to Raphael. She hadn't known Harvester had fallen from grace on purpose, and it was one of Harvester's greatest regrets that her mother hadn't learned the truth before she died.

*Fight this.*

Reaver grunted again as Revenant pounded his fists into his face and body, and this time, Harvester took no pleasure in his suffering.

"Stop it!" she screamed. She scrambled across the

floor toward them, her knees cracking painfully hard on the floor.

She dove for Revenant's legs. She didn't make it. An agonizing pain wrenched her neck as she was jerked to a sudden stop by her hair. Gethel, her fist wrapped around Harvester's ponytail, hurled Harvester through the air.

She hit the wall in a crack of bones and stone, and everything went black.

When she came to, she and Reaver, his face badly bruised and bloodied, were propped against the pillar he'd crashed into, chains connecting their collars to hooks embedded in the stone. Both Gethel and Revenant were gone. The asshole Nightlash, Slag, was sitting on a marble bench a few yards away, a satisfied smirk on his ugly face.

"Only reason you're not both dead is that the Dark Lord wants you alive. You," he said, jabbing his finger at Reaver, "are for his bed until you beg him for death." His smile widened. "He shares with Slag."

"Slag's right," Harvester agreed. "He does share. But I doubt he shares with demon morons who refer to themselves in the third person." She shifted to cast a furtive look at the guard situation near the front entrance. There were three that she could see. "He also likes audiences."

"That was very helpful," Reaver said dryly.

She slid a glance at him, trying to get a bead on what he was thinking, but his expression was shuttered, his attention focused on their surroundings. The familiarity of his expression made her smile. She and Yenrieth—Reaver— had spent a lot of time hunting minor demons, and she knew the look he got when he had a plan.

A Khepri entered, its nasty insect head swiveling. It

drew Slag aside, and the moment they were distracted, Harvester leaned closer to Reaver.

"So . . . what's the plan? Tell me you have one."

"I snagged a key to our collars off Revenant when he was tenderizing me," he said, and she wanted to kiss him. "But lifting the key was too easy, which makes me think it's a trap."

Her heart sank. "It's our only chance."

"Agreed." He rested his head against hers, and again the familiarity came roaring back. They'd propped each other up more times than she could count. "Let me know when Slag turns his back."

"You got it." She kept one eye on Slag and the other on the door her father would use when he arrived. The thought made her throat close. She'd do her best to kill both herself and Reaver if she had to. She couldn't endure more torture, and she couldn't bear the thought of Reaver going through it, either.

And wasn't that a huge shift from just a day ago?

"He turned," she murmured, and Reaver's arm started moving, as if he was fidgeting. Or maybe digging a key out of his pocket as inconspicuously as possible. "Reaver? What do you think Revenant was talking about when he said the Horsemen met with an accident?"

Reaver went as stiff as the pillar they were bound to. "I don't know, but if he was responsible, I'll kill him."

Harvester would help. "What are you going to tell them about me? Do you think they'll get why I did some of the things I had to do?" *Do you think they'll forgive me?*

It was a stupid, sentimental thing to want, but the Horsemen were the closest thing she had to a family. She'd observed them in secret for three thousand years, and she'd been involved with them as their Watcher for two thousand. She'd watched them grow, watched their failures and successes, their joys and miseries. On hundreds of occasions she'd even healed them or their friends and staff, and all without them knowing.

So yeah, she couldn't expect them to welcome her with open arms, but she'd like it if they didn't hate her.

"I think they'll get it," Reaver said gruffly, almost as though he was choked up.

"Reaver, are you okay—shit, Slag's turning."

Reaver stopped moving just as Slag looked them up and down. Harvester waved and gave him a Cheshire cat smile. Asshole.

"He turned back," she said quietly.

A low rumble boiled up from Reaver's chest, startling the crap out of her. She risked a peek at him, but that only made things worse. His head hung low, his blond hair falling across his handsome face. His big shoulders heaved with breaths that made his entire body shudder.

"I'm sorry, Harvester," he said in a broken whisper. "I'm sorry for what I did to you. You need to know that in case I don't get out of here. Promise me you'll tell my kids I'm dead, even if I'm taken alive."

"What?" she whispered harshly. "No." How could he even ask that? "And Slag's looking."

She shot him the finger. He returned the gesture, and then he made a show of using his fuck-you finger to swipe his bracelet. Ten million volts set fire to her blood, her muscles, her brain. Agony shrieked through her in an inferno of lightning. Flashes of light and dark tapped on her eyeballs, and her surroundings became a blur.

When she was done seizing, she found herself in

Reaver's arms, his hands stroking her back. She tasted ash and ozone, and her ears rung, but she was relieved that she wasn't the flaming ball of fire she'd thought she was.

Reaver bent to speak into her ear, making it appear as though he were giving her a kiss, and an unbidden shiver of pleasure went through her.

"Are you okay?" At her nod, he continued. "I got the key out of my pocket. Now I need you to sit up a little so I can unlock your collar. Then you'll unlock mine."

"What then?"

"I'll create a distraction. I want you to run. Get inside the Harrowgate and get out of Sheoul."

"Are you insane?" She started to twist around, but he held her tight. "I'm not abandoning you."

"Shh." His hand slid up to the back of her neck, and the collar loosened. "Don't draw Slag's attention."

She felt him slip a tiny, smooth object into her palm. The key. Casually, he pushed her off him and shifted so she could reach his collar. It took only a mere swipe of the key over the metal and the thing popped open.

"We can do this together," she whispered.

"Trust me, I don't have a death wish, so I'll try for the gate. But if something happens, don't play the hero. Get the fuck out of here."

"Reaver—"

"Hey." He silenced her with a kiss that stunned her into silence and that she felt all the way to her bruised, scarred soul. "Tell the Horsemen everything. About you. About me. You need them, and I don't want them to hate you."

She swallowed a tangled lump of grief and fear, and not a little yearning. She might hate him sometimes, might not ever be able to trust him, but she also didn't want to be separated from him. Didn't want to lose him. It had taken five thousand years to find him again, and even though Reaver wasn't the Yenrieth she remembered, that turned out to be a good thing.

"Okay," she lied. "I'll head straight for the Harrowgate."

"Thank you," he breathed. "Thank you for…everything."

She didn't have time to reply. Hell, she didn't have time to blink. In a blur of motion, Reaver was across the room, his fists and feet putting Slag and the bug-headed freak into the wall.

"Go!" he shouted.

And that was when she felt it. Terror. Horror. A malevolent, oily sensation that permeated every organ and that meant only one thing.

Her father had arrived.

# Twenty-Four

*Fuck.* In an uncoordinated scramble, Harvester came to her feet as demons swarmed into the mansion like an army of ants protecting their hill.

The Harrowgate was just yards away, and even though she'd have to knock a few demons aside to get to it, she could get there.

But not without Reaver.

Reaching deep for every drop of power she could find, she let out her inner demon, gray skin, sharp claws, horns...the whole package that she rarely brought out on purpose. With a roar of fury, she hurled a shockwave of energy that knocked the invaders into walls and pillars. Reaver got caught in the blast, but in a stroke of badly needed luck, he tumbled through the arched opening that went straight to the Harrowgate.

She charged after him, but she skidded to a halt as chaos erupted in the courtyard below. Darkness fell in the distance, screaming toward them like the blackest storm cloud. Giant bolts of crimson lightning zapped anyone who was unfortunate enough to be in the path of the chruning tempest. Bodies exploded like bags of liquefied hamburger, splattering the street, buildings, and other demons.

*Here comes Daddy.*

Harvester let out a juicy curse, but it was nowhere near adequate to describe the terror turning her marrow to jelly and her bones to rubber.

She seized Reaver's wrist and dragged him to his feet. "Come on," she shouted over the din of screams, shouts, and the rumble that came with the storm and her father's approach.

They limped toward the Harrowgate, joining the mass exodus of demons who were desperate to escape the great and terrible king of demons they both worshipped and feared.

"I told you to run," Reaver yelled. "You agreed."

"I lied." She elbowed a dozen different demons, who were either trying to kill them or shoving their way to the Harrowgate.

Suddenly, Reaver became a dead weight. Pivoting midstride, she slipped in a pool of blood. Reaver's blood.

His face was a mask of agony as he went down, a sword impaling him between the shoulder blades. The blade tip erupted from his chest, the telltale sparkle of an *aurial* weapon twinkling even through the wetness of his blood.

"No," she gasped. "*Oh, shit no.*"

"I have another blade with your name on it, Daughter." The ominous, rumbling voice seemed to come from everywhere at once. "Unless you give yourself up without a fight."

In the center of town, the hideous, horned monster that was her father was coming fast, carried by a hell stallion twice the size of a normal beast. Every footprint left a fiery hole in the street, and every puff of breath sent flames at anyone stupid enough to still be in the path.

She eyed the Harrowgate. She could be inside in a few heartbeats, but only if she abandoned Reaver, who would be dead in minutes if he didn't get help.

*"Harvester."*

Satan's voice rattled her to her core and kicked her into high gear. In a frenzied, clumsy rush, she grabbed Reaver's arms and dragged him toward the gate. Something sliced into her back, making her stumble and nearly lose her grip on Reaver. Gritting her teeth against the agony, she battled a storm of daggers, razor discs, and throwing stars, too many of them taking bites out of her flesh.

She risked a look back . . . and wished she hadn't. Satan and Gethel's minions were almost upon them, smashing through the crowds of panicked demons.

It was a messy mass of confusion that saved Harvester, and even though she was bleeding so badly she could hardly see for all the blood in her eyes, she hurled both herself and Reaver into the gate. An ugly tusked demon slipped inside at the last second and slammed his palm onto the wall map.

"No!" she shouted, but the gate closed with a glittering flash of light.

A heartbeat later, the gate opened, spilling them in a heap onto a grassy mountainside.

In the human realm.

Holy hell, they'd done it. Harvester sat up and held Reaver close as she let out a sob of relief. Tears and blood stung her eyes as she inhaled a breath of fresh air she thought she'd never take again.

The demon who'd hitched a ride with them snarled, the tusks jutting from his lower jaw dripping with pink-tinged drool. Bits of raw meat were stuck between his teeth.

"Looks like I brought supper with me." His lips peeled back in what she thought was a smile.

She rose and limped toward him, hoping the fact that she could barely walk didn't diminish her powers of intimidation.

"You will step aside and allow us to leave, or I'll destroy you."

His snarl-smile grew fiercer. "Private Harrowgate, bitch. Anyone can come here, assuming they know the right map sequence, but no one but me can leave."

Oh, wasn't that just perfect. Now what? Reaver was unconscious and would be dead in minutes, and Harvester's injuries were too severe to get them much farther.

"You do know who the Four Horsemen of the Apocalypse are?" She pointed to Reaver. "That's their father. If you don't go get them and he dies, I promise you'll spend the rest of your miserable life suffering in ways you can't even imagine. When they finally let you die, it'll be Thanatos who slaughters you, and then you'll spend eternity in the hell of his armor."

The guy's mouth snapped shut, and after a mere second of hesitation, he disappeared through the Harrowgate.

Practically collapsing with relief, she settled down in the grass next to Reaver and listened to his shallow, rattling breaths, wishing she hadn't spent all her power. If she could channel some healing energy into him, maybe she could remove the sword. Right now, the thing was draining his life, but pulling it free could do even more damage. An *aurial* didn't allow for healing around the site of the wound, and a bleed-out from one could kill.

"Don't you die on me, you bastard." Her voice was shot to hell, thick with emotion that would piss her off if she wasn't so terrified. "I haven't had enough time to make you pay for disappearing for thousands of years."

Reaver didn't even groan. His heartbeat began to fade, and hers went ballistic.

"Don't do it," she cried. "Do *not* die." She shook him, hating him for putting her through this. "You son of a bitch! You can't come back into my life and make me feel something and then go away again. Don't do this!" She choked on a sob. "Please."

A low-level buzz filled the air, and an instant later Thanatos and Reseph, fully armored, burst through the gate. Hatred so fierce Harvester felt it as a wave of stinging heat billowed off Thanatos. He glared, and all around him, the inky, shadowy souls of those he'd killed began to circle at his feet.

"What happened?" he barked as he sank down next to Reaver.

"I'll tell you everything," she swore, hoping he didn't strike her down right then and there. "But we need to get him to UG first."

With tenderness few would expect from the Horseman known as Death, Than scooped up Reaver and cast his own Harrowgate.

Harvester stood, her heart clenching at the sight of Reaver lying limp and pale in Than's arms. "You're going to leave me here?"

"That's up to Reseph." Than stepped through the gate,

leaving her alone with Reseph for the first time since she'd healed his mind by linking it with his mate, a human named Jillian.

And how weird was it that after all the months of torture she'd endured as a guest in Satan's palace, it was the memory of what Pestilence had done to her that wrapped around her like barbed wire and rendered her nearly unable to stand her ground in front of him.

She actually reached for her power before remembering she was tapped out. Defenseless.

"Take me with you." She swallowed, but it did nothing to ease the sudden dryness in her mouth. "Please. Reaver went through hell to save me. It'll all make sense when he's better."

Reseph, who had never taken anything seriously prior to his Seal breaking, looked down at her, his expression eerily blank. "*If* he gets better."

"He will," she insisted. "Reaver is too damned stubborn to die." *Please be too stubborn.*

"Our Watchers said you were working for Heaven. Is that true?" Reseph's blue eyes, so like his father's, were haunted, and she wondered how much of his evil past as Pestilence still had a hold on him.

She understood that more than she'd like to.

"Yes," she said. "From the beginning."

"So all the shit you helped Pestilence with? That was all bullshit?"

"Not all of it," she admitted. "I had to help further his cause sometimes. I couldn't let him get suspicious."

Reseph closed his eyes and exhaled slowly, and she knew he was on the fence. As Pestilence, he'd hurt her, and his guilt still ate at him. She hadn't crossed over into the realm of good so firmly that she felt shame for exploiting his guilt.

"Please," she repeated. "I'm . . . begging you. I need to make sure Reaver's okay."

"If you're lying . . . if you hurt him—"

"I'm not, and I won't." She held her breath, waiting for his answer with as much patience as she could muster. Reaver could be dying while he waffled.

He lifted his lids and resolve gleamed in his eyes. "Let's go."

"*Wait!*" The booming voice shook the ground, and even the air around them vibrated.

In a fluid spin, Reseph produced a sword and put himself between Harvester and Raphael. Gods, he must hate her, and yet, his instinct was to protect her.

So like his father.

Raphael stood imperiously before them, a rich, velvety purple robe draping his body. Silver wings that matched the robe's fur lining rose skyward in an elegant arc.

Reseph didn't sheathe his blade, a blatant insult to any archangel.

Raphael's lips peeled back in a vicious smile. "I still find it hard to believe that you, of all the Horsemen, had the balls to defeat your demon half."

"I still find it hard to believe they let douchebags be archangels," Reseph said in a bring-it-on drawl. "Guess we're even."

At the furious spike of Raphael's brows, Harvester leaped between Reseph and the archangel.

"Go, Reseph," she said calmly, even though her heart was beating so fast she thought it might break out of her rib cage. "Take care of Reaver."

"Still trying to protect Yenrieth's children, I see," Raphael murmured. "You're not their Watcher anymore."

"Thank you for the reminder," she said sourly. "But my oath to watch over them came long before I was officially appointed as a Watcher. My pledge still holds."

Raphael's voice was mocking. "Does it."

Reseph hadn't moved, so Harvester reached behind her and gave him a light shove. "Please. Go."

"I'll give Reaver your best," Reseph said to Raphael. "Your concern for him is just so...overwhelming." Reseph opened a gate and stepped through, but not before shooting Raphael a fuck-you gesture with both hands.

"How did you put up with them for so long?" Raphael stared at the empty space where Reseph had disappeared into. "They're horrible."

She forced a smile when inside she really wanted to punch the angel. The Horsemen might not be the most pleasant of people, but they were what they were because of Raphael and his brethren. And truly, considering their pasts and everything they'd endured, she figured they'd turned out pretty damned well.

"They're horrible only if you're on their bad side." She'd seen what happened to those who pissed off the Horsemen. *Horrible* didn't cover it. She crossed her arms over her chest, wincing at the aches and pains all over her body. "If you're here to apologize for the assassins you sent after us, you're wasting your time."

Raphael snapped his fingers, and all her wounds healed. Power sang through her, bright and vibrant. Even her fallen angel wings had grown back, and she spread them wide, nearly weeping at the sensation of feeling whole again.

"I don't know what you're talking about." He didn't even make a token effort to sound convincing.

"You underestimated me and Reaver. You always have."

A low, dangerous growl erupted from Raphael's broad chest. "And you," he spat out, "have always *over*estimated him in every way. Yenrieth was never good enough for you. As Reaver he's no better."

She clenched her teeth before she said something really stupid. Like, *Neither are you.* Or worse, *Reaver is better than any of you.*

"Do you know how much trouble he's caused?" Raphael asked. "According to our intel, Satan knows he was behind your rescue, and his armies are amassing at Sheoulic exit points all over the world in preparation to invade Heaven when Lucifer is born. We don't have much time to prepare."

They had even less time than he thought. "The game changed while Reaver and I were in Sheoul. Lucifer could be born in just a few days."

The blood drained from his face. "Are you sure?" At her nod, he snarled. Overhead, storm clouds brewed from out of nowhere. "Perfect. And do you know what will make it easier for him...*in a few days*? There are weak spots in the Heavenly fabric, and for the first time in history, demons invaded Heaven."

She gasped. Demons? In *Heaven*?

"And did you know it's your fault? Yours and Reaver's?" Thunder rumbled in the sky above, and Raphael snapped his fingers, putting a big bubble of a rain shield over them.

"Bullshit." She wasn't ready to take anything Raphael said at face value.

"You fed from him. Twice. Both times opened small portals that allowed demons to wander through."

"There's no way you could know that," she croaked out.

"We know because you two share a blood bond."

Oh, God. They shouldn't know that, either. *Bluff*. "Even if you're right, feeding wouldn't cause that."

"It would if you're fallen and Reaver is—" He snapped his mouth shut so fast she heard his teeth crack.

She narrowed her gaze. "Reaver is . . . what?" When he waved away her question, she gave up trying to be civil. "Dammit, why are you here? If you're going to kill me, do it already. And have the balls to do it yourself instead of hiding behind fucking darkmen."

"Your time in Sheoul has wreaked havoc on your vocabulary." Raphael stepped closer, a mountain of Heavenly menace. "You know why we had to send the darkmen. I didn't want to, but you survived, you're here now, and it's over."

He pressed forward, stalking her like a tiger, his gaze hungry and ruthless, and an alarm started clanging in her head. But before she could so much as *think* about flashing out of there, he was on her, backing her against the lone tree on the hilltop.

"What are you doing?" The quaver in her voice more than gave away her anxiety. She'd escaped one enemy just to land on the doorstep of another. She'd gone from the frying pan into the fire. From the claws of a Soulshredder into the jaws of a Gargantua.

She was racking up the clichés for trouble.

One hand slammed into the tree above her head, and the other gripped her shoulder in a bruising hold. Even at full strength, with all the power inherent to a fallen angel of her rank and genetics, she couldn't escape him.

"I'm doing what I should have done a long time ago." The archangel's eyes flamed hot. There was no warning, no slow buildup. He slanted his mouth over hers.

Startled, Harvester went taut as Raphael pressed his big body against hers and savaged her mouth in a demanding, brutal kiss. Under normal circumstances, her response would be swift and lusty. But these weren't normal circumstances by any means.

And Raphael was no Reaver.

Wedging her hands between them, she palmed his chest and shoved, breaking the kiss. "Don't do this."

"I *am* doing this. I'm claiming you." He was so arrogant, so sure she'd fall under his spell.

She shoved him again, but he didn't budge. "No one *claims* me."

Except that wasn't entirely true, was it? When she and Reaver had been in the Boregate, what he'd done to her had felt like a possession, and God help her, she thought maybe that was okay.

"You're mine, Verrine." Raphael's voice throbbed with authority, the kind that made even high-ranking angels cower before him. "You should have been mine thousands of years ago, but you gave everything up for that loser Yenrieth."

She inhaled sharply, a vicious stab of realization piercing her gut. "That's why you didn't want me to fall, isn't it," she said hoarsely. "It had nothing to do with the fact that you thought it was a crazy idea. You didn't want me to go because you wanted me for yourself."

How could she have been so blind? Raphael had been a rakish novice archangel at the time she and Yenrieth were in their training, and he'd made himself available to keep her company when Yenrieth was off either hunting minor demons or looking for a female with a warm bed.

"*He'll never be faithful to you*," Raphael had said. "*It's not in his nature. Battle angels were bred to fight and breed more warriors. They're soldiers. Dumb muscle. You need someone with brains, someone who can stand by your side for life and never look at another female.*"

Like an idiot, she'd been too naive to recognize Raphael's attempts to lure her into his own bed.

"Yes," Raphael said. "I wanted you." His smile was very cat-and-mouse, and she was the mouse. "And now I have you."

"You don't have me." She tried to slip out from under him, but he blocked her with his body and tightened his grip on her shoulder. The sensation of being trapped left her struggling to breathe normally.

"But why now?" she asked, her mind racing to make sense of this. "It's been almost five thousand years. You didn't get over me in that much time?" Not that she had a lot of room to talk, given that she'd carried a torch for Yenrieth for just as long.

"Time runs differently in Heaven. You know that. It feels like yesterday, not centuries."

He had a point. But she wasn't going to acknowledge it. "You didn't want me to be rescued. You wanted me to rot in Satan's torture chambers. How can you claim to want me if you didn't care that I was going to suffer and die?"

"I did care," he said fiercely. "But leaving you there was for the greater good."

"Funny how the *greater good* doesn't feel so good when you're the one with the hot poker in your bowels."

Raphael swallowed audibly, and she swore she saw genuine regret in his expression. "I'm sorry. I never wanted you to suffer. But now that you're here, I can make it up to you."

"That's very touching, but no."

"No ... what?" he prompted.

Was he being deliberately dense? "I won't be your ... whatever it is you want me for."

Reaching out, he brushed a knuckle over her cheek, a gentle gesture that she might have fallen for when she was Verrine. Now she didn't want his attention. Now she knew he could be as cruel as he was tender.

"Oh, I think you will," Raphael drawled, and she broke out in gooseflesh as a sensation of impending doom sank into her gut. "See, I'm going to make you a deal."

She narrowed her eyes. "What kind of deal?"

"I promise to keep you safe from Satan. You're vulnerable while you're in the human realm. Come with me, and he won't be able to touch you ever again. In addition, I won't destroy Reaver for what he's done." Raphael smile was wolfish, a predator that had pinned the deer. "In exchange, you agree to be my consort."

The asshole thought he had her, didn't he? She returned his smile. "Tell you what. I keep myself safe, you don't destroy Reaver, *and* I don't become your consort. In exchange, I tell you where Gethel is."

He laughed. "We know where she is. We nabbed the demon you hitched a ride with in the Harrowgate." He took Harvester's hand and squeezed as if he owned her. "So what's it to be? A ceremony for Reaver's execution, or a ceremony binding us together forever?"

A thought occurred to her, a terrible, ugly thought, and

she drew in a ragged breath. "This isn't about me, is it? This is about hurting Reaver. That's why you wanted me to torture him."

He smoothed his finger over her cheek, and her skin crawled. "You're part right. I did want him to suffer, but this isn't about him. It really is about you. As I said, I've wanted you for a long time." His vile touch moved south, down her neck to her collarbone, where he slid his finger under the strap of her tank top. "But if it makes you feel any better, remember when I threatened to take away your memories of Yenrieth if you didn't torture him?"

"Gee, no," she gritted out. "Totally forgot."

"You'll have to stop with the sarcasm. I don't like it," he said, and yeah, she'd get right on that.

"What does any of this have to do with my memories?"

He shrugged. "I lied. I couldn't have taken your memories," he said, and a blast of betrayal and fury blindsided her. Was the truth so fucking hard for people? "The blood bond with Yenrieth saved you from the full memory wipe everyone else got. Nothing can change that. Not even an archangel." That last part came out with so much bitterness she could practically taste it on her own tongue.

Harvester had spent five thousand years in hell with demons so evil that even Satan contained them. And yet, Raphael, an angel of Heaven, was one of the biggest fiends she'd ever known.

And in order to save Reaver, she was going to be forced to spend the rest of eternity with the fiend.

For a split second, the length of half a heartbeat, her inner evil rose up and considered turning Raphael down. But she squashed the thought immediately. As jumbled as her feelings were about Reaver right now, she was one hundred percent certain that she couldn't see him die.

"You sick, twisted bastard," she rasped. "I *hate* you. No matter how long we're together, I will despise every breath you take."

He grinned. "Then a mating ceremony, it is."

# Twenty-Five

Reaver woke in the triage tent in Underworld General's parking lot. Eidolon hovered next to the bed, Ares, Thanatos, and Reseph flanking him.

"Behold," Eidolon said. "The angel awakens."

"I'm guessing I owe you my life." Owing a demon anything was never ideal, but Reaver knew Eidolon well enough to know the doctor would never abuse leverage. Reaver tried to sit, but heavy straps held him down. "And why am I restrained?"

"Because it took five Sems, including me, to remove the aurial without killing you." Eidolon flipped the releases on the restraints. "You didn't handle it well."

No, a demon channeling power into him while he was unconscious would trigger an angelic instinct to fight. He was lucky his body had accepted Seminus healing energy in the first place. Most angels couldn't be healed by demons. "Where's Harvester? What happened?"

"She sent for us to bring you here," Reseph said. "You almost died."

Thanatos moved closer to the bed, his accusing gaze cutting deep. "Why did you go to Sheoul to save her? Lorelia and Revenant claimed she was a spy." He clenched his fists at his sides, as if wishing Harvester's neck was between them. "But that's bullshit. She plotted with Pestilence to start the Apocalypse and murder my son."

Reseph turned a little green at the mention of Pestilence, while Ares folded his arms across his chest, watching with assessing eyes. Of all the Horsemen, he was the one who could be the most level-headed and would likely approve of everything Harvester did over the centuries for the sake of victory. But he was also the one who would be the least understanding of what Reaver had done, because Reaver had done it out of emotion, not logic.

The bed creaked as Reaver sat up, and oh, look at that. He was naked. He snatched a bed sheet and covered his lap while Eidolon dug a set of scrubs from out of a cabinet.

"Harvester didn't plot to do any of that," Reaver said. "Your Watchers are right. She volunteered to fall from Heaven in order to watch over all of you."

"The hell she did." Thanatos's anger was accompanied by a whoosh of souls escaping his armor to writhe at his feet. Their desire to kill in order to be free of his armor forever had them stretching the limits of their invisible tethers.

Eidolon tossed Reaver the blue scrubs before turning to Than. "Put the souls away, Horseman."

Normally, Thanatos wouldn't be cowed by any demon, but Eidolon had proved himself time and time again, and he'd delivered Than's son. The scorpion tattoo on his neck writhed, its tail stabbing at his jugular a few times before he got hold of his temper, but finally, the souls melted into his armor again.

"It's true," Reaver insisted. "She's been looking out for you since you were infants. When she fell, she worked her way to becoming Watcher and spent her time secretly manipulating events. When Reseph's Seal broke, she pretended to help Pestilence, but everything she did was to help stop the Apocalypse."

Ares frowned. "But it was she who made sure The Aegis sent Regan to seduce Thanatos. She knew the baby was the key to breaking Thanatos's Seal."

Thanatos growled at that, and the souls made an appearance again. This time Eidolon just shot him a dirty look and the souls disappeared.

"She also knew the baby was the one and only person who could *stop* the Apocalypse," Reaver insisted. "It was a risk, but she had faith you'd find a way to end the Apocalypse and save your son."

"But she tortured you. And I…" Anguish darkened Reseph's expression. "She… and I…"

"Hey," Reaver said softly. "We've been through this." He shoved his legs into the scrubs and moved to Reseph, who had gone pale at the memory of what he'd done to both Harvester and Reaver. "You weren't you, and she didn't have a choice. Raphael ordered her to do it. And trust me, she could have hurt me far worse than she did." He pulled on the scrub top. "I'm not asking you to understand. Not yet. But I *am* asking you to give her a chance."

"She means a lot to you, doesn't she?" Reseph asked.

"More than you know." More than even he knew, he suspected. He had a feeling they'd uncover a lot more layers of their relationship if he ever recovered all his memories. "Now, where is she?" Ares and Thanatos both shot Reseph a questioning glance, and Reaver's blood pressure bottomed out. "*Where*?"

"I left her with Raphael," Reseph muttered.

Raphael? Shit. What had he done with her? He looked around for his boots, found them near the door.

"E, did Tavin make it back?" He hoped so. The poor Sem had gone through hell while in...hell. And Reaver had managed to fuck him up even more.

"He's fine. Except for the snake issue. I don't suppose you can shed some light on that?"

"Not really." Reaver jammed his feet into his boots and bent to tie them. "I don't know what it is. I'll see what I can find out."

Eidolon nodded. "I've got Idess on it, and I've got someone else I can consult with."

Relieved, Reaver straightened. If Eidolon was on it, Tav was in good hands. "I need to go." He started toward the tent exit but stopped before he got there. "Where's Limos?"

More exchanged glances. "She's home." Ares's tone dripped with rare emotion, and Reaver's gut clenched as he remembered what Revenant had said about an accident.

Thanatos's gaze was stricken, his pause ominous. "She lost the baby."

"She didn't lose it," Ares growled. "The child was destroyed."

Reaver's heart skidded to a smoking halt and raw, grinding grief carved deep into his chest. *Oh, Limos, I'm so sorry.* His throat constricted into a tube so narrow every breath was like a searing whip of air.

"How?" he croaked.

Thanatos let loose a tirade of curses in several ancient languages. "Our new Heavenly Watcher lost her shit. The bitch took us all down. She even killed one of Ares's hell-hounds." He inhaled a ragged breath. "The baby didn't survive. We've been scouring the globe for Lorelia, but it looks like she's hiding behind archangel skirts."

Rabid fury and ice-hot hatred shot through Reaver with an intensity he hadn't felt since learning Verrine had kept the secret of his children from him. Harvester was missing, was probably being held by the archangels until they decided what to do with her, and the Watcher who had been assigned to watch over Limos had hurt her and killed Reaver's grandchild.

"I have to go," Reaver ground out. "I swear to you, Lorelia will pay for what she's done."

"No, Reaver," came a chorus of voices he knew too well. "It is you who will pay for what *you've* done."

Suddenly, he wasn't standing in Underworld General's triage tent anymore.

He was in standing atop Mount Megiddo, surrounded by archangels. And a few yards away was Harvester, her curvy body wrapped in a skin-tight ivory leather dress that revealed more flesh than he wanted anyone but him to see.

Her eyes were downcast.

And her hand was twined with Raphael's.

The leaden press of foreboding crushed Harvester under its weight. This was going to be bad. She dug her nails into Raphael's hand as hard as she could, hoping to inflict as much pain as possible, hoping to make him feel a small measure of what she was feeling. The dickhead just smiled and watched four archangels escort Reaver into the center of a ritual circle drawn with the blood of three camels bathed in holy water.

Harvester's heart bled as he was forced to his knees on the hard-packed earth where so much history had been made. Tel Megiddo was not only a site important to humans but to angels as well. It was here that fallen angels could summon those in Heaven. It was here that angels were elevated to higher ranks within their orders. And it was here that punishments were carried out.

Clearly, Reaver wasn't here to be elevated. But what kind of punishment would he be forced to endure? Raphael's smile grew wider, and a sudden, terrifying thought came to her.

Tel Megiddo was also where executions took place.

*Oh, dear God, no.* "You promised you wouldn't kill him," she croaked. "You *bastard.*"

Trembling with a combination of fear and anger, she jerked away from Raphael and bolted toward Reaver, but two Enforcers, angels assigned to ensure compliance of angelic law, seized her by the arms and hauled her backward.

"Leave her alone!" Reaver exploded to his feet, but four more Enforcers brutally pinned him to the ground.

"I promised you we wouldn't destroy him," Raphael assured her. "But what he's done can't be forgiven, either." He cupped her cheek with a gentleness that didn't match the ominous tone in his voice. "Calm down. You're only making things worse for him."

*You son of a bitch.* She hated that he was right, hated

that Reaver was going to suffer for saving her. Swallowing dryly, she put on the cool, detatched facade she'd perfected as a fallen angel and forced herself to remain still.

Raphael joined five other archangels who formed a semicircle around Reaver as he lay on the ground, arms and legs held by the Enforcers. Another Enforcer reached under him and dragged his wings out to spread wide in the dirt.

Michael rose above the others as if on an invisible pedestal.

"Reaver, known also as Yenrieth," he began, his rich baritone carrying such power that Harvester wondered if his words were being broadcast in the heavens. "You have defied us for the last time. Because of you, Satan is demanding a hundred thousand souls in payment for our breach of contract. His forces are gathering, and an assault on Heaven is now not a matter of if, but when. We have laws for a reason, and in thousands of years, you haven't learned to obey them."

He produced a golden *treclan* stake, and Harvester slapped her hand over her mouth, cutting off the cry of alarm that coiled in her throat.

Not long ago, Gethel had driven half a dozen of those things into Harvester's body. Every place the stakes had penetrated began to throb anew, as if her muscles remembered the agony of the stakes developed solely to hold an angel for all eternity if one wished.

Michael slammed the stake through Reaver's hand, pinning it to the ground. Reaver's face contorted in agony and sweat beaded on his brow, but he didn't make a sound.

"No!" Harvester screamed. "Don't do this!"

No one listened. She struggled against the Enforcers,

sobbing as the archangels took turns driving stakes into Reaver, one in each hand, foot, thigh, and wing. Reaver never screamed, never made a single noise as his bones broke and his blood ran in rivers on the hard-baked ground.

Uriel punched a stake into Reaver's abdomen, and Harvester's screams hadn't even died away before Gabriel rammed a *treclan* into Reaver's chest. This time, he grunted and coughed blood, and for the first time since the horror began, he closed his eyes.

"I'm so sorry, Reaver," she rasped, tears streaming down her face. She cried out as Raphael lifted the last stake high over his head and plunged it into Reaver's throat.

Reaver gasped, bloody spittle spraying from his pale lips.

"We don't take any pleasure from this," Raphael said to Reaver, and Harvester called bullshit on that. The other archangels seemed either sad or indifferent, but Raphael's glee wasn't well concealed. "Harvester. Come here."

The Enforcers released her, and she half ran, half tumbled toward Reaver. Gabriel caught her before she reached him.

"What are you doing?" She tried to break away, but the other archangels gathered around her, blocking her.

Raphael kneeled next to Reaver and shocked the hell out of her when he gently palmed Reaver's cheek. "Not all is lost, Yenrieth. When one falls, another rises." He dragged his hand through the pool of Reaver's blood and stood to face to Harvester.

All of the archangels began to chant in a deep, hauntingly beautiful song. She felt frozen in place as Raphael came to her. He stopped a foot away.

"I wish it could be my blood that strengthened you," he said gruffly. "But you've already got a blood connection with Yenrieth."

"I don't understand." Anxiety wrapped around her chest and turned her lungs to cement. What were they going to do to her?

Reaching out with his bloody hand, Raphael gripped the back of her neck and joined the chanting. The world around her spun, joined by a muscle-melting peacefulness that made her sag. Several hands caught her and held her upright.

Suddenly, agony hijacked every muscle, every organ, every cell. It was as if every bone was being pulverized while still inside her body. The pain blinded her, took her breath and her voice so she couldn't even scream. She felt her wings crumpling like wadded-up paper, and she thought she must have passed out, because the next thing she knew, the archangels were backing away, heads bowed, and the pain was gone, replaced by the purest, sweetest euphoria she'd ever known.

Blinking, trying to gain her bearings, she tensed the muscles in her back... and felt the weight of wings. New wings.

Was it possible? Had she been returned to full angel status? Afraid to look, she flared her wings and peeked with one eye.

She gasped, her heart soaring at the sight of massive, glossy blue-black wings that rose high into the sky, the tips of each feather dusted with iridescent glitter.

"Only a handful of Unfallen have been raised to Heavenly angel status," Gabriel said. "But never before have we raised a True Fallen. We weren't even sure it could be done." Framing her face in his hands, he kissed her lightly on the mouth. "Welcome home, Verrine. Your service to the human and Heavenly realms has never been equaled, and you can never be thanked enough."

Tears of unfettered elation filled her eyes, and deep in her soul an awareness she hadn't felt in five thousand years filled her heart. The blood bond with Reaver. She could feel him in places that had been so empty for so long.

She turned to him, and although his pain must have been off the charts, he smiled weakly at her, his sapphire-blue eyes glinting with satisfaction. But her own satisfaction was fleeting. She couldn't celebrate, not when Reaver was suffering. Not when he'd just lost everything.

"But," Raphael continued, his tone turned grim, "there is a price for your return." In a coordinated move, both he and Uriel produced golden scythes Harvester knew too well.

"No!" she cried out in horror, her joy forgotten. "Don't—"

The two angels brought the scythes down in silent swoops, and in an instant, Reaver's wings were severed, and with them, the blood-bond sensation she'd gained only seconds before.

Reaver's scream of ultimate agony, of soul-wrenching misery, rocked the entire plateau in an earthquake that would register on the Richter scale. Above them, clouds roiled from out of nowhere, bringing thunder and lightning, and a torrential downpour. The rain came down in buckets, but an angel-made dome over the mount left everyone but Reaver dry.

"*Reaver.*" Harvester ran toward him, her feet slipping in mud created by the rain and his blood. She threw herself at him, tearing at the *treclan* spikes. No one stopped her, and Reaver didn't move. His eyes were open, but he wasn't there.

When she'd pulled free all of the spikes, she gathered him in her arms and held him against her, rocking him, stroking his hair, not caring that her pristine white clothes were now ruined.

"I'm sorry," she whispered. "I'm so sorry." She glared at the archangels through the rain that pelted her and Reaver. "You bastards. You fucking bastards."

Temper flashed in Raphael's eyes, little bolts of crimson lightning. "You may be my consort, but you will never speak to an archangel like that again."

"Don't bet on that," she shot back. "You're right; you should have gotten me thousands of years ago, when I was meek and biddable. Big mistake, Raphael. Huge."

His expression darkened. "Come. We're done here. You're not to see him again."

When she didn't move, he threw his head back and roared. The storm Reaver had created with his agony grew ten times worse, spawning tornadoes that circled the hilltop.

"Now," he growled, his voice amplified to a near-deafening pitch. "Now, or I will pluck Reaver from your arms and dump him in Sheoul."

To do so would complete Reaver's fall from grace, allowing him no chance of redemption, because somehow, she doubted that he'd ever be raised the way she had. She was the first, and likely, the last.

With a sob, she laid Reaver carefully on the ground. Bending, she brushed her lips across his, taking a perverse pleasure at Raphael's growl of jealousy.

"*Now!*"

Harvester came to her feet slowly, defiantly, and without sparing Raphael even a glance, she spread her new wings and took flight.

"Forbidden to see Reaver again? WWRD, asshole," she muttered as she shot upward into a black cloud. What would Reaver do, indeed. He'd break the rules.

So would she.

# Twenty-Six

⌒

Blaspheme hated days off work. Days off meant she had to find something to do with herself, and she'd rather not be that creative. But when Eidolon promoted her from paramedic to doctor a few months ago, she'd been given more duties, and she'd been put on call on her days off.

Awesome. She loved getting called into work, and with all the turmoil going on in Sheoul right now, there was plenty of work to go around.

She'd barely stepped out of the Harrowgate and into the packed emergency department when Eidolon pulled her aside. "Glad you're here. I need you to take a look at Tavin."

"Tavin? Wasn't he released days ago?"

"Yeah." Eidolon frowned. "But he's got something weird going on with his *dermoire*."

She automatically glanced at the sleeve of dermal glyphs on his right arm. "Shouldn't that be your area of expertise?"

"His personal symbol changed. Idess says it's angelic in nature, but there's something wrong with it." He lowered his voice as a Ramreel patient limped past, his hoof wrapped in bandages. "I was hoping you might have some insight."

She stiffened. What would make him think she could give insight into something angelic in nature? False Angels were like false morels. Poisonous copies of the real things and related only in appearance.

"Do you mean *False* Angelic?"

"No." He looked beyond her for a moment before meeting her gaze. "And on the subject of angels, stay away from Revenant."

She frowned. "Who's Revenant?"

"The male who was here about Limos. Tall. Lots of leather. Long black hair. Asshole."

Right. Asshole. Now she remembered him. He'd generously offered to let her suck his cock. As if. Sure, he'd oozed danger and sex, and if she'd met him at a club, she'd probably have taken him home. Except he'd be the one doing the mouth workout. Not her.

"I wasn't planning on hanging out with him or anything. Why do I need to stay away from him?"

The doctor's voice went low again. "He's a fallen angel."

Her gut did a slow slide to her feet. She had a fallen angel interested in her. As much as she didn't like the idea that Eidolon had seen through her False Angel facade, at least she trusted him. But fallen angels were hazardous to people like her.

They hunted her kind for sport.

"Understood," she whispered.

E nodded briskly. "Good. Now go check on Tav. He's in exam three."

Knees wobbling, mind spinning in a haze, she made her way to Tavin's room. He was sitting on the exam table, his black fatigues covering him from neck to ankles. Black combat boots completed his assassin attire. Well, the weapons completed it.

He looked tired, the dark crescents under his eyes swollen with exhaustion. He also looked ready to butcher something.

Just the way Revenant would look if he learned she wasn't really a False Angel.

*Stop it. You're worried about nothing. He hasn't been around in days. He may never come around again.*

She squared her shoulders and put on her cheery doctor face. "Hi, Tavin. Eidolon said you have something to show me."

"You could say that." He tugged down his collar to reveal his personal Seminus symbol, the one his offspring would inherit just beneath their own symbols.

The markings would continue all the way to their fingertips, revealing the history of their paternity for dozens of generations. It was kind of cool, really. One glance at another Sem, and a Sem like Tavin or Eidolon could determine their relationship to each other. Tav and E, in fact, were related by a star symbol far back in their family *dermoire.*

She peered closely at the vaguely familiar snake symbol. The horned head rose up from a body coiled around a skull, and as she looked at it, she swore the tail moved. Squinting, she leaned closer.

"It looks like a—" She reared back. What had Eidolon said? An angelic symbol?

"What?" Tav let go of his shirt collar and twisted around to her. "What is it? Idess said it was an angelic protection symbol gone wrong."

Blas shook her head. "It's not angelic. It's *fallen* angelic."

"What's the difference?"

"Angels and fallen angels draw their power from different sources," she explained. "So they have different abilities and talents. For example, only an angel can create the patron cobra, and only a fallen angel can create what you have. The death cobra."

Tavin snorted. "Well, I hate to tell you this, but it was an angel who did it. Not a fallen angel."

She shook her head. "Impossible."

"I'm telling ya," he said with a shrug.

She wasn't going to argue. Not when she knew she was right. "Just for shits and giggles, let's say it's the death cobra."

"But I don't want it to be the death cobra," Tavin blurted. "That sounds really fucking bad."

"It is. It's a curse."

"A curse? You mean, like a *curse* curse. Like, a *bad* curse?"

There really wasn't any other kind, but seeing how the patient was getting worked up, she didn't point that out.

"Yeah. A bad curse."

Tavin swallowed, and the snake shifted. Damn, that freaked her out. And she was used to weird shit.

"Okay, so what am I cursed with, and how can I get rid of it?"

"I don't know how to get rid of it. As for the curse..." She blew out a long breath. "Poison. I'm sorry, Tav, but it's an ancient assassination curse, not even used anymore. Every time you agitate the snake, it'll bite. You'll eventually die. "

*"Assassination?"*

She nodded. "Ironic, yes?" His flat stare said he didn't appreciate the irony. "I'll see what I can find out about it. We'll all work on this, Tav."

Her name badge should read: DR. BULLSHIT. Curses were not easily broken.

"Fuck." Tavin scrubbed his hands over his face. "Live by the poison, die by the poison. Awesome. I have a new mantra."

Well, she thought, it was better than hers: Live a lie, die a liar.

*Don't borrow trouble. You've survived almost two hundred years without a problem. Keep your head down and your nose clean.*

The curtain swished open, and Gem entered, all perky despite the fact that she'd been on shift for twenty-four hours. She must be getting ready to go home to her hot-as-hell husband and their daughter.

"Hey." Gem thrust a note and a single black rose into Blaspheme's hand. "Someone left this for you. Very romantic." She acknowledged Tavin with a wave. "I'm outta here. See you later."

Blas barely heard a word. Her gaze was glued to the note, to the block script that turned her blood to ice. No, not ice, because thorns on the rose stem dug into her hand, and blood trickled down her wrist and dripped onto the paper.

*I'll see you soon. Very soon.*

It was signed.

*Revenant.*

# Twenty-Seven

"What is it you want, Verrine?" Raphael poured her a glass of ice wine made from the azure grapes that grew in the Demura plains outside Archangel Hall. They were in the expansive kitchen of his palatial home, and she wondered how long she was going to be stuck here.

And what his game was.

They'd just come from the entrance of a hellmouth, where Harvester had been trying to sense Lucifer, but after watching Reaver lose his wings and fall from grace, her heart hadn't been in it. Besides, it appeared that Lucifer had been moved. Now she had to find a place on Earth where she could get a signal, but it was going to take time.

Time they no longer had. So why were they in Raphael's home talking as if they had nothing better to do?

"Harvester," she corrected as she took the glass of the crystal-blue wine without a thank you.

Raphael graced her with a patronizing smile. "You'll

get over that eventually. *Harvester.*" He sipped his own wine and let out a moan of pleasure. "Now, tell me what you want."

*Your head mounted on a pole. That's what I want.* "That's a broad question. I want peace on Earth. Three hundred and sixty-five days of Christmas. A ban on all remakes of eighties songs. Oh, and Reaver's angelic status restored." She traced the rim of her glass with her finger. "Shall I go on?"

"Sheoul has not positively influenced your personality," Raphael said, but she didn't agree. Well, mostly she didn't agree. But he was still an ass. "Would you like to be the Horsemen's Watcher again?"

Her heart skipped a beat. Was he serious? He gazed at her with narrowed eyes, clearly waiting for a reaction that he would, no doubt, use to his advantage.

So she didn't give him one.

With a casual shrug, she tasted the wine. Instant arousal rushed through her veins and concentrated in her breasts and pelvis. Wow. She eyed the glass. Raphael was a sneaky bastard, wasn't he? No more of that for her.

"I don't think the Horsemen would appreciate it."

"They might not like it, but their opinions don't matter, and you know them better than anyone."

"I suppose."

Raphael took another drink from his glass, and his gaze darkened. He probably shouldn't have any more of the wine, either.

"We're going to assign you as Watcher."

*Yes.* She gave another shrug. "Whatever. I suppose I need a job. But I'm telling you, they won't be happy. Not after everything I did as their Sheoulic Watcher."

"But you were helping them."

"I doubt they'll see it that way, and even if they do, it'll take them a while to get over it. Thanatos especially."

He gestured to her glass. "Have more."

"I've never been much of a drinker." Very deliberately, she put the glass on the counter. "Are we done here?"

"Don't you want to know what will make the Horsemen welcome you back with open arms?"

She resisted rolling her eyes. "I give. What will make them suddenly forgive me for everything I've done?"

"A baby." Raphael's voice was low, seductive in a nonsexual way. Seductive in that way that promised you everything you ever wanted. She was drawn in, no doubt exactly the way he'd planned, and it occurred to her that she'd never had the upper hand in this negotiation. He'd only let her think she had.

"What baby?"

"Limos's. You didn't know she lost it?" He smiled, a real I-have-you-now smirk she wanted to slap off his face. "You can give Limos her dream back. You'll be a hero." He picked up her glass and held it out. "Drink up, and I'll tell you how."

Reaver jolted into consciousness, head pounding, eyes filled with sand. Or glass. He dragged them open and peered through slits at Eidolon's concerned face hovering over him.

"How are you feeling?"

He cleared his raw throat, wondering why it was so sore. "Like I went through an industrial meat grinder." He frowned. "Where am I? Why are you here? Why do I keep waking up with you in my face?"

"We're in Israel. I'm here because Harvester sent word. And you keep waking up with me in your face because you keep getting into trouble."

Harvester. Right. She'd gotten her wings back. *Thank you, God.* She'd been so radiant, so full of joy, and so had Reaver. Even through the misery, Reaver's heart had soared for her.

He tried to sit up, but when his skull threatened to implode, he decided that lying on the ground for a few more minutes couldn't hurt. Then he remembered, with sickening clarity, being nailed to the ground, and suddenly he didn't want to be on it anymore.

He struggled to sit up, this time making it past the skull-shattering stage. "My wings are gone, aren't they?" He knew the answer, but he needed to hear it.

Eidolon's eyes were sad. "I'm sorry, Reaver."

He was a fallen angel.

Again.

Didn't matter that he'd expected it. Hell, he expected to be destroyed. Still, pain that extended well beyond the physical wrapped around him, squeezing like a vise. He let himself mourn for a moment, and then he allowed Eidolon to help him to his feet, ignoring the aches that permeated every cell in his body. He couldn't— wouldn't—dwell on this or regret that it happened. The goal had always been to save Harvester from an eternity of torture. He'd have done it even if he'd known with certainty that he'd lose his life or his wings.

What was done was done.

"Thank you, Eidolon." Reaver clasped the doctor's hand in his. "I know you don't normally make house calls."

"Are you kidding? I'm always making damned house calls." Eidolon reached into his medical bag and handed him yet another pair of scrubs to replace the ones currently Swiss cheesed and drenched in rain, mud, and blood. "I'll admit I have an ulterior motive."

"Are you offering me my job back?" Reaver asked as he stripped out of the destroyed clothes.

Eidolon gave him a sheepish shrug. "I'm desperate."

"Wow." Reaver paused to yank on the scrub pants. "You really know how to sweet talk a guy."

Eidolon laughed. "So? Is that a yes?"

"Yeah." Reaver flexed his shoulder blades under the scrub top, feeling the loss of his wings as a distinct, too-light sensation of phantom limbs. "I need a little time first."

He was back in the human realm, but now there was fallout to deal with. He hadn't had a chance to spend time with the Horsemen, and right now Limos, especially, was a priority. And Harvester... he had no way to contact her, but he had to try. His feelings had shifted the moment he learned the truth about her, and then they'd grown during their time in Sheoul. Now, being away from her left a hole in his chest where a ghost organ beat, much like the wings missing from his shoulders.

Then there was the issue of the brewing war between realms. A war that, if it boiled over, would be his fault.

Eidolon walked toward the Harrowgate that sat on the southern edge of the Megiddo plateau, and Reaver joined him. "Come back when you're ready."

They stepped into the gate, and Eidolon selected the caduceus symbol that would open into Underworld General. When the emergency room appeared, E stepped out. "Be safe. There's trouble brewing in Sheoul, but I'm guessing you know that."

"Little bit." Reaver waited for the gate to close. When it was dark inside, with only the glow of Sheoulic symbols and map lines on the wall, he tapped until he found the Harrowgate that was closest to Limos's Hawaiian house.

Losing the ability to flash himself anywhere in the world was one of the worst things about being booted out of Heaven, and Reaver cursed as he walked the sandy path from the gate to Limos's house. When he arrived, it was Arik who met him at the door and surprised him with an enthusiastic embrace.

"Reaver, man, it's good to see you." Arik stepped back. "I heard you spent some time in Sheoul. Is it true that you rescued Harvester? And that she was a spy for our side?"

Reaver followed Arik into the beach themed living room. Limos was conspicuously absent. "Yeah. She's been reinstated as an angel."

"Cool, I guess." Arik gestured beyond the canoe-shaped bookcase to the kitchen. "Offer you a beer?"

"Thanks, no."

Socially required niceties over now, Arik sank onto the wicker couch as if his legs had given out. "Shit." He braced his elbows on his knees and buried his face in his hands. "I'm so glad you're here. Limos is...I don't know. I feel like she's gone."

Reaver's heart squeezed painfully hard. "Where is she?"

"Bedroom." Arik looked up, the shadows under his eyes speaking of a lot of worry and restless nights. "She doesn't come out. I can't get her to eat, and I have to carry her into the shower or she won't even do that. She doesn't talk. She doesn't even cry." He jammed his hand through his hair, leaving unruly grooves in the dark waves. "Help her. Please."

Reaver would do anything in his power to help. He just hoped he could. Steeling himself, he went to the bedroom and found Limos curled under the covers, only her tanned feet sticking out from the lacy pink bedspread. An empty cradle sat in the corner, Thanatos's scrollwork lovingly etched into the wood.

Heart breaking, Reaver sank down on the bed next to his daughter and gently placed his hand on her shoulder.

"Li?"

The Limos-lump moved under the covers. "R-Reaver?"

She clawed her way out of the tangled mess of blankets and sheets and threw herself at him, her arms clamped so tight around him that he could barely breathe. And Limos, who rarely cried, bawled until his neck, shoulder, and chest was wet with her tears.

He said nothing, simply holding her as she wept. If he'd learned anything at all about females . . . mostly from Harvester . . . it was that it was easy to say the wrong thing, and more often than not, saying nothing at all was the right thing.

Finally, Limos's sobs turned to sniffles, and he twisted around to get a box of tissues off the bedside table. Very carefully, he dabbed the wet streaks from her cheeks and brushed the matted hair off her skin. There was nothing Limos liked more than to be pampered, and Reaver was prepared to do whatever it took.

She let him clean her up, and then she scooted backward just enough to give him room to sit more fully on the mattress. "You've been gone." There was no accusation in her voice, simply a statement of fact.

"I'm sorry."

Bloodshot violet eyes met his. "Arik said you were rescuing Harvester. Do you love her?"

Whoa. Talk about being blindsided. But Limos had never been anything but blunt. "It's...complicated."

"Why?"

He really did not want to talk about this, but he sensed that this was a turning point for Limos, a reason to join the living, even if only for a little while before she burrowed back under the covers.

"Back when I was Yenrieth, we were close," he said, and Limos sat up a little straighter.

"Were you lovers?" Beneath her deadly Horseman exterior, Limos had always been a romantic.

"No, but we should have been. We can lay that one on me. I was an idiot. I don't remember much, but I know it was you who told me you were my daughter and that I had three sons."

She frowned. "I don't remember that."

"Because your memory was wiped along with everyone else's." His gaze drifted to the cradle, and sorrow clogged his throat. What he wouldn't do to make things right. "Apparently, I went a little crazy. I still don't know what happened, but I disappeared, and Harvester vowed to watch over all of you because I couldn't." Or wouldn't. He had no idea, but that missing piece of his life was going to drive him mad until he knew. "She gave up everything to Fall and become your Watcher."

"So you feel you owe her."

"I don't feel it," he said quietly. "I know it."

"And you love her." This time, it wasn't a question. It was a proclamation.

"Like I said, it's complicated."

Limos shook her head. "Complicated is when you fall in love with someone while you're engaged to Satan and you're wearing a chastity belt. Does Harvester belong to anyone? Is she wearing a chastity belt that will chop off your body parts? No? Then it's not complicated."

The image of Harvester holding Raphael's hand flashed in his head, and his breath turned raw in his throat. He hadn't thought much of it at the time given that he knew something bad was about to go down on the Megiddo hilltop. But now the idea that Raphael was acting a little too friendly with Harvester skinned him alive.

"She's an angel now," he told her. "I saw her get her wings back." Harvester had glowed like a diamond in a ray of sunshine. She'd been the most beautiful female he'd ever seen. If he hadn't been pinned to the ground like an insect in a display case, he'd have been on her in a heartbeat.

"That's perfect." Limos smiled, and he had feeling it was the first time since losing the baby. "Now there aren't any rules between you—"

"I got the boot, Li," he said, stopping her before she could finish. "I lost my wings."

"Oh my God." Limos's eyes filled with tears again. "No. No, that can't be. You saved her. How can they do that to you?"

"It's okay," he said. "I expected to die."

Limos punched a pillow. "It's still bullshit."

He took her hand, which felt too fragile despite the fact that she was one of the most powerful beings in all the realms. "When I was fallen the first time, I prayed I'd get my wings back. When it happened, it was like I was home." He could still feel the elation, the amazement that he'd done something to deserve entrance into Heaven again. "But you know what I missed? My independence. My freedom."

"The ties that bind also chafe," she mused.

"Exactly." He squeezed her hand. "I'm okay. Seriously." Strangely, he was. Maybe he'd fall into a deep depression the way he had last time, but he doubted it. So much had changed in the last few years, and now he had a family. Only two things were missing.

Harvester and the grandchild he should have had from Limos.

"Limos—"

"I don't want to talk about it, okay?"

He nodded. "If you need anything…"

"I know."

There was a tap at the door, and Reaver stood as Arik poked his head in. When Arik saw Limos sitting up in bed, his eyes lit up, and he came inside in a rush.

"Reaver, you have a visitor." Arik sank down on the bed and drew Limos against him. "It's Harvester."

Reaver's heart skipped a beat. Torn between wanting to stay with Limos and wanting to rush to the female fate had separated him from for thousands of years, Reaver stood frozen to the bamboo floor.

"Go." Limos's voice was muffled against Arik's chest. "Get her."

Arik gave Reaver an *I-got-this* nod just as Limos grabbed his wrist. "Thank you for coming," she whispered. "Dad."

# Twenty-Eight

Harvester stood at the edge of the jungle outside of Limos's remote beach house, her skin caressed by the steamy tropical breeze, her bare feet buried in the sand. The simple pleasure of warm sand on her skin was something she never thought she'd feel again when she was hanging from meat hooks inside a frozen wasteland in her father's realm.

Yeah, this was amazing. And she owed it all to the male in scrubs walking toward her with long, fluid strides. The fact that he was no longer an angel didn't diminish his powerful presence in any way. The mere sight of him made her heart flutter madly.

Technically, he wasn't supposed to look upon an angel who served in Heaven unless he was given permission, but she wanted him to look. As much as he wanted to.

Oh, on many levels, she was still furious with him. Wasn't sure she could ever trust him. But she supposed none of that mattered anymore, and she wasn't going to spend what little time they had fighting. Besides, as the Horsemen's Heavenly Watcher, they'd be seeing a lot of each other.

"Hi," she said lamely.

He didn't say anything. He kept coming at her, his expression serious, and the delicate flutter turned to an ominous thud. Was he angry?

He halted a few yards away, his nostrils flaring, his chest heaving. Burning, raw masculinity emanated from him, and Harvester's body went hot with feminine appreciation.

"First," he said, "thank you for getting me out of Sheoul and saving my life." His voice was guttural, warped with emotion she was afraid to name. But he was wrong. *He'd* saved *her* life. "Second, we're done hurting and hating and going through the bullshit."

She inhaled sharply. After what happened at Tel Megiddo, she should have expected this, and it was inevitable, after all, but it didn't stop sensation of her heart being shredded.

Squaring her shoulders, she tried to hide the hurt. "It's probably for the best."

Especially given that she was going to have to officially give herself to Raphael tomorrow night.

"I'm glad you agree." In three strides Reaver was on her, his mouth crushing hers. "No more bullshit," he said against her lips. "I want you. I think I've always wanted you."

Shock and joy tangled so fiercely inside Harvester that she nearly crumpled to the ground. With a sob of relief, she arched against Reaver and lifted her thigh to hook around his waist as he pushed her backward against a tree.

God, he was a spark and she was dry tinder, and when his hand dropped to her ass to hold her for a slow roll of his hips that rubbed his rigid length against her core, she nearly burst into flame. The cool breeze coming off the ocean did nothing to help ease the heat. If anything, the reality that she was here in this tropical paradise with the male she'd loved and hated for centuries...the same male she'd loved and hated for the past few years...made it all that much hotter.

Reaver pelted her cheeks, jaw, and throat with hungry kisses. His breath fanned her skin, scorching her as he worked his way down, over her clavicle and then lower, to where he flicked his tongue under the V-neck of her silk tank top.

In the distance, Limos's servants' laughter rose above the crash of waves and the calls of the sea birds flying overhead.

"Not here," she whispered.

Reaver dragged his tongue between her breasts as she flashed them deep into the jungle, to a crystal pool off a well-worn path from Limos's house.

"Perfect." Reaver stepped back just enough to help relieve her of her top. When she tried to shove down her matching black leather miniskirt, he circled her wrists and held them against her belly as he dropped to his knees in front of her. "No." His voice was commanding. Hungry. So sexy she didn't mind that he was taking control. "*I* get to do this."

Releasing her wrists, he slipped his hands beneath the hem of her skirt. His palms were smooth and hot, and her thighs quivered as his thumbs stroked her sensitive skin.

Lifting his face, he caught her gaze. His gem-blue eyes

smoldered as he slowly slid his hands upward. Inch by agonizing inch, he caressed her legs, kindling a sensual fire that threatened to set off an inferno. She started to pant before she felt the first brush of his fingers against her tender flesh.

"No panties," he said roughly. "Damn, I'm so going to take advantage of that."

Please, *please* take advantage.

Apparently, Reaver could read minds, because before she could catch her breath, he pushed the skirt up to her waist and eased her back onto a wet boulder. In an effortless surge, he draped her legs over his broad shoulders and opened his mouth over her aching sex.

Never before had she felt exposed when she was naked with a male. Copulation had always been about satisfying a basic urge, but this...this was about emotions and a physical desire so deep she felt it in her soul. She hadn't felt like this since Yenrieth took her virginity.

Anxiety stirred, a protective instinct borne of thousands of years of hard living, and she pushed at him with a soft cry.

"Easy," Reaver said, his soothing tone bringing her down a notch. "I've got you."

He caught her hands, twining her fingers with his as he looked up at her, his gaze so full of promise that she had to lower her lids and turn her face away before he saw the vulnerability that was probably glaringly obvious.

For a long moment, he was still, and then, just as she opened her mouth to tell him to either get on with it or forget it, he lowered his head and nuzzled her inner thigh. His hot breath fanned her skin as he nibbled his way up, the erotic pinches of his teeth followed by velvet soft kisses that made her squirm in anticipation. By the time she felt the first probe of his tongue between her folds, she was so ready she cried out in sheer bliss.

He teased her out, licking in long, slow strokes before devastating her with quick side-to-side motions or a deep plunge of his tongue. She whimpered as he hit a spot that sent a jolt of electric sensation all the way to her womb.

"Reaver." She lifted her hips, chasing his touch with wanton abandon.

"You drive me crazy." He dragged the flat of his tongue through her slit and latched on to her clit, sucking gently. "I need to be inside you."

"Yes," she moaned, her body hovering at the edge of orgasm. "Oh...*yes*." He did something sinfully wicked with his lips, and she came with a shout, bucking and thrashing so hard he had to grip her thighs and hold her down.

He rose up in a surge of flexing muscle, but even as he centered himself between her legs, she flipped him into the shallow water onto his back. Most males would have freaked out at the manhandling, but Reaver only growled his approval as she took his cock in hand and guided it inside her. The cool water countered their molten heat as she rocked on top of him.

He was big, thick enough to stretch her almost to the point of discomfort, and she reveled in it, taking all of him to the root.

Closing his eyes, he gripped her waist and arched to meet her downward strokes. Each thrust lifted her out of the pool, and on the return, little waves lapped at the juncture where their bodies met. Water licked at her clit as

Reaver's cock stroked her on the inside to create a storm of erotic wonder. The musky scent of sex rose up, mingling with the freshness of the ocean breeze and the flowers and leaves surrounding them. It was as if Harvester and Reaver were one with each other, one with nature, and for the first time in centuries, Harvester felt alive, like she was exactly where she was meant to be.

"Damn." Reaver's husky voice rolled through her like thunder. "This is so...good." He opened those amazing eyes, and she lost herself in them and in the moment, letting the sounds of the waterfall and sex take her so high she felt as if she could bump her head on the moon.

She moved faster, the tension inside her building to a fever pitch. She couldn't get enough of him, could never get enough to make up for time lost.

Arching her back, she took him deep, needing to feel him everywhere. He hissed and jerked, his body going taut as his hot flow spilled inside her.

"Yes," he gasped. "Fuck...*yeah*."

His eyes glowed with blue-hot inner fire that sucked her in and triggered an explosion of ecstasy so powerful she screamed with the force of it. Pleasure crashed through her in unrelenting waves.

Beneath her, Reaver peaked again, and they came together in an overwhelming tempest of rapture so fierce that when it was over, neither of them could move. She collapsed on top of him in a heap, hoping no one stumbled upon them, because she didn't have the energy to even lift a finger to say hi.

They lay half in, half out of the water for a long time, sated, breathing hard. Harvester nuzzled Reaver's throat, figuring now would be the best time to break the news. Maybe Reaver was as exhausted as she was.

"There's something I have to tell you."

Reaver stroked her back, his warm fingers stirring her insides again. "This isn't going to be good, is it?"

"No." Dread descended on her like a swarm of ghast-bats as she braced herself for what she was going to say next, but she couldn't stop her stomach from churning. "I agreed to be Raphael's consort."

Reaver sat up so fast she fell into the water. He fetched her, sputtering and spitting, and pulled her onto the sandy bank with him. "Consort? As in...mate?" He brushed her wet hair back from her face. "Harvester? Look at me."

She didn't want to. "He wants a ceremony and shit."

"Why? What the hell—"

Raising her gaze to his, she silenced him with a finger on his lips. "It was a deal to keep you alive."

"Fuck." Reaver fell back into the sand and stared up at the canopy of tree branches and clear blue sky beyond them. "Don't do it. Please don't do it."

"I can't go back on my word," she choked out. "He'll kill you."

"I don't care." He twined his fingers with hers. His hand was shaking. "Don't chain yourself to him for eternity."

He didn't care? He seriously would give up his life to make sure she was happy? Dear God, she'd been so wrong about him for so long.

But she wasn't going to let him die for any reason. She'd put up with far worse than being chained to Raphael if it meant keeping Reaver safe. "There's more."

"More? How can there possibly be more?"

"It's not entirely bad," she said.

"About time," he muttered. "But I don't like the 'entirely' part."

Neither did she. "I'm the Horsemen's new Watcher. This time on the good side." She smiled, letting herself forget Raphael's bargain for a moment. "And it gets better. Brace yourself. I have Limos's baby."

He sat straight up. "You . . . wait . . . say that again?"

Still smiling, because it was rare to see the usually stoic Reaver flustered, Harvester told him the rest. "Lorelia took the baby to exchange it with Lucifer in Gethel's womb. But when—"

"She was going to *what*?" Reaver's roar sent birds exploding out of the trees. His eyes blazed, promising murder, and nope, Harvester wouldn't want to be in Lorelia's shoes right now.

"Reaver." Harvester lowered her voice, shooting for a tone she hadn't used in thousands of years, the tone that had always soothed Yenrieth. Well, almost always. Nothing had calmed him after he learned that she'd kept the existence of his children from him. "They didn't do it. Something went wrong. The exchange won't work. But now only a Watcher can return Limos's baby to the womb, and there's not much time left. If I don't do it within twenty-four hours, the child's soul returns to Heaven and she won't be born."

"She?" Reaver sucked in a sharp breath. "I'm going to have a granddaughter?"

Feminine appreciation shimmered through her, a primitive, basic response she hadn't felt in, well . . . not since before she'd fallen. She'd thought all her tender instincts had been destroyed by her time in Sheoul, but they'd merely been shoved into storage and were now emerging, dusty and unused and utterly foreign.

"You are," she said. "I promise."

"Then do it." Reaver leaped to his feet, his bronzed body gloriously naked, his skin glistening with water droplets she wanted to lick. "Why are you waiting?"

"Because I'm not powerful enough by myself. I need an archangel."

"Let me guess." Reaver's hands clenched at his sides. "Raphael is holding it over your head."

"I agreed to be his consort to save your life. But he didn't specifically say I had to sleep with him." She shoved to her feet and snatched up her clothes. "So he's using the child as leverage. If I screw him, he'll help me give Limos her baby back. I also have to help the archangels locate Lucifer. I'd have done that anyway, but Raphael felt the need to tack it onto our agreement."

"That *bastard*."

She wasn't going to argue that. "I have to do it." She reached out and took his hand. "I'll do anything to keep you alive and give Limos the child she always wanted."

"I know." Reaver wrapped his arms around her and pulled her close, holding her as if he were afraid to let go. "But I don't want you to have to. Somehow I'll fix this, Harvester."

He couldn't fix it. Even he had to know that. Raphael had proven he was willing to stop short of nothing to get what he wanted, and right now, what he wanted was Harvester.

She couldn't put Reaver at risk again. He'd already given up his wings to rescue her. She wouldn't see him give up his life as well.

So while she hoped there was a way out of this mess, she wasn't going to count on it.

She used to believe in fate. She'd been sure that she and Yenrieth were soul mates. Now she wasn't sure of anything.

# Twenty-Nine

Reaver was still reeling with Harvester's revelations as they dressed, his mind churning with a million different things.

"Do you have a place to stay?" Harvester asked.

"I got an apartment in New York when I was fallen the first time." He shrugged. "Kept it when I got my wings back. You never know when you're going to need to get away from prying eyes. Besides, do you know how hard it is to find a decent sized apartment with a view and parking in Manhattan? I'm never giving that sucker up."

"Smart," she mused. "So what now?"

"Now, I'm going to see Ares."

"You have a lot to catch up on with your sons."

Yes, but that wasn't why he was going. "Can you give me a lift?"

Man, he hated asking for shit that, as an angel, was so simple, but in an instant, they were inside Ares and Cara's

Greek mansion. The two of them were half-clothed and rolling around on the floor.

"Ah…" Reaver cleared his throat.

Cara screamed and grabbed a throw from off the couch to cover up. A young hellhound rushed into the room, skidded across the floor, and crashed into a marble pedestal. The pedestal toppled, sending the two books on display tumbling onto the tiles. Ares cursed and stood, blocking his wife from view. At least he had on shorts.

"There's a thing called a door," he said flatly. "It comes complete with a doorbell, and it's right behind you."

Harvester snorted. "You know I don't knock or ring doorbells. Also, I'm your new Watcher. Be nice."

Ares bent to pick up the copy of the *Daemonica* that landed near his feet. "Switching teams hasn't improved your temperament, obviously."

"Obviously," she drawled.

So getting her halo back hadn't changed *everything*. Reaver kind of liked that, but he still drew her aside before the fur started flying. He carefully picked up the Bible off the floor and set it on the coffee table as Ares and Cara discreetly dressed.

"I'm going to ask Ares to—"

"The Bible." Harvester grasped his wrist as if he hadn't spoken. "I got it! Oh, damn, Reaver, I thought of a way out of this mess with Raphael."

His heart kicked into high gear. "How?"

She bounced on her toes excitedly. "He can't kill you. He lied about that." At what must have been a perplexed expression on his face, she explained. "You're the Horsemen's father. Their father is supposed to break their Seals when it comes time for the biblical Apocalypse."

He inhaled sharply. "You're right. He wouldn't dare kill me and interfere with such a history-altering prophecy that favors Heaven in the Final Battle." *Yes*. He lowered his voice so Ares and Cara wouldn't hear the rest. "He can't force you to be his consort...at least, not with that threat. But there's still the issue with Limos's baby. He's still got you over a barrel."

"But only for sex."

Only. There was no such thing as *only* sex. Not when it was Harvester with anyone but Reaver.

"You can't let him know you're aware that he can't kill me, or he'll use the baby as leverage to get both sex and your consent to a mating ceremony."

"So what do we do?"

"Stall for time."

"Reaver, we don't *have* much time." She pegged him with serious eyes. "I'm going to give Limos her baby back, even if it means—"

"I know what it means," he growled, and a searing, almost uncontrollable anger flared in his chest. Harvester was his, and the thought of her fucking Raphael was enough to make his head explode. "We'll find a way to get you out of fucking him. Just...stall."

Harvester nodded and flashed away in a sparkle of light.

"So what's this about?" Ares asked, as Reaver turned back to him. Cara had slipped away, but the clumsy hellhound had remained to keep an eye on Ares. The things were rarely more than a few seconds away from either one of them, and they always sensed when an angel was near. Ex-angels, too, apparently.

"I need you to summon Revenant."

Ares's eyebrows shot up, but he didn't ask any questions. He merely called out with both formal protocol, and a less formal, "Yo, Rev. Get your ass over here." He grinned. "Revenant hates informality. He's a stickler for the rules. You two would really not get along."

"We didn't get along for the *five minutes* we were both Watchers together," Reaver muttered. Not to mention the five minutes of ass-kicking Revenant had given him in Gethel's Sheoulic palace.

Ares scratched the hellhound's ears. "He was pissed about what Lorelia did to Limos. He reported her to his Watcher Council and recommended execution as punishment. It won't happen, but he tried."

Well, that was unexpected. But then, a Watcher's duty included making sure the other Watcher didn't screw up. "He was probably more interested in seeing an angel die than in avenging Limos."

Ares shrugged. "His motives don't interest me. I'm just glad he did it." He looked past Reaver, and the hound snarled. "Speak of the fallen angel. White hair today, huh?"

Damn, but Reaver missed the warning tingle that accompanied the arrival of another angel or powerful supernatural being. It was going to take some time to get used to his Unfallen status again.

"Oh, look," Revenant said. "It's the newly fallen angel everyone in the underworld is trying to find." He strode over, his boots clomping on the hard tiles, his leather pants and jacket creaking with every step. "If I took you to the Dark Lord right now, I'd be the richest male in Sheoul."

"Touch him," Ares said, "and you'll live the rest of your sorry life looking over your shoulder."

"Yeah, yeah," Revenant said, sounding utterly bored. "The wrath of the Horsemen will come down on me. Every hellhound in Sheoul will be hunting me, blah-fuckity-blah. Don't worry your little pony heads about it." He punched Reaver in the shoulder. "Your father is off-limits for Watchers to grab, torture, kill, or molest in any way. Not that I'd molest him. I like my bedmates with bigger breasts and fewer balls."

"What a relief," Reaver said dryly.

Revenant grinned, flashing fangs as shiny and white as the hair that fell past his shoulders. "I knew you'd appreciate that. But a word of advice. You're only off limits while you're in the human realm. Step into Sheoul, and Satan will want you. Watcher rules or not, I can't disobey his command." He turned to Ares. "Why did you summon me?"

"I asked him to," Reaver said. "I need to know what can stop Satan from starting a war with Heaven."

"The war you put into motion? That one?" Revenant shrugged. "You can't do anything. You fucked up."

Which was why Reaver needed to stop it. And now they had only days to do it.

Ares strode over to the wet bar and poured a shot of whiskey. "Reaver, why the hell would you think Revenant would help you with this?" He held up the bottle. "Anyone?"

Ares must be seriously grateful to Revenant for what he'd recommended to his Watcher Council, because he wasn't usually so free with niceties for the evil Watchers.

"Hells, yeah," Revenant said.

Reaver, to be contrary, turned it down and returned to the subject at hand. "I was hoping he'd want to prevent a battle that could rage on for centuries and destroy both our worlds."

Revenant took a glass from Ares and knocked back half the contents. "Maybe the prospect of war excites me."

"Maybe," Reaver said. "But I've learned enough about demons in my time to know that most of them aren't gung ho for war. They want to live their lives, the same as everyone else."

"I'm not a demon."

Not technically, but sometimes being a demon had more to do with behavior than DNA. Reaver knew a lot of decent demons... and a lot of humans who were far more evil than almost anyone who lived in Sheoul.

"You're a fallen angel who must want to protect someone you cared about in Heaven before you fell," Reaver said.

Revenant shrugged. "If I ever cared about anyone there, I don't remember, so preventing your war is none of my concern."

"You don't remember?" Ares came around the bar with his glass and the bottle of whiskey. "Are you that old?"

"No idea. My memory was taken from me."

And here Reaver thought he was special. "Why? Who'd *you* sleep with?"

"Dunno—" Revenant went taut, as if every muscle had turned to stone, and the glass in his hand shattered. "I... have to go," he rasped.

"Wait." Reaver grasped Revenant's arm, and a sense of familiarity rippled through him, as if a memory was on the verge of coming to life. Had they known each other in the past? "Why did you let me lift the collar key off you?"

Revenant scowled. "I didn't." He leaned and then

righted himself, the unsteady sway of a drunk man. Even his gaze had gone glassy. "I . . . why did I do that?"

Then he was gone, leaving Reaver with more questions than he'd started with.

"That was weird." Ares snapped his fingers at the hellhound who rushed over to see if the broken glass was edible. The beast got a quick lick of whiskey before sullenly slinking away. "Damned mutts will eat anything. Cara is always dealing with grumpy-ass hellhounds and their bellyaches."

"They get grumpier?"

Ares snorted. "You have no idea—"

Suddenly, Ares was armed and armored, and the hellhound that just took off with its tail tucked was back, crouched in the doorway with its hind legs gathered and ready to launch. Reaver wheeled around to come face to face with Gethel's image. Like last time, when she'd appeared at Than's place, she was a phantom, completely protected by the spawn in her belly.

"I'm really getting sick of this new power of yours, Gethel," Ares growled.

"Yes, well, I've been sick of you for decades."

"Why are you here?" Reaver asked, his teeth clenched so hard they hurt. "Or not here."

"I have an offer for Reaver." She stepped closer, her eyes glittering with anticipation, and Reaver knew the offer was going to be a sucky one with a high price. "Arrange for Raphael to meet you at the Dome of the Rock tomorrow at dawn. If you agree, Satan will call off the war."

"What happens to Raphael?"

Gethel's smile was so cold Reaver's spinal fluid froze. "That," she said, "is none of your concern."

"Tell me what Satan wants with him," he shot back, so not in the mood to deal with vague offers and secret agendas.

"Let's just say there's a score to settle."

Man, it was tempting. Raphael had screwed with Reaver's life hard, had forced Harvester to torture him, and had blackmailed her into becoming his mate. Getting that archangel bastard out of the way would be awesome.

But it would also make Reaver a traitor. And as much as he hated Raphael, the archangel *was* an angel, and while Reaver might play fast and loose with Heavenly rules, he would never betray Heaven to Satan.

"Well?" Gethel huffed. "I don't have all day." She cranked her head around in an *Exorcist* move and hissed at Ares. "Keep your mutts back, or I'll burst their skulls like popcorn."

Ares barked out a command, and the five hellhounds that had been stalking Gethel halted midstep. They couldn't harm her, but clearly, Gethel had a thing against hellhounds.

Could she really kill them even if she was no more substantial than a ghost? If so, Lucifer had grown unbelievably strong. Not good.

Gethel jammed her fists on her hips and pivoted back to Reaver. "Your answer, *Fallen*."

She must be loving this, the bitch. "My answer is no."

"Think about this very carefully," she said.

"I did. No."

Her soiled wings shot up from her back, and the hounds growled. "Idiot! You will be condemning Heaven to a war it can't win, which means it will spill over into the human realm." Her wings quivered with her zealous excitement.

"But before any of that happens, you, and everyone you care about, will pay for your foolish choice to not deliver Raphael to the Dark Lord." She spat on the floor, and even though she wasn't physically in the room, her wet spit splattered on the tiles. "You have until dawn."

She disappeared, and Reaver cursed. He was so sick of the games both Heaven and Sheoul played with lives, the way they used loved ones to get what they wanted.

"So what are we going to do?" Ares's gaze was steely, his stance squared and aggressive. He was ready for battle, and Reaver knew the Horseman would fight until his last breath if Reaver asked him to.

"*We* aren't going to do anything." Reaver scrubbed his hand over his face. Fuck, he was screwed. "I started this, and I'll finish it. I can't put anyone else at risk."

Ares came over and laid a big hand on his shoulder. "Don't worry about us. Just don't do anything stupid, like rescuing Harvester and leaving us in the dark about it." Irritation rumbled in Ares's voice, but Reaver didn't regret the choice he'd made to keep the Horsemen safe. "You're our father, and we'll do anything to help you. Especially if it means a chance to feed Gethel to the hellhounds."

Reaver knew that, and he was grateful. But he also didn't see any way for the Horsemen to help. He couldn't hand an archangel over to the forces of evil, but he couldn't risk his family, either.

"Ares!" Clutching a cell phone, Cara ran into the great room, wrapped in a fluffy pink robe, her hair dripping wet. "It's Regan. Than's castle is under attack." The cell buzzed before she could say more. She glanced at it and looked at Reaver. "It's Shade. Underworld General is under siege, too."

Nothing could attack the inside of the hospital, but if the parking lot filled with demons, they could wreak havoc on the outside. Once the structure was compromised, the antiviolence spell would break, and the hospital, which had barely recovered from Pestilence's rampage, would fall.

"Are you going to Than's?" Reaver asked.

Ares threw a gate open. "Yup. Wanna lift?" At Reaver's nod, Ares turned to Cara. "Call Reseph. Send him to UG."

"Call Limos, too." Ares and Cara both gave Reaver looks edged with doubt, but Reaver shook his head. "She's okay."

"Ares." Cara ran over and kissed him, a kiss so full of love that Reaver nearly swayed from the force of it. He thought of Harvester, and how they'd finally found each other...but was it too late?

"Be careful," she said to both of them. "I'll send some hounds."

"If these are Satan's forces, the hounds won't fight," Reaver said.

"I know." Cara patted Ares on his boiled-leather breastplate. "But they'll defend. And they look really scary."

Reaver laughed despite the seriousness of the situation. "They are that."

Ares cast a personal Harrowgate, and with a wave to Cara, Reaver entered with the Horseman...and stepped out into complete chaos.

# Thirty

Reaver stood on the outer wall of Thanatos's keep, looking out at the charred remains of the evil army that had besieged them. The battle had been tough, but brief… which meant this had been a demonstration of intent, rather than a full-scale assault on Reaver's loved ones.

But tough, he knew, was a matter of perspective. With no powers, Reaver had been forced to fight with his hands. He was good at it, more than a match for a similarly sized demon, but… he'd hated the way everyone felt as though they needed to protect him.

He felt like such a failure, unable to contribute much to battle. Even Thanatos's vampire servants had been of more help. Just a day ago Reaver could have crushed any one of them like an insect under his boot.

Now he was the bug waiting for a foot. A foot that was coming for him soon. The attack had made that clear. It had made a lot of things clear, and as he gazed out at the sparse vegetation surrounding the countryside where Thanatos's children would play, Reaver knew what he had to do.

Footsteps approached, and Reaver turned to see Thanatos and Ares top the stone steps that led to the wall walkway. No longer armed, Ares was in the blue board shorts he'd worn at his manor, and Thanatos was in workout pants and a T-shirt. The 3-D tattoos that covered him from chin to toe shimmered on his skin as he walked.

"Got a text from Limos," Than said. "Underworld General is safe. Minor casualties." He smirked. "Eidolon refuses to help the injured enemies. Funny, I'm always torn between wanting to kill that guy and wanting to high-five him."

"I know what you mean," Reaver muttered. "All Sems have that effect."

Than snorted. "I've noticed. Which reminds me that I need to text Wraith and cancel our playdate for the kids today."

Reaver just shook his head. It was so bizarre that Thanatos found the most exasperating of the Sem brothers to be the least annoying. Even more bizarre was hearing the Horseman known as Death talking about playdates.

"Never thought I'd say I was glad to see Harvester show up," Ares said. "Man, she smoked that ice troll."

Reaver tried not to be petty and bitter about the fact that he'd barely been able to make the ice troll flinch.

"Yeah," Than said, "but wasn't that against Watcher rules?"

Reaver glanced down into the courtyard at the troll, which hadn't dissolved into a greasy stain yet. In the human realm all demons that didn't appear human would, upon death, dissappear. But rate of disintegration varied depending on species and where they died.

"She didn't violate Watcher rules," Reaver said. "This wasn't about Horsemen. It was about the conflict between Sheoul and Heaven."

"Exactly." Harvester appeared next to Reaver in a glittering shimmer of light, and instant lust kindled in his groin at the sight of her in a short black leather skirt, a black leather bra top, and thigh-high fuck-me boots. Damn, he was happy that her taste in clothing had survived the transition from fallen angel to angel.

"But I'll still get in trouble." A breeze made her ebony hair swirl around her slender shoulders, and Reaver's fingers flexed with the desire to wrap her silky locks around his hands and hold her for a sensual onslaught. "I'm not supposed to be on the front lines, since I'll be a target for capture or kill."

"Then why are you here?" Ares asked. "It's a foolish risk. You never expose your most important assets to the enemy. That's how wars are lost."

"Foolish?" Harvester cocked a dark eyebrow. "I swore an oath to watch over you. Not to put up with your shit. I'm not evil anymore, but I'm still not nice. Keep that in mind."

Well, *that* wasn't going to help the relationship between Harvester and the Horsemen at all. "He's right," Reaver said before Ares could blow his stack. "You shouldn't have come."

"Would you have come?" she shot back. He didn't need to answer that, and she knew it. "Thought so." She looked past Reaver at Than and Ares. "Boys, can I have a minute with your father?"

Warmth engulfed Reaver at the way she'd said *your father*. His family had begun with one impulsive roll in the grass with a demon, but Reaver couldn't be sorry. The Horsemen's existence had caused countless tragedies and measureless destruction, but angelic intuition told Reaver everything had happened the way it was supposed to.

Than and Ares left, miraculously without an argument, leaving Reaver in the cool Greenland breeze with the female he wanted to prop against the battlements and ravish. The burn of battle still rushed through his veins, heightening his senses and laying a fine line between bloodlust and good old-fashioned sexual lust.

Fuck it. He wasn't an angel anymore, didn't have to play nice. Not that he ever had.

Before Harvester could so much as blink, he lifted her onto a merlon and stepped between her legs to kiss her.

"Now this," she murmured against his mouth, "is the way to come down from a fight."

He couldn't agree more, and while she tore open his jeans, he shoved up her skirt. They didn't waste time with foreplay; this was going to be raw and swift, as much a needed release of tension as a way to mark his female in a way she'd never forget.

Because this would be the last time.

He entered her in a powerful surge that made them both cry out. He didn't pause, didn't let either of them get accustomed to her tightness or his size. There was only a single, driving instinct to possess. As if she felt his desperation, she clung to his neck with her arms and wrapped her legs so tightly around his hips that he couldn't have broken free if he'd wanted to.

He thrust against her, fueled by the way she met every

pump of his hips with a frantic roll of hers. And when she whispered hot, dirty things in his ear, things she wanted to do him and that she wanted him to do to her, he nearly short-circuited with lust. She wanted to do *what* with a pair of stiletto heels? Harvester might have a halo, but dear, sweet Lord, she was no angel in the sack.

Awesome.

Voices drifted from below, but he wouldn't have cared if they were coming from a few feet away. Nothing was stopping him, nothing was getting between him and the female he loved. Not yet. Right now, in this very moment, she was his, and he didn't share.

"Yes," she moaned. "Oh...yes." She wedged her hand between their bodies and cupped his balls. A wicked vibration hummed through his sac and up his shaft, and holy...*damn*, he nearly went over the edge.

"I'm glad," he said between panting breaths, "that you still have that power."

"Oh," she purred, "you haven't seen anything yet."

Groaning, he melded their mouths together as he rocked against her. Sweat broke out all over his body and his pulse drummed loudly in his ears. They were out in the open, in a precarious position and right there for anyone to see, but it was perfect. He had no doubt that no matter where or when he and Harvester made love, it would always be perfect.

Except that it wouldn't happen again.

Harvester clung to him as if she heard his thoughts, her nails digging into his back. Stiffening, she clenched around him and let out a keening cry of sheer pleasure. Her core rippled along his cock as she came, and he was done for.

The orgasm tore him in two. He threw his head back and roared her name, engulfed in an churning maelstrom of ecstasy that went on and on. Harvester came again, arching her spine so violently that she tipped backward, her upper body hanging perilously forty feet above the ground. Panicked even though he knew the fall wouldn't kill her, he gripped her thighs tight as her wings shot out, leaving her supported on a raft of air. He hissed with pleasure, the crazy position forcing him so deep inside her that he swore he felt her soul.

"Mine," he moaned. Another release gathered, his come boiling in his shaft as his balls pulsed, filling her again. "You've always been mine."

Harvester panted through yet another climax, and this time when she finished, she sagged in his arms and let him haul her back up onto the castle wall.

"Oh, Reaver," she whispered against his chest. "Our lives have been so fucked up."

"I'm sorry for everything I did to you as Yenrieth," he murmured into her hair.

"But will you still be sorry if you remember?" She pulled back, creating distance between them he wasn't ready for yet. "You're okay with what you remember so far, but you're still missing so much. What happens if you remember more to hate me for?"

"Is there more?"

"No." Her lips flattened into a thin, grim line. "But with all the blanks filled in, maybe it'll change how you feel."

"I don't see that happening, but if it does, we'll work through it." Shit, now she'd gotten him to talk as if they had a future together.

A wave of doubt came off her, and it occurred to him that even if he'd found a way for them to be together, she'd never fully trust him. Not until he got his memories back and dealt with what he and Verrine had gone through.

But none of that mattered, and reluctantly, he withdrew from Harvester's warm body.

"Reaver?" She jerked her skirt down and watched him with growing alarm. "What is it?"

"Nothing," he lied. "I'm still working on a way for us to be together."

"You need to hurry. I have to go to Raphael in a few hours."

"I know." He cupped her cheek, committing her soft skin to memory. "I know I have no right to ask you this, especially after everything you've done for me already." He inhaled her scent, memorizing that, as well. "But if anything happens to me, I need you to promise to take care of the Horsemen."

"Of course." She frowned. "You know I will."

"And Limos's baby."

She closed her eyes, and when she opened them, they were liquid with unshed tears. "I swear to you, I'll make sure she gets her baby back. But I will hate Raphael forever."

"That," he said, "I can deal with."

The idea that she'd hate Raphael made the fact that she was going to have to have sex with him tolerable. Okay, not tolerable. Not even close. The mere thought made him want to rip the archangel's head off and shove it up a Gerunti demon's slimy ass.

Because the reality was that after Limos's child was restored to her, Harvester wouldn't be off the hook with

Raphael. There was no way the bastard was going to sit idly by and let her get away. He'd gone to extremes to get her. Without Reaver's life to hold over her head, he'd find another way, and Harvester would once again be blackmailed into being with him.

Damn, but he hoped she'd make his life a living hell.

Abruptly, shame washed over him. In the fantasyland of his head, the prospect of her hating Raphael forever was awesome. But Harvester deserved better. She deserved to be happy and to be in love. He'd rather she grew to love Raphael—the fucking bastard—than live for eternity with someone she hated.

And wasn't that just magnanimous as all hell, he thought sourly.

"Why are you asking me this?" Harvester rubbed her face against his palm. "Nothing is going to happen to you. We know Raphael won't kill you—"

"It doesn't matter. He's not going to let you go, and you know it. He'll blackmail you with something else, and you'll be forced to accept his offer."

"I'll find a way out of it," she swore. "I won't stop looking for a way to be free of him."

"You'll have to give your word, Verrine," Reaver said, reminding her of who she was, who she'd always been. "You aren't one to break an oath, and I'd rather see you with him than suffering with a broken promise. It would eat you alive, and you'd grow to resent me."

But would she resent him even if he wasn't around? Because he was going to the Dome of the Rock as scheduled. It just wasn't going to be Raphael who he offered up as a sacrifice.

"Reaver—"

"Shh." He silenced her with a kiss. A kiss he hoped conveyed every soul-deep ounce of his love and respect for her. A kiss good-bye. "I have one last favor to ask," he murmured against her velvet lips.

"Anything," she breathed.

"Go to the Watcher Council." He held her body firmly against his as he stroked the creamy skin of her neck, wishing they could stay like this forever. "Find out what you can about Lorelia's punishment. The Horsemen deserve to know what's going on. She might even be able to tell you if there's a way to restore Limos's baby without Raphael."

It was a bullshit favor, designed to get Harvester out of the way so he could do what he had to do without her interference. Because he had no doubt that if she knew about his plan, if she even *suspected*, she'd try to stop him. And if she enlisted the Horsemen's help to do it, everything Reaver was trying to avoid—death, destruction, and misery—would come to pass.

"I'll go now." She threaded her fingers through his hair, a bittersweet smile curving her lips. "And you?"

"I'm going to meet with the archangels," he lied. "I've been to places in Sheoul no angel has ever gone. I'm hoping I can help them nail Gethel."

She grinned. "And then they'll be so grateful they'll give you your wings back."

Guilt pricked at him for getting her hopes up, but he forced himself to smile. "Exactly."

"Good luck," she said, and for the first time since all of this began, hope made her voice sing and her eyes glitter with optimism. This was the Verrine he remembered, finally breaking through five thousand years of walls.

In a matter of hours, all of that would be snuffed. She'd

be alive and safe, but once again, he'd have disappeared without a word, without explanation.

Reaver's gut slid to his feet. Fuck Satan, because there was no torture the demon could devise that could match the torment Reaver was going to put himself through on his own.

As Harvester dematerialized, Reaver cast one last look around the keep and said a silent good-bye to his family. Then he took a deep, bracing breath and switched into battle mode. There was no turning back.

*Okay, Satan, buddy. Let's do this thing.*

# Thirty-One

~

Reaver stepped out of the Israeli Harrowgate closest to the Dome of the Rock, but the moment his feet hit the ground, he knew something was terribly wrong.

He wasn't at the right place.

He was at Megiddo.

Which meant someone had brought him here. Again. The blood from his wingectomy still stained the ground.

A stab of light blasted the earth in front of him, and suddenly, Metatron was there, all sparkly and glowy, his massive wings stretching impossibly high into the pre-dawn sky.

"Hello, Reaver."

Reaver sighed. "I'm getting tired of you guys jerking me from one place to another. And if you're here to cut off my wings and give me the boot from Heaven, you're too late."

"I'm here because you intend to hand yourself over to Satan in return for peace."

Reaver jerked as if Metatron had reached into his head and yanked his brain out. "I'm not going to ask how you know. I'm going to ask that you don't interfere." He gestured to the land around them. "Though I guess you already have. Can you flash me to the Dome of the Rock? I have only about three minutes before the meeting takes place."

"A meeting where you're supposed to turn over Raphael, yes?"

No use in denying it. "Yes."

"Why did you choose not to do it?"

Reaver crossed his arms over his chest, impatient with this conversation already. He had a sacrifice to go to, and he couldn't be late, seeing how he was going to be the guest of honor.

"Why don't you tell me, since you seem to know everything."

"I want to hear it from you." It was a command, not a suggestion, and Reaver anxiously glanced at the widening sliver of reddish light on the horizon.

*Red in the morning means blood will be flowing.* The ancient angelic weather wisdom was going to be one hundred percent accurate today.

"Because as douchey as Raphael is, he's an angel," Reaver said. "I might not have wings, but I'll never betray Heaven."

Metatron cocked one eyebrow. "You don't consider all your rebellious acts and broken rules to be betrayals?"

Reaver considered his words very carefully, because he'd rather they not be his last. "I've made mistakes. I admit that. But some of the things I did I wouldn't take back. They needed to be done. I can't explain how I knew, just that I did. And nothing I did betrayed Heaven to Sheoul."

"Good answer. Now, what makes you think you'd be an equal exchange for Raphael?"

"Because," Reaver explained, "I'm the angel who is supposed to break the Horsemen's Seals. Satan won't kill me. He'll torture the fuck out of me for eons, but he'll need me alive in order to fulfill the biblical prophecy. He'll probably spend centuries trying to figure out how to use me to make it happen as soon as possible. It'll buy Heaven and Earth a lot more time than if the war starts in a few days, the moment Lucifer is born."

"You realize that when Satan takes you into Sheoul you'll become a fallen angel, right? A True Fallen?"

He shuddered. Becoming a True Fallen was the one thing he swore would never happen to him, the one thing he'd willingly kill himself to prevent. And now, becoming a True Fallen was the one thing he had to do.

"I know."

For some reason, Metatron smiled. "Excellent. But it isn't going to happen. Instead, I'm going to offer you something, but even if you refuse, I won't allow you to give yourself up to Satan. Understood?"

Confused as hell, Reaver stared. "Not really."

"I'll make it simple," Metatron drawled. "Would you like your memory back?"

Reaver blinked. Wasn't sure he heard the archangel right. "I just told you I planned to waltz off to become a fallen angel and Satan's prisoner, and instead you want to give me my memory back?"

Metatron looked up at the heavens, as if seeking answers from above. Which had always seemed so strange to Reaver, since Heaven itself was much like Sheoul—an overlay occupying the same space as the human realm but on a different plane. Angels and human souls crossed over into Heaven. They didn't fly upward to it unless they wanted to cross over in Heaven's airspace.

"You will be given a choice, but first, I'll give you a little about your past that should help you decide."

Finally. After all this time, he was going to learn why his life had been taken away from him. And for the first time, he was actually having second thoughts. What if the truth was so horrible he couldn't handle it?

"But the war—"

Metatron silenced him with a wave of his hand. "This is more important."

More important than a war between Heaven and hell? Holy shit.

"I'm ready," he said, even though he wasn't. Not even close.

"I know you've pieced together your history with Verrine, but she doesn't remember everything either. It's odd that she remembers anything at all, although we've determined that the blood bond with you is the root of that."

"How do you even know about the blood bond?"

"Long story." Metatron started to prowl, his long strides eating up the ground as he strode back and forth, his hands locked behind his back. "Did you know that Radiants are recognized while still in the womb?"

"I'd heard that."

Metatron nodded. "Your mother was an angel named Mariel. She mated with Sandalphon. I assume you knew of this."

"I researched it after I learned the truth of who I was, yes." Reaver narrowed his eyes at the archangel. "The records don't say anything except that Sandalphon was destroyed by Satan's forces, and after Mariel gave birth, she met the same fate."

It was all very odd that their deaths hadn't been chronicled in vivid detail, especially given that one of them, Sandalphon, had been considered a prince among angels. Princes didn't just die and go forgotten.

"The truth about you, and about them, is in a private library to which very few have access."

"Ah. Secrets among angels. Who would have thought," Reaver said dryly.

Metatron pursed his lips, and Reaver prepared to be blasted by some painful angel weapon for his flippant response.

"Unlike most of my brethren, I've always liked your spirit." He jabbed a finger at Reaver. "But be careful how far you push me. I do have limits."

Well, that was a surprise. Reaver would have thought the guy hated him. He inclined his head in a rare, respectful nod.

"Now," Metatron continued, "like I said, Radiants are recognized in the womb, but the moment the baby is born, they are no different than any other angel." He shot Reaver a stern look. "That's important to remember later in the story."

"So that was like foreshadowing in a movie. Gotcha. Committed to memory."

"Your association with demons and humans has made you vexing at times."

"Funny, I tell *them* they're annoying."

Metatron didn't quite roll his eyes, but the desire practically radiated from him. "We sensed a Radiant in your mother's womb."

Reaver's breath caught. "The womb I was in?"

"No, the womb Mickey Mouse was in," Metatron snapped. "Of course the womb you were in. Why else would I be telling you this story?"

Reaver didn't say anything, which was a measure of how hard the news had hit him.

"Your mother was pleased by the news, but she didn't change her habits. As a battle angel, she needed to fight, and Sandalphon remained at her side." Metatron resumed pacing. "But we had a traitor among us, and Satan learned of your mother's pregnancy. He captured her and destroyed your father. We tried to rescue her, but we lost legions of angels in the efforts."

"None of this is in our histories," Reaver said.

"No, it's not. We erased it."

"Wow. You guys are real fucking free with playing with people's memories, aren't you?" *That* earned him a lightning strike that put him on his ass with steam hissing off his skin. He wheezed, and when he finally found his voice, it was as smoky and cooked as his body. "I'm guessing I hit your limit?"

Metatron just smiled. "With all our efforts wasted and many lives lost, it was time for more extreme measures. We were to go to war with Sheoul. But on the eve of battle, Lucifer met with me. Your mother had given birth." He pegged Reaver with a hard stare. "To fraternal twins."

Reaver had been in the process of trying to stand, but at the news, his knees buckled and he went back down. Hard. On his ass.

"Twins?"

Metatron nodded. "They run in the family. These twins were males. But there was no way of knowing which boy was the potential Radiant. Lucifer brought a deal to the table. We would return four very powerful fallen angels we'd captured and agree to never create another *sheoulghul*." He cocked an eyebrow. "*Sheoulghuls* are made from fallen angels. One per fallen. You can see why Satan would want that practice stopped." Reaver could only nod dumbly. He hadn't known how they were made. He'd had two dead fallen angels in his pocket for days. "In trade, they would give us one of the boys and they would keep the other."

Reaver could hardly breathe. So many questions rattled in his skull, but he couldn't speak. He could only listen, and even then, processing all of this was happening far too slowly.

Metatron continued. "Obviously, it was you we got back. Your mother, knowing you would be safe, chose to stay with your brother to protect him. To this day, we have no idea what became of her."

"Who raised me?"

"My mate and I raised you."

*Okaaaay.* Reaver hadn't seen that coming. "Why you?"

"Because," Metatron replied, "Sandalphon was my brother. As I said, twins run in the family."

So Metatron was Reaver's uncle? It was a good thing he was still seated. He should probably just stay that way. He had a feeling the shocks were going to keep knocking him on his ass.

"Did I know about my real parents?"

"You believed my mate and I were your birth parents."

Reaver closed his eyes, trying to find even the smallest sliver of memory to help him sort this all out, but he might as well have been feeling around inside an empty box. "So I didn't know about my brother, either?"

"No." Metatron flared his wings just a little, a sign of his irritation with the matter. "We raised you as a battle angel, suspecting you were the potential Radiant. Your powers, even as a child, were stronger than most fully trained adult battle angels." He smiled fondly. "You were a handful."

Somehow, Reaver wasn't surprised by that.

Metatron took a deep breath, and Reaver braced himself for whatever was coming next. "Your temper was legendary. Let me repeat the handful thing." He shot Reaver an accusing look, as if Reaver could do anything about being a pain in the ass when he was young. "By the time you started battle angel training, we had to curb your powers. Then, when you were taken to Sheoul for your first lesson in fighting in the demon realm, we learned that you had the ability to draw power from evil sources. Again, a talent unique to Radiants. We had to seal it to prevent you from abusing the ability."

Harvester had said she'd noticed something similar. "Sounds a little extreme," Reaver muttered.

He got a full-fledged *you're a dumbass* look from the archangel. "Have you even met yourself?" Metatron sighed. "Things went well until you slept with Lilith. When you learned what you'd done, you went on a bender, destroying every demon you came across, disobeying direct orders, and, in general, being an asshat. Verrine was the sole calming influence on you, but after you learned that she kept the existence of your sons and daughter from you, we lost even that." He blew out a long breath. "Then you met your brother, and that was the beginning of the downward spiral no one could pull you out of."

# Thirty-Two

⌒

Reaver could really use a bottle of tequila right now. Maybe two. He stared at Metatron, the male who had raised him as his own, and then decided he didn't need the alcohol, because his head was already spinning.

"So I met my brother. Did I know he was my brother at the time?"

"No, but he knew you," Metatron said. "He, too, had been raised to think he was an only child. But somehow he learned about you, and he arranged a meeting. We don't know what went down between the two of you, only that your anger was so formidable that you leveled entire cities at the height of your wrath. Your brother, too, was angry, and he barged into Heaven as if he'd lived there all his life."

Reaver frowned. "How could he get in? Fallen angels can't enter Heaven."

"Ah, but think about it. He wasn't fallen. He was a full

angel raised in Sheoul, but the fact that he could also draw power from Sheoul made us suspect that you were both Radiants." Metatron went back to wearing a path in the dirt. "One of the terms in the deal that gave you to us said that what was done to one of you must be done to both, so his ability to draw power from Heaven was sealed... and then we erased you both from all memories."

Reaver's stomach churned. "So he forgot who I was, and I forgot him?"

"Exactly." Metatron's boots hit the hard-packed earth with the force of thunderclaps.

"But why? I get that I deserved punishment, but why the memories?"

Metatron's expression turned sour. "Because people began to talk. They began to suspect the truth, including the fact that one or both of you were potentially Radiants. We learned our lesson with Satan. He was a potential Radiant, but his anger over not being Raised— promoted—to Radiant status filled him with hatred. His hatred leaked out of every pore, and those around him began to resent his power and his potential. Envy is poison for angels, infecting huge populations like decay. We couldn't afford another internal uprising, so we did what we had to do."

Reaver supposed that made sense. "Then what?"

"Angels cannot be *given* the honor of becoming a Radiant; they must earn it. You weren't going to earn it until you learned to control your temper and your powers, and the only way to do that was to give you a clean slate and let you reinvent yourself. We named you Reaver and let you continue on with your life." He shook his head. "You were still a challenge. Maybe even more of one. You were like a dog that doesn't get enough exercise or discipline and turns destructive. There wasn't a rule you didn't break. And when you transferred the Marked Sentinel charm from Serena's mom to Serena thirty years ago, it was the last straw. We took away your wings and once again took your memory, and that of your brother, and you have both lived without memories since. Honestly, we all wrote you off. None of us believed you would earn your way back into Heaven by saving the world with that Seminus demon."

Reaver had offered himself up as a meal to Serena's mate, Wraith, allowing the demon to destroy a fallen angel who was hellbent on opening a portal from Sheoul into Heaven. He hadn't counted on surviving, let alone being raised to full angel status again.

"Bet you didn't believe I'd manage to lose my wings again, either."

Metatron shook his head. "You've always been unpredictable. But now I'm giving you a choice."

"And what is that?"

"Do you want your memory back?"

"Is that really a choice? Because...ah, yeah. Who wouldn't want their memory back?"

"Someone who did terrible things."

Okay, there was that. Reaver was happy with who he was now. He loved his sons, his daughter, his grandchildren—born and unborn. And then there was Harvester. The very thought of her made his heart trip all over itself. Would all of that be ruined if he remembered all his stupid, horrible mistakes? He thought about Reseph, and how happy he'd been before the memories of what he'd done as Pestilence turned him into a tortured, drooling mess. If not for his mate, Jillian, Reseph would probably still be insane.

But Reseph was also making amends. The people Reaver wronged deserved nothing less. Harvester deserved nothing less.

"I want them back."

"And that," Metatron said, "was the right answer. Stand." He made a rising gesture with his hand, and Reaver rose to his feet without any effort of his own. "You, Yenrieth, also called Reaver, for your numerous sacrifices, will be Raised."

A massive stream of light blasted down from the heavens, bathing Reaver in gold. Ecstasy infused every fiber with strength and bliss. He swore he could feel each individual cell in his body come alive, could feel his wings knit back together in a matter of seconds.

The light retreated back into the clouds, and when Reaver took his first breath, it was as if he was no longer breathing air, but power. It detonated inside him, filling him with electric euphoria. He flared his wings and nearly dropped his jaw when he took in their new magnificence. No longer layered with white, sapphire-tipped feathers, they were pure gold, and as he tested their might, golden, glittery dust settled around him.

An echo of awareness tingled deep inside him, familiar and warm. *Harvester.* Damn, he could almost feel what she was feeling. Sense what she was sensing. And right now, she was happy, was with Limos's child. It was as if she were standing right next to him, and his eyes stung with pure, unadulterated joy.

"You are a Radiant," Metatron said softly, and Reaver gasped.

He remembered Metatron. Remembered how the angel had taught him to swim, to heal a rabbit with a broken leg, to fly when Reaver's first feathers grew in. He'd loved the archangel like a father.

Then his memories had been taken, and Reaver had lived for thousands of years seeing Metatron from only a distance, never knowing how important the angel had been to him. Then, thirty years ago, even those memories had been taken, and Reaver didn't lay eyes on Metatron again. Not until Reaver had earned his wings back. His regular wings. Not these golden beauties.

"New memories will come back to you in waves," Metatron said. "Even a Radiant can't handle thousands of years' worth all at once."

"What…" Reaver swallowed a rare lump of emotion. "What does being a Radiant mean?"

"It means there are very few whose powers can match yours, let alone exceed them. Those who can exceed include me, Satan, and God himself."

Reaver could barely catch his breath to speak. "Who can match?"

Metatron's eyebrows shot up. "You know that there must be a balance between Heaven and Sheoul. My equal was Lucifer."

Metatron, as the Lord's right-hand man, had always been in an angelic class by himself. A lightbulb went off in Reaver's head. "That's why Gethel is pregnant. Without your equal, there's an imbalance that needs to be corrected."

"Precisely. We need to prevent his reincarnation for as long as possible to avoid destruction and more demon invasions in Heaven, but eventually, he *will* be reborn or another equally powerful fallen angel will take his place." He looked down, uncharacteristically hesitant. "Balance is important, and part of the deal with Satan when we got you back was that if you were Raised as a Radiant, your brother must be Raised as well, though in Sheoul they call the equivalent a Shadow Angel."

Reaver's mouth went dry. All around, there was a rumble, as if a thunderstorm had started in the bowels of hell and had broken through Earth's crust. Suddenly, something streaked out of the sky and hit the plateau like a bomb. Rock and dirt exploded into the air, and when the dust cleared, the massive form of a dark-haired male crouched in the center of the crater took shape.

"Reaver, meet your brother." Metatron gestured to the male, who unfurled to his full height. "Revenant."

# Thirty-Three

Revenant's presence triggered another memory blast that knocked Reaver backward several steps. Images tore through his head, everything from his childhood with Metatron and Caila to his history with Verrine to his fits of temper that destroyed entire cities. Oh, there were good things, too, like the time he rescued a village from demons who had been bent on eating the town's children.

In fact, there was more good than bad in the massive memory dump. But the bad, especially the things that involved Verrine, ripped his heart in half.

"Reaver." Gripping his head with both hands, Revenant stepped out of the crater. "Fuck . . . Yenrieth . . . I remember you. I remember . . . everything."

So did Reaver. The memories kept coming, and if Revenant's grunts were any indication, it was happening to him, too.

In his head, he saw Revenant standing on a boulder in

a plain brown robe that matched his uneven mop of plain brown hair.

*"Yenrieth." The brown-haired male held out his hand. "Finally we meet."*

*"Finally?"* Reaver ignored the offered hand. *"Who are you?"*

*"I'm Revenant. I'm your twin brother."*

*Yenrieth snorted. "I have no brother."*

*Sadness swam in Revenant's black eyes as he dropped his hand to his side. "Your life is a lie. Just like mine."*

"We met. Here. On this very spot." Reaver took in the landscape, seeing it in a whole new light. "You told me you were my brother, and that everything I'd ever known was a lie." Revenant's words rang in his ears as if they were spoken only moments ago. "You told me our father was dead and that Metatron was really my uncle." He sucked in a sharp breath as he remembered what else Revenant revealed that day.

*"How do you know all of this?" Yenrieth asked. "Who told you?"*

*"Our mother."*

*Yenrieth grappled with his surprise and all the new information as Revenant leaped off the boulder he'd been standing on, his sandals hitting the hard ground with twin slaps of leather on dirt.*

*"Our...mother? You know her?" Yenrieth's heart pounded wildly. "Where is she?"*

*"Dead."*

*Yenrieth hadn't known her, but the fact that now he would never have the chance to meet her left him shattered. If Revenant was telling the truth, Yenrieth's entire life had been a lie, and the people he'd loved, the people*

*he'd believed were his parents, had deceived him since*
*infancy. He had so many questions, but right now, the*
*female who had given birth to him was his only focus.*

"When?"

"Recently."

"How?"

*Revenant met Yenrieth's gaze. "I killed her."*

"You killed our mother," Reaver breathed, the anger
coming back to him as sharp and clear as the memory.

Reaver had already been in a rage after learning what
Verrine had done, and his brother's revelations had tipped
him all the way off the ledge. He'd gone insane, furious at
Revenant for murdering the mother Reaver hadn't even met,
angry at everyone in Heaven for lying to him. Betraying him.

Metatron's head whipped around to Revenant. "You?
*You* killed her?"

Revenant snarled, his raven wings, now marbled with
gold and silver streaks, snapped out to eclipse the rising sun.

"And *you*," he shot back at Metatron. "You left me to
rot in Sheoul, while you took *him*." He jabbed his finger
at Reaver.

"We had no choice," Metatron yelled. "It was one or
neither."

Revenant's hair changed color to match Reaver's as
he ignored Metatron and rounded on Reaver again. "You
didn't give me a chance to tell you about our mother. I
was young and alone, and the very day I learned about
you, I came to you as a brother. But all you saw was an
enemy and a fiend." Revenant's eyes went crimson, and
black veins marbled his skin as he rose off the ground in a
whirlwind of lightning. His voice was a cannon boom that

would have shattered lesser beings' eardrums. "Now that is all you will *ever* see."

Revenant shot into the sky, and when the high cloud layer engulfed him, the heavens churned and blood began to fall as rain.

Metatron ground his teeth, muscles leaping under skin dripping with red. "That could have gone better."

Probably. But right now, worrying about rocky family reunions was the least of Reaver's concerns. Heaven and hell were about to square off for a battle in which no one would win, and the deadline had passed for him to offer himself up to Satan in place of Raphael.

"You said I can go anywhere in Sheoul?"

"Anywhere but Satan's region and any region he's visiting." Metatron reached skyward, and the blood-rain stopped. "You can go places even I can't. But beware, Yenrieth. There are limits to your powers. You can't heal demons anymore. Positive energy from you will harm them. Some species of demons will burn to ash in your very presence. You'll need to spend a month every year in Heaven or you'll lose your most powerful abilities. And Revenant can sense you in Sheoul, as you'll be able to sense him in Heaven. His job will be to keep you away, and he'll have a power advantage on his home turf."

"Will I have an advantage on mine?"

"Yes, but remember, he isn't a fallen angel, so no one else, including archangels, can sense him in Heaven. You'll be our only line of defense should he get in to steal records or assassinate angels...or worse, to open the gates of Heaven to Sheoul from the inside."

The not-so-subtle subtext there was that Reaver needed to not let them down. And he wouldn't.

Overhead, a pitch-black cloud roiled, but instead of pitching thunder and lightning, Reaver heard growls and screams.

"Demons are in Heaven," Metatron barked. "I have to go."

In a flash, Metatron was gone. Reaver stretched his wings and took flight, amazed at the power and grace that flowed through the veins of his new body.

Now it was time to test that power.

He banked a hard right and dove toward Jerusalem and the Dome of the Rock, where demons were spilling from a Harrowgate nearby. Angels soared in from the opposite direction, dozens of them, their hands gripping ancient Heavenly weapons.

With no more than a thought, he burned the first wave of demons to ash on a flyby. Then he took out the second wave, then the third. The other angels didn't even have a chance to fight, but he sensed demons rising from Harrowgates all over the world, and he couldn't stop them all.

Their target wasn't humankind; they were on a mission to destroy Earthly holy places and draw angels from Heaven. Then, after enough angelic blood was spilled, the demons could open a hole in the barrier that separated the Heavenly and Sheoulic realms.

The birth of Lucifer would be the death blow, collapsing sections of Heaven itself and, in turn, demolishing huge expanses of the barrier.

But Lucifer was also the solution to stopping this. Leaving the next wave of demons to the waiting angels, he searched his senses for... there. Harvester was picking up on Lucifer's life force. Quickly, before he lost the signal, he locked onto Harvester's vibe and flashed himself into Sheoul and directly into a region he was sure he'd never been to. Into a palace built of bones and gold, and where the corpses of demons hung in decorative cages from the ceiing.

And there in front of him was Gethel.

She was feeding from an infant werewolf, and if the pile of bodies in the corner was any indication, she wasn't ready to stop sucking blood to feed the unholy spawn in her belly anytime soon.

"*Bitch.*"

With a yelp, she spun around. The baby fell from her hands, tumbling headfirst toward the stone floor. Reaver darted in and snatched the little boy' a mere centimeter from the tiles.

"Reaver," she gasped. "You're a—"

"Yeah," he snarled. "I am."

He blasted her with a bolt of supercharged Heavenly light that enveloped her in blistering acid. She tried to scream, but the light entered her open mouth, scouring away her voice and leaving her nothing to spill but blood.

He dove for her, preparing to snatch her up and whisk her out of Sheoul. But as his fingers brushed the fabric of her gown, what felt like a wrecking ball smashed into him, knocking him into a pillar that broke in half and came down in massive chunks. He shielded the infant against his chest as Revenant nailed him with another invisible ball of pain.

"Oh, brother," Revenant hissed. "We're off to a great sibling rivalry, aren't we?" He sent a fiery streak at Reaver, but Reaver leaped out of its path and returned fire with a blast of razor shards that drilled a dozen holes through Revenant's body.

His brother didn't even blink.

*His job will be to keep you away, and he'll have a power advantage on his home turf.*

No shit, Metatron.

As Revenant came at him with a massive flame-sword, Reaver tucked the infant under his arm and did a midair roll that smashed him into Gethel. She was screaming in silence, her skin so blistered that she was barely recognizable. He grabbed her and flashed to Megiddo, where he dropped her in a pool of the blood-rain Revenant had left behind.

As expected, Brother Dearest arrived a split-second later. "Give her to me."

"Tell your boss that you can have her back if he stops this war and forfeits the souls he wants to claim for breach of contract."

Revenant snorted. "He'll never agree."

"Oh, I think he will." Reaver fed waves of agony into Gethel, waves that also sucked life away. "You know our power. You know I can destroy both Lucifer and Gethel right now."

Revenant's wings flared. "A minor setback. Lucifer will be reborn again."

"But it'll take time," Reaver pointed out. "Finding the right vessel to carry him could take centuries. Psychotic traitor angels willing to give up their lives so they can give birth to Satan's spawn are pretty rare. Even you must know that."

Reaver's scalp prickled and half a dozen archangels, followed by two dozen fallen angels Reaver had never before seen, appeared in a circle around him, Revenant, and Gethel.

Metatron came forward, meeting one of the fallens inside the circle. "Caim." Metatron halted a yard away from the white-haired male. "It's been a long time."

"Not long enough." Caim flashed fangs as long as Reaver's index finger. "Give us our Dark Mother."

Metatron eyed Gethel as she writhed at Reaver's feet. "I don't think so."

Caim's snarl was echoed by the other fallen angels. An ominous tingling sensation whispered across Reaver's skin as the evil angels loaded themselves to the brim with power, readying for a fight.

Reaver snapped his fingers and a bolt of azure lightning scorched the earth mere inches from Caim's feet. Caim leaped backward with a hiss.

"What the fuck." He hurled a ball of fire in response, but Reaver knocked it away with a thought, and the thing fizzled out.

"Call off the demon army," Reaver said. "Then we'll talk."

Caim balled his clawed hands at his sides so fiercely that blood dripped from his palms. "I'll put in a request," he gritted out. "But make your choice, angels. Kill Gethel, and you'll witness a war that will spill into your precious human realm. Give her to us, and we'll stand down."

They'd stand down, but it would be a temporary measure at best. Lucifer's birth would result in Heavenly destruction, and Satan would once again launch an attack.

Either way, Heaven and Earth were going to lose.

*I feel you, Reaver.*

Harvester swallowed at the intense sensation of having Reaver's life force buzzing through her, more powerful and more vibrant than ever before. He was an angel again, of that she was sure. But how?

She pondered the question as she paced outside of Watcher headquarters, waiting to hear the decision regarding Lorelia's punishment. In many ways, she actually felt bad for the female, who had been operating under orders while knowing her actions would get her into trouble.

Harvester had done the same thing when she'd kidnapped Reaver and held him captive at Raphael's command. And Harvester had, indeed, paid the price.

The door opened and Modran, a senior Watcher Councilmember, appeared, his short dark hair partially covered by a brown hooded mantle. It was quite the medieval monk fashion statement.

"Verrine. I wasn't expecting you."

"It's Harvester." She'd been Harvester far longer than she'd been Verrine, and besides, Verrine had been pure and innocent. Harvester could never be Verrine again, and she didn't want to be. She didn't want to be the Harvester she'd been as a fallen angel either, but in time, she hoped to find a nice balance of good and...experience. "I want to know what's happening to Lorelia."

"All you need to know is that we've met with the Sheoulic Watcher Council, and we've agreed on a punishment."

"Does that include punishing Raphael for his role in ripping Limos's baby from her womb?"

Modran's brown eyes went chilly. "Archangel business is none of ours, and I'd suggest you make it none of yours, as well."

Hard to do, considering she was supposed to get naked with an archangel in about ten minutes. "I'll be returning the infant today—"

She broke off with a gasp, her inner Satanic alarm

screeching in her head so forcefully she felt the ground shake.

Lucifer was in the human realm. Which meant Gethel was, too. But how could she feel him so far away?

Unless . . . Reaver. He was with Gethel.

"Ver—ah, Harvester?" Modran glanced nervously around. "What's going on? Did you feel that?"

She blinked. "You felt it, too?"

Before the other angel could answer, the ground shook again, this time hard enough to put a crack in the great support pillar carved with images of famous angels of the past.

Was Gethel in labor? Or was she in another kind of pain? If so, Lucifer would be in agony as well, and the quakes they were experiencing now would be nothing compared to what was coming when he was born.

Harvester swore, which earned her a sharp glare from Modran. She wished she could flash to wherever Gethel was and end her now, but damned Raphael had restricted her movements to Heaven only. It was his way of ensuring she wouldn't see Reaver again until Raphael had bedded her, the bastard.

She had a feeling he knew about her trysts in the Hawaiian pool and on the battlements of Thanatos's castle. Good. She hoped he got an eyeful.

The complex rocked, sending angels streaming out of chambers and running for outside. But one angel was running in.

Michael jogged over to her, looking as frazzled as she'd ever seen him. "Reaver captured Gethel," he said. "We have an opportunity to destroy her, and Lucifer with her. But Reaver is refusing. We need you to talk to him."

"Why would he refuse? And why does he have any say in it? You took his wings."

"Long story," Michael said with an impatient wave of his hand. "As for why he's refusing, we have a choice. War or Heavenly destruction. Apparently, Reaver would rather see Heaven leveled than lose a few humans."

"Of course Reaver would choose the humans. Have you learned nothing about him at all? After everything Heaven has done to him and his family, why would he choose you?"

Michael flared his wings in annoyance. "It doesn't matter. We need to do something. Now. Lucifer will be born fully grown, which is going to magnify the destruction beyond even what we'd initially believed—"

"Wait," Harvester broke in. Gethel had talked about Lucifer being born fully grown, and now something was flitting at the far edges of her mind.

"Harvester?"

"I said wait!" she snapped. Grabbing her head, she paced in a circle, trying to coax the elusive thought into something tangible. "How many fallen angels have been reborn?"

"I don't know," Michael said in a voice overflowing with exasperation. "A hundred, maybe. Why?"

The why didn't matter yet, because Harvester wasn't sure of it herself. "How many have been born fully grown?" And ew. What a mess that would make.

"One." Michael glanced up at a micro-fissure in the gold-flecked ceiling. "Nine hundred years ago. His birth collapsed an entire Heavenly mountain range, and he wasn't a quarter as powerful as Lucifer."

"The mother," Harvester said, excitement building as the thought she'd been chasing started to solidify. "Who was she?"

"A nun," he barked. "*Why?*"

Her breath caught and held. That was it! She knew how to stop the destruction *and* stop the war.

"Michael, you have to cut off Gethel's wings."

He frowned. "Her wings? Why—" His eyes shot wide, and then a broad grin spread across his face. "Of course!" And then Michael, who was known for his aloof nature, hugged her. "If I didn't have a mate, I'd take you right now."

And that was the problem with archangels. They took what they wanted, even if what they wanted didn't want them back.

Michael flashed away, leaving her to answer the new buzz in her head.

Raphael's summons. It was time.

Tel Megiddo had seen more angelic history happen on its earthen mound than any other place on Earth, but Reaver would bet the tension on its hilltop had never been greater than it was at this very moment.

Long, strained minutes passed as the two sides engaged in an epic stare-off. Even the clouds overhead had frozen in place. The only noises were Gethel's agonized bleats and the werewolf cub's whimpers.

Finally, Caim inclined his head in the shallowest of nods as if taking orders from some invisible supervisor. "The demons have retreated. Give us Gethel, and the Dark Lord will let Harvester's rescue slide." He flapped his leathery wings. "But this isn't over. The slightest interference with Sheoul will shatter this fragile truce, and you will know Satan's wrath."

"Blah, blah." Reaver rolled his eyes.

Revenant popped Reaver on the back of the head with a flare of power. "Asshole."

"I can feel the brotherly love radiating from you." Reaver returned the not-so-gentle gesture, except from the front, and Revenant's head snapped back as if he'd been punched.

"Stop it!" Metatron barked. "Reaver, release the traitorous whore."

"No!" Gabriel flashed from the sidelines to the center of the circle. "If we let her go now, we'll never have a shot at her again."

Gabby was right. Satan would ensconce her in his realm where she'd be safe from anyone, including Reaver.

But Reaver was siding with Metatron on this. The fallout, and the damage to Heaven, would rest on his shoulders.

And he was okay with that. If he'd learned anything at all in his long and weird life, it was that if you made a decision, you owned it. Even if it was the wrong decision.

"Wait!" Michael materialized next to Reaver, a set of golden scythes in his hands. Instinctively, Reaver growled. He'd been on the sharp edge of those things twice, and they were a little too close for comfort, even if they wouldn't work on him. He'd turn Michael into sausage if he tried.

Gabriel spun to Michael and gestured to the scythes. "What are you doing with those?"

"Something we should have done a long time ago." Michael turned to Reaver. "It was Harvester's idea."

That was all Michael needed to say. Reaver stepped back from Gethel, and when the fallen angels tried to rush to her, he knocked them back with an invisible barrier formed by his thoughts.

Revenant tackled him like a linebacker, slamming them both into the ground. Pain streaked through Reaver's shoulder, but he healed in a heartbeat and used his freshly healed arm to punch his brother in the face.

Blood spurted from Rev's nose, but as with Reaver, the injury healed instantaneously, disappearing even the blood.

They rolled around on the packed earth, trading punches in a fight that was far more personal than using special powers would have allowed. For all the amazing upgrades they'd been given, there was nothing more satisfying than a good old-fashioned brawl between brothers.

Through the sound of flesh striking flesh, growls, and curses, Reaver heard Gethel scream. Heard the sickening crunch of wings being separated from her body.

And then, as if a veil had been lifted. Revenant was gone. All the fallen angels were gone. Team Evil had collected its prize and left, leaving Reaver with Metatron and his colleagues.

Shaking his head, Reaver cleaned himself of the blood, dirt, and injuries, and came to his feet.

"I'll be damned," Metatron murmured, his gaze fixed on the set of bloody wings lying on the ground, the dull, frayed feathers ruffling in the hot breeze.

"What happened?"

"Harvester figured it out." Michael made the scythes disappear. "Lucifer's birth was all about the vessel. In order to be reborn with even greater powers than he had before, the vessel carrying him needed to be someone pure and holy, but who fell from grace." Everyone gave him blank stares. "Fell from grace," he prompted. "But not *fell from Heaven*."

Of course! Reaver damned near conked himself on the head. "Gethel wasn't fallen, so she still counted as pure and holy despite all her vile actions."

Michael nodded. "Harvester realized that if we gave Gethel an official boot out of Heaven, she would no longer be fit to give birth to a fully formed, adult Lucifer."

"Clever," Metatron mused. "She's still pregnant with Lucifer, but he's been downgraded. We still have time to kill him, but even if we don't, his birth isn't going to cause cataclysmic destruction."

Reaver grinned. "So Harvester stopped the war *and* saved Heaven. Not bad for an angel you all wanted to let rot in Satan's prison."

That earned him a lot of scowls and a few insults, all of which he ignored. The fact that he was more powerful by far than any of them except Metatron made him feel extraordinarily magnanimous.

Michael, who Reaver had always thought was a bit of a dick, strode over. And held out his hand. Wary, Reaver took it, but the archangel merely clasped their hands together as he leaned in.

"I've judged you harshly. Deservedly so," he added. Of course. "But you've proven yourself. You and Harvester are meant for each other." His voice dipped low. "You should hurry."

Reaver's breath clogged in his throat. Harvester was with Raphael. Right now. Was it too late?

Heart pounding, Reaver spread his wings. "I'm out of here. Send me your thanks for grabbing Gethel and helping to end the war later."

"You started it, you arrogant ass!" Uriel shouted.

"Right. Forgot." Reaver shrugged. "You never thanked me for the last time. I'll take your apologies later."

He left them open-mouthed and fury-faced. All except Metatron, whose laughter followed Reaver all the way to Heaven.

# Thirty-Four

⌒

Harvester once again entered Raphael's home high in the Covenant mountains that stretched across the endless outer regions of Heaven. It always surprised newcomers that Heaven wasn't composed of clouds and golden gates. It resembled Earth. Except cleaner. With no biting insects, venomous reptiles, or allergy-inducing pollen. And even in the snow and the desert, there was no uncomfortable cold or heat.

He was waiting for her in the bedroom.

Stomach churning, she walked inside.

"Look at you," he said. "How many layers of clothing do you have on?"

About a million. She'd taken her time getting ready for this, which included crying, showering, and crying some more. Getting dressed had been a major ordeal, but she had to admit that she'd smiled when she'd put on the ugly pink underwear and bra Reaver had gotten for her. It would be a silent defiance, but she'd love that Raphael would be forced to remove something that belonged to Reaver.

Leggings and a tank top had followed, then sweats, then a robe. But with the way Raphael was undressing her with his eyes, she wished she'd put on armor, too. And a chastity belt.

The cock-severing chastity belt Limos had been forced to wear when she'd been betrothed to Satan would be perfect.

For his part, Raphael was wearing only a pair of crimson silk lounge pants, and she had a sneaky suspicion he was commando underneath.

"Let's just do this," she ground out.

"So eager." He smiled, but it wasn't a nice one. "I'd think you'd be worn out from your earlier activities with Reaver." He moved toward her, his predatory intent clear. "That ends now. If he so much as kisses you, I'll destroy him."

She hissed. "I'm coming to you because we had a bargain, and this is for Limos. But if you ever lay finger on Reaver, know that you will have to take me by force for the rest of my life."

Reaching out, he hooked his arm around her waist and tugged her against him. "Oh, I don't think so." He nuzzled her ear, and it took everything she had to not recoil. "Once you've had me, you'll beg to join me in my bed."

What. A. Douche. "My loins are aquiver with anticipation."

His tongue traced the shell of her ear as he guided them toward the massive bed in the center of the room. With every step, her heart sank and her gut twisted, and a bleak, wintery feeling washed through her.

Over the thousands of years she'd been a fallen angel, she'd had to bed some extremely unpleasant males, and she'd learned to cope, usually by playing a role that allowed her to separate herself from her actions. But she couldn't do that with Raphael. She didn't think she could ever do it again.

Not when Reaver was the one on her mind and in her heart. Just like when she'd lost her wings, she knew this had to happen. But it felt like the worst betrayal she could imagine, and she wondered what would be left of her when it was done.

Raphael's hand slipped between them to cup her breast, and a sob wedged in her throat. Panic closed around her like shrink-wrap. Blindly, without thinking, she shoved against him with all her strength. He released her and she stumbled backward, her breaths coming in ragged gulps.

Anger twisted Raphael's beautiful face into something dark and terrible. "How could you have lain with demons and animals, and yet, you find me repulsive?"

Animals? He thought she'd slept with animals? It took her a moment of thinking through her panic attack to realize he meant shapeshifters and weres. Angels had never considered human-animal hybrids to be anything other than abominations.

"I find you repulsive," she ground out, "because you're holding lives over my head."

He snorted. "And no demon has ever done that to you?"

"Of course they have," she shot back. "But they're *demons*. It's what they do. You?" She looked at him with loathing. "You think you're superior, but ultimately, you're worse. I don't know what happened to you while I was gone, but you're not the male I remember." She moved closer to him, not wanting to miss every emotion play out on his handsome face. *"I've fucked demons who were less disgusting than you."*

*Thank you for that one, Yenrieth.*

Raphael's fury rose up, becoming a tangible storm in the room. Electricity sizzled on the surface of his skin, little streaks of lightning that made him glow like someone had plugged him into a wall outlet.

*"You* are what happened." His voice warped with the force of his anger, and an icy tremor of fear rippled down her spine. "You should have been mine a long time ago."

Damn, she'd screwed up by taunting him. This wasn't about her, and she needed to remember that. This was about keeping a promise and giving Limos back her baby.

*Suck it up. Apologize. Give him the best damned night of his life, even if you have to throw up afterward.*

"I'm sorry." Her voice was halting, stale. Apologies had never been something she'd offered easily, and if she'd said those two words more than a dozen times in the last five thousand years, she'd be shocked. "I'm just... nervous." She fluttered her eyelashes and played contrite and cowed.

His expression softened. "Understandable. It's your first time with an archangel."

Oh, gag. How could he walk around with a head that big and not lose his balance? "Yes." She forced a smile. "That's it."

He returned the smile. "Come here." When she hesitated, only for a heartbeat, he repeated his command, but this time with a sharp edge. "Come. Here." He snapped his fingers, and suddenly, she was standing in front of him.

Wearing only her bra and underwear.

Closing his eyes, he inhaled. A rumble came up from his chest, and he lifted his lids. The crystal blue of his eyes was stained by angry crimson flecks.

"I can smell him on you."

"Not *on* me." She lifted chin and met his gaze with defiance that flew in the face of the apology she'd just offered. But dammit, she wasn't going to apologize for being with Reaver. "*In* me."

"I will erase him." The dark, dangerous tone in his voice accompanied a menacing step into her.

His intent was clear, and she felt herself slide into acceptance. This was it. She'd given herself over to Sheoul once, knowing she was condemning herself to an eternity of absolute hell.

Somehow, this was harder.

Raphael wrapped his fist in her hair and yanked her head back. She closed her eyes so he wouldn't see how much she despised him as he slanted his mouth over hers.

"*Raphael.*" The impossibly deep voice rattled the entire room and made every organ in Harvester's body quiver with raw terror. "Release her. *Now.*"

An invisible, electric force pulled them apart. Raphael flew backward, crashing into a marble table that held what was likely a priceless Chinese vase.

Priceless before it shattered on the floor.

Harvester spun toward the newcomer, her initial terror turning to shock at the sight of the male filling the room with the sheer force of his presence.

"R-Reaver?"

He sauntered over to Raphael, who was sitting, stunned, in the splintered remains of his vase. Power, as potent as the sun, radiated from Reaver. With a flick of one finger, he lifted Raphael off the ground and suspended him in the air.

"I could have handed you over to Satan." Reaver flared his wings, and Harvester gaped. Gold. They were . . . gold. Never before had she seen such a thing, but she knew angelic history the same as everyone else.

Only Radiants possessed gold wings.

Dark spots appeared before her eyes, and she swayed. In an instant, Reaver caught her, lifting her into his arms and holding her protectively against him. Still, his gaze was locked on Raphael.

"Obviously," he told Raphael, "I didn't betray you."

Raphael swallowed, and the sound echoed as if they were in a canyon. "I didn't destroy you. I could have, but I didn't."

"Actually," Reaver drawled, "you couldn't have. But that's not important. What's important is that I *can* destroy you. It would be wise to keep that in mind." Very gently, Reaver put Harvester down and eyed her clothing. Or lack thereof. "You're wearing my lingerie for him?"

She shrugged. "I believe in subtle protests."

His lips twitched. "You've never been subtle in your life."

"Yes, well—" She broke off with a gasp. "You have your memory back."

"I do. I'm not sure it's a good thing, but it gives me a starting point for making amends. To you, especially."

He waved his hand, and suddenly she was clad in a slinky black dress and knee-high leather boots. A sensual breeze blew up her skirt and between her thighs, and wow, the naughty boy had outfitted her with crotchless underwear as well.

"That's better," Reaver said. He turned to Raphael. "As for you, I don't owe you jack shit. But I'll be the bigger angel and forgive you for having me tortured. I'll also give you the courtesy of a warning." Raphael dropped to the ground in an ungainly heap. "Touch Harvester again, and I'll castrate you. She's mine. She can't break the deal she made with you, but I can."

Harvester's heart soared. Reaver had offered to castrate an archangel for her. How sweet was that? As Yenrieth he'd only brought her flowers and honey cakes. Oh, yes, she liked the way Reaver rolled.

Raphael settled himself on his knees and bowed his head. "She's yours."

"Yes," Reaver said roughly, as he hooked her around the waist and tugged her close. "She is."

⌐

Reaver flashed Harvester from Raphael's obnoxiously opulent mansion to Limos's place, popping right into the living room. They didn't have much time to spare, and he wasn't going to waste a second. Harvester had a million questions, he knew, but they'd have to wait. After they were done here, he'd explain everything.

And then he'd make love to her for a solid month.

Arik padded out of the kitchen, a platter of sandwiches in one hand, a TV remote in the other.

"Jesus Christ!" He nearly jumped out of his skin at the sight of Reaver and Harvester in the living room. The sandwiches flipped into the air, but with his super-duper mind powers, Reaver caught them and plopped the plate onto the coffee table.

This Radiant thing was so cool.

Apparently, Arik wasn't as impressed. He rounded on them, one hand clutching his chest. "What the hell? Are you trying to give me a fucking heart attack?"

"I could fix it if you had one," Reaver said. Yup, *so* cool.

"I've always said angels were assholes," Arik muttered.

Limos darted into the room, clad in her samurai armor and wielding a katana. When she saw Reaver and Harvester, she grinned and put away her blade.

"I knew it!" she said. "Ares and Than were all, 'Dad is acting funny. I think he's going to do something crazy.' But I knew you wouldn't leave us again. Reseph did, too."

*Dad.* The word melted him on the inside. Oh, he knew she wasn't telling the story right; Ares and Than would have called him Reaver. But Limos had made the switch, and he knew she wasn't going back.

That was even cooler than the Radiant thing.

"I never wanted to leave you," he said, leaving it at that. He gestured to Harvester. "Harvester has something for you."

Limos loved presents, and behind the lingering sorrow in her eyes, a spark lit. "What is it?"

Harvester held out her hand. "Come here."

Thousands of years of distrust sat heavily in the space between them, and Limos hesitated. Reaver didn't blame her for that, and when she shot him a questioning glance, he nodded, hoping this would be the first step toward a fresh start.

Warily, Limos lay her palm in Harvester's. Reaver took Limos's other hand and summoned his power.

Worry etched deep lines in Arik's face as he moved behind Limos and gripped her shoulders protectively. "What's going on?"

"Shh." Harvester produced a cloudy marble and very gently pressed it against Limos's abdomen. "Close your eyes."

A low-pitched hum filled the room, and Reaver's energy flowed in a hot stream into Limos, where it twined with Harvester's into a massive, undulating ribbon of power. The life Harvester had been carrying in the little marble settled inside Limos's womb, and under Harvester's hand, Limos's belly began to swell.

Harvester smiled, her genuine delight in returning Limos and Arik's child to them radiating in an angelic aura all around her. It was just as he remembered her so long ago, and his heart tripped all over itself.

As if she knew he was watching, she cut him a glance that was *nothing* like he remembered from Verrine. No, the wicked gleam in Harvester's eyes promised the exact opposite of *angelic*, and he flushed hot. He couldn't wait to get her alone. Couldn't wait to start making up for five thousand years apart.

Limos gasped as Harvester cut off her power and stepped back. "Do you want to know if it's a girl or a boy?"

Arik, looking poleaxed, stared at Limos, who was staring at her belly. "What just happened?"

"Your baby didn't die when Lorelia punished Limos," Harvester explained. "She stole it as part of a plan to destroy Lucifer. Only a Watcher could replace it, and only with a very powerful angel's help. So...you have your baby back—*oof*!"

Harvester broke off as Limos tackled her in a huge hug. "Thank you, thank you...oh my god, thank you!" Limos hit Reaver next, throwing herself into his arms and squeezing the breath out of him. Arik got the final embrace, knocking him off his feet so the two of them tumbled onto the couch in a tangle of limbs, laughter, and kisses.

"I think it's time for us to go," Harvester murmured.

"Hell, no!" Limos popped up, but she didn't release Arik. "We'll call my brothers and all our friends and have a big fucking party."

"Maybe," Reaver suggested, as he turned to Harvester and took her hand, "we could make it a mating ceremony, too."

Harvester inhaled sharply. "I . . . ah . . ."

Ah, damn. Reaver might be a gazillion years old, but he hadn't learned a thing about females in all that time, had he?

"Wait," he blurted. "Don't say anything. Hear me out." He sucked in a bracing breath and went for it. "I remember me. And you. I remember *us*." Closing his eyes, he took himself back in time, to a place where he and Verrine had shared their first kiss. "I wanted you, but I wasn't ready for you. I was young, impulsive. Full of piss and vinegar and way too much power." Metatron had been right to seal his abilities. Reaver had been irresponsible and indestructible, and eventually, he'd have become corrupted by his own arrogance.

He opened his eyes and caught Limos and Arik trying to make a silent getaway. "No," he said. "Stay. You should hear this, too."

Arik looked like he wanted to get the hell out of there, like he'd walked in on something intimate he shouldn't see or hear, but Limos perked up.

"I remember being with Lilith and how stupid I

felt later when I learned she was a succubus. My pride wouldn't let me let it go." He took Harvester's hand. "I neglected you and our friendship for decades. While you were out scouring the globe for my children, I was too self-absorbed to notice how busy you were." His heart pounded as the worst time of his life rolled through his head in a wave of fresh images. "Heaven was abuzz about these three men and a woman who were marshaling armies of humans together to destroy demons. It was the biggest thing to happen since Satan's rebellion. When I learned that those four people were my children and that you knew all along . . ."

"I know." Her nails dug into his palms. "You don't have to say anything more."

"I do," he insisted. "I do and you know it." He blew out a breath, ready to spill the rest, even if it cost him the female he loved. "I hated you. I hated you more than I hated Lilith."

But even though he'd been out of his mind with rage, the thought of killing her hadn't occurred to him. On some level, he'd still wanted her, even if he'd also wanted to hurt her the way she'd hurt him.

"So I told you I'd forgiven you, and I seduced you." Crushing pain compressed his chest, the weight of a lifetime of shame.

*Heavenly sunlight shone down into Verrine's frilly, open-air bedroom, warming Yenrieth's back as he panted through an orgasm he'd tried to hold back. Verrine had screamed or moaned through at least three, which had been the plan. His climax had not been in the plan, and his anger scorched his throat with every breath.*

*The instant it was over, he rolled off her, leaving her in a messy sprawl on her bed. He dressed while she watched him with drowsy eyes. When she sat up and discovered the blood on the sheets, she scrambled to hide it, and her embarrassment.*

*"What's the matter?" he asked. "Ashamed?"*

*"No." She wrapped a blanket around her naked body. "Of course not."*

*Ice filled the hole she'd drilled in his heart with her lies. "You should be."*

*She blinked, her emerald eyes shifting from drowsy to confused. "W-what?"*

*"Virginity isn't something to be given over lightly."*

*"You think I did this lightly?" She tugged the blanket more securely around her, as if the cold in his body was radiating outward. Maybe it was. "I've wanted you for decades. I saved myself for you."*

*"You shouldn't have." He leaned in close, taking pleasure in how quickly she paled. "I despise you." Snarling, he ripped the blanket away and left her exposed and vulnerable, the way she'd left him when she'd admitted to knowing about his children. "You took my sons and daughter away from me, so I took something from you."*

*Her mouth worked silently. "I—I... Yenrieth, we've been over this. I thought you understood. I did it for you."*

*"You did it for me? You kept my children away from me for decades to what? To help me?" His voice was at a low roar now, and all around him, the building trembled. "They grew up without me! Limos was raised in hell, Reseph was raised by a wench who is undeserving of raising a puppy, let alone a child, and Ares was beaten until he lost all compassion.* Because of you.*"*

*Tears spilled down her cheeks as she grabbed for*

*him, but he stepped aside, unable to bear her touch. Just looking at her was hard enough. "Please...you have to understand—"*

*"Understand?" he bellowed. "Understand this, Verrine. I've fucked demons who were less disgusting than you."*

The memory knocked Reaver back a step, made him wobble, and Harvester caught him. She'd always caught him. He'd just been too much of an asshole to realize it.

"I'm sorry, Verrine," he whispered. He knew it was Harvester in front of him and not the innocent young angel she used to be. But he'd never apologized to that trusting angel. And after what he'd just remembered, he knew no apology would be enough. "I'm so sorry. You didn't deserve that. Yenrieth was a dick. I was a dick. I don't deserve you, and if you can't accept my apology, I understand. But I'll never stop trying to make it up to you."

"I forgive you." Harvester's voice cracked. "And I should have told you about your children."

"No." He shook his head. "No, you were right not to. We can play the what-if game for a century, but what it comes down to is that we can't know what would have happened if you had. But I can almost guarantee that it wouldn't have been anything good. You did what you thought was right, and that's all that matters. You were right. I was wrong. So very wrong."

"So," she said, in a voice that was as shaky as his emotions, "you're saying you remember everything, and you're still sorry, and you still want to have a mating ceremony?"

With all his heart. "If you'll have me. Someday when

you're ready. *If* you're ready. I'll always be here for you. I'll wait as long as it takes." He locked his eyes with hers. "You were *always* the one."

For several agonizing moments, Harvester said nothing, and Reaver began to sweat. He might be one of the most powerful beings in existence, but all the power in the universe wouldn't make Harvester budge if she didn't want to do something. Like mate him.

Finally, Harvester lifted her chin in that muley way that drove him mad. "I'm not getting mated in any absurd formal angel ceremony."

He suppressed a smile. "I'm fine with that."

She sniffed. "And I won't wear a ridiculous gown."

"Agreed." She'd be about as comfortable in a gown as a nun would be in a brothel.

Harvester, who had always loved torturing him, wound her long hair around her finger and made a long production out of studying the seashell paintings on the walls.

"Harvester..." At his growl she smiled, and then she was on him, throwing her arms around his neck and hanging on for dear life.

"I hope you know what you're getting into," she murmured in his ear. "I love you, Reaver, but if you piss me off, remember that I can chain you with your own bones."

Damn, that was sexy. Oh, at the time when she'd actually done that to him, it had hurt like hell. But he loved that her shiny new halo hadn't crushed her horns.

"I'll keep that in mind." He lowered his voice to a whisper. "But you should keep in mind that with my new powers I can fuck you until you pass out, and I don't even have to be in the same room."

To prove his point, he sent a stroke of sensation between

her legs. All he had to do was think about what he wanted to do, and she'd feel it as if he were there with his hands, his tongue, his cock. He imagined licking her from her clit to her core before thrusting his tongue deep, and she had to bite into his shoulder to keep from crying out.

"That," she breathed, "was evil. Do it again."

He laughed. "Later. I promise."

They pulled apart, their secret smiles and her passion-glazed eyes sure to give them away, but Limos and Arik were too busy texting—presumably their brothers, sisters, and in-laws.

"Yay!" Limos tossed aside her phone and called for one of her servants to bring Champagne. "You know, Harvester, I kind of hated you before. You were such a bitch." Limos wasn't exactly known for her tact. She looked down at her belly, her expression steeped in con-templation. "But I know what it's like to live in Sheoul. I know what it does to you. And I know that if it hadn't been for you, I wouldn't have been able to get out of my betrothal with Satan." She looked up, her eyes glisten-ing with happy tears. "So even if you hadn't given me my baby, I'd still welcome you to the family."

Harvester gave Limos a hug—brief and awkward, but Reaver had a feeling it was the first time she'd initiated an embrace since she'd been a young angel.

"Thank you, Limos." Stepping back, Harvester cleared her throat of an emotional hitch and glanced down at Limos's newly restored baby bump. "Do you want to know? Boy or girl?"

Limos and Arik exchanged glances, and then they both shook their heads.

"We'll wait. You can taunt me for the next few months."

Harvester snorted. "You really do know me."

Limos scanned Harvester from head to toe as if deciding how true Harvester's observation was. "It's going to be weird having you be our Heavenly Watcher after centuries of being our Sheoulic one."

"Speaking of your Sheoulic Watcher," Reaver said, taking Harvester's hand, "you should probably know that Revenant is my evil twin brother."

"*What?*" The question came as a chorus from Arik, Harvester, and Limos.

"Yeah. Long story. I'll tell you all over margaritas." Reaver grinned. "Let's get this party started."

# Thirty-Five

⌒

The sunset ceremony, performed by Idess on the beach outside Limos's house, was perfect. Harvester had never been into "girly wedding dresses and crap," so she wore a slinky black and white—the white part at Limos's insistence—sundress with stiletto-heeled black boots that Reaver wanted her to wear later.

"Just the boots," he'd whispered into her ear.

"What about the garter," she whispered back, and he'd groaned. "That can stay."

And just for him, she'd worn skimpy hot pink panties under the dress. He was going to eat them off of her.

Now the Horsemen and their families were partying into the night with the Underworld General crew. Hellhounds patrolled the perimeter, although Cara's hound, Hal, and Thanatos and Regan's son's pup, Cujo, were in the center of the action and creating trouble, as usual. Currently, Cujo was playing keep away with the pit-roasted pig's head while Hal chased after, knocking over people, tables, and chairs.

The Horsemen had all taken an opportunity to welcome Harvester to the family—even Thanatos, who had more reason than any of them to harbor a grudge. Reaver suspected it would be a while before he trusted Harvester completely, but she was okay with that.

Reaver watched her from the deck, where he'd come to check on Tavin. Earlier, Harvester had confirmed Blaspheme's theory that the symbol was an ancient fallen angel assassination curse, and now that Reaver knew the truth about himself, he understood why he'd been able to conjure a fallen angel curse. As a Radiant, he possessed both angel and fallen angel powers, so even though he hadn't been Raised at the time, the ability had been inside him and released thanks to the *lasher* implants.

Not that the reason for Reaver's ability to create an ancient assassination symbol meant anything to Tavin. It wasn't all bad news, though. According to Harvester, the snake curse had to be programmed to kill at a specific time.

"No program, no kill," she'd said. "You should be safe."

"*Bullshit. The fucker* is *trying to kill me,*" Tavin ground out.

"*That's because you haven't made friends with it.*"

*Tavin swore.* "*How the fuck am I supposed to make friends with an assassination snake that's permanently attached to me?*"

"*I have no idea,*" Harvester said. "*Good luck. I have to go get mated now.*"

Getting her angel wings back hadn't changed Harvester's personality much. And Reaver was fine with that. She wouldn't be the same frustrating, bold, sexy angel if it had.

She'd left Tavin to hang out with his brothers, who were all surveying the female guests and calculating their odds of getting laid.

Too bad Tav was still pissed about the whole "ruining his life" thing, and he'd let Reaver in on that fact by punching him in the face. The dude hadn't even cared that Reaver could destroy him with a mere thought.

Seminus demons were seriously the most obnoxious species of demon *ever*.

Reaver made an attempt to repair the damage he'd done, but it turned out that Metatron was right, and he couldn't channel any kind of positive energy into the demon. In fact, when he tried, Tavin had screamed in agony and the snake had bitten into his throat. Reaver had been forced to fork the serpent in the eye to make it let go.

Tavin punched Reaver again and muttered something about trying to tame a pissed-off fork-faced snake.

You couldn't please some demons.

But Reaver would make it a priority to help the guy. Without him, Reaver never would have been able to rescue Harvester. They both owed him their lives.

As if she heard his thoughts, Harvester looked over her shoulder at him, her ebony hair cascading over breasts he couldn't wait to have all to himself very soon. Maybe now, if the naughty glint in her eyes was telling him something.

He was about to kidnap her for a quick repeat of the pool incident when Eidolon came over and clapped him on the shoulder. The clap was followed by a hiss and an abrupt step back.

"Damn," he said, shaking out his hand. "Angels give me the willies. And you're an angel on steroids now. Reaver 2.0."

"Wraith called me Angelicus Prime. I'm not sure if that's an insult or not."

E laughed. "It's from Wraith and Stewie's current obsession with the Transformers."

"Ah."

Eidolon gazed out at the cast and crew of one of the strangest and most amazing episodes in Reaver's life. "It's kind of crazy how everything has worked out, isn't it? When I first met you, you were angling to get your wings back, and I was up to my eyeballs dealing with two brothers who couldn't have been more messed up."

Yeah, Reaver could now relate to the messed up brother thing, and the strangest part was that he wasn't reeling in surprise over it. Or over anything Metatron had told him. Once his memories had been restored and after the initial shock of each memory's revelation, it was as if they'd always been with him. As if he'd always known that during the five thousand years Harvester was in Sheoul he'd been assigned to odd jobs around Heaven. As if he'd always known Harvester liked to swim in the nude—because he'd spied on her when she was Verrine. As if he'd always known he had a brother.

But where did they go from here? How did he deal with an evil brother who clearly hated him? He'd have to ask Eidolon how he'd done it someday.

"We've come a long way," Reaver agreed.

"I can't believe we're all mated now." Eidolon grinned, and Reaver went on alert. That was E's evil grin. "Which means you have to tattoo my caduceus on your ass."

Reaver groaned. "You're going to hold me to that, aren't you?"

Eidolon shrugged. "Tell you what. Get it anywhere you want. I'm generous that way." Near the surf, Tayla held up their son, Sabre, and waved his little hand at Eidolon. E waved back, a fiercely proud smile on his face. "So... now that you're all Angelicus Primed, will we still see you?"

Reaver scowled. "Are you taking back your job offer?"

A volleyball came at them, and E batted it back to Wraith and Than, who were having a one-on-one no one seemed to be winning.

"I assumed you'd have other duties. And angels can't enter the hospital."

Reaver grinned. "I can enter anywhere I damned well please. That's the thing about this Radiant gig. I can do whatever I want."

Eidolon raised a skeptical eyebrow. "And what you want is to work at a demon hospital?"

Yeah, Reaver was surprised by that, too. He turned to the doctor, propping his hip against the deck railing. "When I lost my wings again, I thought I'd be miserable. But the screwed-up thing was that I was actually kind of relieved." He'd loved the power that went with being an angel, but not the regiment. He'd liked the responsibility, but not the rules.

"But when you were fallen the first time, all you wanted was to get your wings back."

"I did," he said. "But after I got them back, I realized I missed healing." He smirked. "Even if it was demons."

"Aw, I've missed your backhanded compliments," Eidolon drawled.

Reaver laughed. "So? What do you say? My angel duties are light. I pretty much exist to put down huge demon problems and counter everything Revenant does, so as long as things stay calm, I'll need something to do. I can't use my powers to heal demons, but I'm a damned good doctor, and you know it."

"Fine. Get the tat and report for duty next week." Eidolon glanced over at Harvester, who had kicked off her boots and was walking toward them, her gaze locked on Reaver and promising very, very bad things. "Or, you know, when you're done with the honeymoon."

"That might be a while." Reaver's focus narrowed on the female coming at him, her stride purposeful, predatory, and his body hardened. "A long while."

Unable to stand another second without Harvester, he gave Eidolon a "see ya," and flashed to her, scooped her up before she could blink, and flashed them both to the jungle pool. Shifting to wrap her legs around his waist, she brought her mouth down on his. She kissed him passionately, her tongue sweeping his mouth and sliding against his, making him groan with need.

"We can go someplace else if you want," he murmured against her lips.

"Can't wait." She rolled her hips against his erection, and he hissed at the intense friction.

"Agreed." He left her lips to kiss his way to her neck, loving how she arched back to allow him more access. "We've waited too long as it is." He drew back, pausing things for just a moment, because this was too important to ignore. "I didn't realize it, but I've been looking for you for five thousand years."

Harvester's eyes shimmered wetly, like dew clinging to meadow grass. "And I've been waiting for you for five thousand years."

"No more waiting or looking," he whispered.

"No more," she agreed. "But there's still the little matter of our deal."

"You released me from that."

"I changed my mind." She shrugged. "I decided that what we did in Sheoul doesn't count. I want my twenty-four hours of pleasure."

"Do you," he mused. "Hmm. I guess I can do that. You know, if I have to."

"You have to." She playfully dragged her finger down his chest. "And remember how I said I appreciate a talented tongue?"

Heat flooded him, and it took every ounce of self-control to not drop her to the ground and take her right that second. "I remember." His voice was a ragged croak.

"Good. Let's put that tongue to use."

Grinning, he dropped her to the ground and did just that. With his new powers.

Yep, this Radiant thing was *very* cool. Reaver couldn't wait to explore all his new upgrades.

But what he wanted to explore the most was Harvester. And he had an eternity to do it.

# One

Revenant was one fucked-up fallen angel.

No, wait…*angel*. He'd only *believed* he was a fallen angel.

For five thousand fucking years.

But he wasn't an angel, either. Maybe technically, but how could someone born and raised in Sheoul, the demon realm some humans called hell, be considered a holy-rolling, shiny-haloed angel? He might have a halo, but the shine was long gone, tarnished since his first taste of mother's milk, mixed with demon blood, when he was only hours old.

*Five thousand fucking years.*

It had been two weeks since he'd learned the truth and the memories that had been taken away from him were returned. Now he remembered everything that had happened over the centuries.

He'd been a bad, bad angel. Or a very, very good fallen angel, depending on how you looked at it.

Toxic anger rushed through his veins as he paced the parking lot outside Underworld General Hospital. Maybe the doctors inside had some kind of magical drug that could take his memories away again. Life had been way easier when he'd believed he was pure evil, a fallen angel with no redeeming qualities.

Okay, he probably still didn't have any redeeming qualities, but now, what he did have were conflicted feelings. Questions. A twin brother who couldn't be more opposite of him.

With a vicious snarl, he strode toward the entrance to the emergency department, determined to find a certain False Angel doctor he was sure could help him forget the last five thousand years, if only for a couple of hours.

The sliding glass doors swished open, and the very female he'd come for sauntered out, her blue-and-yellow-duckie-spotted scrubs clinging to a killer body. Instant lust fired in his loins, and fuck yeah, screw the drugs, she was exactly what the doctor ordered.

*Take her twice and call me in the morning.*

He watched her long legs eat up the asphalt as she walked, and he imagined them wrapped around his waist as he pounded into her. The closer she got, the harder his body got, and he cursed with disappointment when she dropped her keys and had to stop to pick them up. Then he decided she could drop her keychain as often as she wanted to, because he got a fucking primo view of her deep cleavage when her top gaped open as she bent over.

She straightened, looped the keychain around her finger, and started toward him again, humming a Duran Duran song.

"Blaspheme." He stepped out from between two black ambulances, blocking her path.

She jumped, a startled gasp escaping full crimson lips made to propel a male to ecstasy. "Revenant." Her gaze darted to the hospital doors, and he got the impression she was plotting her escape route. How cute that she thought she could get away from him. "What are you doing lurking in the parking lot?"

Lurking? Well, some might call it that, he supposed. "I was on my way to see you."

She smiled sweetly. "Well, you've seen me. Buh-bye." Pivoting, her blonde ponytail bouncing, she headed in the opposite direction.

Back to the hospital.

He flashed around in front of her, once again blocking her path. "Come home with me."

"Wow." She crossed her arms over her chest, which only drew his attention to her rack. *Niiice.* "You get right to the point."

He shrugged. "Saves time."

"Were you planning to wine and dine me at least? You know, before the sex."

"No. Just sex." Lots and lots of sex. He could already imagine her husky voice deepening in the throes of passion. Could imagine her head between his legs, her mouth on his cock, her hands on his balls. He nearly groaned at the imaginary skin flick playing in his head.

"Oh," she said, her voice dripping with sarcasm. "You're a charmer, you are."

Not once in his five thousand years had anyone ever called him a charmer. But even uttered with sarcasm, it was the nicest thing anyone had ever said to him.

"Don't do that," he growled.

"Do what?" She stared at him like he was a loon.

"Never mind." Dying to touch her, he held out his hand in invitation. "You'll love my play room."

She wheeled away like he was offering her the plague instead of his hand. "Go to hell, asshole. I don't date fallen angels."

"Good news, then, because it's not a date." And he wasn't a fallen angel.

"Right. Well, I don't fuck fallen angels either." She made a shooing motion with her hand. "Go away."

She was rejecting him? The sudden reality was like a blow that left him completely off balance. No one rejected him. *No one.*

She started to take off again, and an abrupt, almost crushing panic squeezed his chest. This wasn't right. He had his sights set on her, and she was supposed to surrender. This was something new. Something... titillating. The crushing panic morphed into a sensation he welcomed and knew well: the jacked-up high of the hunt.

Instantly, his senses sharpened and focused. His sense of smell brought a whiff of her vanilla-honey scent. His sense of hearing brought her rapid, pounding heartbeat. And his sense of sight narrowed in on the tick of her pulse at the base of her throat.

The urge to pounce, to take her down and get carnal right here, right now, was nearly overwhelming. Instead, he moved in slowly, enjoying how she backed up, but he didn't catch the scent of fear from her.

"What are you doing?" She swallowed as she bumped up against a support beam.

"I'm going to show you why you need to come home with me." He planted both palms on either side of her head and leaned in until his lips brushed the tender skin of her ear. "You won't regret it."

"I already told you. I don't fuck fallen angels."

"So you said," he murmured. "Do you kiss them?"

"Ah...n—"

He didn't give her the chance to finish her sentence. Pulling back slightly, he closed his mouth over hers.

Strawberry gloss coated his lips as he kissed her, and he swore he'd never liked fruit as much as he did right now.

Her hands came up to grip his biceps, tugging him closer as she deepened the kiss. "You're good," she whispered against his mouth.

"I know," he whispered back.

Suddenly, pain tore into his arms as her nails scored his skin. "But you're not that good." Before he could even blink, she shoved hard and ducked out from under the cage of his arms. With a wink, she strutted away, her fine ass swinging in her form-fitting scrub bottoms. She stopped at the door of a candy-apple-red Mustang and gave him a sultry look that made his cock throb. "Give up now, buddy. I can out-stubborn anyone."

And with that, she hopped into her car and peeled out of her parking stall, leaving him in the dust.

Do you love fiction with a supernatural twist?

Want the chance to hear news about your favourite authors
(and the chance to win free books)?

Keri Arthur
S. G. Browne
P.C. Cast
Christine Feehan
Jacquelyn Frank
Thea Harrison
Larissa Ione
Darynda Jones
Sherrilyn Kenyon
Jackie Kessler
Jayne Ann Krentz and Jayne Castle
Martin Millar
Kat Richardson
J.R. Ward
David Wellington
Laura Wright

Then visit the Piatkus website and blog
www.piatkus.co.uk | www.piatkusbooks.net

And follow us on Facebook and Twitter
www.facebook.com/piatkusfiction | www.twitter.com/piatkusbooks

piatkus